this

might

hurt

OTHER TITLE BY STEPHANIE WROBEL

Darling Rose Gold

this

might

hurt

STEPHANIE WROBEL

Berkley
New York

BERKLEY
An imprint of Penguin Random House LLC
penguinrandomhouse.com

Library of Congress Cataloging-in-Publication Data

Names: Wrobel, Stephanie, author.
Title: This might hurt / Stephanie Wrobel.
Description: First Edition. | New York : Berkley, 2022.
Identifiers: LCCN 2021020988 (print) | LCCN 2021020989 (ebook) |
ISBN 9780593100080 (hardcover) | ISBN 9780593100110 (ebook)
Classification: LCC PS3623.R628 T48 2022 (print) | LCC PS3623.R628 (ebook) |
DDC 813/.6--dc23
LC record available at https://lccn.loc.gov/2021020988
LC ebook record available at https://lccn.loc.gov/2021020989

Printed in the United States of America
1st Printing

Book design by Alison Cnockaert
Map by David Lindroth

For my sisters,
Jackie and Vicki

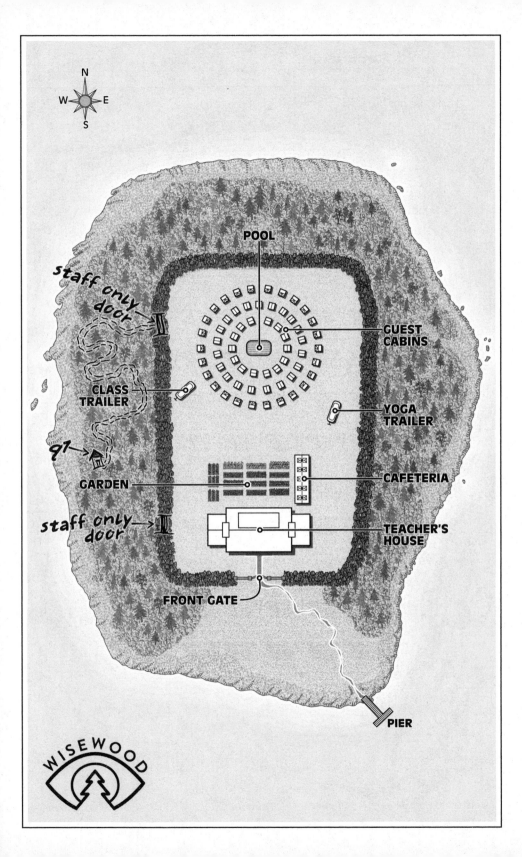

Look down at me and you see a fool.
Look up at me and you see a god.
Look straight at me and you see yourself.

—CHARLES MANSON

this

might

hurt

Split

THE GALLERY IS the size of a high school gym. Vaulted ceiling, white walls, movie screens on two of them. A dozen visitors line the perimeter of the dim room. Shoulder blades tap the walls. A low buzz fills the space while the spectators wait.

In the middle of the room is a chair and table. On the table is a medical tray: gloves, gauze, gardening shears. A spotlight illuminates the empty chair.

Waiting with a briefcase-sized camcorder on his shoulder is a crooked-nosed cameraman.

A door opens. When the artist enters, a hush falls. She glides to the center of the room. The cameraman focuses his lens on her. The movie screens fill with her image: thick lashes, long neck, steely gaze. This is not her first stunt, will be far from her last.

She puts on the gloves and stares straight into the camera. "Fear is not real," she says, "unless we make it so."

She sits down.

Picks up the shears.

Extends her tongue.

Cuts.

Gasps but does not cry.

The camera catches it all. On the screens the audience watches a tongue split in half. Someone faints. Others wail. Not the artist. She remains steady.

Blood pours from her mouth.

I

I want to live a life in which I am free.

THE WORLD'S GONE mad. People always say that.

On the contrary, we're much too sane. We're going to die someday, every single one of us. Never again the touch of a soft breeze. Never again the pinks of a setting sun. Yet we still rake the leaves come fall. We mow the grass and plow the snow. We spend all our time on all the wrong things. We act like we'll live forever.

Then again, what should a time bomb do? It has only two options.

Tick or explode.

1

Natalie

I S T A N D A T the head of the conference table. The chairs around me are filled with men: short, tall, fat, bald, polite, skeptical. I direct the close of my pitch to the CEO, who has spent fifty minutes of my sixty-minute presentation playing with his phone and the other ten frowning at me. He is past his prime, trying to disguise the fact with hair plugs and a bottled tan.

"Using this new strategy," I say, "we're confident we will make your brand the number one beer with men twenty-one to thirty-four years old."

The CEO leans forward, mouth slightly ajar as if a cigar is usually perched there. He oversees a household-name beer that's been losing market share to craft breweries for years. As sales have slipped, my new agency has found itself on thinner and thinner ice with this client.

He looks me up and down, sneers a little. "With all due respect, what makes you think *you*"—he spits the word like it's a shit sandwich—"can get inside the mind of our man?"

I glance out the conference room window, squint at the Charles River in the distance, and count to three. My team warned me about this guy, a dinosaur of corporate America who still believes business belongs on the golf course.

What I want to say: *Yes, however will I peel back the layers of such compli-*

cated minds? Can a simpleton ever truly understand the genius of the noble frat star? For now they crush empties against their foreheads, but someday they will command boardrooms. Someday they will be you *and insist they got to where they are through nothing but sheer hard work. By then they'll have traded the watery swill you call beer for three-hundred-dollar bottles of pinot noir. They'll still spend their weekends falling down and throwing up, only now they'll do it in hotel rooms with their best friends' wives. When Monday rolls around, they'll slump at this table and wonder why I don't smile more often. They will root for me to break the glass ceiling as long as none of the shards nick them. They will lament the fact they can no longer say these things aloud, except on golf courses.*

What I actually say: "To get up to speed on your business, I've spent the past two months conducting focus groups with six hundred men who fit your target demo." I scroll to the appendix of my PowerPoint deck, containing forty slides of detailed tables and graphs. "I've spent my weeknights collating the data and my weekends analyzing what all of it means. I know these men's occupations and income. I know their levels of education, their religion, their race. I know where your guys live, their lifestyles and personal values, their attitudes toward your brand as well as toward all of your competitors' brands. I know their usage frequency, their buyer readiness, and the occasions when they buy your beer. I know their degree of loyalty to you. When I get on the train to go to work or am lying in bed at night, I relisten to my interviews, searching for any insight I might've missed. I can say with confidence, I know your guy as well as I know my own father." I wince involuntarily. "Which means I know him as well as you do. I don't *think* I can get inside the mind of your customer. I know I can. Because I already have. With all due respect." I grin so the jab sounds playful instead of aggressive.

Everyone else in the room appears impressed. My assistant, Tyler, forgets himself and claps. I shift my eyes in his direction, and that's enough to make him stop, but by then the others have joined in, both the clients and my account team. The CEO watches me, amused but undecided. It was a risk, publicly challenging him in order to galvanize the rest, but I'll rarely interact with him; I'm told he shows up to advertising meetings only when he has no one else to antagonize. The marketing team members are the ones I need on my side. The CEO sits back and lets his underlings finish the session. He leaves halfway through the Q&A.

Five minutes later the clients have signed off on our strategy brief for the year. Handshakes and back pats are exchanged. Invitations to lunch are extended for the first time in months. The account team stays with the clients but I bow out. My lunch hour is for catching up on e-mail. If my inbox is empty, I spend the hour at the gym.

Tyler and I take the elevator forty floors down to the lobby of the Prudential Tower. I smirk while he raves about how awesome the presentation was. I didn't choose him as my assistant; he was assigned to me. What he lacks in ambition (or any set of demonstrable skills, really) he tries to make up for with personality.

On Boylston Street I shiver in the cold while Tyler books an Uber. Once we're nestled in the car, I turn toward him. "I want you to buy a box of Cohibas from the cigar parlor on Hanover. Wrap the box in navy blue paper. Send it with a note on the back of one of my business cards. Not the shitty agency-issued ones but the thick card stock I had made with the nice embossing. Do you have a pen? Then get your phone out. I want the note to say this exactly: 'To a productive partnership.' End that sentence with a period, not an exclamation point. Then, under that line, a dash followed by 'Natalie.' Got it? No 'Yours truly' or 'All my best' or 'Cheers.' Just a dash with my name. Send it to the CEO."

Tyler gapes at me. "But he was so rude to you. In front of all those people."

I tap a list of post-meeting to-dos on my phone. Without glancing up, I say, "When I was coming up in this industry, you know what I spent most of my time doing? Listening. And taking notes."

Out of the corner of my eye I see his expression sour slightly. He's only three years younger than I am.

"I want the minutes of today's meeting on my desk within the hour. Please."

"In my two years at DCV no one has ever done meeting minutes," he mumbles.

"Maybe that's why you almost lost the client that pays all of our salaries." I wait for a snappy comeback. When I don't get one, I pull a folder from my bag. "I glanced through your Starburst brief. It's riddled with typos." I find the marked-up pages and hand them to him. "It reflects poorly on both of us when the work is subpar. More careful proofreading next time, okay?" His jaw tightens. "And I told you: section headings in all caps and bolded. Not one or the other. Both. You'd be surprised how far attention to detail will take you."

The car pulls up to our office building. We ride another elevator together, this time in silence. On the sixth floor we get off. As we're about to part ways, Tyler sniffs. "If you've never met the CEO before today, how can we be sure he smokes cigars?"

"I know my target." I head into the women's bathroom.

A minute later I walk down the hallway, scrolling through my calendar (three more meetings this afternoon). I'm about to round the corner to my office when hushed voices in a nearby cubicle catch my ear. I recognize the first as that of one of the assistants, a woman who doesn't know she's being considered for a promotion. "I would love to work for her. She's such a boss bitch."

"Or your run-of-the-mill bitch." That one is Tyler.

The other assistants titter.

"She treats me like a child," he says, gaining steam from his friends' reactions. He affects a shrill voice. *"Tyler, I want you to go to the bathroom. When you wipe your ass, use four squares of toilet paper, but make sure it's three-ply, not two. If it's two, you're fired."* They all giggle, these people who are almost my age but make a third of what I do.

I straighten, pull back my shoulders, and stride past the cubicle. Without slowing down I say, "I don't think my voice is that high-pitched."

Someone gasps. The last thing I hear before closing my office door is total silence.

AT MY DESK I remove the lid of my scratched-up Tupperware and stare at my lunch, the same one I've eaten every day for years: a cup of kale, two slices of bacon, toasted walnuts, chickpeas, and Parmesan cheese, tossed in a shallot vinaigrette. I eagerly await the day scientists discover kale's worse for your health than nicotine; for now, a superfood's a superfood. I sigh and dig in.

I had a lot of time to think through my New Year's resolutions over

Christmas break. Last year I put an additional two and a half percent of my pay into savings. The year before that, I started washing my bed linens twice a month instead of once. Every January (except this one) Kit tells me I should resolve to have more fun. Every January (except this one) I want to snap at her that resolutions have to be measurable or you can't tell whether you've achieved them, but that would do little to disprove her point.

On New Year's Eve, as I sat alone in my apartment, staring at the needles falling off my three-foot Fraser fir while snow pelted my window, I was loath to admit my sister might be onto something. I don't know a soul in my new city other than my coworkers. How does a thirty-one-year-old make friends if not through her job? I'd rather be eaten by a bear than go to one of those Meetups, standing around with a bunch of strangers, trying to figure out who's least likely to make a skin suit out of me.

I'd resolved to try harder my first day back at work, focus less on the job, more on the people. Three hours in, I veto the resolution. Why waste my time with dolts like Tyler?

I allow myself a moment to wish Kit were here, then brush the weakness away.

I check the time back home (nine a.m.) and text my best friend, Jamie: *Still not making any progress with work people.* No response; must be busy with the baby. I stab a chickpea with my fork and jiggle my finger across my laptop's track pad.

Once I've cleared my work inbox, I move on to my personal account. I scan the subject lines: a few newsletters, a grocery coupon, spam from someone named Merlin Magic Booty. Plus a message from info@wisewood.com. I pause.

Kit went to Wisewood six months ago.

My sister didn't tell me much before she left, just called last July to explain she'd found this self-improvement program on an island in Maine. The courses are six months. During that time you aren't supposed to contact family or friends because inward focus is the goal, and oh, by the way, she had already signed up and was leaving for Maine the following week, so she wouldn't be able to call or text me for a while.

I had balked. She couldn't afford to go half a year without income. What about health insurance? How was she okay with cutting off everyone she knew for such a long time?

I pictured her shrugging on the other end of the line. If I had a dollar for every time Kit answered me with a shrug, I could pay for her to live at Wisewood forever.

"What are you thinking?" I'd asked. "You finally have a dependable job, benefits, an apartment, and you're going to throw it all away on a whim?"

Her tone cooled. "I'm not saying Wisewood is the answer to all my problems, but at least I'm trying to figure it out."

"Your job is the answer." I was incredulous that she didn't get it. "How much is this program? How are you going to afford it with that student loan?"

"Why don't you worry about yourself for once, Natalie?" She never calls me that, so I knew she was furious. "Why can't you be happy for me?"

I couldn't be happy for her because I knew exactly how this would end: Kit disillusioned with Wisewood and stranded on the island, begging me to save her. My sister needs rescuing more often than most people. Last year she called me sobbing over a scarf she'd misplaced. (I found it an hour later in her closet.) On the other hand, she's known to get in hot water on occasion. She once found herself stuck in the desert after her loser guitarist boyfriend dumped her in the middle of his tour, which she had dropped out of college to follow him on. Another time a misunderstanding with her best friend ended with me picking both of them up from a police station. My sister doesn't want me to hover until the exact moment she needs me, and then she expects me to drop everything to save her.

We ended the call still snapping at each other. I haven't heard from her since. She doesn't even know I moved across the country to Boston, taking a page out of her playbook that mandates when the going gets tough, the tough flee the situation. Back when I started toying with the idea of moving, I had pictured more frequent sisterly get-togethers; I would be only a train ride away now. She left New York before I got the chance. On my more honest days, I can admit her absence is a relief. The less often I talk to her, the less guilty I feel.

The e-mail has no subject line. I open it.

Would you like to come tell your sister what you did—or should we?

Hairs rise on the back of my neck. On the track pad my hand trembles. The note is unsigned but has a phone number at the bottom. Attached are two pdfs. The first lists directions to the island: various routes involving buses, trains, and planes, all leading to a harbor in Rockland, Maine. From there I'd have to take a ferry. The next one leaves Wednesday at noon.

I click on the second attachment and frown at the heading in bold letters. As I scan the typed words I start to feel sick. Halfway down the page a hand-written note in blue ink catches my eye. The blood drains from my face. I push my chair away from the computer. Who could've sent this? How would they know? What if they've already told her? I shove the heels of my palms into my eye sockets, wait for my body to still.

I'm in control. All I need is a plan.

I read the message twice, three times, then dial the number listed at the bottom of the e-mail.

A throaty, relaxed voice answers. "Wisewood Wellness and Therapy Center. Gordon speaking."

I launch straight in. "My sister's been at Wisewood for almost six months—"

"Sorry, ma'am," Gordon interrupts. "We don't connect family members with guests. Our guests are free to get in touch with loved ones once they're ready."

I blink, stung. Kit never told me that, nor has she reached out a single time. I force myself to focus on the task at hand. He might put me through if he thinks she made first contact. "She did get in touch. She sent an e-mail, asking me to come there."

"Well, don't do that. Only approved guests are allowed here."

I keep pushing. "Her name is Kit Collins."

He's quiet for so long I think he's hung up on me.

"You must be Natalie."

I startle. "Has Kit mentioned me?"

"I know all about you."

I swallow. Is he part of the "we" from the e-mail, this group making threats? I wait, not wanting to show my hand. He doesn't elaborate. I lift my chin, project confidence into the receiver. "Can you put her on the phone?"

"I think you've done enough, don't you?" he says pleasantly.

"What's that supposed to mean?"

"Perhaps your sister needs less interference with her happiness. You have a maximized day, now."

The line goes dead.

What has she told these people about me?

Gordon sounded like he knows something, but if he's behind the e-mail, why solicit me to come to Wisewood only to discourage me over the phone? I watch my screen until it turns off, thinking. First I'll reply to the message. If I don't get a response, I'll call Wisewood a second time. If I can't get through . . .

I skim the directions in the pdf again. Kit is a hundred and ninety miles of driving plus a seventy-five-minute ferry ride away. I could complain about her until I was blue in the face, but she's still my little sister. Besides, it's time. Over and over I've sworn to tell her the truth but have been too chickenshit to confess.

I have no idea what Kit will do when she finds out.

2

NO ONE HAD said a word the entire car ride. We were off to a good start.

No, a *fortuitous* start. *Fortuitous: happening by a lucky chance,* and also today's word of the day from my bright yellow word-of-the-day calendar, which was last year's Christmas gift from my parents.

I clutched Mr. Bear, climbed out of the station wagon, and stood in the driveway, staring. Aunt Carol's one-story lake house had red clapboard siding and dark green shutters. It wasn't as big or fancy as some homes we'd passed on our drive, but it had three whole bedrooms. I was going to have my own room for an entire week.

"Help your mother and sister with the groceries," Sir said, carrying armfuls of luggage to the front door. I tossed Mr. Bear in the backseat and walked to the trunk, where Mother handed me a paper bag of food.

"Take two bags," Jack said.

"They're too heavy." I scuttled toward the house before she could hand me another.

Sir opened the door. I peered around him. The cottage was musty but clean. I carried the groceries into the homey kitchen. Sunlight streamed through the open windows. I picked up a handwritten welcome note off the counter and sensed Sir reading over my shoulder.

"Of course she has house rules." He snickered, then elbowed me and lowered his voice. "We'll make sure we break every single one." I couldn't tell whether he was serious, so I made a noise that could have meant anything.

Sir didn't like Aunt Carol because she was related to Mother and had the nerve to afford a second home without a man's help. He rarely let us see her anymore, but I guessed he didn't hate her enough to say no when she offered to loan us her house.

I barely had enough time to unpack and snoop through the garage before Sir called a meeting in the cozy living room. There were throw pillows everywhere, embroidered with sayings like *Live, Laugh, Love* and *I just want to drink wine and pet my cat.*

Sir clapped, eyes twinkling. "What do you say we have ourselves a family outing?"

Jack and I bobbed our heads. Nobody called my sister by her actual name. Sir had been hoping for a son. When the nurse handed him a baby girl instead, that didn't stop him from using the name he'd picked out for his boy. The nickname had stuck, much to my sister's and mother's horror.

Mother wrapped her arms around herself. "I think I'll say a rosary, then lie down while you three explore."

Sir's face darkened. "Our first family vacation and you're going to sleep through it?"

"We have plenty of time, don't we?" Mother said. "I only need an hour or so. The drive took it out of me." She turned and walked down the hallway before he could respond, and closed a bedroom door gently behind her. Jack watched our father nervously, twirling a strand of brown hair between her fingers.

Sir shook his head. "Unbelievable."

He walked out the back door. Jack and I followed, letting the screen door slam. The three of us waded through the ankle-high grass past centuries-old trees that made the flagpole in the yard look small. The Stars and Stripes waved merrily from their perch. "Woman is always tired," Sir grumbled.

Thirty feet ahead was the man-made lake, olive green and murky. A pier and boathouse stood over the water. Aunt Carol's motorboat was nestled inside.

Sir clocked the boat and grinned at us. "What do you say, girls?"

"I saw horseshoes in the garage," I said.

He adjusted his thin-framed glasses and sucked his teeth, glaring at me. He wore his buzz cut so short you could barely see the white-blond hairs.

"I want to learn how to play," I lied.

"I drove two hours and you want to stay on land? I don't think so."

Sir sauntered toward the boathouse, calling over his shoulder, "Jack, let's get this thing in the water." She followed him across the overgrown lawn. My sister was only three years older than me, but our bodies had begun to look different. Sir called us his toothpicks when we were little, but that label no longer applied to Jack. She'd started growing curves. I was beyond jealous.

Leaving those two alone was a bad idea. I never knew when she might be in the mood to rat me out. I hurried after them onto the pier.

Like Aunt Carol's house, the boat was no-frills but well cared for. Sir and Jack hoisted it into the water. He hopped in, and she followed suit. They turned to me, waiting. Angry waves beat the sides of the boat. With seating for four, it was smaller than I'd expected. I chewed my lip.

"Ain't got all day, sweetheart." Sir started the engine.

I opened my mouth, swallowed. "I'll just . . ."

"Get your sister in the boat," Sir said to Jack. He walked away and glanced around the lake, shielding his eyes from the sun.

Jack reached for my hand. I gave a tiny shake of the head. She exaggerated her reach, stretching toward me. I shook my head again. Her eyes widened, first with fury, then in fear. *Now,* she mouthed.

I can't, I mouthed back.

Her eyes darted from my face to Sir's. He was studying the boat's dashboard. I could see her doing the calculations: How much longer would he be distracted? What would he do when he realized she hadn't done what he'd said?

Please, she pleaded.

On one seat, I spotted a bright orange life vest. I could put it on as soon as I stepped aboard. I didn't want to get my sister in trouble again; you never knew how bad the punishment might be.

I gave her my hand. Relief flooded her face. She pulled me into the boat. "You'll be okay," she said.

I was too busy racing to the back to respond. The life vest was halfway over my head when Sir boomed over the roar of the engine, "Take that thing off."

I froze, then turned to him.

He arched a blond eyebrow. "Does my driving concern you?"

"No," I squeaked, tightening my grip on the vest.

He jabbed a thumb toward the house. "We left all the cowards behind today. No daughter of mine needs that thing."

I didn't move. The vest lingered above my head.

"I'm not gonna tell you again," Sir said. Jack lunged toward me, ripped the life vest from my hands, and tossed it back on the seat.

"Let's get going," she said.

Sir edged the boat away from Aunt Carol's pier toward the middle of long and skinny Lake Minnich. *Ten miles of shoreline,* Mother had told us while we packed yesterday. Sir had worried that the water would be swamped with families taking advantage of the dwindling summer weather, but Mother had reassured him most kids would be back at school by now, didn't have a late start like our district did. She was right. On this Monday in early September, the lake was empty. While Sir and Jack waved at the few boats we passed, I gripped the metal rail with both hands.

"How about this for a view?" Sir crowed, gesturing at our surroundings. My sister and I obediently took it all in: a few small beaches, cabins and trailers set back off the shoreline, sycamores so big they threatened to swallow the houses whole. One squirrel chased another. A frog croaked. For a second I forgot to be afraid.

After twenty minutes, my fingers loosened around the rail. I sat back in the cushioned chair, letting the sun warm my face. I hardly flinched when a drop of water splashed me.

The boat slowed. I opened my eyes. We were in a cove, tucked away from the main waterway. Jack was kneeling next to my chair, dragging her fingers through the water. I winced at the way she was angled over the side of the boat, grabbed the back of her shirt to be safe. She glanced at me and winked.

Sir stopped the boat in the middle of the cove and pulled a bag of food from under his seat. Jack made us bologna sandwiches, carefully taking the crust off mine the way I liked, which she almost never did. After scarfing down the sandwiches, we lounged on our backs and gazed at the sky. Sir gave me his jacket to use as a pillow. Jack lay there, nibbling her lip and waiting, I didn't know what for, while Sir and I pointed out animal shapes in the clouds.

He gestured at one wending its way toward us. "That there's a unicorn."

I giggled. "Unicorns aren't real."

He mocked offense. "What would you call it, then?"

I considered. "A rhino?"

"A rhine-er-ocerous?" he said, pronouncing it the way I had when I was a little kid. I glanced at him. He kept watching the sky but nudged my shoulder with his. I imagined my heart growing two sizes like the Grinch's. Perhaps this would be one of those days I always remembered. Did we know we were making our favorite memories while they were happening?

Sir's knees cracked as he pulled himself to standing. He put his hands on his hips, lips pursed as he scanned the water. He was almost handsome standing there. Six feet tall, strong and tan from building rich families' pools all summer. From this angle, you couldn't see the jowls starting to form, the growing gut on his otherwise lean body. I wondered what he was thinking.

He crouched in front of me, sitting on his heels. "Tell you what, sweets." I warmed. He called me that only when he was especially pleased with me. "If you can stay afloat in this lake for an hour, you can skip swim lessons."

Jack's shoulders stiffened next to mine.

"I'll give you six points." Sir stroked his stubble. "You won't get a better offer than that."

I already had nine points today. I could get to fifteen by helping with dinner and finishing that book Sir was making me read, the one by the Carnegie guy. I sat up and forced myself to meet his eye. "I'll take the lessons."

"You've put them off for two years." He screwed up his face. "Almost nine years old and no clue how to swim. It's embarrassing."

My face burned. "I'm only eight and three-quarters."

He gestured to Jack. "Your sister sailed through all six levels and is set to lifeguard in a couple summers."

Jack avoided my eyes.

I gulped. "But I don't have my swimsuit with me."

He waved me off. "What you've got on is fine. You got plenty of dry clothes back at the house."

I trembled. I knew when it was time to reason and when it was time to beg. "Please, Sir. Please don't make me do it."

He pulled me to my feet. "The fact you're so afraid of the water is proof you gotta go in. You gonna avoid bathtubs your entire life? I know it's scary now, but you'll see it's not so bad."

I turned to Jack, silently pleading with her to stick up for me. She rolled over onto her stomach. A tear ran down my cheek (–4).

"Minus four," Sir said as I thought it. "I don't want to have to push you in."

He wasn't going to back down. My eyes darted around, landing on the life vest.

Sir scoffed before I could say a word. "That'd kinda defeat the purpose."

I was going to have to get into the water. My teeth rattled, then my shoulders, then my arms, until every body part was shaking.

"You've gotta calm down or you'll never make it. I've shown you how to doggy paddle. You know what to do. You're letting fear control you now. Your imagination is telling you it's gonna be worse than it actually is. You'll see."

I nodded, though I didn't believe him. I took off my sneakers but left on my socks, then shuffled toward the small ladder he'd hung off the back of the boat. I stepped onto the highest rung, searching the lake for creatures with sharp teeth and scaly skin. Were there piranhas in Lake Minnich? I turned around on the ladder so I wouldn't have to face the water. In two great strides, Sir was standing over me, not amused.

Paradox: any person, thing, or situation exhibiting an apparently contradictory nature. Last Monday's word.

I lowered myself to the second rung. Chilly water soaked my socks and bare calves.

Sir clucked his tongue.

I stepped down another rung, sending my knees and the ends of my pink shorts into the water. I prayed to Mother's god.

Sir's nostrils flared.

I moved to the last step, flinching as my shorts went completely under-water. They were heavy now, pulling me down. Staring up at my father, I prayed he might change his mind, that this would be enough. I could get over my fear some other time. I was still dry from the waist up.

His face hardened. "Goddamn you." He nudged my fingers with his shoe. Shocked, I let both hands go and fell into the water. I cried out at the burst of cold up to my neck. When I reached for the ladder, Sir threw it clat-tering to the boat's floor.

He wasn't going to let me back in.

My bladder let go, warming the icy water around me. I flailed my arms and kicked away from the boat, terrified he'd somehow know. I wasn't sure how many points wetting your pants cost you but bet it'd be a lot.

He pulled the horrible stopwatch out of his pocket. Did he go anywhere without it? "You so much as touch this boat, the count starts over." He pressed a button. The watch beeped.

I panted, trying to slow my pounding heart. The water wasn't actually slimy. It was all in my head. I pointed my toes to see if I could touch bottom. I couldn't. I imagined my ankles getting caught in weeds that would snag me, saw myself sinking, sinking, sinking to my forever home at the bottom of the lake, the strands of my hair trembling like kelp, my skin decomposing to flakes of fish food, the meat of me picked clean down to skull and teeth. Sir would scoop out what was left of me with a fishing net, the biggest prey he'd ever subdued. Or he might leave me there, rotting and fluttering in my bed of silt, too ashamed of my spinelessness to stake his claim.

Shaking, I paddled my arms and kicked my legs like Sir had shown me. He stared at me from a chair at the back of the boat.

"You think I *enjoy* spending my first vacation in ten years teaching my daughter the meaning of discipline?"

I'd learned what a rhetorical question was years ago.

I kicked and splashed and fought the water, eyes never leaving the boat.

I pushed away thoughts of what was behind and below me, of how it would feel to have my skin peeled away strip by strip from my muscles.

"Lord knows you're not gonna get by on talent or gifts. God skipped our ancestors when he was handing out presents, that's for sure. If your grandfather had an idea, it would've died of loneliness. Not that your dear old dad is much better off. We can't control the brains we were given, but what can we control?"

He waited long enough that I sensed he wanted an answer this time. "How hard we work," I puffed.

"Speak up."

"How hard we work," I repeated, louder this time.

"What's the only way you're going to succeed?"

"Through my willingness to endure," I recited.

Sir nodded, satisfied. "I don't believe in destiny, but I do believe in potential. You got all the potential in the world for greatness, sweetheart. Don't let anyone tell you any different." He checked the stopwatch. "Ten minutes."

After another few minutes, he looked bored. He stood and stretched his arms overhead. Perhaps he'd call the whole thing off and drive us home. I'd be willing to give up this entire vacation if it meant I could get out of the water.

"You're doing great, sweets. Up to fifteen minutes. I'm gonna have Jack take over while I snooze."

My heart leapt as I watched Jack make her way toward the back of the boat. She slumped in the chair Sir had been holding court in a few seconds ago, then studied the stopwatch, both anxious and annoyed.

"Let me—"

She flashed me a dirty look, glanced over her shoulder, and put a finger to her lips. My heart picked up.

Nothing happened. He must not have heard me.

She leaned her head back and stared at the sky, refusing to look at me. I kicked and kicked, waiting for what felt like hours, trying not to panic as my fingers and toes numbed. Surely he would be asleep by now.

"Let me rest," I called to my sister.

Her eyes flicked to Sir, then to me, then back at the sky. "I can't."

"I'm tired."

"Sorry." She closed her eyes. This was the thanks I got for getting on the boat, for helping her stay out of trouble.

I slowly edged closer, then lunged for the boat's side. Jack jumped out of her chair, ready to stop me, but the side was too slippery for me to hang on to. I slid all the way under, gasped at the shock of cold on my soaking face. I swallowed water, and by the time I resurfaced I was choking.

"If you do that again, I'll start the count over."

"Please. We won't tell him."

"He'll know." She peeked over her shoulder again. "He always does."

I coughed, trying to get the water out. "I'll be quiet."

"Shh. You'll get us both in trouble."

"I can't do this," I wailed, shivering.

She consulted the stopwatch. "You're already thirty-five minutes in. More than halfway there."

My side was cramping. One of my socks had slipped off, leaving my toes exposed to fangs and claws. Something was pulling me toward the bottom of the lake, I knew it. Whatever it was wouldn't eat me in strips but in chunks, a half limb at a time. I felt the sharp teeth sever my arm, imagined the lake turning a rusty red. Quietly I cried.

Jack welled up too. She swiveled her chair so I could only see her profile. "Don't be such a baby." She wiped her face.

A baby? I'd seen Jack bawl her eyes out when Sir had pushed her into easier challenges than this. What did my sister know about being brave? Everything came easily to her: making friends, getting good grades, learning to swim. It was easy not being scared when you were good at everything.

A creature slithered through the water right by the boat. I screeched, thrashing backward, trying to get as far away from it as I could. I turned in circles, searching for it, my chin dragging through the water. Out of the corner of my eye I saw it again. I shrieked and paddled away from the spot, kicking hard until I lost my breath.

I pictured the thing touching my feet and curled my toes. How big was it? Did it bite? How bad would the pain be compared to losing a tooth? Sir made us use the string and doorknob every time, said wiggling was for wussies. Was getting eaten like that? Would the fear be worse than the pain? How long until I couldn't feel anything at all?

Something brushed my right calf. I screamed again and slipped under the water. I was too afraid to open my eyes. I cried out, but it sounded like a mumble. I got my head above water and gulped air, gurgling and shouting and spinning, scanning for the boat. How had it gotten so far away? The chair at the back was empty. Where was Jack? I coughed before slipping under again.

This time I opened my eyes. The water was a cloudy vomit green. I swallowed more of it, making my throat burn and my head spin. My arms and legs were concrete. I couldn't make them do what I wanted anymore. They were too tired. I was freezing, couldn't see or hear anything, felt myself sinking, alone. Was this dying? I begged for numbness.

Everything went black.

I came to, already heaving, sucking in lungfuls of air. I opened my eyes and was blinded by the sun. Sir's and Jack's faces came into focus, hovering over me. I was lying on the boat floor. Jack's eyes were bloodshot. Her soaking hair dripped on my face. I blinked.

With his hands on his knees, Sir grinned at me. "Looks like you're taking them swim lessons after all, sweetheart."

3

Natalie

THE BUS PULLS into the parking lot of the Rockland Ferry Terminal after a three-and-a-half-hour drive. Along the way we passed farm stands, diners, lobster-fishing supply stores, plus a craft store called Maine-ly Sewing. A sign next to a food cart boasted of selling more than five million hot dogs. Normally I would have appreciated the whimsy, but I couldn't stop thinking about my sister.

Our last FaceTime had been standard fare until Kit announced she was leaving for Wisewood. We'd debated who would win the current season of *Survivor*. (We didn't care that we were the last two fans of the show; our support for Jeff Probst was unwavering.) I had told her about a security app I liked since she'd lost all her passwords again. (It makes me stress-twitch too.) She mentioned a personal-styling startup that sends clothes to your house so you don't have to put up with the exquisite torture that is shopping in a store. She was even-keeled, in good spirits. Until I lambasted her decision to leave.

Would you like to come tell your sister what you did—or should we?

I wince. The only thing worse than admitting my secret to Kit would be letting the e-mail sender or anyone else do it. I have to shoulder her pain, defend myself if she'll listen.

That's a big if.

I rise from my seat, legs shaking, and clamber off the bus into the sunny but cold morning. A few inches of filthy snow have been plowed to the outskirts of the parking lot. Immediately, I feel exposed. What if the Wisewood staff is already here, watching me? I squint at the few cars in the lot, then duck my head and rush with my duffel bag toward the terminal building.

After Gordon hung up on me two days ago, I replied to the e-mail, short and simple: *Who is this? Please ask my sister to call me.* Then I googled Wisewood. Up came an address and phone number, which matched the one I'd called, plus links to directions and three Google reviews. The first URL in the search results was ihatemyblank.com. I clicked it.

It took me to an empty black landing page. I stared at it, waiting for something to happen. After a few seconds, large white letters appeared one at a time, as though they were being typed onto the screen.

I HATE MY _____

At the end of the blank space, the cursor blinked. Was I supposed to fill it in? I leaned toward my computer, squinting. The typing started again: j-o-b. As soon as "job" had been finished, a new word replaced it. Words filled the blank faster and faster, cycling so quickly I almost missed a few.

I HATE MY_____JOB_____

I HATE MY___PARTNER___

I HATE MY___FRIENDS___

I HATE MY____FAMILY____

I HATE MY___SCHOOL___

I HATE MY____DEBT____

I HATE MY ILLNESS

I HATE MY BODY

I HATE MY CITY

I HATE MY ADDICTION

I HATE MY DEPRESSION

I HATE MY ANXIETY

I HATE MY _____ GRIEF _____

I HATE MY _____ LIFE _____

At "life," the letters shook, subtly at first but then more violently, until they exploded into a bunch of specks. Once all the specks had blended into the black screen, a new sentence appeared.

ISN'T IT TIME TO MAKE A CHANGE?

WHAT ARE YOU SO AFRAID OF?

WHAT WOULD YOUR LIFE LOOK LIKE

IF YOU STARTED LIVING IT?

COME FIND OUT.

A form field appeared, asking for my e-mail address with a submit button underneath labeled BECOME FEARLESS. I sat back in my chair and exhaled, imagining Kit watching this pitch. I tried to guess which part had sucked her in, what she had hated: Her job? Her grief? Our family? I left the website without signing up, not in the mood for weekly pep talks or years in unsubscribe-me purgatory.

Instead, I returned to the search results page and clicked on the Google reviews. Two gave five stars, the third only one. The anonymous users left no explanations, only the ratings. I looked up Wisewood on Tripadvisor and Booking.com. The resort had listings on those sites but no reviews. How could Wisewood be in business if they had so few customers? It occurred to me that if you were someone willing to forgo all technology for six months, you probably weren't running to your computer to post a travel review when you returned home.

I checked my inbox every few minutes, spacing out through the rest of my Monday meetings. When I didn't receive any messages, a knot formed in my stomach. Tuesday morning rolled around. I called Wisewood again; this time no one picked up. Another workday passed. At five o'clock I called a third time, but still no answer. The knot tightened. I considered filing a missing persons report, but Kit wasn't missing. I imagined walking into a police station, explaining that I knew where my sister was, but she refused to contact me. They'd point me to the nearest counselor's office.

By the time I left work yesterday, I knew I wouldn't hear from Kit or Gordon. At home, I sat in the kitchen and stared at my phone. My clock tick, tick, ticked in admonition until I was ready to rip the thing off the wall. I e-mailed my boss to say I had a family emergency and wouldn't be in the office for a few days, worst case a week. He told me to take the time I needed. When you work long hours and have no social life, the higher-ups learn to love you pretty quickly.

The Rockland terminal building is clean and quiet. The American and Maine State flags hang from a rafter. Four rows of benches face the port. On the walls are small stained-glass window scenes of birds and plants that must be significant to Maine.

After using the bathroom, I head back outside. Gray clouds creep toward the harbor. I jam my hands in my pockets and exhale, watching the puff of condensation drift from my mouth. I pause at two H-shaped loading ramps. On the first ramp, the public ferry to Vinalhaven Island is preparing to depart. Men in jeans and neon yellow sweatshirts guide truckers as they drive their vehicles onto the ferry. The water glistens, bluer than I expected considering all the traffic.

On the other side of the harbor bob dozens of sailboats. A red lobster shack, concrete tables, and red barstools stand nearby. Secured to a lamppost is a handwritten sign: GUESTS OF WISEWOOD, PLEASE WAIT HERE. I sit on one of the stools, trying to convince myself I'm not in danger. I hope I'm not the sole passenger on this boat; it would be my luck to try to save my sister only to wind up in a body bag on the ocean floor.

I tap my foot and check my phone. The water taxi should be here in six minutes. I consider squeaking out a few e-mails while I wait (Tyler will spend the day sharpening his stand-up routine if I don't keep him busy) but I'm too wired to focus. A sixty-something woman wearing a khaki sun hat and dragging a purple suitcase heads toward me. I sigh with relief. Even small talk is preferable to imagining Wisewood's skipper folding me into a tarp like a ham and cream cheese roll-up.

The woman waves, the fanny pack around her waist jiggling. "Here for the Wisewood ferry?"

I nod.

"Me too." She extends her hand. "I'm Cheryl."

"Natalie," I say as we shake. "What brings you to Wisewood?"

"A little R and R, some self-reflection." She chews her lip, thinking. "Oh, what the hell? This place is all about honesty." She leans in and lowers her voice. "My business partner and I were going to retire next year, sell our flower shop. Instead, she threw me out on my bottom and had me replaced. After twenty years together." Cheryl squeezes her suitcase handle hard enough to break it in half. With great effort, she forces her jaw to relax and rolls her head around her shoulders. "I've tried meditation. Exercise. Therapy. Lots and lots of therapy." She laughs bitterly. "Can't let it go. I'll sit down on the couch for a minute and next thing I know, hours have gone by without me realizing it." Her expression blackens. "You should see the severance she gave me, the nerve of her. The shop was *my* idea—we opened it with *my* life savings. I'd be starting over at sixty-four if it weren't for my husband's pension."

Cheryl's shoulders have crept back up to her ears.

"I'm so sorry."

She touches my arm. "Thank you, dear. I figure if traditional therapy hasn't done the trick, maybe I need something less conventional. My sister's the one who told me about Wisewood. She joined after a rough divorce. Husband's a real prick. I told her as much before they married thirty years ago, but does she ever listen to me? Anyway, Wisewood doesn't seem like your average retreat, some glorified vacation with sunrise yoga thrown in. You know that application we had to fill out? I haven't written something that long since I was in school." She raises an eyebrow. "I heard they only accept ten percent of applicants. I liked that line from their brochure: *We are not your first resort.*"

What story did Kit's application tell? I wonder whether the ten percent approval rate is accurate or a marketing ploy to make the place sound exclusive.

"I liked that," Cheryl repeats. "Sends a message that Wisewood is for people who really need help. It won't be four days of trust falls and self-empowerment babble and then back home we go. Kinda hard to change your life in a week, don't you think? I'm talking real, lasting change."

I nod, distracted. Kit must have been desperate. Guilt stabs me; I had no idea she was so miserable.

"My sister's never been happier, so I thought I'd try Wisewood too."

I should have been honest with Kit from the start. No, I never should have done what I did in the first place.

She'll hate you if you tell her.

I rub my face as a group walks over: two adults in their fifties and a teenage girl. The couple reveals they've enrolled their daughter Chloe before she starts college in the fall but don't share why.

"This will be the longest she's ever been away from us," her father says, putting his arm around Chloe, who's a cross between Wednesday Addams and Cousin Itt with her colorless skin and bushel of dark hair.

Chloe wriggles out of his grip. "I'll be fine."

At the sound of an engine, we all twist toward the harbor. I search for the source of the noise, but fog cloaks the horizon, turning once-cerulean water an icy gray. The haze has stilled the sailboats and engulfed the ferry workers.

We are alone in this port. I turn the same question over for the hundredth time: if people at Wisewood have no problem threatening strangers, how have they been treating my sister these past six months? In my pockets my hands clench. We wait, frozen, until a white motorboat with navy trim skulks through the mist. I check the time again: twelve on the dot.

Two men are aboard. The driver is pushing seventy and short, barrel-chested with a shaved head. His companion is around my height, five-nine, wears baggy jeans, an oversized logger coat, and thick work gloves. Underneath the coat is a purple sweatshirt with the hood pulled up. I'd put him in his late twenties, the perfect example of my beer client's target. The two men are staring straight at me.

What if these men are the ones who e-mailed me?

The driver climbs out of the boat. When Hooded Guy tries to follow, the driver glowers at him. Hooded Guy flinches and sinks back into his chair. The driver ties the boat to a cleat, finger jabs a warning at his partner, then heads toward us at the pace of a man decades younger than himself. My pulse hammers in my throat. When he reaches our circle, the driver puts his hands behind his back and inclines his head.

"Welcome to Wisewood. My colleague and I will be taking you to the island today. I'm Gordon."

Shit.

Gordon gestures to the boat behind him, which has a black-and-white winged hourglass on its side. "This is the *Hourglass*. Unless there are questions, now's the time to say goodbye to your loved ones. Then we'll get going."

Gordon taps his foot while Chloe quickly hugs her parents. Once they've left, he scans our three faces and frowns. I put a hand on my hip, straighten my spine.

"We're expecting Cheryl Douglas"—he peers at Cheryl before she raises her hand—"and Chloe Sullivan." He glances at Chloe, as if he knows who she is too. He turns to me with a thin smile. "Who are you?"

Based on our phone chat, I'm guessing friendliness won't work here, but I grin at him anyway. "Natalie Collins."

A flicker of something unpleasant crosses Gordon's face. "Why don't you ladies climb aboard?" he says to Cheryl and Chloe. They glance at me curiously but pull their luggage toward the water. Gordon nods at Hooded Guy, who's been watching us from the boat with a forlorn expression. Hooded Guy takes the women's bags, then helps them onto the *Hourglass*. Gordon stares at him until he returns heavily to his seat.

Once the three settle, he shifts back to me. "We offered Kit a staff position."

My breath hitches. "She works there?"

"For three months now. She's perfectly fine."

In three months she never once thought to tell me.

I refuse to let a lump form in my throat. "Then why did I get this e-mail?"

The wind claws at us. It takes all my self-control not to shudder, but the weather doesn't bother Gordon. He studies me. "You never told me the contents of this supposed e-mail."

I've decided to share what the e-mail says with as few people as possible; it'll lead only to the question I don't want to answer.

I drop the treacly shtick. "Nothing supposed about it. I told you on the phone, she asked me to come to Wisewood. I want to make sure she's okay."

"I checked the Sent folder of our company e-mail. There was no message to you in there."

"I never said she sent it from the company e-mail."

"That's the only account our guests and staff have access to."

I backtrack. "Someone must have deleted it, then."

"Or you've created an excuse to interfere," he says, losing patience. "You wouldn't be the first."

"I have better things to do with my time."

"In that case, take my word for it. I saw her at this morning's staff meeting, and as I've already told you, she's grand."

If Gordon had something to do with the e-mail, surely he'd want me to come to the island rather than fight tooth and nail to keep me away. "I need to see her myself. In person."

Gordon glances over his shoulder. On the boat, Hooded Guy makes small talk with Cheryl and Chloe while scanning the parking lot. Gordon turns back to me. "As I told you over the phone, only approved guests can come to Wisewood."

I clench my cell in my pocket. I could forget the e-mailed threat, take Gordon's word for it that my sister is flourishing. I'd love nothing more than to head back to Boston; if I leave now, I might make this afternoon's creative meeting. Nobody's going to deliver that brief better than I will.

But if the roles were reversed, Kit wouldn't give up. She would attach herself to Gordon's back like a koala if that's what she had to do to get to me. She may struggle to stand up for herself, but she never, ever fails to defend her people.

Kit never would have lied to me in the first place.

With matching composure I say, "Then approve me."

"The approval process requires—"

"I don't care. Bend your rules."

"I'm telling you, there's nothing wrong with her," he snaps.

The crack in his poise terrifies me. Why is he so insistent? I unleash the stress, the panic, the guilt I've been tamping down. "How do I know she's not hurt or in danger?" I explode. "If you won't take me to Wisewood, I'm going to the cops."

He stills. "Wait a minute."

"I'm not wasting another second with you."

I turn on my heel. Gordon yanks my wrist so hard that I yelp. "Get your hands off me." I pull free of his grip, backpedal a few steps. He peeks again at the boat. Hooded Guy is on his feet now, pacing and fidgeting. Gordon stiffens.

"Fine." He eyes his companion. "You'll leave Wisewood first thing to-morrow."

"Gladly." I rub my wrist, glaring at him.

"You'll pay the night's room and board."

"Not a problem."

"You'll follow our rules."

I make no effort to hide my eye roll but nod anyway.

Gordon steps aside. "Hurry and get on."

The boat bounces like a toy on the churning water. Cheryl and Chloe watch me with enormous eyes as I walk. Even Hooded Guy snaps out of his reverie to gaze my way. I stop halfway there, my boots glued to the concrete.

Gordon clears his throat. I feel his eyes drilling into the back of my neck and I lurch toward the dueling musks of brine and gasoline. With each step, I try to ignore my gut. Everything will be fine. I have to tell her the truth.

Hooded Guy scrambles to the front of the *Hourglass* to make room for me. I climb on board and nearly lose my footing. Beneath me, the water thrashes. My stomach twists.

I'm coming, Kit.

4

I WORRIED I might hurl the puffed rice cereal I'd had for breakfast that morning. The swim teacher watched me expectantly. I peered at my classmates, most of them a humiliating foot shorter than I was. They splashed around the pool like sea otters, all of their faces already wet. I held my breath, cupped water in my hands, and splashed it across my face (+1). My heart jerked.

"Very good!"

I wiped my face and opened my eyes. The swim teacher, a teenager at the high school I'd attend someday, patted me on the shoulder.

He grinned. "You've come so far these past couple weeks."

Considering I'd thrown up in the locker room before my first three classes, I supposed he was right. I stood in the chest-high water, wishing I were as carefree as the younger kids. On the one hand, I wanted to move up class levels as soon as possible to get away from the six-year-olds. On the other, I could see the students in the more advanced levels at the deep end of the pool. They were ducking underwater and staying there for way too long. And they were doing it on purpose. I shuddered.

"One last drill," my teacher called out. "We're going to practice floating on our backs."

I sighed with relief. I could handle floating on my back. It was floating on my front that made me want to jump out of my skin.

After the class finished the final drill, we all sat around the edge of the pool so the teacher could give us pointers. The other kids dangled their legs in the water, but I kept mine crossed. Logically I understood there couldn't be any finned monsters at the bottom of a public pool, but that didn't stop my brain from insisting that something was slithering toward my legs, waiting to sting my arms, pull me under, wrap me in its tentacles, hold me until I stopped fighting.

I shook the thoughts from my head. It was easier to spend as little time in the water as possible.

I pulled off my swim cap and squeezed water from my hair, white-blond no matter the season, like Sir's. A pale, chubby kid sat next to me. He was the only other nine-year-old in level one. As far as I could tell, the main reason Alan talked to me was because I too knew how to tie my shoes.

When class finished, Alan said, "I can't wait 'til we get to level two and start using kickboards. I hope I get the red one my first time. Or the blue one. The blue one's cool too. I think we'll both get moved up soon, don't you? What was your favorite part of class?"

I squinted at Alan like he was crazy. "Right now."

"Now?" he asked, confused. Most of our classmates were dashing across the slippery tiled floor to greet their parents. They slowed when our teacher scolded them to *Walk, please.* Mother never came inside the community center to pick me up. She claimed she used those spare minutes in her car to pray, but I suspected she was avoiding the other moms. She was sure they whispered behind her back, spreading rumors she spent all day in bed.

"My favorite part is when it's over."

His eyebrows rose. He considered what I'd said, kicking his legs in the water, splashing me a little. I scooted over a few feet.

"Why do you take lessons if you hate them so much?"

"Because my dad makes me." I couldn't wait to get the smell of chlorine off me.

"Why don't you tell your dad no?"

Perhaps Alan actually *was* crazy. "He's not that kind of dad."

"What kind of dad is he?" Alan stared at me, scratching his baby nose.

Naïve: showing a lack of experience, wisdom, or judgment.

I debated how best to answer. "One who makes you do stuff you don't want to because he thinks it's good for you."

"What if it's not good for you, though?"

I shrugged. "He's the dad."

Alan shrugged too. "Sounds like you need an escape trick."

"What do you mean?"

"I mean like Houdini."

"What's a Houdini?"

"Are you serious?" Alan's eyes widened. "You don't know who Houdini is?"

"That's what I said, isn't it?"

"Sorry, sorry. He was this famous magician from a long time ago. My dad bought a book about him. Sometimes he reads parts to us."

Aunt Carol took Jack and me to a magic show once, back when Sir let her babysit. The magician called me onstage to be his assistant, which was still the single most exciting thing that had ever happened to me. He pulled a quarter out of my ear and said I could keep it. Then he turned a fake dove into a real one and let it fly away. I always wondered where that dove went, if the magician had trained it to return to him somehow. After the show, Aunt Carol bought popcorn and threw kernels in the air for us to catch in our mouths. No one noted who'd caught more kernels or gave long lectures about self-control. It was one of my favorite days ever.

Alan took my silence as encouragement to keep talking. "Houdini started out with card tricks, but what made him famous is all these crazy escapes he did. He could get out of any pair of handcuffs in the world."

I stared at Alan. "You're lying."

"Am not. He let people put shackles on him and then nail him up inside a crate and then someone would throw the crate into the sea and he'd escape from it."

I felt sick imagining it. I couldn't even handle being thrown into the sea with my arms and legs unrestrained. Who was this impossibly brave man? He couldn't be real.

"I don't believe you," I said.

"I'll bring the book next time. You can read it for yourself. You'll see."

I nodded, trying to act indifferent, already plotting how I would hide the book from Sir. What Alan claimed couldn't be true. There was no way this book would tell me how to dodge my father or his challenges. You couldn't find answers to something like that in any book.

Still, it wouldn't hurt to check.

Just in case.

5

Natalie

THE *HOURGLASS'S* INTERIOR looks like it's been doused in bleach. Every surface sparkles: white leather seats with tan trim, white sundeck, white floor. A folded map sits on the dashboard. I join Cheryl and Chloe on the L-shaped cushions. Gordon unties the boat, then hops in behind me. Hooded Guy watches Gordon, who lowers himself to the captain's chair.

"Once again, welcome," Gordon says to the three of us. "I'm Gordon, and this is my friend Sanderson. Normally he does these trips on his own, but he's under the weather today. To be safe, I'll do the driving, but he'll still tell you about the area. Pretend I'm not even here."

While Gordon talks, Sanderson scratches at his facial hair, which doesn't quite come together to form a mustache or goatee but grows in ornery patches around his face. He has the general appearance of a stray cat.

Sanderson wrinkles his brow as Gordon steers the boat out of Rockland Harbor. "Maximized morning," he says in a daze. "I'm Mike Sanderson. Been at Wisewood three and a half years."

"Three years, wow," Cheryl says. "You must love it here."

Sanderson swallows. "Wisewood saved me. Hang tight—we're about to pick up speed."

The cold is even more punishing once we've left the marina. My teeth chatter; hair whips my face. I pull a fleece hat from my bag and watch the coast recede, feeling an irrational pull toward the harbor.

I wonder whether Kit has ever driven the *Hourglass*. God, this is so like her: throwing herself headfirst into an endeavor with no regard for how it affects anyone else. As long as she's pursuing her true north, she doesn't mind, probably doesn't even notice, when she leaves people adrift. She can afford that selfishness; no one has ever depended on her. She's always had someone to lean on: me.

Letting out a deep breath, I try to break up the ball of queasiness in my abdomen. I have no room to talk when it comes to brushing away the consequences of my actions; I am the blackest of pots. I try to relax my hands, but they keep clutching each other when I'm not paying attention.

"None of you are from Maine, right?" Sanderson asks, eyes losing that glazed-over quality. "Me neither. Check it: there are over forty-six hundred islands in this state."

Cheryl gasps. I lift my eyebrows. Chloe doesn't react, completely indifferent.

"Right now we're on Penobscot Bay, which opens into the Atlantic. You might have heard of Vinalhaven, the most crowded island in the area, if you can call twelve hundred people a crowd. We only make the seven-mile trip from Wisewood to Vinalhaven to pick up mail—"

Cheryl squeals, pointing at the water. "Is that a seal?"

While everyone else peers where she's pointing, Gordon watches me. I pretend not to notice. A gray blob bounces in the distance.

"Excellent spot, Cheryl," Sanderson cheers, pulling out a pair of binoculars and doing his best Steve Irwin. He's a different person now than he was in the harbor, chatty and happy, no longer nervously glancing at Gordon every thirty seconds. "We see tons of seals around here, otters and porpoises too. You should all keep an eye out. Once a bunch of dolphins even swam alongside the boat. So dope."

Cheryl oohs and aahs while Chloe leans over the rail. The mention of marine life makes me think of Kit's walrus impression, assisted by breadsticks. She would do anything to get a chuckle out of Mom and me: that goofy butt dance, corny dad jokes, the way she rode her bike with no hands while belting Mariah Carey, dead serious that she thought she sounded good when in reality her voice sounded like a crow in distress. When I realize I'm thinking of her in the past tense, my breath catches.

By now Maine's coastline has disappeared. Wild islands surround us. At their shorelines are slabs of granite so monstrous a person could fall between two and disappear forever. Towering evergreens have consumed every inch of land beyond the granite, huddling in such thick clusters you can't see past them. They lean away from the water, recoiling as one, and it's no wonder. The sea roars and roils, steel in color and resolve. A wispy fog envelops us, dancing on the surface of the bay. Instead of descending from the silver sky, the vapors climb out of the water, otherworldly. I peer over the side of the boat, trying to find their source. I sense something is down there, watching, waiting.

"What's the deal with the fog, Sanderson?" Cheryl asks.

"It's sea smoke. Super-cold air moving over warmer water."

"Does that mean we can swim at Wisewood?" says Chloe, who I'm relieved still has a pulse. "If the water is warm?"

Sanderson frowns. "It only reaches the high fifties, even in summer, so I don't think you'd want to. But we have a class for advanced students called Mastering Extreme Elements that includes some gnarly cold-water swimming."

"How deep is it out here?" Cheryl asks.

"Twelve feet."

Cheryl gestures to Chloe, herself, and me. "And are your guest groups usually this small?"

"Depends on the time of year. Not many peeps want to come here in winter. If the wind kicks up too much, the water becomes unpassable. That means no leaving the island for weeks at a time. Not that you dudes would notice. We have plenty of food and medical supplies—nothing to worry about."

Cheryl bobs her head.

"Check out my three o'clock," Sanderson says. "See the bald eagle on top of that tree? We have a lot of these guys in the area."

From wildlife Sanderson moves on to naming the landmasses around us: Hurricane, White, Spectacle, Crotch (yes, seriously), Lawrys, Cedar, Dogfish. Some islands he points out have houses on them, but most don't. Every new isle is identical to the last: an army of spruce trees trying to spear the sky, granite breakwaters guarding the perimeter. Out here you can't hear an ambulance siren or the ping of a new e-mail. Already we're too far away.

After a lengthy silence, I sneak a peek at Sanderson. He's gazing at the horizon, mind a million miles away again.

"Are you all right, son?" Cheryl asks him.

For the second time since leaving the harbor, Gordon turns around. "Tell them about your setback today. What we discussed on the ride over."

Sanderson grimaces. "I've been sober three and a half years. Not a single drop." He gnaws on his lips like he's trying to stop the words from coming out. "This morning I woke up, and the urge was strong. Stronger than usual. I thought I'd take the boat ashore, find the nearest bar, have a drink. Just one." He closes his eyes. "Instead I told Gordon about it. He offered to make the ride with me, so I didn't have to face temptation alone."

"We're all about helping one another here," Gordon says, his attention back on the wheel.

Sanderson forces a smile, pale and sweaty despite the temperature.

"It must be so hard changing old habits," Cheryl says.

"The key to recovery isn't fixing your old life," Sanderson says. "It's starting a new one."

Gordon points at an isle in the distance. "Here we are." He glares at Sanderson. "Home sweet home."

Wisewood has the same thick forest as the other islands, with a coastline of boulders, but as we make our way around the island, the forest gives way to a manicured hedge wall at least eight feet tall. In the middle of it is a wrought iron gate. Past the gate, a long path leads to a silent misshapen structure.

The geometric building appears to be two stories, but it's hard to tell. Walls jut from more walls, as if the house has grown tumors. Some sides are floor-to-ceiling glass, while others are painted the same deep green as the forest.

"This is Teacher's home," Sanderson says.

Teacher? Is that what they call the guy who runs this place? I can already picture him: perpetually barefoot, wavy brown Jesus hair, wire-rimmed glasses, eyes open a little too wide. I've seen the documentaries.

What has he done to inspire such devotion in these people?

The boat passes the gate, and the hedge wall obscures most of the building once more. Ahead of us, an aluminum pier protrudes from the water, unyielding as waves crash against it. A small lump rests on the end of the jetty. I squint. It's a backpack.

Gordon stops the *Hourglass*, and both men tie her up. With Sanderson's help, the three of us wobble onto the snow-powdered pier with our luggage. A gust of wind mauls us, nearly blowing Chloe into the water. I hold her arm until she steadies. Sanderson puts on the backpack. It appears heavy, packed to the gills. Embroidered on the top strap is *MS*. Mike Sanderson.

"I'll take that." Gordon reaches for the bag.

"I've got it," Sanderson says.

"I insist." Gordon yanks it off his back. Bag clenched in one hand, he gestures to Sanderson with the other. "Please. Lead the way."

Sanderson opens his mouth and closes it again. He ducks his head from the wind, then leads us to the start of the pier. What did he need that huge backpack for? Why did he leave it behind? Why won't Gordon let him carry it?

We step onto the island, cloaked in several inches of snow. Someone has shoveled a path wide enough for one person from the pier all the way to the front gate. Frozen earth and dead grass crunch beneath our feet as we bustle up the path single file, Sanderson in front and Gordon in back. Once again, I sense his eyes crawling over me.

When we reach the gate, Sanderson punches a code into the security system. The doors open. Cheryl, Chloe, and Sanderson dash through. I spin a slow circle. At the pier, the *Hourglass* flails on the water. I can't see another blot of land from here.

That's all Wisewood is: a crumb in the middle of a savage ocean.

"Let's go, Ms. Collins," Gordon says.

I run to join the others as the gate closes behind me.

The front yard is a modernist garden, snow-covered topiary in the shapes of cones, cubes, and spheres. Every shrub is just so. The wind shrieks like a woman being stabbed over and over, shoving us up the path. I tighten my scarf around my neck, reminded of nooses and snares. I squint at the lair of grotesque angles ahead.

We rush toward the house. Sanderson yells to be heard over the wind. "Let's jet straight to the cafeteria and get you out of this weather."

I stop at the house's front steps. The person who threatened me might sleep within these four walls. The windows rattle in their frames, but there's no movement behind any of them. I could be standing in front of a painting. It's impossible to imagine people healing, growing, loving, here.

Everyone inside is dead.

"Ms. Collins," Gordon says behind me.

I blink away the bizarre thought and see the others are walking toward the side of the house. Just before the hedge wall they turn left, disappearing out of sight. I take a deep, smothering breath of pine and hurry to catch up.

The path between the house and wall is narrow enough that I could touch both if I extend my arms. I turn back to Gordon.

"I'll skip orientation," I say. "Tell me where Kit's room is and I'll be out of your hair—"

The five of us freeze on the path. I'm cut short by a scream so long and loud and bloodcurdling I think my knees might give out.

It comes from the other side of the wall.

6

I PULLED THE cream-colored paperback from our bookshelf and sat on my twin bed. Illustrations of long chains wrapped the front and back of the book. HOUDINI was printed in bold black letters across the cover. Under his name was a drawing of the man himself in an olden-day straitjacket and full-body restraints. The spine was cracked. Gingerly I flipped to the chapter about handcuff escapes. Some of the pages were close to falling out.

"How many times are you going to read that dumb book?" Jack asked from her bed a few feet away. She was doodling in a notebook, probably drawing hearts around the names of boys she'd never tell me about.

"As many times as it takes to master every one of his tricks," I said without glancing up. "And it's not dumb."

"I don't get what's so great about the guy."

This time I looked up. "He performed in front of thousands of people, pulling off stunts no one ever had before." I closed the book. "He wasn't afraid to do them either. Imagine not being scared of anything."

My sister didn't seem impressed.

"He made ten-thousand-pound elephants disappear like that." I snapped my fingers.

That got her attention. "How?"

I waved the book in her face.

"No, thanks." She scrunched her nose. "You've read that thing every day for a year."

"And two months."

"You must have memorized every paragraph by now."

"Memorizing instructions and being a great magician are not the same thing." I grabbed my deck of cards off the bookshelf. "Harry Houdini made people believe magic is real."

When Alan lent me his copy after swim class, I tore through the book in three days. I read it a second and third time before Alan said his dad wanted the book back. I convinced Mother to buy me my own copy, saying I needed it for school.

I shuffled my deck. "Want to see my latest trick?"

"Not really." Jack returned to her doodles.

Apathetic: not interested, even when someone is trying to show you something super cool.

"Point check," Sir called from downstairs.

I stilled and peeked at my sister.

"Already did mine," she said.

"Coming," I called back.

I scooped my small black notebook off the floor, shoved the deck of cards into my back pocket, and took the stairs two at a time. I stopped next to Sir's recliner in the living room and waited. The sooner I wrapped this up, the sooner I could get started on rope practice, if I ever found the thing.

Sir didn't acknowledge me as I stood by his side with perfect posture. He kept right on reading some old Western, holding the book in one hand and balancing a bag of frozen peas on the other. He'd brought a hammer down on his thumb again while working on a customer's house. I didn't dare clear my throat to get his attention.

I could hear Mother opening cupboards and wiping down counters in the kitchen. We'd had pot roast again, the meat dry and rubbery. Mother served the same handful of flavorless meals over and over; Sir wouldn't let her waste money on spices or condiments. He said only the weak live to eat, that eating to live instead built moral fiber.

When he reached the end of the chapter he was reading, Sir closed the novel. "Think you've got fifteen?"

I consulted my notebook, though I'd already quadruple-checked the math. You lost two points for an inaccurate tally.

"I do, Sir." I rattled them off. "Two points for making my bed this morning, two for going to school, three for bringing home an 'Excellent' on my *Charlotte's Web* book report." I showed the pristine white pages to him. "One for setting the table before dinner, one for clearing my plate after dinner, two for mastering the three-card prediction trick, three for graduating to level five in swim class, and one for folding laundry."

I handed the notebook to him so he could check my math. He stared at it awhile, so long that I began getting nervous I had, in fact, messed up the count. Mother shuffled into the living room, settled in the other recliner, and picked up her cross-stitch with a tired sigh.

Sir looked up. "Let's see the three-card trick, then."

I kneeled at the coffee table in front of his recliner and moved a stack of old newspapers out of the way. Underneath them was the rope I'd misplaced. I set it on top of the papers. Sir closed the footrest and leaned forward, eagle-eyed, as I pulled the deck from my pocket. I spread the cards out in front of him, restacked them, cut the deck, and shuffled it with the ease of a Vegas dealer. I fanned the deck out in my hands, chose a card, and placed it face-down. I let him choose a card. He plucked the seven of hearts and put it faceup next to the first card. I chose a second card and handed him the deck to pick another. We repeated the process a second time. Six cards sat on the table in three pairs. Sir's picks lay faceup, mine facedown.

By this point my mother was watching. I paused for a dramatic flourish, then started with the card next to the seven of hearts. I flipped it over to reveal the seven of diamonds. Next to the four of spades was a four of clubs. And next to the jack of hearts was a jack of diamonds. I had performed the entire trick in under two minutes without any fumbles or hesitation (+2). I resisted the urge to preen. Two months ago I had mastered the one-card prediction trick, and now I'd already graduated to three.

Mother clapped enthusiastically but Sir kept his cool. He ran a hand over his buzz cut and gave a single nod—"I'd call that good as mastered"—then inspected my notebook. I bit my lips to keep from grinning and gathered my deck back into its sleeve.

Sir pulled his glasses from his plaid shirt pocket and settled them on the crook of his nose. "We got some issues with the math here, though."

I froze.

"Two points for going to school? Every nimrod on the block has to do that. That might've been well and good when you were in kindergarten and afraid to leave the house, but you're, what, eleven now?"

"Ten," I whispered.

"No more rewards for things you have to do. Like setting the table and cleaning up after dinner. We're not charging you room and board here, are we? We expect you and your sister to pay your dues in other ways. What kind of father would I be if I raised two loafers? You'll grow up expecting government handouts instead of making a good, honest living. And two points for making your bed? I don't think so, sweetheart. By my count, this puts you at nine. What else you got?"

I stared blankly. He had never invalidated activities.

He raised his eyebrows.

"I don't—I don't have anything else. Sir."

He sighed and glanced at his watch. "You're going to have to do something big if you want to get to bed before midnight."

I tried to recall the highest-value task I'd ever completed. I had once earned four points for sitting in the snow without a coat for an hour. Four for the time I'd held my breath for two minutes. Five for kneeling on broken glass. I waited for what he would conjure this time, wished fleetingly that my sister had come downstairs with me. Not that she'd ever stood up to Sir. Why would she start now?

His eyes searched the room, stopping on my dead grandmother's serving platter. It was my mother's most treasured possession, her only belonging of any value, made of fine bone china with English roses painted on it. We never actually used the platter; Mother didn't want to risk any scratches. Though it clashed with the shag rug and tattered furniture, she had hung it on the wall as a decoration after my grandmother passed.

Panic filled me, but I kept my face neutral. Showing you were scared only made things worse, something Mother never understood. I channeled my inner Houdini. How would the master of escapes get himself out of this fix?

Sir rose from his chair and pulled the platter off the wall. He spun it around on his finger like pizza dough. Mother gasped. He silenced her with a warning stare.

"I've got a six-pointer, if you think you're up for it," he said.

I glanced from him to Mother, searching for a clue. She was too busy watching him twirl her plate to come up with a solution. She clutched the armrests of her chair, her face turning as white as her hair. She'd gone gray years before I was born.

"Don't worry about her, sweetheart," Sir said. "The Barbers were born with no guts. She don't get it."

"The Bible tells us to honor our mothers and fathers," Mother said, eyes downcast. "That platter is a sacred family heirloom."

He stopped spinning the plate. "Don't start with your preaching bullshit." He took two steps toward her. "Funny how God's wants always line up with yours."

I rose from my spot on the floor. "I'm up for it."

Distracted, he turned away from her and winked at me. I was faint with relief. "Now, you know all this magician stuff you're interested in needs a lot of stamina, the mental and physical kinds. These exercises'll make you big and strong like I am now, so when you're my age, you'll be bigger and stronger than I ever was."

I nodded. I'd heard this speech a thousand times.

"How's about a balance challenge? You keep this plate on your head for forty minutes, I'll give you six points, and we can both go to bed. How's that sound?"

It was either do the challenge or he'd keep me awake all night. That was the rule: you needed fifteen points by the end of every day in order to go to sleep. I had a math test first thing in the morning.

I chewed my lip, thinking. "If I do it for an hour, can I also get one thing from the magic store tomorrow?" Sir favored boldness. If you agreed to his challenges too slowly, he'd strip you a point or two.

"When did you turn into a little wheeler and dealer?" He grinned. "All right, you're on."

I nodded. Mother screeched.

He left to riffle through a drawer in the kitchen, searching for God knew what. A minute later he returned with a roll of masking tape. A forgotten memory flared: half a day spent with my mouth taped shut. Had that been a five-pointer? Couldn't have been six. Might've been four.

He saw the question on my face. "To guarantee no cheating. Barbers might cheat but we sure as heck don't."

I glanced at the rope on the newspaper stack and picked it up. I pulled it taut in front of him. "This would be sturdier." He nodded, impressed.

Sir placed the platter on my head so I could get used to it. My mother fled upstairs to her bedroom. He watched her go, his lips curled in disgust. I set the platter down, wrapped the rope around my right wrist a few times, then let Sir tie both wrists together behind my back. He double knotted it, satisfied. At least I was standing on carpet. If the platter fell, there was a chance it wouldn't break. I was only four feet two inches tall.

As if he could read my thoughts, Sir moved me to the tiled floor in the kitchen. He brought the platter, holding it solemnly before me, like a baby about to be baptized.

He steadied it on my head, watching me. "Nod when you're ready," he joked. "You all good, sweets?"

I steeled myself. "You can let go."

He backed away and started the stopwatch. Ten minutes in, the lecture began. Sir circled me, a gunslinger ready for a duel. "What's the only way you're going to succeed?"

I wondered if the vibration of my voice would be enough to tip the platter, which, up to this point, I had kept steady. My neck was already beginning to ache.

"Through my willingness to endure."

"Your future audience ain't gonna hear you with a little church-mouse whisper like that. You're not gonna sell out theaters or find your name on posters. You better find your voice, girl, and find it quick. It don't take the world long to decide you're unexceptional. You love magic?"

It was a ridiculous question, like asking a person if they loved breathing or swallowing. The feelings I'd grown for magic in the past fourteen months went beyond something as fragile as love. My mistake had been confiding that to Sir, who'd thought magic was dumb until he realized he could use it for his challenges.

"Of course."

He nodded and squatted in front of me, voice low. "You keep your eye on the prize and you're gonna be somebody someday. I can feel it." His hand twitched as if to highlight the point. "The world's never seen the likes of you, sweets." He returned to full height, stretched his back, then settled into a kitchen chair.

"Sir?" Jack called from the stairs as soon as he'd gotten comfortable. "Can you come up here?"

"Whatever it is, ask your mother," he said without moving.

"Her door's locked."

"Come down here, then."

"I can't." She hesitated. "I was trying that jump-rope trick you taught me. I think I twisted my ankle." When Sir didn't say anything, she added, "It really hurts."

He heaved himself out of the chair and grabbed the watch. "Fifteen to go." He sauntered out of the kitchen, climbed the stairs, and began scolding my sister.

I resisted the urge to relax. The platter was steady. All I had to do was keep it exactly where it was for fifteen more minutes. I could do anything for that long, couldn't I?

The task ahead of me was easy compared to Houdini's work. For the Upside Down Trick, he locked his feet in stocks, then had himself lowered upside down into a tank filled with water. He stayed in there for two minutes until he escaped. He performed the trick hundreds of times.

In the Underwater Box Escape, he was handcuffed and put in leg-irons before climbing into a wooden crate. The crate was weighed down with two hundred pounds of lead, nailed and chained shut, then hoisted off the side of a barge into New York's East River, like Alan said. It sank immediately. Fifty-seven seconds later, Houdini resurfaced, free of the restraints. When the crate was brought ashore, it was intact, shackles still inside.

These were the lengths I'd have to go to in order to make it as a performer. Sir was right: I had to be head and shoulders above everyone else. I pretended that I barely felt the rope chafing my wrists, the platter weighing down my skull.

Still, I considered shifting ten steps to my left so that I'd be in the living room and positioned over the couch to give the platter somewhere soft to land, just in case. Sir warned against just-in-case thinking all the time. Only losers thought that way, and in doing so, they predetermined their failure. But he'd never said I had to complete the sixty minutes standing in this exact spot.

I decided to stay where I was. No sense disturbing the peace.

Then: I felt it. Sometimes they built slowly, giving you time to press your tongue to the roof of your mouth or say "pickles." Other times, like this one, they came out of nowhere.

I had to sneeze.

I hurried toward the carpet at the same time my nose and mouth erupted. All of a sudden my head was horribly light. In slow motion I watched the platter falling, falling, falling. With three quick flicks of the wrist, I freed my hands from the trick rope and caught the platter right before it crashed to the floor.

I stood there for a minute, doubled over and gasping. When my breathing returned to normal, I noticed how quiet the second floor had become.

Sir's sermon had stopped.

A wave of something stronger than nausea rushed through me. I would've heard him coming down the stairs, wouldn't I? I stopped breathing but could still feel my heartbeat in my hands. My knees went weak. I saw myself locked in the coat closet, a dog cage, a casket, in the pitch black, in white light, in seeping red. I was too frightened to cry or whine. I tightened my sweaty grip on the platter. I forced myself to peek at the staircase behind me.

He wasn't there. He was still upstairs.

I exhaled heavily, then tiptoed back to my spot on the tile and rebalanced the platter on my head. Once I was positive it was steady, I refastened the ropes around my wrists.

Thanks, Houdini.

I listened for my father's footsteps. Half a minute later he marched down the stairs, grumbling.

"That sister of yours is destined for the stage." He pulled the stopwatch from his pocket and tossed it on the table. "Nothing wrong with that ankle."

Several minutes later the watch beeped and vibrated. Sir glanced at the screen, then my head. He pressed the stop button.

"I'll be damned, sweets. See what happens when you put your mind to something?"

I smiled. He took his time making his way over to me. When he lifted the platter, my head felt light enough to float away. I held my breath as he removed the rope from my wrists. If I hadn't tied it exactly as he'd left it, he didn't notice.

"Bet that feels good." He set the rope on the dining table.

I rubbed the reddened skin on my wrists.

"We'll go to the magic shop after school tomorrow." He picked up the platter and began spinning it again. "What do you want from there, anyway?"

"Handcuffs." I kept my eyes on the dish.

He nodded. The platter slowed, wobbling on his finger. My father sighed once like he was bored and, without warning, dropped his arm. Mother's platter crashed to the floor before I even thought to move.

It shattered into a hundred pieces.

My knees buckled; my chin slumped to my chest. I picked up a few shards as though they might glue themselves back together. I thought of my mother alone upstairs. She must have heard the crash, must be crying her eyes out now, asking God why she hadn't been given a better family, a stronger daughter. I dug my fingernails into my palms to stop the tears. I couldn't bear to lose four points right now. I closed my eyes, willed myself to escape like Houdini had.

When I was positive I wouldn't cry, I peered up from the floor at my father. He was watching me with curiosity, like I was a science experiment.

"Why?" was all I could manage. Did he know I'd cheated?

"Don't you worry, sweetheart. A deal's a deal. We'll still hit the shop tomorrow."

I nodded, confused, and began to gather the fragments in a pile.

"Leave it. You got your fifteen points. Go on to bed."

"But . . ." I gestured at the surrounding mess.

He winked. "She'll clean it up in the morning."

7

Natalie

JANUARY 8, 2020

WE STAND IN silence, waiting, but hear nothing else from the forest on the other side of the wall. Gordon and Sanderson exchange a glance.

"What the heck was that?" Cheryl clutches her suitcase.

Chloe peers backward, like she's thinking of making a run for it.

I examine the hedge, the tightly wound leaves an unnaturally perky green. I reach out and finger them. Fake. My eyes climb the eight feet of wall. On the top are small metal spikes.

"For the birds," Gordon says in my ear. I jump, then picture a bird impaled on every spear, sparrows and warblers and yellowthroats trapped in the land of progress. I let go of the leaves.

Sanderson continues down the narrow path between the house and wall. When he realizes no one's behind him, that we're all ashen with fright after that scream, he stops. "Don't worry about that. Probably a class exercise."

"Probably?" I ask.

"In the woods?" Chloe says.

Cheryl's voice quavers. "It sounded like someone was being tortured."

Sanderson raises his hands in mock surrender. "We never claimed to be ordinary."

"Isn't that why you've signed up?" Gordon says.

Come for the self-improvement; stay for the waking nightmares.

Sanderson keeps walking. The rest of us hesitate before following. "Have you heard of exposure therapy? Wisewood's all about conquering fear. To do that, we gotta be vulnerable. Sometimes vulnerability means silly dances, and sometimes it means screaming at the top of your lungs. I've done both. You wouldn't believe how free you feel after."

I picture Kit deep in the woods, shrieking until her lungs give out, until her throat is raw and ruined. My knees wobble again. The ever-present knot in the pit of my stomach tightens, but Cheryl and Chloe are lightening up. They no longer share my concern. Here is the rationalization they've been waiting for: weirdness with a purpose. Eccentricity as medicine.

When we reach the back of the big house, I survey the grounds. Everything is buried under snow. Pewter clouds have infested the morning's blue sky, and without the sun the cold is brutal. A dense fog creeps our way again, like it's patiently followed us all the way from Rockland. The wind wails, rattling my teeth. Though footprints are scattered across the grounds, there's still no sight of human beings besides us. I feel their eyes, though, sense their presence.

The island is big, the size of at least four or five football fields from what I can see. A pole with cream-colored arrows stands before us. One slants left to the cafeteria, a long, dark green building that extends from the big house. Other arrows face right, one to a classroom in a single-wide trailer. Another is labeled GUESTHOUSES, pointing to rings of cabins. I turn a slow circle. In every direction looms the eight-foot wall. The trees beyond the wall dwarf it in size. Together they cut off any ocean view. You can't even hear the waves from here; the wind overpowers every other sound. I bite my thumbnail.

Gordon turns to Sanderson. "Please take Mrs. Douglas and Miss Sullivan to the cafeteria for lunch, and then drop their bags off in rooms forty-two and forty-three. After lunch you'll give them the usual tour of the island and show them to their cabins." He glances at the women and bows his head. "Enjoy your stay."

Then he turns to me. "I'll take care of you."

Sanderson rushes away from Gordon's scrutiny, leading Cheryl and

Chloe toward the cafeteria as instructed. He holds the door open for the women. The three disappear inside.

Once they're gone, Gordon, as eerily quiet as the grounds, fixes his attention on me. Where are all the guests? I debate taking off, sprinting from building to building until I find my sister. Gordon may be fit, but he can't possibly outrun me.

The doors to the cafeteria burst open. People pour out: twentysome-things, the sprightliest elderly I've ever seen, and every generation in between. My shoulders sag with relief. Lunch must have just finished. I scan every face for Kit. The residents of Wisewood wear jeans and puffy jackets, bundled up against the cold. Some of them carry stacks of books; others have cleaning equipment in hand. They appear relaxed but move with purpose. Two young women walk with their heads back and tongues out, giggling as they try to catch snowflakes. Everyone seems . . . normal.

Happier than normal, if I'm being honest. Few dark circles lurk under eyes. Their skin shines. They beam as they pass us. There are no flowing white robes, no blood dripping down faces. Maybe Wisewood isn't to blame for Kit cutting me off. Her decision to join might not have been tough at all. Maybe she was sick of her know-it-all big sister criticizing her every decision.

Kit and I bickered about a lot of things (crayons, bikes, boys, the importance of saving for retirement), but most of all, we fought about Mom. Kit tiptoed around our mother. She let her lie in bed for days, whereas I tugged her out of it and nudged her into the shower. Kit was the favorite because she never pushed, because she made room for weakness like it was a member of our family. She was soft on Mom, so Mom was soft on her. They rubbed each other's backs and finished each other's sentences. They never missed a Puzzle Tuesday; they knew I hated puzzles. The two of them seemed like one mind split between two bodies. I tried to win my mother's affection through achievement, breaking school reading program records and lifeguarding at the local pool. She'd pat me on the back, then return to her puzzle.

When I was six, I lost my first tooth and carefully hid it under my pillow. The tooth fairy never came. By the time Kit lost hers a few years later, I'd discovered who the tooth fairy was, or who was supposed to play her. I couldn't bear to see the disappointment on Kit's face that I knew had been on mine. Since I didn't have any money, I tucked my favorite toy (a small stuffed elephant that Kit had long coveted) under my sister's sleeping head, putting her tiny incisor in my pocket. I tried to pick up Mom's slack wherever I could, putting Eggo waffles in the toaster before school, checking that my sister had finished all her homework and washed her face. Maybe that's why Kit forgave my mother's shortcomings; she at least had a childhood.

When a doctor diagnosed Mom with lung cancer three years ago, Kit's and my fighting intensified. A year after the funeral, Kit announced she was moving to Wisewood. I know the way I'd handled Mom's illnesses disgusted her. She doesn't know the half of it. For two years, this virus has been eating me from the inside out.

I watch the cafeteria group disperse. They may appear harmless, but at least one of them has threatened me. I focus, turn to Gordon. "Any idea where Kit is?"

He shakes his head.

I cross my arms, tired of his reticence. "What's the name of your supervisor?"

He smirks at me. "My what?"

"Who do you report to?"

"We all *report* to Teacher," he mocks me.

"If you won't help, then I want to talk to him."

His voice drips with condescension. "You know nothing about this place."

"I'm all ears," I snap.

"I can tell you're a woman used to getting her way, but this is not some customer service hotline, where you demand to speak to more and more senior managers until you get what you want. Here we're all equals. I've been here longer than anyone, yet I still attend classes like everyone else."

I try to interrupt, but he speaks over me. "Teacher is much too busy and important to worry about the likes of you, as are the rest of us. Kit works all over this island. Since she doesn't wear a tracking device, I don't know where she is at the moment. In the hope of making your visit as expeditious as possible, I will direct her to your room when I see her next." He points toward the cabins. "Shall we?"

Arguing with Gordon is a waste of my time; clearly he's determined to be useless. I'll scour the grounds on my own instead. If Kit is on staff, I'm bound to run into her. "Where are we going?"

He points at the duffel bag over my shoulder. "I thought you might like to drop that off."

We weave through the guest accommodations, positioned in four concentric circles. The cabins are basic but sturdy, with windows on three of the four walls. Given how close the houses are to one another, snooping must be easy. Unless there are curtains I can't see, someone could watch you sleep.

"Watch your step," Gordon says as we pass a big hole in the ground in the center of the rings. That must be a pool. With snow covering every surface, it would be easy to fall into the drained concrete pit if you weren't paying attention. Or if someone pushed you.

"I'll need two things before I let you go." Gordon cracks his knuckles. "The first is your phone."

I bite the inside of my cheek. "I didn't bring mine."

He watches me. "Where is it, then?"

"I left it at home."

He purses his lips.

"I figured I wouldn't have service out here."

He's about to follow up when a deep voice behind us calls his name. We both turn.

"Where have you been?" the man demands. He's in his forties, tall, burly, and bald. His beard gives Hagrid's a run for its money.

Gordon's wrinkled face sours. "I'm busy at the moment. Your theatrics will have to wait."

The man blinks furiously. "You go off on these long jaunts where no one hears from you for days."

"I was only gone for a couple hours, bringing new guests to the island." He glances sideways at me.

"That's Sanderson's job."

"Yes, well, he's out of sorts today. Now, if you'll excuse us . . ." He steps away from the big guy and continues up the path. I follow suit, peeking over my shoulder as I do. The man storms off in the opposite direction.

The fog has thinned, hanging around us like tattered curtains, but the snow falls faster and clouds loom lower, suffocatingly close now.

"So your hospitality extends to employees as well as guests," I say.

Gordon works his jaw. "You Collins girls are nothing but trouble, you know that?"

I wonder what Kit has done to piss this guy off. "Does that mean I should cancel the tandem bike reservation I made for us?"

He ignores that, stops at cabin sixteen, and pulls a key card from his pocket. "You'll stay here for the night."

"Fine." I reach for the card.

"It's strange." He holds on to it, scrutinizing me. "You said you left your phone at home, yet I have it on good authority you were using it in the harbor parking lot this afternoon."

Startled, I drop my purse. Gordon and I both bend to pick it up, but he gets to it first. He peeks inside, then holds on for a second before letting me take it from him. Our eyes meet.

"Better get your story straight." He hands me the key. "Around here we don't take kindly to liars."

8

I STARED AT the burgundy velvet curtains. A bead of sweat ran down my hairline. When the curtains opened, I stifled the urge to run offstage and forced a grin on my face.

I clutched my wand, then stepped forward on the polished wood floor. A month ago, the spotlights had blinded me. Now I hardly noticed them. I glanced around my high school auditorium. Half of the three hundred seats were filled, the most spectators I'd ever had. Few performers came to my small town. Word had spread.

In the front row at house center sat Sir and Mother. Jack wasn't there. She had departed for college earlier that year, not that she would have attended my show anyway. She'd chosen a university out west, determined to move as far from home as she could. I tried to bother her as little as possible, saving my calls for the nights when I was truly scared of what our father might do. Not once did she pick up.

Mother had put on her Sunday best tonight. Sir wore denim and a T-shirt. I'd held them off as long as I could, wanting to hone my performance first, but last night he'd put his foot down. Now Mother waved at me. Sir winked.

They were the least of my worries.

I stepped up to the microphone stand and introduced myself. "Welcome to *Earthly Delights*." I scanned the crowd for four pimpled faces, then grabbed the microphone and gesticulated around the stage, where I'd scattered empty flower pots earlier.

"Let's brighten this place up before we get started." I pointed my wand at a pot. A lipstick-red tulip bloomed. Someone gasped. I strolled from pot to pot, sprouting a different flower in each one, the next prettier than the last. The audience cooed with pleasure. I could have done this trick in my sleep by now, had roused from more than one dream brandishing my index finger like a wand. Once every pot held a flower, I raised my arms and turned to the crowd. I reveled in their raucous applause and exhaled, a grin breaking out on my face for the first time that night.

I still hadn't located them. Perhaps they had rehearsals.

After the flower trick, I sashayed to the cardboard table at stage left, buoyed by my guests' enthusiasm. I settled into the familiar rhythm of my show, a forty-minute routine that had taken me six months to assemble and practice. From the table I grabbed my old rope, cutting it in two before making it whole again. Golf balls appeared between my fingers, then vanished as quickly. I did a series of scarf tricks, first pulling one long rainbow-striped piece of fabric from my mouth. I separated it into five smaller scarves, each one an individual color, then turned them back into one tie-dyed piece. Though the stunts were hardly innovative, the audience went wild. According to the new book I was reading, magic wasn't about the tricks. It was about selling your audience, making them believe in what you were doing.

Show after show, I kept working at the basics. I was impatient to move on to more difficult executions but had vowed not to do so until I perfected the routine I'd already put together. I'd worked that rope until my palms bled. Blisters bloomed on the fingers that wielded my wand. Most nights I hardly remembered my head hitting the pillow when I got into bed. I didn't concern myself with boyfriends or best friends. I was singular in focus, and my hard work was paying dividends. Onstage I was growing more confident. This was the best crowd response I'd ever had.

I was about to transition to my favorite part of the show when a low "boo" rumbled at the back of the theater. My stomach turned. I squinted. A few spectators peered around, trying to find the source of the noise. The four faces I'd been searching for slowly came into view in the back row. They'd been hiding low in their seats the entire time, waiting for an opportune moment. Normally they sat in front. My heart sank.

Not tonight. Not while Sir is here.

Perhaps he wouldn't hear them. He was slightly deaf in his left ear.

I returned the microphone to its stand and held up a pair of complicated-looking handcuffs, the same pair Sir had bought me the day after the incident with Mother's platter. "For my next trick, I'll need an assistant. Any volunteers?"

Hands shot up in the crowd.

"Why don't you make yourself disappear?" one of the four called. I knew it was Alan, my old swim classmate, by his nasal voice.

I wiped my forehead and scanned the crowd. Behind my parents was a family with two boys. The older one was spellbound, had honey eyes and a crooked nose. He looked like the type to sit at home reading books about Houdini, memorizing every performance, every clue, like I had. Like I still did. I called him up while wondering whether crowds had booed Houdini in his early days. The books never said.

Houdini's first taste of success came from handcuff escapes. In one of his earliest acts, he boasted he could break free from any handcuffs the audience or local police supplied. He made good on his word. From there he transitioned to jail getaways, then leaping off bridges, then locking himself in boxes underwater. At fifteen, I had no idea how I would even buy the provisions necessary to attempt his later feats. How would I get inside a jail? Did one need permission to jump off a bridge? These tasks were impossibly gargantuan to someone who had never traveled more than two hours from her hometown. A lack of other options forced me to take my performances one step at a time. As a child I'd taught myself card tricks, like Houdini had. If simple handcuff escapes accelerated Houdini's career, then I would master them too.

The spellbound boy joined me onstage. "What's your name?"

"Gabriel."

I thought of the magician who had chosen me all those years ago. "Did your family drive far to be here, Gabriel?"

He stared at his mom, fear plain on his face. She nodded encouragingly. He opened his mouth. "W- . . . w-we're from Aldsville."

Aldsville was a couple of towns over. I winked at Gabriel's parents. Gabriel's little brother was on the literal edge of his seat, eyes shining. "Thank you for coming to see me today." I turned back to Gabriel. "How would you like to be my assistant for this next trick?"

He nodded eagerly, alarm subsiding.

I held my handcuffs in the air. I'd been practicing with this pair for almost five years, knew every scratch and dent in the metal. Escape had become second nature.

I handed Gabriel the handcuffs. He locked them around my wrists, then showed the audience the key so they could see it was he, not I, who held it. The drama club students had been quiet while Gabriel introduced himself and assisted me but were jeering loudly enough now that even my father would hear them.

"Let's see you conjure some friends," Alan said.

Sir's lips tightened, but his eyes remained on the stage. The rest of the crowd stole continual glances over their shoulders. Some of them chuckled uncertainly, hoping this was part of my act. Some grimaced at my classmates. One woman shushed them. Most of the audience was confused, their attention split between my performance and the teenagers in the back row, who were whispering and poking one another when they weren't mocking me. My face burned.

Onstage Gabriel watched me, the only person in the auditorium paying no mind to the bullies. The handcuffs rattled, drawing attention to my shaking hands. I fumbled as I worked the lock. The audience stared. Surely they could tell I was struggling, that I wasn't faking it for dramatic effect. Mistakes were not part of my act.

Over the past month, I had attempted every solution I could think of to stop the drama club students. First, I appealed to them privately. Then I demanded mid-act that they cut it out, my voice booming over the microphone. Next I involved a teacher, who stood guard for a couple of performances but was spread too thin to come to every show. Without fail, my peers kept heckling me. They weren't concerned about detention. Ms. Kravitz usually fought their battles anyway. Finally I had settled on ignoring them. This made the catcalling stop the quickest, although nothing about these thrice-weekly humiliations was fast.

"No one likes you," Alan said.

I blundered my way through the handcuff trick, unable to escape. Normally this took me half the time it had already taken. The crowd's eyes crawled over my body. I could hear my heartbeat in my ears. Sweat spread like a mustache across my upper lip. My breathing was too loud, throat parched. Could the rest of them hear my telltale heart?

Finally I got the damned handcuffs off. I gave them to Gabriel, who had grown less impressed as the minutes ticked by. I asked him to hold up the cuffs for the audience to see, then told him to verify there were no trick springs or secret unlocking mechanisms. While he did, I rubbed my raw wrists. I'd broken skin on the left one. Blood trickled from the cut (–2). This whole miserable performance deserved a big fat minus ten. I glanced at Sir. He'd slumped lower in his seat, as if he didn't want anyone to know we were related.

I gestured to Gabriel and spoke into the microphone. "How about a round of applause for my assistant?"

The crowd clapped, more weakly this time. By now those who were confused earlier had realized the booing was not part of the act or some masochistic teenage impulse they didn't understand. I patted Gabriel's shoulder, and he beamed at me before scuttling offstage. When he returned to his seat, his younger brother shook him by the arm, thrilled. They would relive this show over and over in the weeks to come.

"That's all from me tonight." I swiped blood off my wrist. "I perform here every Monday, Wednesday, and Friday, and I add new tricks to my act every few weeks, so please come see me again. Thank you."

I bowed deeply at center stage, letting every ounce of blood rush to my head so I'd have an excuse for my red face. My guests clapped politely, then quickly fled the auditorium, like failure might be contagious.

I snuck a peek at the back row. Empty. They always left before the final round of applause, letting me hear a few claps that weren't overpowered by taunts. They parceled out enough hope to keep me coming back to the stage a few days later. I shifted my gaze to the front row. Mother's eyebrows furrowed. Sir was hard-faced. The curtains closed. I trembled, squeezed my eyes shut.

It will never hurt worse than it does right now.

Sir used to tell us that all the time whenever we stubbed our toes or bit our lips. Fresh pain was the worst pain; it would only get better with every passing second. We'd repeat abbreviated versions of the refrain in our heads, *never hurt worse, never hurt worse,* waiting for the pain to subside. He was right. It always went away.

I squared my shoulders, walked offstage and into the auditorium. The rest of the theater had emptied, but my parents remained in their seats. "Thanks for coming," I managed.

Mother patted my shoulder once, as if she was afraid of being too comforting. "You were wonderful. God must have been guiding your hand."

Sir gave her a quizzical look and stabbed a thumb at the stage. "Don't blame what happened up there on a bogeyman." He turned to me. "That how these shows usually go?"

I was too exhausted to play dumb. "You mean the booing? Those were some kids from the drama club. They're mad because everyone came to my show instead of their opening night. They want me to stop doing my act, but I won't, so they keep heckling me."

When I'd pitched *Earthly Delights* to the school principal, he agreed to let me stage it in the gymnasium and gave me three dates to choose from for my premiere. I probably wouldn't have chosen the same Friday night in December that the drama club opened *Bye Bye Birdie* if the drama club director, Ms. Kravitz, hadn't called me dim in front of her entire physics class earlier that day. That was not the first time she'd disparaged me, so I didn't shy away from her sacred Friday night opening. How was I supposed to know the entire town and student body would rather see my magic show than her talentless troupe? The auditorium usually filled to the gills for the school musical, which my peers attributed to their genius. When they saw the lackluster turnout this time, it forced them to face reality. The size and enthusiasm of their Saturday and Sunday crowds—I didn't perform on weekends—couldn't make up for the disappointment of opening night. The damage was done. They were out for blood.

I had hoped we would wipe the slate clean over winter break. New semester, new play. On the same day as auditions for *You Can't Take It with You,* the principal called me into his office. He said my show was so popular he wanted to move it from the gymnasium to the theater. Three nights a week I'd get to do my show on an actual stage with curtains and spotlights instead of risers. I couldn't believe my luck. Did I consider that my upgrade would force the drama club to change their schedule and move a few rehearsals elsewhere? Not at the time, no. I was busy shaking the principal's hand and thanking him effusively. I didn't realize what I'd done until they showed up at my first performance later that week. The bullying continued, but I wasn't about to slink back to the gym, tail between my legs. Who knew when I'd next get the chance to perform on a stage? If my classmates redirected half the energy they spent booing me into learning how to act, people might actually show up to their stupid plays.

Sir gnashed his teeth. "Let's go home."

The fifteen-minute drive was a silent one. I wished he'd come out and tell me my punishment already. Not knowing was the worst part. He wouldn't call it a punishment; instead he'd mask it as a "point opportunity," make it seem like we were doing this for my welfare, all in the name of self-betterment.

By now I was old enough to know better, but when would I be old enough to stand up to him? Three and a half years until I could leave for college. I would go far, far away like Jack had. Not to the same school, obviously. Somewhere the opposite of the West Coast. Florida, perhaps. I'd have to research the farthest city from our town.

When I daydreamed about my escape, I tried not to think about leaving Mother alone with Sir. That hadn't stopped Jack, so why should it give me pause? Besides, if Mother had ever had any fight in her, it had evaporated a long time ago. Once, while Sir was out on a job, I asked her why she didn't leave him. She had cried out like I'd punched her, said she'd taken a vow, that this was God's plan for her. When I observed it wasn't a very good one, she asked how I dared challenge his wisdom, began ranting about my impudence and faithlessness. She was still fuming as she marched to her bedroom, slammed the door, and locked it. That was the angriest I'd ever seen her.

The three of us shuffled wearily into the house. The paint on the front door had chipped that year, but no one bothered to fix it. I took my time removing my shoes in the foyer; if I dashed to my bedroom, he'd only call me back down as soon as I settled. I stole a glance his way. He'd sunk into his recliner and flicked open the newspaper. Was I actually going to make it through the evening unscathed? I tiptoed up the stairs.

"Sweetheart," he called when I reached the threshold of my bedroom. I gripped the doorframe, stewing in the irony that I'd wished for my own room my entire life, but now that Jack had left, I wanted nothing more than to share it with my sister. The house was a graveyard without her.

"Coming." Dread built in the pit of my belly. What would it be like to have an ordinary father who made your eyes roll instead of dilate when he called you? I padded back down the stairs, heart thumping with every step. What did he want? I was too shattered to attempt one of his challenges. I'd been awake since four thirty that morning so I could squeeze in an hour of magic practice before heading to the pool (+1).

I stood in front of his recliner, the fabric stained and fraying. He steepled his fingers, as though considering me for the first time, as though we didn't see each other's ugly, bitter face every single day.

Please, not the sandpaper.

"You practice backstroke today?"

I blinked in surprise. You never knew what was going to spew from Sir's mouth, but rarely was it a normal question. "Yes," I said, sure I was walking into a trap.

"Time?"

"One fifteen."

He frowned. "That's your best time yet" (+2).

Why was he frowning, then?

After I'd made my way through all six levels of swim class, a month faster than Jack had, that still hadn't been enough. I had to be better, faster, stronger. He decided I would join the high school swim team.

"It's about time you started thinking on the future," Sir said. "Enough of this magic bullshit." My jaw dropped. "Your sister got an academic scholarship. You certainly ain't gonna qualify on that front. How you planning to pay for college? Pulling dollar bills out of people's ears?"

Jack had gotten a *partial* academic scholarship. She was paying most of her tuition with waitressing tips. I doubted my parents had the means to help us with college, but they wouldn't even if they could. Sir was determined to teach self-sufficiency.

"You push harder at swim practice, you might get an athletic scholarship. Nowhere good, but maybe at a small school wanting to improve their program."

I fumed. My progress would have thrilled any other parent: I no longer feared water, be it in a bathtub, pool, or ocean. I was a more-than-proficient swimmer, strong enough to swim someone else to safety. But swimming was a chore. I had no intention of continuing the sport after I graduated. I was on the godforsaken swim team only because he'd signed me up.

I cleared my throat. "I don't want to swim in college."

"Yeah, well, I don't want to work for a living, but adulthood is about doing shit you'd rather not. What are you planning to do with your life? Your sister's getting a business degree while you're getting booed out of theaters."

"Those were some mean classmates retaliating. Everyone else loved the show."

"Those hooligans were the most interesting part." I flinched, suddenly yearning for the sandpaper. "Now, listen, I supported this little hobby while you were a kid, but it's time to get serious. You're not gonna put food on the table by grabbing rabbits out of hats."

"If I get good enough, I can. I'm still learning."

"Not anymore, you're not."

I sucked in a breath.

"No more magic shows 'til you get your backstroke down to 1:02."

My eyes nearly bugged out of my head. "Thirteen seconds off? My teammates are pushing to shave a single second."

"Them girls were in swim clubs while you were farting around Lake Minnich."

That was one way to describe a near drowning.

"You got a helluva lot more room for improvement than they do." My father sniffed. "And we don't lower ourselves to other people's standards, sweetheart. I say thirteen seconds by end of senior year is doable."

"How?"

He shrugged. "Better technique. Muscle buildup. Cardio. You can be awful resourceful when you want to be. You'll figure it out."

I gaped at him, refusing to cave to this insurmountable demand.

He narrowed his eyes. "I mean it. No more shows, no more practice, no more magic. Not unless you get your times down."

I gritted my teeth. "I can do both. I'll get better at swim and magic at the same time."

"Like hell you will. Try to get this through that thick skull: there's no future in magic here. You gotta go to New York or somewhere for shit like that. You're staying"—he jabbed his finger on the tray table—"right here."

In less than a year, I would earn my driver's license. I could leave this house and drive as far as I wanted. I could drop out of high school, find a couch to sleep on, devise a way to get my GED.

"You're done with magic."

His glare dared me to challenge him. There was no use arguing.

My chin dropped. "Yes, sir."

"How many times have I said, if you only applied yourself, you could be somebody someday? But you've gotta get focused. Enough horsing around." His eyes flicked to the television. "Bring your points notebook down here."

"Yes, sir," I repeated.

I trudged upstairs to my room and flopped on the bed, squeezing Mr. Bear's head until my arms ached. I opened the nightstand drawer and pulled out my notebook, thought about hurling it out the window.

From now on, I would practice before Sir woke. I'd perform impromptu shows for smaller crowds in secret venues. I'd do all my reading and research at the library, tell my parents I was working on group projects. I would sharpen my craft, losing blood, gaining bruises, until I was flawless and fearless like Houdini. I would move to New York if that was what it took. Sir could threaten me all he wanted, but I wasn't going to stop.

I would never, ever give up performing.

9

Natalie

"*I* DON'T TAKE kindly to being called a liar." I flash Gordon a withering glare, put the key card to the scanner, and hear the door unlock. "Whoever you talked to has their facts wrong." Heart racing, I push the door open and haul my duffel bag inside, not giving him a chance to respond.

What do I know about any of these people, what they're capable of? Who's to say they'll limit their threats to e-mail? I press the bruise on my wrist, picture Gordon dragging me by the hair to the water and holding me under until I fall limp. Who would know where I've gone?

Who would care enough to look?

I shake my head clear and glance around the cabin. The room is spotless, not a dust bunny in sight. It's set up like Paul Bunyan's dorm room: heavy on function, light on decor. A twin bed rests against the far wall, crisp white sheets tucked into perfect corners. Across from the bed stands a bare oak desk and hard-backed chair. Sliding doors conceal a small closet. No rug on the floor, gadgets on the nightstand, art on the walls. Just knots in the pine that look like swarms of bees.

"One more thing," Gordon says. I jerk and spin around. He has crossed the threshold, is standing inside my room. He closes the door and reaches into his messenger bag. From it he pulls a stapled packet. "I need you to sign this."

I flip through the pages of the contract. It says I can't sue Wisewood for injuries or emotional distress, that I promise not to share anything that happens here with the "outside world." No posting ratings or reviews on travel sites or elsewhere on the web.

We do not want anyone disclosing trade secrets or spoiling the experience for future visitors.

That explains why there are so few reviews of Wisewood online. I turn to the last of twenty pages of mind-numbing legalese. When I look up, Gordon is staring at me expectantly. He's waiting for me to sign right here and now. It's not like I read Apple's terms and conditions before updating my iPhone, but for all I know, Wisewood's contract includes a nightly animal sacrifice.

"I'll need to read this in depth," I say. He nods but makes no move to leave. "Privately."

"Take your time." Gordon taps his foot. "You just have to stay in this room until you've signed. We need to protect our intellectual property."

I clutch the packet. The longer I stand here reading, the longer it'll take me to find Kit. Not to mention I haven't checked my e-mail in hours. Though my phone is off, I'm sure I can hear the pings of panicked messages pouring in, in my absence.

I speed-read the pages. Nothing crazy jumps out. I sign on the dotted line and hand the contract to Gordon.

"You can pay for the night's stay when you check out tomorrow. We serve dinner at six in the cafeteria." He heads for the door.

"Hey, what did you mean on the phone?" I worry my lower lip with my teeth. "When you said I'd done enough?"

"You fidget with your mouth when nervous. I presume you wear a mouth guard at night to stop from grinding your teeth." I immediately stop. He clasps his bear-paw hands behind his back. "Kit's talked a lot about your family in class."

I flinch. "What's she said?"

"Ask her yourself." With that, he opens the door and leaves. I lean against it. "Maximized day, Ms. Collins," he calls quietly.

I wait for my heart to slow. After a minute, I realize I never asked which room is Kit's. I yank open the door, but Gordon is long gone.

I curse, then scan the room. Next to the closet is the bathroom, which is so small I can wash my hands in the sink while sitting on the toilet. I sigh and shift my gaze above the sink to check the damage this weather is undoubtedly inflicting on my hair.

There's no mirror on the wall.

I inspect the tiny bathroom. There's no mirror anywhere. I leave the bathroom and examine the walls of my temporary home, which can't be more than a hundred square feet. I open drawers, check closets, even peek under the bed. Not a single mirror.

I give up on the mirror, search the windows for blinds or curtains instead. There aren't any of those either. When I peer outside I don't see anyone, but that doesn't mean no one's there, lurking behind a cabin or tree. I back away from the window, take my coat to the bathroom, and close the door. Making sure it's silenced first, I pull out my phone and turn it on. I cross my fingers and check the screen.

No service.

I groan, then tap the settings app. Of course there isn't any Wi-Fi.

I wait a minute to see if the phone will find a signal, but the no-service status doesn't budge. My skin crawls at the thought of the red notification number climbing higher and higher. I'll have to find service elsewhere on the island. I search the walls for power outlets to charge the phone and learn there are none. Befuddled, I stand in the middle of the room until I realize guests don't need outlets if they can't have electronics. The alarm clock on the nightstand is battery-powered.

I pull enough clothes out of my duffel bag for an overnight stay. Bra and underwear always go on the top closet shelf, pajamas on the second, jeans and my favorite turquoise sweater on the third. I used to hang my sweaters until I read that stretches out the shoulders; now I fold them in half, then in thirds. If this cabin doesn't have a mirror or power outlets, there's a zero percent chance it has an iron, but I check anyway, for the sake of my jeans. Inevitably, I come up empty and sigh. For the life of me, I cannot understand why most people are too lazy to take three minutes out of their day to make themselves presentable. I hide the phone in my pajamas and close the closet door.

In the desk drawer, I find a map of the property. I put it and the key card in my pocket and tug my heavy jacket back on. I step outside, making sure the door is locked before setting out. I find myself absurdly relieved that the lurking fog has vanished. In its place, crystal flakes twirl toward the earth. I tip my head and watch them fly. For a second this world is peaceful, safe. Then a blast of wind whistles past me and the spell breaks. I head toward the outermost circle of cabins. Traipsing through the fresh powder reminds me of Kit. She loathes walking through untouched snow, hates to see it disturbed, used to insist we avoid it no matter how circuitous our route became. I wonder how she deals with that on an island. I smile, imagining her waking up early every morning to clear the walkways. Kit has always known how to keep magic alive.

I search every window for a glimpse of my sister or her belongings. All the rooms are empty and orderly, like a hotel that hasn't yet opened. Where is the guests' stuff? Surely they can't all be neat freaks. I find no swimsuit or goggles, no deck of cards or well-worn paperback on the desks. Trappings of Kit are nowhere in sight. Sweat pools in my armpits despite the cold.

Where is everyone? I sense them nearby, beady eyes on me, but every time I glance over my shoulder, I find nothing, no one.

Once I've finished the first ring, I move on to the second. I feel like the Night Stalker peeping in strangers' rooms, but this method is quicker than knocking on every door. Outside, the grounds are still. No one wanders the island. It strikes me how rare it is to be out in the world without another person in sight. A natural disaster could wipe humanity off the face of the earth at this moment, and I would have no idea. The thumping in my chest picks up.

What if Kit is desperate to get out of here when I find her? The mainland is more than an hour away. What if the *Hourglass* flips over in a storm? I have no clue where the nearest piece of land is, let alone how to get to it. What if this island sinks and sinks, gobbled whole by the Atlantic?

What if I never get to tell her? What if someone else does first?

In between houses I stop and put my hands on my knees, panting. I have always hated secrets: having them, learning them, holding them. This one burrows like a maggot into my chest, chewing a hole through my heart. I take a breath. I can't be the Collins sister who loses her head. I wait for my breathing to slow.

An odd sense that I'm being watched forces me to lift my chin. Several feet away, two women stand on the path, observing me. The older one has a kind face; the other is middle-aged and vibrates with nervous energy. They're bundled in winter clothing, but neither wears a hat, which highlights their identical hairstyles.

Both of their heads are shaved bald.

The skin stretches taut, revealing every dent, bump, and ridge on their skulls. Liver spots afflict the elderly woman's scalp, but the other is the un- sightlier of the two with her oblong dome and uneven ears. Together they're fun house mirror reflections, two eggs waiting to crack. I wince at their ex- posed crowns, at the fragile gray matter waiting beneath the crust.

The older woman smiles. "Are you all right, honey?"

They might know where I can find Kit. I walk over to them. "Fine, thanks."

The second woman examines me, almond eyes shining. Up close, her lips are full, cheekbones defined. "Are you new blood?"

Before I can answer, the older woman says, "What she means is, we haven't seen you around here? I'm Ruth?" She dips her head, phrasing state- ments as questions. "I teach our introductory course to every guest, and I haven't had you in class? Are you Chloe or Cheryl by chance?"

I shake my head. "I'm not here to stay, just visiting."

Ruth blinks. "A visitor?"

The other woman twitches. "Wisewood doesn't have visitors."

"How did you get here?" Ruth asks.

"Wisewood doesn't have visitors," the other one repeats more insistently, bouncing a little on the balls of her feet.

"I came on the ferry with Gordon. This afternoon," I say to Ruth, trying to ignore the crazy one.

Ruth squeaks, "Only Gordon?"

"No, a guy named Sanderson too."

Ruth exhales, then studies her shoes.

"Do you know where I can find Kit Collins?" I ask.

Ruth's head whips up. "Is that who you're here to see?"

"Friends and family aren't allowed at Wisewood together," the other woman warns.

Ruth rubs her brow like a headache is coming on.

"Have you seen her?" I prod.

"Sorry, honey, I haven't. I wish I could be more helpful."

I nod, about to turn and go, when the younger one says, "I know where she is."

I wait.

"On the path to fearlessness." She winks at Ruth.

I scowl. "How about a place you can find on a map?"

"Who do we look like? Lewis and Clark?" She shrieks like a banshee, her laugh so high-pitched it hurts my ears.

"For Pete's sake, Sofia, enough already. You're going to give her the wrong impression."

Sofia stares pointedly at me. I think I have exactly the right impression: unhinged.

"You're welcome to sit in on one of my classes," Ruth offers. "My beginners' course meets at seven tomorrow morning."

Sounds like about as much fun as the day in junior high when a tampon fell out of my pocket in front of the entire class.

"Thanks. I should get going." I wave and begin walking away from the twosome.

"If you change your mind," Ruth calls, "I think I can help with all the loneliness you're shouldering."

Where'd she come up with that? I twist around to see the women standing stock-still, watching me. Any trace of laughter is gone. I keep walking, unable to imagine Kit fitting in here, loving it so much she's taken a job with these people. Kit is trusting but has a bullshit detector. She assumes the best in a person until they give her a reason not to. She'll let you use her, but only to a point. How could she think this place is the answer? Throughout our lives I've tried to teach her to be more skeptical, even heartless when necessary. She won't have it; she wants to believe in the inherent goodness of humanity. Which is why I find myself in places like this, dragging my sister back to reality. She loses sight of it more than anyone I've ever met.

Since I have little daylight left, I decide to skip the rest of the guest rooms. I hurry to the northwest corner of the property, where a second trailer stands. I creep toward it, wary of being caught prying, and the blinds are down. Why are there blinds for the classrooms but not for the cabins? I listen outside but can't make out any words. Instead of impassioned speeches or a guided meditation, moans and cries pour from under the door. A tremor darts down my spine. I hurry past the trailer.

By now my goose bumps have goose bumps. The snow falls in grumpy clumps. Slushy flakes dart into my boots, licking my socks. I scold myself for not dressing warmly enough, decide to swing by my room for another layer before continuing the search.

I jog across the island to my cabin, kick the snow from my boots, and leave them on the welcome mat. Inside I pull off my coat and gloves, and rub my hands together. The room might be sterile, but at least it's toasty.

I stop short when I notice an unfamiliar scent. It's a woman's perfume, crisp with notes I can't identify.

Has someone been in here?

I shake off the feeling. I'm being paranoid. This island has made me jumpy.

I walk to the closet and slide open the door. One more sweater should do the trick. I crouch to the third shelf but find only jeans. There's an empty spot where my sweater should be. I frown.

As I pull myself to standing, a strip of turquoise catches my eye. I turn toward it, then back away from the closet like it's on fire. My heart snags in my throat, blocking the cry that wants to come out.

Gently swinging on a hanger is my favorite sweater.

10

ONE MORE LAP. I ducked underwater and emerged on my back, slicing the water pinkies first.

That the best you got?

I pushed him away but quickened my pace.

Red and white pennants, strung wall to wall over all six pool lanes, fluttered as I swam past. Emblazoned on each red one was my university's logo. When I reached the end of the lane, I glanced at the clock. This lap had been a second slower than the last one. I docked myself a point, then pushed the thought away.

I would go again.

Inhaling deeply, I began another lap. I'd grown to love the clean, chemical scent of chlorine, the way it overpowered and purified. I was halfway down the lane when someone in neon yellow shorts and a T-shirt approached the edge of the pool. I waved at my roommate and sped up. By the time I reached Lisa's feet, I was huffing and puffing. I lifted my goggles and rested them on my swim cap.

"Leave some gas in the tank for tonight," she said.

"Which run-down warehouse are we going to this time?" I teased.

"Evelyn Luminescence is brilliant. You'll see."

"Was that pun intentional?"

She stuck out her tongue. "See you back at the dorm."

I nodded and set off for a couple more laps, vowing to set a new personal best for the day.

Thirty minutes later and PB achieved, I slogged back to my room, no longer eager for a night on the town. When I walked through the door, Lisa, whose dark hair and skin looked perfect sans beauty products, was fussing with her eye makeup. She would fight me tooth and nail on this.

The sheets had come loose from one end of my twin mattress. I ignored the (–1) demanding to be counted, tucked the sheets back into hospital corners, and dropped onto my bed. "I think I might stay in tonight."

Lisa spun away from the mirror, mascara wand in one hand, tube in the other. "No way. I went to that awful magic show you picked last weekend. Need I remind you the guy tried to pull a dove out from under my skirt?" I chuckled at the memory. "This art show is the least you can do to pay me back."

I had recently tracked down a new Houdini biography and wanted nothing more than to spend the night lost in his world. "I'm tired."

"What are you pushing so hard for in the pool? It's not like you're on the dang swim team."

I'd stuck with swimming through all four years of high school like Sir had demanded. When I crossed the stage at graduation, my primary source of happiness derived from the realization that I'd never again have to don a cap and goggles. Imagine how stunned I was, after six months out of the pool, to find that I actually missed swimming. I'd made a tentative return a few weeks ago and hadn't missed a day since. The sport was much more pleasant when I was the one deciding how hard to push.

"Old habits die hard."

Lisa returned to her mascara application. "Then form some new habits. You're nineteen years old and, last I checked, don't belong to a convent. I love you, girl, but sometimes you live like life is a punishment."

I knew she was right but I said nothing.

"What's the point of living half an hour from New York City if you're going to sit in the dorm on a Friday night?"

To escape from a box in the East River like Houdini had?

I raised my arms in surrender and slipped on my shower sandals. "I'm going, I'm going."

LISA AND I waited in a long line outside a nondescript brick building on a seedy Manhattan sidewalk. It was a warm night in late March, the first springlike day of the year. I glanced at my roommate and linked my arm through hers, glad she'd pestered me into fraternizing. Lisa was the closest friend I'd ever had. She was an art major who wanted to run a gallery someday. She loved karaoke and dogs and Greek food. She didn't laugh when I told her I wanted to be a magician. We'd known each other only two months before she invited me to her family's house in Pennsylvania for Thanksgiving and then Christmas, so I didn't have to go home. She didn't say that was the reason, just explained her little brother drove her crazy and I'd make a good buffer. When her dad asked about my major—psychology—and what I wanted to do after school, I hesitantly admitted I was an aspiring magician. Her family didn't laugh either. "She's not aspiring," Lisa butted in. "She's been doing her own shows for four years. She *is* a magician." She winked across the table. Over and over she insisted none of the labels Sir had assigned me fit. She was the first person I'd ever heard call him an asshole.

I hadn't been home since starting college, would never again have to eat bologna sandwiches or puffed rice. I talked to Mother every couple of weeks and had gotten Jack on the phone once or twice a semester. Each time, she ended the conversation after five minutes, citing homework or parties. I could tell from her awkward, clipped tone that she didn't want to talk, that she had looped me in with the dysfunction of our childhood. She was ashamed of us, I realized. After a while I stopped trying. I would not beg her to act like my sister.

Sir I had not spoken to since move-in day. By the end of high school I'd shaved seven seconds off my backstroke for him, but he'd still chewed me out for not being good enough. He didn't know that I'd won the high school talent show with my magic routines sophomore, junior, and senior years. He wouldn't have cared.

By the time I moved out, I was six feet tall, same as him, with arms ropy from swimming. I had gradually come to understand my father was neither wise nor brave. I stopped giving him the benefit of the doubt, quit hoping his punishments would somehow empower me. I admitted to myself what he was: a sadist, a man so pathetic that the only power he successfully wielded was over two little girls who wanted nothing more than to please their daddy. I was finished counting points for him, couldn't get far enough away.

Remnants of his control lingered. I still found it difficult to relax. If I heard footsteps outside my dorm room, I'd jump off the bed and pretend I'd been organizing my desk or cleaning the room. I had to remind myself, or Lisa would, that no one was going to yell or call me lazy. I didn't have to earn the right to relax. I hoped that impulse would wear off.

A door to the brick building opened. The line of people began shuffling through the entryway. Lisa clapped giddily. I smiled at her excitement.

"Sometimes her shows are interactive," Lisa said as we filed inside.

Was that a good thing? I studied the space: concrete floor, white walls, high ceiling. Other than the warm bodies filling the gallery, the building was empty. Usually when Lisa dragged me to art installations, there was . . . art.

I nudged her and gestured at the barren walls. "Isn't something missing?" Lisa shrugged, eyes flitting around the room, trying to take in every inch.

The bouncer closed the door. As the minutes ticked by sans any action, reverence faded. Voices crept higher. Then the door opened again. In walked a woman I assumed was the artist.

She was petite, in her sixties, had waist-length, unkempt jet-black hair with a thick silver streak. She wore a billowing rainbow-colored dress that resembled a parachute. Her expression was solemn, even grave. She drifted barefoot to the middle of the room as if in a trance. She held a black piece of fabric in one hand.

Lisa elbowed me. "That's her! That's Evelyn."

I patted my friend's hand.

Evelyn stopped in the dead center of the room. When she spoke, her tone was hypnotic. She turned in a circle, making eye contact with every patron. "We have become accustomed to violence. When we hear that more than one million people have died in a war, we hardly flinch. Are we proportionately more upset over one million than one hundred thousand casualties?

No. Should we be?" She paused. "What number would it take to make us put an end to this senselessness?"

She stopped turning and locked eyes with me. "What about one? What if we make violence personal by putting ourselves on the receiving end of it?"

Evelyn looked away from me, fingering the black cloth in her hand. "I invite you now to insult me. The criticisms may pertain to anything. My art, my physical appearance, things you imagine to be true about me. Whether you believe the things you're saying is immaterial. Do not hold back." She bent her head. "Please begin."

People in the crowd exchanged glances, shifting their weight uneasily. Some of them must have known what they were signing up for. I glared at Lisa, who already looked guilty, was undoubtedly aware of the ribbing she'd take from me back in the dorm tonight. Who was this deranged woman asking people to denigrate her?

No one spoke.

"I thought that might be the case." Evelyn tugged the black fabric over her head and around her eyes. "How about now? Is this better?"

Another twenty or thirty seconds passed, the room holding a collective breath. No one wanted to throw a punch, but no one wanted the awkward silence to continue either.

Finally, a man across the room timidly offered, "You could use a haircut."

Several people sniggered. Evelyn bowed, as if in thanks.

"Your nose is too big."

Evelyn nodded.

"Your smock is hideous."

"I can't believe I came all the way out here for this."

On and on they came, like a dam had burst. I glanced at Lisa again. She bit her fingernails.

"Are you on drugs?"

"I find your beliefs offensive."

"My father died fighting for your freedom to do this show. Sometimes violence is necessary."

"Your husband doesn't love you."

"No one likes you."

I froze, then craned my neck to locate the source of the barb, half expecting it to be Alan sneering at me onstage again: *No one likes you.*

The jabs at Evelyn continued, but I no longer heard them. My face burned as I remembered Sir's shame in the front row while Alan high-fived his friends in the back. Show after show he had taunted me. He was merciless.

Until the day I rescued him.

It was the last week of freshman year. I'd stayed after algebra class to ask my teacher a question. When the bell rang, announcing the beginning of our next class, I hoofed it down the hallway, hoping I wouldn't be too late to history. I whipped around a corner and spotted two students at the other end. They were Alan and Peter Levine, an eighteen-year-old junior who was perfectly sized for the football team but too much of a delinquent to qualify for extracurricular activities. Peter Levine had trapped Alan by the water fountain and was holding his face in the stream of water while Alan thrashed helplessly.

I turned back the way I'd come. I wouldn't have won any popularity contests in high school but had a just-hostile-enough demeanor that my peers, drama club notwithstanding, generally respected. I kept my nose out of others' business, and they returned the favor. I could handle the occasional nuisance like Alan. The last thing I needed was an actual bully after me.

As I walked the long route to class, I admit to being satisfied that Alan was getting his comeuppance. He deserved the humiliation. No one would have been more surprised than I was when I wound up heading back to the water fountain. Peter Levine had only an inch or two on me but had half a foot on Alan. Alan wasn't going anywhere until Peter Levine got bored.

"Hey, Walking Cliche," I said when I was within earshot of the fountain, not daring to get much closer. If anyone would strike a girl, it'd be Peter Levine. "Leave him alone."

Understand that I didn't stick my neck out for Alan because it was the right thing to do. I didn't come from a home that put much stock in altruism. I stepped in because I saw an opportunity to save my show. I wanted to spend the next three years practicing in peace.

Peter Levine, still gripping Alan's hair, turned to me. "Beat it. No one asked you."

I took a couple of steps closer and put my hands on my hips, trying to live up to the rumors that swirled through the classrooms: I kept a pet bat; I slept in a coffin; I had a serpent's tongue. All because I wore black clothing and makeup. Alan choked on the water, blubbering and flailing.

"Don't you have a test to fail or an underage girl to impregnate?"

Peter Levine's grin morphed to an expression of rage. His hold on Alan loosened for a moment. "Why don't you fuck right off?"

Alan saw his chance, shook free, and sprinted down the hallway faster than I'd ever seen him move, without so much as a backward glance. A vein bulged on Peter Levine's forehead. It was just him and me.

I relaxed my shoulders and affected a tone of nonchalance. Peter Levine was small potatoes compared to the bully I faced at home every day. "I'll take that under advisement." I walked past him into my classroom. He didn't move a muscle.

The next morning I found a first edition of a hard-to-find Houdini manual in my locker. No one in the drama club ever bothered me again.

Back in the art gallery, the onslaught of abuse had continued unabated for ten minutes. I had assumed the crowd would tire of the charade and lose steam, but they were still shouting with enthusiasm.

All the while Evelyn stood in the middle of the room, blindfolded, with a serene expression on her face. The longer she stood there, the more curious they were. Her refusal to quit intrigued them. A realization struck me like a father's fist: the best performances weren't about escaping as fast as you could. Anyone with bluster and a key could do that.

They were about enduring as long as you could.

Houdini's tricks were just that. He employed secret panels and trapdoors and concealed keys. He was an inventor, a salesman above all else. He sold his magic so well his crowds were blind to the smoke and mirrors right in front of them.

What if I could create true magic instead? An act without easy answers or trapdoors. A performance that involved no key. I didn't want my work to be replicable by any average joe with a toolbox. It took minutes to reproduce

Houdini's feats. It would take months of discipline to copy mine. Suddenly I was bursting with ideas.

Even then I understood that the danger Houdini put himself in was only part of his draw. What audiences craved was the "ta-da." They wanted bravery in the face of said danger, a hero to cheer on, someone who pulled off the impossible sans trembling chin or lips chewed to a pulp. Who was a more devoted student of fearlessness than I? I no longer scared easily, having spent most of my childhood summoning the nerve to complete whatever insane exploit Sir conjured next. Then again, I wasn't infallible. I wanted to be. How was Evelyn immune to pain? How could I harden myself to it?

The artist held up a hand, and the room quieted instantly. She removed the blindfold to reveal red eyes and tear-streaked cheeks. Our words *had* hurt her.

My fellow spectators' faces filled with sheepishness, even horror. They were sorry for what they'd said, even though she'd asked them to say it. Now that they could see her eyes again, they remembered there was a person under that blindfold. Our humanity poured from, was trapped in, those two small orbs.

You could have heard a pin drop.

"Now we see how violence feels at the individual level." Evelyn held out the blindfold. "Would anyone else like to brave a turn?"

The crowd took a step back. It was one thing to ridicule a stranger; it was another to be forced under the spotlight yourself. But I was more like Evelyn than like the rest of them. I knew what it was to be booed, to stand my ground anyway. This crowd might hurt me, but nothing anyone said here would deliver a fatal blow. Perhaps I would pass my lessons on someday, teach others how to be unafraid.

Calm washed over me. I raised my hand. "I will."

11

Natalie

I REACH FOR the hanger to stop its swinging and stare slack-jawed at my sweater.

Someone has been in this room. Someone has gone through my things.

I hold my breath as I dig through my pajamas. My phone is still here. I exhale, close my eyes.

The peace lasts only seconds before a new thought strikes: whoever did this could be watching right now. Dread wrenches my stomach. I rise and turn to each window.

The first is empty.

So is the second.

Through the third, I glimpse a shadow slinking out of sight. My temples throb. I march to the window. But when I open it, the intruder is gone.

"What do you want?" I shout. I'm answered with silence.

I clench my fists, muttering every four-letter word I know. I ransack my duffel bag, the nightstand drawer, the bathroom, cataloguing my stuff, trying to figure out what's missing. Something has to be, but nothing is. Not a single item has been stolen. Nothing new left behind either. The room is exactly as I left it, except for the sweater.

Whoever came in here did it only to screw with me.

The realization brings anger, which is much more comfortable than fear. Anger I can use. I think of the e-mail, the staff's hostility, my sister's irresponsibility. All of it is fuel.

I will keep going. I will find her. I will tell her what she needs to know, and then I'll get out of this godforsaken place. I yank on the sweater and put my outer layers back on. I debate bringing my phone with me, then imagine it falling out of my pocket or someone patting me down for contraband. I left it here once, and no one took it. It's safer here than on me. I leave it in its hiding place, lock the cabin door, and stomp toward the northern edge of the property.

To keep my bearings, I stay close to the hedge wall. Other than the cabins in the distance, there's nothing to see out here. The sky is a furious shade of iron. Beyond the wall the wind bends the spruces, threatening to rip them from the earth, fling them into the surf. For a moment I'm sure I can hear the churning sea itself, snapping at the granite shoreline, clamoring for a fight. I walk until my nose runs, fingers and toes frozen. Snow blows over my boots. Every few minutes the wind forces me to stop and brace against the hedge. I cling to the fake leaves as they tremble. The going is slow, draining, uneasy. Despite my anger, I wish Kit were here. She'd make this fun: challenge me to sing the *Full House* theme song backward or make up her own version of the chicken dance. Then again, if Kit were here, I wouldn't be searching.

When I reach a corner of the hedge, I notice a door built into the shrubbery. I almost missed it; it's painted the same shade of green as the surrounding leaves. On the door in black letters are the words STAFF ONLY.

I reach for the handle.

THE DOOR IS locked. I swear under my breath.

I follow the hedge back toward the cabins. I'm getting a better lay of the land, but still no sign of Kit. Barely a sign of anyone. Sanderson said this was low season. I wiggle my toes in my shoes. I should have packed wool socks.

I try to prepare for how my sister will look when I find her. I tell myself to be positive, to picture that contagious grin, her dimples, but insidious images overpower the pleasant ones. Tear-soaked cheeks and dripping chin.

A face full of blood, features bashed beyond recognition. A nose poking out of wet soil. Eyes without light. No eyes at all.

I tell myself to stop being ridiculous. There have been no signs that she's hurt.

Let me find her. I'll tell her everything. I will do better.

I wonder if other sisters leave as much unsaid as we have. We've never apologized for our slights against each other as kids. Some of the inflicted pain was accidental, but most of it was intended. I still feel bad about all the times I refused to let her play with me and my friends, yelled at her to leave us alone. Once I offered to do her makeup. She jumped up and down with anticipation, but I did a terrible job on purpose, turning her into a clown. She was thrilled when I handed her the mirror, too young to understand my betrayal. All she'd wanted was to spend an hour with me. Another time I locked her out of the house while we were home alone. I'd meant it as an innocent prank but forgot about her. Thirty minutes later, I found her curled up and weeping on the front stoop.

There's so much we've never talked about. We haven't talked about the boy in high school who she liked but I dated anyway. We haven't talked about the night I caught her talking shit about me with her friends. We don't talk about sex. Do other sisters? We don't talk about Mom's death. We don't talk about our father. Kit has never taken the time to understand my pain, and I guess I haven't bothered with hers either. When you've known someone your entire life, it's easy to assume you understand the way their mind works. Most of the time I know not only what she'll say before she says it, but the exact tone and gestures she'll use as well. Part of me will always see her as the rug rat I need to keep in line, like part of her sees me as a humorless taskmaster. Do the big and small ways she's hurt me still weigh on her too? I take solace in the fact that I can remember almost none of her wrongdoings, only my own. I hope the same is true for her. Why haven't we said we're sorry?

Because "sorry" is woefully inadequate in my case. If I knew which words would make what I've done okay, I would have said them years ago.

The snow keeps tumbling like a levee in the sky has burst. It piles on my head, clutching my shoulders, promising to bury me alive no matter how fast I walk. Charcoal clouds part, revealing an aloof moon. I check my watch and decide to break for dinner. The big house looms ahead, soundless, watching. I hurry toward the dark void.

Ten minutes later I reach a garden. Tiny lights illuminate the walkways, casting ghostly shadows in the snow. The vegetable plots are barren. I try to imagine Wisewood in the summer. It might look less like a Tim Burton movie set once everything is in bloom.

Bones aching with cold, I open the door to the cafeteria. A blast of heat hits my face. After an unsuccessful attempt to pat my flyaways into submission, I decide the absence of mirrors might be a good thing.

In the cafeteria stand six long wooden tables. Serving counters are at the far end of the room. Behind them is an industrial kitchen. The room is bustling, all the tables occupied, though not full. I'd guess there are around twenty people inside. Most of them know one another, chatting and laughing as they return from the counter with trays full of steaming food. Traces of thyme, oregano, and basil waft through the room. My stomach growls.

I search the tables for Kit, heart sinking a little more with every unfamiliar face. The guests watch as I pass. I hurry to the counter and grab a plate, getting in line behind four others. Two chafing dishes hold penne and red sauce. A third offers dinner rolls. I start when I see the staff member standing behind all the food.

She too is bald.

The fluorescent lights bounce off her shiny scalp. What are the odds that every employee here is part of a cancer support group? My stomach turns when I reach the front of the line.

"I love your hair," she says. "How do you get it so shiny?"

The ordinariness of the question throws me. "Hair masks. It sounds crazy, but once a week I beat an egg, comb it through my hair, rinse it out after fifteen minutes. Lot cheaper than the salon versions."

"Gosh, it's beautiful." She runs a hand over her own smooth head. "You must be new here. Welcome to Wisewood. I'm Debbie. I prep all the food."

Debbie is in her fifties with whiskey-brown eyes that droop at the corners like they're weighted down by the shit they've seen.

"Natalie." I reach for Debbie's hand, but she keeps her arms at her sides. Awkwardly I gesture at the food. "The sauce smells delicious."

Debbie avoids eye contact, says to the vat of red liquid, "Oh, it's not. I'm a horrible cook. Not for a lack of trying."

"I'm sure it's fantastic." I hand her my plate. "You work with Kit, right?"

She stiffens. "How do you know her?"

"Any idea where I can find her?"

Debbie clutches my dinner plate. I bet she looks fried even after ten hours of sleep. "What did you say your name was?"

I hesitate. "Natalie Collins."

Debbie does a double take, then busies herself with filling my plate. I peer beyond her into the kitchen, hunting for my sister. Debbie hands the loaded plate back to me. "I don't know where she is, but you won't find her here. She's too important for kitchen work."

She twists her wrists, then strikes up a conversation with the next person in line, dismissing me.

I turn to the dining room, reeling. What the hell does "too important for kitchen work" mean? My plate shakes when I picture my sister as one of a dozen concubines, all belonging to this Teacher guy. If I can find him, I bet I'll find her.

I scan the tables again and am relieved to spot Chloe sitting with a couple of young women.

"Mind if I join you?" I ask.

Chloe pats the chair next to her, much warmer now than she was on the boat. She introduces me to the two girls she's sitting with, April and Georgina. They appear to be around Kit's age (late twenties) and are well-dressed, clearly have money.

Chloe speaks again. "April and Georgina go home tomorrow."

April (short, plump, cheerful, dressed like a store mannequin at Lululemon) nods and tosses her brown bob. "This place has been life changing, but I'm ready to go home."

Georgina, lithe in a silk dress, with giant sunglasses perched on her head (a ridiculous getup in this weather), says with a laugh, "I know this makes me sound terrible, but I think I'm almost as excited to get my phone back as I am to see my family."

Finally, normal people.

"Why did you sign up?" I ask them.

They work in different industries but have similar stories. Georgina is an investment banker working eighty-hour weeks. April is an IP attorney doing the same. They both had panic attacks in the weeks leading to their applications.

Georgina fingers a thin silver hoop in her cartilage. "This is the first vacation I've taken since I joined the company six years ago. I resisted the time off at first; I knew it would fuck up my annual target. When my boss wouldn't let it go, I pushed for one of those weeklong retreats, somewhere in Greece or Monaco, ideally with a gin and tonic in hand. She stared me dead in the eye and said, 'George, you've been having panic attacks for six years. You think one week on a European beach is gonna fix this problem?' She suggested Wisewood." She lifts her arms. "Here I am."

"I, on the other hand," April says, "am a self-improvement junkie. I've read most of the self-help books and tried pretty much every variety of retreat. Silent, yoga, female empowerment, a couple of the luxury ones Georgina's talking about. Even in the glamorous places, I'd get heartburn every time I reached for my phone. As long as I was tied to my everyday life, I kept getting stuck. I was kicking the anxiety can down the road but couldn't reset."

"Are you glad you came?"

They both nod enthusiastically.

"I haven't had a panic attack since I got here. That alone was worth the money," Georgina says. "Plus, I learned how to quit worrying about them."

"To stop equating achievement with self-worth," April says.

"And I made an okay friend." Georgina winks at April.

"This was the most intense six months of my life." April beams. "But a good intense. You're trying to work through your own issues every day and help other people with theirs, but then you're also doing all of this crazy stuff, like tree swinging and fire limbo." Chloe's eyes bulge. "Sounds nuts, I know. Every single one of my classmates said no to at least one challenge, yet every single one of us did them all. You don't realize how much fear rules your decisions until you come here. The longer I've stayed, the more sure I've been that I can do anything."

"But." Georgina holds up a finger. "Some people take the program too far. They think fearlessness can fix everything. Sounds great in theory, but when you see them put it into practice, they seem crazy." April nods.

An edgy silence settles over the table.

"Where would I find the guy who runs Wisewood?" I ask.

April and Georgina exchange a glance.

"Her name is Rebecca," April says.

I startle. Don't men typically lead this type of place, these strange communes full of people who believe they're too morally superior to partake in regular society? Relief courses through me.

Georgina snorts. "And good luck."

I turn to her, questioning.

"We haven't seen her in weeks," April says. "When we first started here, we saw her all the time."

Georgina butts in. "Now she's too important for us, working on some big new thing. Supposedly running the show behind the scenes. Sounds like some Wizard of Oz bullshit to me."

Georgina has a Jordan Belfort vibe to her, à la *The Wolf of Wall Street*, an assessment she'd probably respond to with a smirking "fuck you very much."

"Georgina," April protests.

"She said Wisewood was her number one priority."

"What's your point?" April asks. She's clearly more loyal to the cause than her friend. I'm sure if I shared one or two more meals with April, she would proclaim *Lean In* has changed her life and profess her love of all things pumpkin-flavored.

"My point is, people are paying good money to come to this island and work with *her*, not Ruth. Anyway," Georgina says, "you have to be a huge kiss-ass to get time with her now."

April sighs. "Like this one poor girl we used to be friends with."

Georgina brightens. "Supercool chick. Our age, lived in Brooklyn before coming here. Has these insane life stories but you can tell they're true. Like she dropped out of college to join her boyfriend's band on tour. Who does that?"

My stomach drops.

"I remember being jealous. Her life was so spontaneous compared to mine. The three of us became close fast. There aren't a lot of women our age here," April says. "But after a few weeks . . ."

"Suddenly, all she cared about was Rebecca. She would do anything to impress her." Georgina grimaces, and I feel nauseous. "Kind of pathetic to watch her become this drudge. Don't get me wrong; we all appreciate what Rebecca has set up here. But she's not a god.

"Some people guzzle the Kool-Aid when they should take sips."

12

IN THE GLORIFIED closet that was my dressing room, I gripped the arms of the chair and willed my heart to decelerate. I'd performed in front of crowds hundreds of times, spent an entire year in venues bigger than this one.

I wasn't the headliner then.

A knock sounded at the door. I wiped my hands on my pants. "Come in."

In the doorway stood Evelyn Luminescence, dressed in an indigo muu-muu and flower crown. She beamed.

"Evie?" I wrapped her in a hug. "What are you doing here?"

"I couldn't miss your first solo act, could I?" She plunked herself on the threadbare couch, wincing as she glanced around the small quarters. "Nowhere to go but up."

"How do I look?" I gestured to my outfit.

She gave me a once-over. "Like a funeral-goer." She pulled a bundle of herbs and a lighter from her frock. "As always."

I glanced down at my black cigarette pants and black cotton sweater and frowned.

She waved off my concern before I voiced it. "The all-black vibe is your thing. Aura-reading earth mother is mine."

I laughed. She lit the herbs and began wafting the smoke around the room with a feather. For the hundredth time, I wondered how deep her smock pockets were. She owned more trinkets than everyone I knew combined. I had stopped asking the meaning behind all her rituals a while ago. Invariably they were for good luck or warding off demons.

"How do you feel?"

"Apprehensive," I admitted, palms already saturated.

"That's normal. At my first show I sweat through three caftans before I even set foot onstage."

Evie had been on the road with her art shows for twenty years. The summer between my freshman and sophomore years of college, I'd attended another performance and convinced her afterward to let me open for her with a ten-minute act. When she said yes, I dropped out of school to join her. She was mildly prominent on the East Coast, so that was where we spent most of our time. After a year together, she'd told me it was time she settled somewhere. Now she limited her shows to New York's greater metropolitan area.

The day before she told me about her impending retirement from the road, an agent offered me representation. He'd seen my opener for Evie's tour and promised he could turn me into a headliner. Ten months later, he had proved true to his word. Here I was, twenty-one and minutes away from my embryonic performance.

"I have a lot riding on this," I said. No one had approved of my decision to drop out of school. When I told Jack the news, she had asked why I couldn't choose a less embarrassing career. Lisa, my supposed bastion of support, had confronted me on three separate occasions, arguing that my magic should wait until I had my degree. *You're going to need something to fall back on when this goes south,* she'd said, then quickly corrected the "when" to an "if." We hadn't spoken since. I didn't even bother with Sir or Mother.

"You can always go back to school," Evie said. "Opportunities like this don't come along often."

Exactly. What was I doing despairing about college when I was knocking on the door of my first real shot? I finally had the chance to effect change, to help others like me who'd had harrowing childhoods. Billions of people around the world were drowning in the wide-ranging fears that came with being human, with the pain of living. I could lessen that load for them, alleviate said fears. All they had to do was let me in and listen.

Many, perhaps even most, would dismiss me. They would say I was nothing more than a magician, a charlatan, a witch. Let them sneer. Their pain would find no salve.

I still must have looked nervous, because Evie leaned in. "A word of advice." She shook her mop of black hair. "You need a mantra."

She sat back, self-satisfied, as though she'd told me where the Ark of the Covenant was.

"What?" I checked my watch. Evie was better known for sage cleansing than sage wisdom.

"You come up with a saying to build you up, you know, grow your confidence. Then you repeat it over and over, I'm talking an hour every day, until you believe it. Anytime you're low, boom"—she snapped her fingers—"you summon that phrase."

Intrigued, I asked, "What's yours?"

She mocked an affronted expression. "Bad luck to share your mantra."

I checked my watch again.

She took the hint this time. "All right." She returned her feather, sage bundle, and lighter to the folds of her dress. "I better get going. I'll be right there in the front row, cheering you on the whole time." She patted my shoulder. "You've worked your tush off, kiddo. Enjoy it."

Then she was gone.

I checked my reflection and took a deep breath. I'd practiced this routine thousands of times. It was impeccable, revolutionary. No one I knew of had done anything like it. I thought about my potential, the number of lives waiting to be changed beyond the stage. I wouldn't let them down. A sureness washed over me: *I am goddamn invincible.*

I liked the sound of that. I pushed my shoulders back and lifted my chin. Most days I didn't feel six feet tall. Today I would own every inch.

I am goddamn invincible.

I strode toward the stage, waited in the wings, and glanced down at the new tattoo on the inside of my left wrist, written in white ink. You couldn't see the single word carved there unless you were searching for it. I rubbed the letters.

I am goddamn invincible.

The announcer boomed over the sound system. "Ladies and gentlemen, thank you for joining us tonight at the Luke Gillespie Theater."

I am goddamn invincible.

He told the audience to put their hands together. My legs carried me forward to center stage. I stared at my old friend, the spotlight, and waited for the applause to die down. I gazed at my new pupils, eager to compel them.

"Allow me to introduce myself. My name is Madame Fearless."

13

Natalie

I SWALLOW, THROAT dry. "What's her name?"

Georgina's and April's eyes meet across the table. "I don't want to gossip about her." April scratches her neck. "All we're saying is some people here get carried away."

Georgina seems disappointed, like she'd relish a roast. "You'll know her when you see her. She has a crazy gleam in her eye."

April scowls at Georgina, who shrugs.

What has Wisewood done to Kit? To the little sister who always let me sing the girl parts of Disney songs, who knew when to crack a joke and when to hold my hand?

I'm almost positive they're talking about her and not surprised they don't recognize me as her sister. While Kit has long blond hair, mine is dark brown. Her face is round with apple cheeks where mine is long with sharp angles. My eyes are brown; hers are green. We don't even look related, let alone like sisters. She takes after our father. I take after Mom.

"Is it Kit Collins?" I ask.

Their mouths fall open.

"I'm trying to find her. Do you know where she is?"

Georgina examines me. "You're on the hunt for all kinds of people here."

I shrug.

"How do you know Kit?"

I don't answer, turn to April.

"We don't see her much anymore," she says. "But her cabin is number four."

The innermost ring. I didn't get that far during my search. I rise from the table, taking my tray with me. "Nice to meet you both." I glance at Chloe. "See you around."

"We should take a class together," Chloe says.

I think of the scream from the forest earlier. Hard pass on any self-help reminiscent of *The Blair Witch Project*. "Sure, we'll see."

I imagine the puzzled expressions they must be sharing after my abrupt departure but am too elated to care. I dump my plate and tray in the kitchen and hurry out of the cafeteria back into the feral night. Stars fall from the sky, rushing toward me. Dizzily, I realize they're snow. From here I can't pinpoint the thousands of flecks holding up the black sky, can't distinguish star from snowflake.

Someone has recently shoveled the paths, but already new powder coats the stone. As fast as I can in heavy boots, I run along the walkways to the circles of cabins, then weave my way through the rings, feeling watched, naked. Each house has an exterior light illuminating the number on the building. I rush past one, two, and three, stopping short at four. My arms shake as I raise a fist to the door. I knock and hold my breath.

Inside Kit will be sitting on the bed with her legs tucked under her, fuzzy red socks on her feet. Now she'll be putting her version of a bookmark (an old receipt or scrap of toilet paper) in that cream-colored paperback she's read a million times. She'll be wearing boxer shorts and two sweaters but will throw on a third before answering. Whatever awaits her on the other side of the door, she will be up for it. She always is.

But I hear no padding of footsteps. The door doesn't swing open. No light leaks from the room. I knock again, louder this time. Still nothing. "Shit."

I walk around the side of the building toward the window at the rear, gripping my hat as the wind rages. Not bothering with discretion, I cup my hands around my eyes and put my nose up to the glass. I can barely see, but what I can make out is tidy, like in every other room. I wait for my eyes to adjust, desperate to identify something as hers, but other than a bath towel laid over the back of the desk chair, the room doesn't even appear lived in.

I blink several times, exhausted. My eyes are dry from the wind. I've spent most of the day unable to feel my fingers and toes. I have no idea where the nearest staff member is and, based on my experience so far, doubt they'd help me anyway. It's time to call it quits. Tomorrow I will find this Rebecca person and demand to see my sister. I will find Kit no matter what, come clean, let her call me every name in the book and vow never to speak to me again. I will accept whatever punishment she deems appropriate. Maybe then I'll stop dreaming that my rib cage is caving in, quit picking my cuticles until they bleed.

Behind me, a twig cracks. I whirl around at the same time a dark figure darts behind a cabin. Through the snowfall I can't make out any attributes other than short and fit, definitely a man. Gordon? Was he the one peeping in my window earlier? I step toward him, acting braver than I feel. When I round the corner, he's gone.

I spin 360 degrees but don't see him, circle the nearby cabins but still can't find him. Where has he gone? Why was he watching me? Is he still out here?

The courage I summoned in my cabin fails me in the darkness. I run back to my room, number sixteen. When I reach the WELCOME mat, I fish for the key card in my pocket. I pause. Light spills out from under the door. I try to remember whether I left a lamp on. I couldn't have; the key card switch powers the lights in the room. I put my ear to the door, and the room is silent.

I don't know the policies in this place. Maybe they have automatic lights that activate after dark or someone is doing turndown service, though I doubt it. Or maybe the person who broke into my room earlier is in there right now.

I put my key to the reader while the wind beats my back, unrelenting. The door unlocks. I take a deep breath, shudder, and push it open. When I step inside, I screech.

Sitting on my bed, eyes glowing, is my sister.

II

As long as I fear, I cannot be free.

WHY I'M APPLYING

I wake with a headache more often than not. I live for forty-eight hours of every one hundred and sixty-eight. Sometimes I forget how old I am, what year it is. My name appears only in e-mails and tax forms—it will disappear altogether after I die. My Social Security number has summarized my earthly contribution to date: person number X of seven billion.

I want to join to prove my sister wrong. There are more important things in life than a steady paycheck.

I want to join to untether from likes and stories and filters and followers.

I want to join to figure out whether my mom is in a place I can reach with my feet on the ground.

To figure out whether I want to be aboveground or under it.

I'm scared of wanting to be under it.

To get out of my head. I would prefer anyone else's.

To determine whether I can be more than a receptacle. If I can do more than accept other people's lunches and bouquets.

I want to join because travel, therapy, religion, acupuncture, new cities, new jobs, new friends, puzzles, journals, candles, thick socks, face masks, long hikes, baths, drugs, sex, sports, stretching, sleeping, drinking, running, and meditating haven't worked.

Because I like the sound of fearlessness.

Because there has to be more.

14

Kit

I SWUNG THE trailer door open and peered around the dim, stuffy room. The blinds had been drawn over the windows. Motivational posters covered the walls. A burning incense stick filled the space with a heady scent. Seven chairs formed a circle. All but one were occupied. I rushed toward it. April and Georgina, two women I'd met on the ferry ride, waved at me. I beamed at them.

When I'd climbed out of the *Hourglass* yesterday and planted both feet on Wisewood's pier, a stillness took hold of my body, a calm I had not known in all my adult life. The chatter of my fellow newcomers faded to the background. I took in a lungful of pine, then tipped my head toward the bright-eyed sky. A bird soared and sang to the sea life below. Lazy clouds gazed at their reflection in the aquamarine glass that stretched miles and miles. Jade, kelly, lime, moss: I had never seen such a rainbow of greens. Yet an odd sense of déjà vu washed over me, like I'd known this place forever, like I'd find my blood and veins inside these tree trunks.

The thrill of potential, the possibility that my answer was here, made me tremble. I wasn't even sure what I was searching for—all I knew was that life was happening *to* me, that I was a minor character in my own story. During those first moments on the pier, I suddenly had in my sights the thing all of us are hunting.

Hope.

In the trailer, an older woman stood. Except for her shaved head, she could have been the grandmother of every friend or classmate I'd ever had. Between her capris, buttoned pink cardigan, and floral scarf, she was *Leave It to Beaver* wholesome, the type of person who called shirts "blouses." She probably excelled at Scrabble, had volunteered at her local library before the move to Wisewood. I wondered what had brought her here—she was hardly the type to stray off the beaten path.

"Now that we're all here, shall we begin, my lovelies?" She beamed as she gazed at each of us, her voice warm and tinkling. "Welcome to day one of Identifying Your Maximized Self. My name is Ruth? If you're willing, let's go around the circle, say our names, where we're from, and why we've joined Wisewood? What we're hoping to get out of the experience?"

Ruth gestured for the lady on her right to introduce herself. I considered what to say when my turn came. I'd first heard about Wisewood while eavesdropping on two accountants in the office cafeteria. The women had been sitting at the table next to mine, chatting and scrolling on their phones while they dug into Burger King sandwiches. I didn't recognize either of them—thousands of people worked in the New York office—but the excitement in one of their voices caught my ear.

The first woman set down her phone. "I'm not kidding, Amy. This was better than that night with the Italian gymnast." She chuckled. "For the first time in my life, I could be myself. Warts and all." She played with a *J* that dangled from a thin gold chain around her neck. "You know I went there to give myself six months to get over you know who, but after a month I was barely thinking about her. My reason for being there completely changed."

"Good for you." Amy patted J's arm. She let one of her black pumps dangle from her toes. "I still can't believe you stuck it out the entire time, though. You hate talking to strangers."

"It was oddly freeing. No one knew me from my actual life, so I could be anyone I wanted. Instead of the boring accountant who watches *The Crown* and is in bed by ten, there I was a daredevil. The life of the party, even."

Amy looked amused and slightly skeptical.

J leaned in. "I climbed a twenty-foot tree using nothing but my bare hands and feet. I swam naked in the ocean and convinced a handful of other people to join me. Me! The woman who hates public speaking and hasn't lain on a beach in half a decade because she despises bathing suits that much. It's like this wilder, more alive version of me has been waiting for her chance to break free." She paused, then said, "I'm going to quit."

Amy's eyes widened when she understood what her friend was telling her. "Your job? Here?" she squealed. J shushed her and nodded. "What'll you do instead?"

"I might finally apply to that French cooking school." Amy clapped a hand over her mouth. J munched on a fry, thinking. "I've been at this career twenty years and I'm not even sure why. What am I so scared of? People judging me for starting over at forty? Failing at whatever I do next? Before Wisewood I could rationalize the steady job, the comfortable but slightly dull life. I'm a different person now. The world is teeming with possibilities, and I get to pick which ones I want."

The spark in J's eyes sold me, her newfound conviction that life was so much more than a bunch of pointless routines. The piecemeal efforts I'd been incorporating into my daily life—ten minutes of deep breathing here, a therapy session there, no drinking on weeknights—hadn't gotten me far enough. I was healthier but no more revved up about my future. I wanted a big change. I wanted to blow up my life like this woman had.

I ran back to my desk, googled Wisewood, and signed up for more information. An e-brochure landed in my inbox soon after. I stared at the words until I had them memorized: *Weeks 1–8: Discovery; Weeks 9–16: Application; Weeks 17–24: Mastery.* Each phase outlined course work, one-on-ones, and workshops. Splashed throughout were gushing testimonials. At the end of it all was the price tag: four thousand dollars for six months, including room and board and all programming.

I sucked in a breath, nearly clicked away until I started doing the math. Six months of rent on my Brooklyn studio cost more than that. The therapist I'd seen once or twice charged a hundred dollars per session. To see her every day for six months would cost me 18,400 dollars. Wisewood was one-quarter of that price, plus it included lodging and meals. I would actually save money living there, as long as I could get out of my lease.

At the end of the brochure was a link to a three-page online application, asking for basic personal information, family and medical histories, and an essay. *What are you struggling with?* the application wanted to know. *How have you tried to resolve your problems in the past? What are you hoping to get out of your time at Wisewood?*

I let the e-mail sit for a week, even deleted it once before dragging it back to my inbox twelve hours later. I couldn't leave the idea alone—a blank slate, a fresh start somewhere no one knew me. A chance to build a life I wanted. I might not have known what that life looked like yet, but maybe Wisewood could tell me. I filled out the form at two in the morning one sleepless Friday, pressing send before I could change my mind. *Thank you for your application,* the confirmation e-mail said. *We aim to respond to all applicants within 48 hours. If you are approved, you will receive a follow-up e-mail informing you of your stay dates. If these dates do not work for you, we'll give you two alternatives. You must pick from one of those three options. Payment is due upon arrival.*

I woke up the next morning to an invitation to join. I'd been walking on air ever since.

That explained how I'd come to Wisewood but hardly clarified why. Why did I want to blow up my life? Because I'd sobbed in the shower every morning for the past year and a half? Because people said the grief would come in waves, but for me it had been a thirty-foot surge that never let up? Because the only way I could stop the guilt was by drowning myself in so many commitments that I didn't have time to think? I snapped the elastic band on my wrist against already-pink skin.

The person to Ruth's right said she'd struggled with anxiety for forty years. The second was lonely—he had retired in Maine last year and wanted to build a community of active seniors. The third hoped to be less afraid of death. He had a slow-moving terminal illness.

While they spoke, I studied the motivational posters on the walls. Some were conventional—a kitten hung from a tree limb by its claws with big bubble letters encouraging us to HANG IN THERE! Others had been made specifically for and by Wisewood staff or guests. One illustrated a compli-cated Maslowesque pyramid with MAXIMIZED SELF printed in big letters at the top. Another listed the three principles of Wisewood:

I. I WANT TO LIVE A LIFE IN WHICH I AM FREE.

II. AS LONG AS I FEAR, I CANNOT BE FREE.

**III. I MUST ELIMINATE ANY OBSTACLES THAT
IMPEDE MY PATH TO FREEDOM.**

Georgina's turn. Tall and lean, she resembled a runway model, dressed in leather pants and a white tee. "I'm Georgina." She smoothed stick-straight hair with a hand full of chunky gold rings. "I live in New York and keep having panic attacks. I brushed them away for a while, but the last one was bad." She closed her eyes. "I need to make some lifestyle changes. I don't know how to do that on my own, so here I am." She opened her eyes and shrugged. The group welcomed her.

The small woman sitting between Georgina and me picked at nails already bitten to the quick. "I'm April." She blushed. "I'm from Boston. I have the same issue as Georgina." She kept her gaze on the floor. "I only had one panic attack, but it scared me into action." We greeted April, and then everyone turned to me.

I ran a hand through my own long blond hair. "I'm Kit. Most recently, I lived in Brooklyn. My last job was as a receptionist at an accounting firm. I guess my issue is"—I searched for the right words—"I'm not sure what my purpose is." I fidgeted with the rubber band. "In the past, I've relied on people like my sister or partners to solve my problems. After I dropped out of college, I followed my boyfriend on tour, expecting he'd magically make me happy. You can imagine how that worked out." I forced a chuckle. "By coming here I'm trying to take control of my life."

April and Georgina flashed me sympathetic glances. After yesterday's boat ride, we'd settled into our rooms and eaten dinner together. I liked Georgina's dry wit and April's warmth. I could see the three of us becoming friends.

Across the circle, Ruth spoke up. "You're all so brave for sharing your stories. Thank you." She crossed her ankles, rested her hands in her lap, and twiddled her thumbs. "As I said at the beginning of class, I'm Ruth. I joined

Wisewood six years ago because, well, frankly, my life fell apart. My husband of thirty years found out I was having an affair." I did a double take, couldn't believe that of all people this sweet woman had strayed. The others appeared as shocked as I was.

"I'll spare you the gory details, but everyone in my life cut me off." She reached for something at her collarbone, but there was no jewelry there. "My sons, neighbors, friends. My brother too. Even the man I loved." She sniffed. "We were a close-knit community, religious. And since I was a homemaker, you know, I had nowhere to turn. From the time I was twenty years old, I'd given my husband and sons everything."

She stroked her throat. "It was an awful three months. I stopped eating and lost a bunch of weight. Eventually I couldn't take the dirty looks, so I quit going out in public."

The trailer was silent—I couldn't even hear the others breathing.

She moved on to fiddling with a button of her cardigan, then stopped herself, returned her hands to her lap. "I decided it was high time I got out of Utah. I'd always wanted to visit Maine. The ocean views, the lighthouses, the lobster shacks—it was all so different from what I knew."

Her posture softened. "I wasn't sure whether this was God's plan for me, but I moved to Rockland anyway. I'd been living there a month when I met Gordon at a farmers' market in town. Back then Wisewood wasn't listed on travel whatchamacallits but he told me all about it, this new community he was helping build." She smiled. "It sounded perfect. I canceled my rental and signed up."

Her eyes gleamed. "When I got here, I met Teacher. She listened and listened"—she smirked—"then listened some more. I poured out everything I was afraid of: that the boys would never forgive me, that the best days of my life were behind me, that I was as rotten as everyone said. She dried my tears and came up with a plan. Teacher said I have so much to offer." I peeked at April and Georgina to see if Ruth's use of "Teacher" weirded them out, but they were both hanging on her every word. "She said I could help ease others' suffering, that of course my best days weren't behind me. She promised I'd find a new family here." Ruth studied us. I wondered what she saw in each pair of eyes.

"She was right. After six months, Wisewood felt more like home than

Utah." She leaned back in her chair. "My fellow students love me unconditionally, and I love them too—a couple as if they were my own children. I
see now that I didn't deserve to have my life ruined. I'm not afraid anymore.
Of anything." She jutted out her chin.

April gave Ruth hearty applause. The rest of us joined in. We had all
glossed over our issues, presenting them tidily so as not to come off as too
broken. Ruth, on the other hand, had confided her darkest secrets to a roomful of strangers with her head held high. She wasn't perfect, but she was
brave.

Ruth inclined her head. "You'll all get here, trust me. It helps when you
have to air your dirty laundry in front of a new class every couple weeks."
We laughed. "Now that we know a little about each other, I'd like to tell you
more about Wisewood." She stood, smoothing the wrinkles in her capris.
"So, what is Wisewood? Why are we here?" She steepled her fingers. "Our
mission is to help our students eliminate their fears." She was speaking slowly
now, giving every word equal weight. "By eliminating fears, we believe you
can become a more fulfilled and joyful version of yourself. We call this state
the Maximized Self."

She pursed her lips. "We'll spend the first week of class identifying what
your Maximized Self looks like. The answer will differ for each of you, but
we'll work together to figure out what those answers are. Before we get to
work, I need to walk you through Wisewood's rules."

April was leaning so far forward I thought she might fall out of her chair.
Georgina sat back with her arms and legs crossed, ankle resting on knee.

"Since we're all about inward focus at Wisewood, we like to eliminate
potential distractions. Rather than think of our rules as restrictions, we consider them freedoms. Instead of saying *No drinking or smoking*, for example,
we say we're a campus free of drugs. When you're free of drugs, you can focus
on the work that will help you reach your Maximized Self. Some of our
guests are recovering addicts, so we have a zero-tolerance policy with this
rule." The woman next to Ruth nodded seriously.

"We're also free of electronics and media. I think the reason is pretty
self-explanatory. Once guests understand the benefits, most are happy to
turn off their phones for six months."

"Amen," said April.

Ruth peered at her. April flushed. "We're also passionate about our encouragement of abstinence. It's pretty hard to focus on yourself when you're thinking about someone else's body." Georgina raised an eyebrow but said nothing. "That's why we don't allow couples to join Wisewood."

"In that same spirit, we discourage kissing, hugging, and touching—for staff too—even in platonic cases. Some retreats forbid smiling, saying hello, and looking at one another, but we find these rules too drastic for our own community. Because we *are* nurturing a community here." Ruth locked eyes with me, making my chest flutter. "We want you to help each other work the path, but we want to emphasize relationship with self over others. Make sense?"

We nodded. Ruth beamed. "Let's move on to my favorite rule: ladies, we get to be free of makeup. Makeup was invented to create fear in women— that our blemishes need to be hidden, that our features require improvement. We disagree. We value you as you were born and hope you won't waste a single moment of your time here worrying about society's impossible beauty standards. Take care of basic personal hygiene, but other than that don't concern yourself with styling your hair or wearing jewelry or perfume." Ruth eyed Georgina. "Consider us your excuse not to worry about shaving for six months."

April wrinkled her nose but caught herself before Ruth noticed.

"The last topic I want to address is responsibilities. We're able to keep the program fees so low by asking our guests to chip in with Wisewood's upkeep. I hope it's obvious that Wisewood's primary goal is not to turn a profit. Teacher regularly donates program spaces to women's refuges and emergency shelters, helping those who have fallen on hard times to get back on their feet." Ruth glanced at a bulletin board filled with photos of grinning people.

She turned back to us. "We find most of our guests are desperate to give back somehow. Chores take a couple of hours each day, and this exchange of labor for self-improvement gets everyone even more invested in Wisewood's cause. All we ask is that you show up on time and do a good job. Remember too that we count on our guests to self-police the community. Believe me when I say they always do."

Ruth returned to her seat, recrossed her ankles. "It's a lot to remember, I know, but you'll get the hang of it." She winked. "Next week will be your first one-on-ones with Teacher. She'll expect you to have the rules down pat by then." People started shifting in their chairs—excited, nervous, both. Ruth checked her watch. "That's all the time we have for today. Save your questions for tomorrow."

We began gathering our things. Nat would be apoplectic if she'd heard some of these rules. *What's next?* she would lecture. *No deodorant? No laughing? No individual thought? What the fuck is this place?*

I snapped the elastic band again—harder this time.

15

A SINGLE BLACK stool, illuminated by a spotlight, stood in the middle of the stage. The audience was quiet, holding their breath and squinting at the shadows. Pink sparks burst from stage right. The crowd gasped. Another burst on the left. They gasped again. The spotlight cut out for a second.

When it brightened again, I was standing center stage, stock-still with outstretched arms.

The audience cheered, unable to believe their eyes. I hadn't walked onstage, had not been lowered or lifted to it. I had simply materialized.

"Ladies and gentlemen," I purred, "thank you for being here tonight. I'm Madame Fearless. Before we begin, let me remind you I do not use actors or plants in my audience. Everything you will see in this theater is one hundred percent real." Affixed to my black floor-length dress was a cape bejeweled with a giant phoenix, wings spread. I swept it aside. "Let me also remind you I do not perform magic. Rather, I am a mentalist. Before you dismiss the difference as some snobbish technicality, I will explain. Tonight I won't saw a person in half, though there are a few men on which I would like to attempt such a feat." I arched an eyebrow and let the audience laugh. "I can't guarantee I'd put them back together."

The crowd continued to chuckle. I took a few steps to my right, the spotlight following me. "Nor will I endeavor any card tricks, sleight-of-hand maneuvers, or pull a never-ending knot of scarves from my mouth." I touched my throat, as if imagining the attempt, then took several steps to the left. The audience had quieted again.

"If you insist on calling what I do magic, then it must be considered mental magic." I returned to the middle of the stage and steepled my fingers, contemplating the sea of faces. "Let us begin. Is anyone willing to join me onstage?"

Hundreds of hands rocketed into the air.

In the two and a half years I had been performing this show, I'd discovered there was an art to selecting assistants. In my early days I called upon only the most appetent participants, the ones who wagged their arms and lifted their backsides off the seats, dying to be chosen. I learned the hard way that many of those people had an agenda. They wanted a chance to ham it up, pilfer my spotlight. As I worked night after night, tweaking aspects of the performance, I realized the key to selection was in the eyes. Sometimes I came down from the stage and walked the aisles in search of the widest, shiniest eyes I could find. I knew them the instant I saw them: the ones who were desperate to believe. Those were the aides I wanted.

While I patrolled the edge of the stage, searching the crowd, two theater employees set up a long table behind me. A third staff member wheeled a cart with an assortment of items next to the table. They had all exited stage left by the time I'd made my first selection. I welcomed a young woman with curly red hair and a shoulder-padded jacket, asked her to tell everyone her name and where she was from. Since all my shows to date had been on the East Coast, most of my participants hailed from New England, sometimes the Midwest. That was about to change. Last week my agent had secured a national tour of my show.

I handed Red a glass vase with a single white rose but no water. "Would you mind holding on to this for me?" She nodded, clutching the vase.

I shielded my eyes from the spotlight, scanning the crowd as if deep in thought, when in fact I'd already spotted my other targets. I called an older man with a big mole on his cheek to my stage and gave him a toolbox.

Last but certainly not least, because the third pick was the most critical, I chose a middle-aged man with bifocals. After Bifocals introduced himself,

I offered him a small package wrapped in robin's egg blue paper. The scene was set, the players in place. My spine tingled with anticipation. The three spectators stood side by side, jittery.

I turned to the crowd. "Since I'm the ambitious type, when I began putting my show together, I thought, 'How wonderful would it be if I could not only entertain people but also improve their lives?' I started thinking about how I could help, about what it means to be human. I thought of love and joy and compassion." I paused, let the smile slide off my face millimeter by millimeter. "But some of us are not lucky enough to experience one of those things, let alone all of them. What's something we can all relate to?

"Pain."

Melancholy engulfed the auditorium. So much of a performer's art was in the invisible work: the ability to read the room, to add touches here and remove others there like a chef over a pot of bouillabaisse. A true artist could manipulate the emotions of hundreds of people within the space of a sentence.

I smirked. "Some of you are thinking, 'I'm not here for a philosophy lesson. Get on with the tricks already.'"

The crowd tittered, lightening a little.

"There is a point to all of this preface. I cannot promise to ease all pain. If you were shot in the gut or punched in the jaw, I cannot say you would not feel it. If I could, I would be standing on a much bigger stage and have a lot more money."

The crowd laughed louder this time. The contract between performer and audience was a promise of seduction. I had them again.

I said to the older man with the mole, "Please open that toolbox. Inside it you will find a hammer."

Mole quickly located the tool. I asked him to hand it to Red, then turned to her. "You will notice there's a beach towel on the table in front of you. I want you to remove the rose from the vase and set it aside. Then you will wrap the vase inside the towel and break it with the hammer."

Red did a double take, as if she'd misheard. I urged her on, gesturing to the audience. "These fine people paid good money for their tickets, and we only have"—I checked my watch—"forty-seven minutes left." Red lifted the hammer and smashed the vase into smaller and smaller pieces inside the towel, wincing as she went about the task. I asked her to unwrap it so the audience could see the broken glass.

I positioned my microphone in front of Red's mouth. "Can you confirm this is actual glass you've obliterated?"

"Yes."

"Hand one of the smaller shards to me."

Red did as instructed. I held the piece of glass in the air for the audience to see. A big screen above our heads projected everything happening onstage for those in the back of the theater.

"You'll recall we were talking about pain a moment ago. Are you aware that studies have shown pain is exaggerated by fear?" I glanced at Red, waiting for an answer. She shook her head, more focused on the glass in my hand than on anything I was saying.

I brought the shard close to my face, twirling it between my fingers. "If you're relaxed and believe whatever you're about to go through won't be painful, then you'll feel none or only a fraction of the pain you'd experience if you were anxious."

I extended my tongue and placed the piece of glass on it, prompting gasps around the auditorium. I closed my eyes, exhaled deeply, then brought the glass into my mouth and swallowed.

"Thus, the key to eliminating much of the world's pain is to first eliminate its fear." I opened my eyes and flaunted my empty tongue. I hadn't even felt the glass traverse my esophagus.

The audience went wild, hooting and clapping. Their faith was mine to lose.

I asked Mole to hand Red a pair of shears from the toolbox. I told Red to cut off a piece of the rose's stem, then guided the young woman into swallowing it, thorns and all. She trembled at the beginning, but with my whispered reassurances, she pulled off the feat without a hitch. By the end, she was grinning. I asked the crowd to give Red a round of applause, then thanked her for her participation and dismissed her.

When she returned to her seat, her friends fussed over her, impressed by her thimbleful of courage. They patted her shoulder and squeezed her hand, aching for an iota of magic to rub off on them. I'd seen it a thousand times. I would see it a thousand more.

For the next year I would perform in front of the entire country, at least one stop in every state. The long hours and late nights were finally paying off. Soon I would need an assistant, someone to book my travel, see to my meals, and ensure every stage was properly set up. In two months' time I would perform in a theater twenty minutes from my hometown. I had not yet decided whether to invite my father; we hadn't spoken in five years.

I shifted my attention to Mole, asking him to remove the drill bit set from his toolbox. He handed me one of the smaller pieces, which I swallowed whole. The audience gasped again, equal parts horrified and delighted. Mole ingested a tiny screw with my calm direction. I thanked and released him.

I moved on to the last student. Bifocals had been patiently holding the small blue box all this time. I wrapped my arm around the reluctant man's neck. Participants always assumed this chumminess was genuine. It comforted them to consider us partners.

"If I were you, I'd feel good about my odds. That's a small box you're holding. How big of an item could be inside of it?"

Bifocals bobbed his head.

I removed my arm. "Open it." I walked away, and waited with my back to him, a grin spreading across my face as I watched the tense audience.

Bifocals did as he was told, prying off the lid. When he saw what was inside, he nearly dropped the box. His quivering unsettled the audience, hushing them to silence.

I returned to Bifocals' side, patting his arm. "Share with them the contents." I held the microphone to his mouth. He was so scared he couldn't speak.

"Spider."

"How many?"

"Two." He wiped his forehead, hand shaking. The cameraman zoomed in on the box's contents so the audience could see the two spiders scurrying around.

A shudder rolled through the crowd. In the front row, a spectator covered her eyes, then peeked through the gaps between her fingers.

I took the box from Bifocals and squeezed his hand. "Consider everything I've told you about pain. It's exaggerated by worry."

He relaxed some once the box of spiders was no longer in his palm.

"Dread is more painful to the brain than the thing you are actually dreading. Let me repeat that: dread is more painful to the brain than the thing you are actually dreading."

With that, I plucked a spider from the box, held it up for the audience to see, tilted my head back, dropped the spider in my mouth, and swallowed.

Dozens of spectators screeched. Several clamped hands over their lips.

Again I showed the audience my empty mouth. Again they roared.

Anyone who claims she wouldn't revel in the face of adulation is a liar. But performing these feats myself was far from the toughest part of the show. Convincing perfect strangers to do them was the real trick.

Over the course of three minutes, through a combination of coaching and taunting, I coaxed Bifocals into eating the other spider. He appeared not entirely pleased with me afterward, and more than a little queasy, as did many of his observers. I often wondered as to their ruminations by this point in the show.

Thank God I didn't raise my hand.

Imagine all the spiders crawling around the broken glass and drill bits inside her.

She couldn't have pressured me like that.

I could and would have, by the way. The average person vastly overrated their own willpower or vastly underrated mine. Let us also credit the power of public shame and the lengths to which individuals will go in order to avoid it. In 650 shows, the second spider had not once gone uneaten.

I asked the crowd to give Bifocals a hand, then sent him back to his seat. Once the group had settled, I spoke in a hushed tone. "Close your eyes."

Rousing music played from the theater's loudspeakers. I boomed over it. "I want every one of you to envision the person you are. Watch yourself move through a typical day: you wake up in the morning, go to work, gather with friends or family or whatever it is you do in your free time." I paused, let them conjure the vision. "Now picture the person you want to become. What would be different? Would you seek a new job? Spend more time with your spouse? Find a new partner altogether? Run that marathon you always swore you would?"

I waited again. The silences were as crucial as the address. "Visualize what's been holding you back. Focus on the parts of your minds and bodies in pain. Has an achy knee stopped you from running? Shyness prevented you from pursuing new love? What is the obstacle that stands in your way?

"Helplessness is self-invented, a matter of perspective. Internal organs and tissues are insensitive to pain. Your brain is telling you the pain is there. I am telling you that if you can change your mind about the pain, then you can change the pain itself."

I knew it to be true, had experienced such a transformation. How else could you explain all the glass I'd swallowed without so much as a scratch? How else could I have severed my father's grip? Pain was an illusion, a crutch.

"When you open your eyes, I will release you from the hold of that pain. You will be ready to start a new life. A life of fearlessness."

Naturally this speech would not cure what ailed every audience member. Hypnosis worked only if you wanted to be hypnotized. The skeptics would claim haughty immunity to my sorcery. Then again, they'd return home with the same hip pain and crushing anxiety they'd hobbled along with for years. Who had been outsmarted?

The music stopped. "Open your eyes." The audience obeyed, blinking slowly, dazed. "Roll your head from side to side. Stretch your arms and legs." I paused. "If your pain is gone, please stand."

Goose bumps sprouted on the back of my neck. This was my favorite part of the show.

As one, as if I'd summoned the dead—and hadn't I, in a way?—hundreds rose from their seats. The audience exploded with joy when they recognized the number of Lazaruses among them. This was why I suffered the nomadic lifestyle of the performer: gas station hot dogs and untoward motel owners and inevitable relationship fizzles. Yes, it was fun to play God, to see how far I could push an individual, but the real reason I kept showing up night after night was to help, to teach people how to lessen their pain, so they might put on a tougher face when next they had to brave the world. *I have been where you are,* I wanted to shout. *If you can be a little stronger for a little while longer . . .*

The cameraperson turned his lens from the stage to the throng of dazzled faces. It wouldn't be long before I was commanding the stage at Madison Square Garden. No, what was I thinking? MSG was much too small, with its measly capacity of twenty thousand. The football stadium at the University of Michigan seated 107,000. That was more like it. I beamed.

The projection screen overhead displayed the crowd's delight up close before fading to black. I bowed deeply at center stage. "Thank you."

On the dark screen flashed a single word in bold white letters.

FEARLESS

The crowd roared. The curtain fell.

I am goddamn invincible.

16

Kit

GEORGINA GRIMACED AT the bowl of puffed rice in front of her. She glanced up at me. "Nervous?"

After breakfast was my first one-on-one with Rebecca. "Mostly excited."

"You should be," April said. "She's wonderful." She had had her first session yesterday and hadn't stopped raving about Rebecca since.

I fiddled with my bowl. "What should I talk to her about?"

"Your mom?" Georgina said.

What would I say? That I'd lost my only parent and best friend in one day? That the guilt of not being there when she passed was eating me alive? That seemed intense for a first meeting. Then again, I was tired of putting on a happy face. I'd always had to be the fun one. Even when I was miserable, I'd sing or invent silly dances to cheer up my mom and sister. I fulfilled my role as the family clown, keeping up the charade until Mom was dead and I was exhausted, no magic tricks left up my sleeve. These days I wanted to cry in peace—violently, unapologetically. I was sick to death of silver linings.

"You think?" I said.

April took a bite of cereal, mulling it over. "She's the issue you're struggling with most. Right?"

I nodded. I had told no one here about Mom besides April and Georgina.

Even with them, I shared only an overview, none of the details that made her sparkle. I hadn't told them about her ice-cream challenges. We'd chase the ice-cream truck down the block, scarf our cones, and whoever got brain freeze first won. I hadn't told them that while other kids got quarters from the tooth fairy, I'd gotten a stuffed elephant toy, like the one Nat had. I hadn't told them about Puzzle Tuesdays. No matter how low she was feeling, Mom never missed a Puzzle Tuesday. We'd invite Nat to help, but she always refused. She didn't understand how I could want nothing more from Mom than to sit by her side.

"Maybe I'll stick to career stuff," I said.

April nodded. "Yesterday Rebecca helped me understand I've only stuck with this job because I'm afraid of who I am without it, without all the money. Makes me wonder what I'd do with my life if I wasn't so afraid of everyone else's opinions." I thought of the accountant who was going to become a chef in France.

"This is step one of five of April moving into a yurt," Georgina said. I laughed. April swatted at her.

A tall woman with a shaved head rose from her stool in the corner. "No touching."

April waved an apology. The rules here would take some getting used to.

Georgina gestured for us to lean in. "How long do you think it's been since Raeanne got laid?"

I choked on the sip of water I'd taken.

"Vulturine" was the best way to describe Raeanne—fifties, beaky nose, permanent frown, perpetually on the hunt for mistakes. Her complexion was golden, but not with a healthful glow; rather, she appeared shriveled, like she'd been tanning on the surface of the sun. I found her more than a little terrifying.

April stifled a giggle. "She's just doing her job."

"I bet she's got mothballs down there," Georgina said.

I grinned and stood to clear my tray. "I'll catch you guys later."

"Good luck," Georgina called.

I left the cafeteria and walked toward Rebecca's house. It was my favorite kind of July day: warm enough for shorts, cool enough for jeans. Every day since I'd arrived, the sky had been blindingly blue, scattered with drifting

Monet clouds. The sun's rays cast buttery light across the garden. A few of the plots overflowed with forsythia, magnolia, and goldenrod. From the rest sprouted tomatoes, green beans, turnips, and summer squash. This rainbow of bounty would make a gorgeous photo. I reached into my back pocket, potential captions already running through my head—but my phone wasn't there. Would I ever lose that urge?

I inhaled a deep breath of pine mixed with sea salt. I'd been here only one week. I had to be patient. A tern with silver wings soared through the sunbeams. That was her, watching over me.

I was exactly where I was meant to be.

During my first week at Wisewood, I had met a lot of friendly people and folded dozens of loads of laundry. In class, we'd each made a list of what scared us and read it aloud. Mine included public speaking, wasting my life, and death—my own or my loved ones'. We'd spent the following class coming up with solutions to conquer these fears. I was eager to get started.

With a deep breath, I opened the sliding glass door to the back of the house, stepping inside. The ground floor was bright, minimalist, and monochromatic—bare walls, twelve-foot ceilings, open floor plan. To my left was an immaculate kitchen.

"What about Raeanne makes you nervous, I wonder?"

I jumped. Gordon was leaning against the counter, arms crossed against a firm chest. I had seen Rebecca's second-in-command around the island once or twice, but he'd never spoken to me directly. He studied me for what seemed like hours. Not once did I catch a blink behind those thick-rimmed glasses.

"Who said she does?" I asked when my heart had slowed.

"You become subdued in her presence, while everywhere else you're cheerful, even sprightly. Could be a coincidence." He shrugged. "Only the smallest of brains feels the need to bark as loud as she does." He gestured to the hallway. "I'll show you to your meeting now."

How closely had he been watching me?

Gordon walked with the gait of a man a foot taller. I followed him through the kitchen and into the foyer. Rebecca's home was the architectural opposite of our spartan cabins—she had spared no expense here. To our left was a dining room with a table big enough to seat twenty. Ahead was an elegant spiral staircase. Beyond the staircase was a great room with a couple of oversized sunken couches.

The house was museum-like, spacious and silent. No coats, scarves, or shoes littered the doorway. No keys on a hook or purse tossed on the sideboard. No mirror for me to check my reflection, to make sure I didn't have remnants of breakfast stuck in my teeth.

Gordon stopped at the foot of the spiral steps. The staircase was sculptural with white plaster walls and plush carpeting. Cascading from the ceiling and through the center of the spiral was a light installation: gossamer-thread pendants with glowing round orbs fixed at varying heights. My guide gazed up at it reverently.

"What brought you to Wisewood?" I asked.

"I prefer to focus on the present," he said without looking at me. I felt as if I'd crossed some unspoken line. Everyone else here was so forthcoming about their past—Gordon was the first to be cagey about his.

"I didn't mean to pry."

"Yes, you did."

Gordon began to climb. At the top of the stairs, there were hallways to our right and left with several closed doors each way. "Her office is the last door on the right. We come here for all one-on-one sessions."

I was debating whether to apologize, unsure if doing so would make things worse. "Sorry" was always on the tip of my tongue, had probably lodged itself in place on the stupid day of my stupid birth. I'm sure I slid out of the womb apologizing to my mom and the doctor for the inconvenience. I wanted nothing more than to walk through life without annoying anyone, to not leave a single smudge on the glass or footprint in the snow. Some people acknowledged that a little conflict was necessary to progress. Most people accepted that not everyone would like them.

I was not one of them.

We stopped in front of the office. "Ready?" He scanned me up and down. I nodded nervously. He rapped three times on the door—swift, distinct knocks, like a pass code—then pushed it open.

Waiting posed at her desk was Rebecca. She stood and made her way toward us. The three of us met in the middle of the office.

I noticed her height first. She was taller than I'd imagined, would have been six feet barefoot, but wore four-inch stilettos and towered over me. She had a ballerina's posture.

She reached out and clasped my hand with both of hers. "Kit, I have so been anticipating this meeting."

Her skin was smooth alabaster, almost unblemished, except for the burn scars on her hands. Her eyes were violet-gray, which must have been because of contacts—I'd never seen such a color. I couldn't decide if her shoulder-length hair was platinum blond or white. She had a long, hooked nose and lips stained a deep purple—I guessed the no-makeup rule didn't apply to her. She wore perfectly tailored black trousers and a black cashmere sweater. Embroidered into the left shoulder of the sweater was a sequined lion's face, its teeth bared. The way she held herself gave the impression of floating.

She watched me so intensely that I had to look away. I hadn't said a word but already felt exposed, like she had downloaded all my thoughts into her brain.

"Please." She gestured to the sofa across from her desk, eyes never leaving my face. "Take a seat."

I did as she said. She turned away, and it was like someone had moved a spotlight off me. My shoulders relaxed several inches. I exhaled.

"Thank you, Gordon. Make today a fearless one."

"Certainly, Teacher," he said with a slight bow.

There was that nickname again.

Gordon backed out of the room and closed the door, leaving me both relieved and trapped. Rebecca made her way toward the couch, movements slow, smooth.

She studied me. "Would you like something to drink?"

I swallowed. "Water, please."

"She speaks." A smirk played on Rebecca's lips. She glided to the bar cart next to her desk. On it were a porcelain tea set, a crystal pitcher of water with cucumber slices, an ice bucket, and a dozen tall glasses. She filled two glasses with water and handed one to me. I thanked her.

Rebecca set her drink on the coffee table between us, putting down a slate coaster first. She crossed her legs. I glanced around the room. Her mid-century desk had a walnut finish. The walls behind the desk and to my right had built-in bookshelves, filled floor to ceiling. Behind me, near the door where I'd entered, was a tall cabinet—a sign affixed to it had bold red letter-ing: AUTHORIZED PERSONNEL ONLY. On my left were French doors that opened onto a balcony. I could see the grounds beyond.

I turned back to the coffee table. In the middle of it was a glass bowl that held shards of what appeared to be a broken china platter. Some pieces had dainty English roses painted on them.

Rebecca broke the silence. "It reminds me of weakness."

I glanced up at her.

"You find it odd that they call me Teacher."

"I didn't say that," I stammered.

She leaned in. "I find it strange too."

Curiosity got the best of me. "You didn't ask them to?"

"The guests made it up. I referred to them as my students once, in a classroom setting. One of them started calling me Teacher. The name stuck." She shrugged, then went back to watching me. I squirmed.

"Your scarf is beautiful."

I played with the colorful silk around my neck. The scarf had orange trim with bright dashes of green, pink, turquoise, yellow, and white. When you unfolded it, the pattern was one big flower in the center with a bunch of paintbrush strokes around it. I thought the strokes resembled seashells; Nat said they were claws.

"It was my mom's," I said without thinking. "She left it to me."

Rebecca rested her chin in her hand. "Where did she go?"

I studied my feet. "She died."

"Oh, Kit." Rebecca rose from her armchair and joined me on the couch. She squeezed my hand. "I am so sorry. That must be one of your most trea-sured possessions, then."

I nodded, burying my nose in the scarf. I knew it was juvenile to pretend that after a year and a half it still smelled like Mom—freesia and cheap hairspray—but I wanted to believe it did and washed it as little as possible. Once, I thought I'd lost the scarf and, sobbing, called Nat. She acted like I was being ridiculous, as if it were any old thing I could replace at Target.

Rebecca flipped my palm up and began stroking it with her thumb. She leaned in so our faces were a foot apart. Her breath smelled like mint. The hair on my arms rose. I hoped she couldn't see.

"What are you most afraid of?"

I hesitated, uncomfortable with getting personal so fast.

"We'll save ourselves a lot of time if we move past the comfort of lies and into the discomfort of truth. The world out there indoctrinates us to believe that white lies or omissions are for the best, but I think lies of any magnitude erect walls between us. Society has taught us to fear uneasy social interactions, as if they can actually hurt us. I'm asking you to dive into the discomfort. Dwell in it so that I can help you."

I took a deep breath. "I'm scared that I don't matter. That my life is meaningless." There, I'd said it. I lifted my eyes to hers, afraid of what I'd find there—pity, scorn, disgust.

They were filled with love.

Rebecca enveloped me in her arms. "Dear girl, you matter. Of course you do. You matter to me. We all need you here. You may not see it yet, but you will soon. I promise you." I let my face relax into her shoulder. My own shoulders heaved, though my eyes were dry.

You matter. You matter. You matter. The two words would carousel through my mind as I lay in bed that night. I wanted nothing more than to believe her.

"Do you think yourself brave, Kit?"

I shook my head. I knew I should pull away from her, put a more appropriate distance between us on the couch—what was I doing, letting a stranger hold me?—but I wanted to stay in that cocoon. She didn't feel unfamiliar, and I was sure that once I detached myself from her, the spell would break. The sense of safety, of belonging, would melt away. I would be normal, sparkleless Kit again.

"You don't have to go anywhere. You can stay right where you are." She petted my hair, and I relaxed back into her arms, relieved. "I know for a fact you're braver than you think. Let me prove it to you."

I waited, listening. Her voice was piano music, ocean waves, raindrops on leaves.

"Tell me one brave thing you've done."

"I went BASE jumping while living in Thailand. I jumped off a cliff in Krabi with nothing but a parachute strapped to my back."

"A formidable challenge. How long did you live in Thailand?"

"Three months."

"You moved to the other side of the world, where you didn't know a single living soul. Does that not also strike you as brave?"

I shrugged. "I ran away after my mom died. I have a tendency to take off when things get hard or scary." How many times had Nat said as much? "I wouldn't call that brave."

"Sometimes the bravest thing one can do is run away." She stopped stroking my hair, and I sat back. The doubt must have been plain on my face, because she prompted, "Would you say a woman fleeing her abuser is cowardly?"

"Of course not. That's not the same."

"You're too hard on yourself, Kit."

I flushed and reached for my hair, then changed course, giving the elastic band a hard snap against my wrist. I winced.

Rebecca stared at the band. Her violet eyes flitted to mine. "What else have you run away from?"

"I dropped out of college." Guilt lodged in my throat.

"So did I." I glanced at her, surprised. "I ran away from family, from college, from the concepts of marriage and motherhood. Refusing to accept what society expects doesn't make us cowards."

I thought about that while staring out the French windows, trying to decide whether I agreed. Suddenly something crashed into the glass, rattling the pane in its frame. I leapt to my feet and glimpsed silver wings sliding down the window. Rebecca gently took my hands, sat me back down.

She guided my chin toward her. "You have absolutely nothing to be ashamed or afraid of. You are warm, thoughtful, and compassionate, brimming with potential. I can help you."

I didn't speak, distracted by the bird but unable to see where it had gone. What if she had broken a wing, never flew again?

"Let me help you."

"How?" I asked, scared of the hope building in my chest, aware that the idea of happiness frightened me but unsure why.

"I've been working the path for a long time. I have many tools to offer." She watched me. "You're a tidal wave, Kit, and you don't even know it."

I opened my mouth, but she closed it gently. She left her thumb on my bottom lip, then dragged it down my chin, my voice box, my neck. She fingered my mother's scarf.

Our eyes met. She leaned toward me. My mouth went dry.

She laughed and gripped both of my thighs, using them to push herself to standing. She strode to the door. "It's time to reframe the story you tell about yourself. We'll start with no more speaking ill, then move on to no more thinking ill. Before our next session, I want you to come up with a mantra—a phrase to instill self-confidence, something you can summon when you're down. Once you have that mantra, you'll spend twenty minutes every morning—ideally when you first wake up—repeating that phrase aloud in your room."

She stood there, waiting.

I rose on shaky legs and made my way toward her.

Her eyes sparkled. "I can't wait to see what you come up with."

17

Kit

JULY 2019

"ALL I'M SAYING is it's a little weird," Georgina said, "that she doesn't follow the rules she made up."

April shrugged. "Rebecca's been doing this a lot longer than we have. The no-touching rule might not serve her anymore."

I considered this as my friends and I left the cafeteria after breakfast. My first meeting with Rebecca had been two days ago. After forty-eight hours of reflection, I'd concluded that Wisewood's leader was offbeat—but in a good way. Sure, she broke her own rules, but she was so confident in what she'd built here, so sure of my potential. I couldn't believe she pored over me and saw something besides failure.

I wanted to be that tidal wave.

"That's true." Georgina shielded her eyes from the sun. Thick, muggy air glued my long hair to the back of my neck. "I came this close to crying during my session, so she must be onto something." She paused, thinking. "God, I haven't cried since that bitch Kim Johnson told everyone I had an eating disorder."

"What made you so upset?" April asked.

"For one, the entire school called me Purge-gina for months. It was a crock of shit, obviously."

"I mean yesterday," April said. "With Rebecca."

Georgina shrugged, avoiding our gazes. "I gotta go. Wouldn't want to be late for chores." She pulled a goofy face and waved goodbye.

April and I watched her disappear inside Rebecca's house, then headed toward the northwest corner of the island for class. We fanned ourselves as we walked, talking about nothing, laughing at newly formed inside jokes. I felt like I'd known her forever.

A few minutes later we'd reached the class trailer. April grabbed the door handle. Before I followed her inside, a flash of movement near the hedge caught my eye. I turned to see a segment of the wall open—I hadn't realized it had doors. Gordon walked through the entryway. I stared. During the grounds tour, we'd been told there was nothing beyond the hedge but a forest. So what was he doing out there? Gordon locked the door behind him, then turned to glower at me like he'd known all along that I was watching.

I averted my eyes—heart racing, face flushed—but the damage was done. He'd definitely seen me. I scurried into the trailer behind April.

The air inside the room was even more humid, like the windows hadn't been opened in weeks. Floor pillows, grouped in twos, had replaced the chairs. The other guests were chatting among themselves.

Ruth greeted us warmly. "Go ahead and mingle while we wait for a couple other students."

April turned to two twenty-something guys. One of them was Sanderson, the ferry driver whom I had yet to see without his hood pulled up, even in this heat. He had been chatty enough on the boat, so when I spotted him weeding the vegetable garden the other day, I'd kneeled beside him and struck up a conversation. While we worked, I learned that he'd come here after getting kicked out of multiple rehab programs, that even after three years at Wisewood he still harbored guilt for the way he'd taken advantage of his parents. His voice quavered when he talked about his mom, so I didn't push the subject. He told me at least four times how much he loved Wisewood.

Before I could join April and the guys, a man and woman in their forties approached me. He wore a Cleveland Cavaliers baseball cap, was portly with a thick but neatly trimmed beard. "Maximized day. I'm Jeremiah."

The woman was bald with a mild twitch on the left side of her face. "And I'm Sofia." She fidgeted like a teenager on a first date.

"Nice to meet you. I'm Kit."

Jeremiah lifted and resettled the hat. I glimpsed bare skin, wondered whether he was bald too. "You enjoying Wisewood so far?" I nodded. "Good. I've only been here a few months but can't imagine living anywhere else."

"Oh, same," Sofia said with wide eyes. "I joined three and a half years ago. I provide basic medical care here."

"She's being modest." Jeremiah grinned. "Sofia is a brilliant doctor."

"I did good work at Tufts, but I wish I'd come home to Wisewood sooner. Lots of overworked and exhausted years out there." She gestured toward the trailer door, like an unsustainable workweek was hunting her beyond it.

"But because of those overworked years," Jeremiah pointed out, "you've been able to donate some of your savings here, right?"

"Not just *some*." She gazed at me. "I would do anything for Teacher. She saved me."

"As for me," Jeremiah said, "I was a CPA at a small firm in Chicago. It was like living in a *Dilbert* cartoon."

"Oh." I smiled. "I work in accounting too, in New York. Well, just as a receptionist."

"Get outta town," he said. "At which firm?"

As I explained my background I tried not to feel inferior, but Jeremiah and Sofia didn't care that I held no advanced degrees—or any degree. They listened intently to every word.

"I'm so sorry about your mom," Jeremiah said when I'd finished. "My brother passed fourteen years ago, and I still miss him like hell. There're a lot of things I wish I'd done differently while he was alive." He stared at his shoes.

"Me too."

He glanced up, about to say something else when the trailer door bounced

open. In walked Raeanne, a toothpick propped between her lips. She sauntered to the middle of the room.

"Raeanne, shoes," Ruth said. "You're tracking mud everywhere." Raeanne twirled the toothpick, then bent down to unlace her boots. Ruth
sighed. "Leave them on. Have you seen Gordon?" Raeanne shook her head.

"We'll have to get started without him, then." Ruth clapped. "All right,
class, today we're working on parental transference. Everyone find a partner
and sit across from them, please?"

I scanned the room for April and hurried to her side. "Be my partner?"

She wiggled her eyebrows and nodded. We sat on the nearest couple of
floor pillows. I glanced around the room at the other pairs. Jeremiah and
Sofia. Sanderson and his friend. Debbie and Raeanne. They were all seated
cross-legged, knees almost touching their partners'. April noticed this too
and moved her pillow closer to mine. Dank heat emanated off her.

Ruth walked to one of the windows and lowered the blind. She spoke in
a soothing tone. "At Wisewood, we work tirelessly to eliminate our fears so
we can reach our Maximized Selves. Many of our deepest fears are rooted in
childhood, whether they be lessons we've internalized from unpleasant experiences or explicit warnings and abuses we've suff—"

"Hey, Ruth." Raeanne raised her hand. "I think Jeremiah and Sofia
should switch partners."

We all glanced at the two of them. Both appeared bewildered.

"Why?" Jeremiah asked.

Raeanne dug her pinkie finger into her ear. "You're awfully interested in
getting close to her these days." She put her finger to her nose and sniffed.
"Rules are rules: no romances allowed."

Jeremiah blushed. "I don't know what you're talking about."

"I'm happy to give examples." Raeanne smirked.

Sofia leaned back from Jeremiah, who looked horrified. "I want a new
partner."

Ruth took a deep breath. "April, will you please switch spots with Jeremiah?"

April shrugged an apology at me and traded places with the big guy.

"Just watching out for your path." Raeanne snickered.

"You've made your point, Raeanne," Ruth said. "Let's move on." She crossed the room and let down the other blind. Jeremiah's face was shadowed, lips a flat line. "Transference is the redirection of feelings toward a new person. The purpose of this exercise is to simulate one or both of your parents sitting across from you. We will unleash negative memories you've all been holding on to. This can be anything from 'I hate the way you criticized my friends' to 'I was never good enough for you' to 'Why did you hurt me?' You don't need to get everything out in one session." Ruth chuckled. "Some of our longtime members have done this exercise dozens of times, and they know we never quite run out of things to say to our parents." People in the room muttered their agreement. "You are free to focus on any issue, however big or small. In a minute, I'll turn out the lights and you won't be able to see your partner."

The trailer door opened again, flooding the room with sunlight. At the threshold stood Gordon. He closed the door behind him quietly.

"Thanks for gracing us with your presence," Raeanne grumbled.

Gordon nodded at Ruth and took a seat near the door, his back to the wall.

"Mind telling us where you been?" Raeanne said.

The room stilled while Gordon stared her down. "Yes. I would."

Raeanne didn't push him.

Ruth flicked the light switch, and we were enveloped in darkness. The room quieted. I listened to the others' faint inhalations and exhalations.

"Your partner is here to encourage you if yo need it, to keep you on track," Ruth said. "Now please close your eyes and keep them that way for the entire exercise. Focus on my voice and what I am telling you. If anyone has any final questions or concerns before we begin, voice them now."

"Good luck," Jeremiah whispered.

"You too," I whispered back.

He smiled, then closed his eyes. Somewhere in the trailer knuckles cracked. I shivered in the heat.

"Picture your mother or father," Ruth said in a hypnotic tone. "Envision the color of their eyes, the wrinkle between their brows, the curve of their smiles, the cut of their teeth. Think about the physical detail you love most about this person's face." She paused. "Now think about the detail you like least. Is the smile more of a sneer? Are the teeth overly yellowed? Are the eyes hard, disapproving? Capture this person's face in your mind. Imagine he or she is sitting across from you, that you're touching Mom's or Dad's or whatever-you-called-them's knees. Can you picture them?"

"Yes," someone whispered.

"Good." Ruth lowered her voice. "Now think of a bad memory of that parent. Don't strain yourself. It doesn't have to be the worst of your memories, although it can be."

The date popped into my mind before Ruth had finished speaking: January 12, 2017. I'd spent the final hour of my afternoon shift at Corrigan's being called unimaginative slurs by a few day-drunk college kids after I ignored their pickup lines. I drove home, drained. It had been five years since I'd dropped out of college. All I'd managed in half a decade was to jump from bar to bar around Scottsdale, hoping the tips would be more generous at the next place. They never were.

Fifteen minutes later I was back in Tempe. I parked my car in the driveway and trudged through the front door of our house, fuming over the poor decisions of my past. Standing in the foyer, I sighed at the peeling wallpaper and months of bills stacked on the chipped console table. I tossed my purse on the floor and padded to the kitchen, stopping short when I saw Nat hunched over the dining table. She was wiping it down with a rag and antibacterial spray.

"What are you doing here?" I said.

"This used to be my house too."

I glanced at the oven clock. "I thought you'd be at work."

"Mom had her doctor's appointment today, remember?" she asked, irritated that I wasn't thinking about the exact thing she wanted me to at any point of every day. *It must have slipped my mind,* I wanted to snap, *when three of my patrons started chanting the C-word at me.* But I didn't say a thing because Nat would have snapped back, *You know where you wouldn't get called the C-word all the time? A hospital, if you'd finished your degree. Or an office job.* She was constantly on my case about getting out of bartending.

"I left early to come hear the results." She eyed me wearily. "She's in the bathroom."

As if on cue, Mom emerged from the hallway, ghostly and grim. "I'm so happy to see you girls." She'd spent a lifetime forcing smiles across her face— I considered how tired her cheeks must be. I was exhausted for her.

Nat quit cleaning. I stepped forward. "Did you get the biopsy results?"

Mom glanced back and forth between us, trying to delay answering. My stomach turned. "You may want to sit down."

"Mom, come on," Nat said. "What'd the doctor say?"

We stared at our mother. She squirmed, squinting at the ceiling.

My world tipped sideways.

She sighed. "It's cancer. I'm sorry, girls."

A wail escaped my throat. I darted toward my mother and clutched her— an already-thin woman shrinking ever smaller. Nat collapsed into a chair.

Mom caressed my hair for a while, sniffling. I let the tears fall, burying my nose in the colorful scarf she wore every day. The three of us stilled in the kitchen, waiting for something to happen, for someone to tell us how to go on. It had to be Nat. It was always Nat.

She cleared her throat at the table. When she spoke, I could tell without peeking that she was trying not to cry. "What are the treatment options?"

"I'm declining treatment."

"What?" Nat jumped to her feet. I winced and reluctantly pulled away from Mom in protest.

"Baby, I don't want them cutting into me or poisoning my body. I don't want to become a shell of myself. I've made peace with it."

"What if you die?"

"So be it." Mom met my sister's eyes. "At least I'll go on my own terms."

My mouth went chalky. My legs shook.

"You both know I've always wanted to live near the ocean. I've been researching condos in San Diego."

"This is the excuse you've been waiting for, isn't it?" Nat raged, wiping the tears that now streamed down her face. "After all these years, you're finally going to let the depression win."

"Honey, I didn't choose to have cancer."

"You have to fight." Nat pounded her fist on the table to emphasize the last word. "You have to be strong."

"I've been fighting my whole life." Mom hung her head. "I'm tired."

Nat came around the table and gripped Mom's shoulders, eyes wild. "I'll fight *for* you, then. I'll drive you to every appointment. Get a leave of absence so I can take care of you. Shave my head. Whatever it takes. I'll fix this."

Mom fingered Nat's glossy dark locks, then pulled her into a hug. "I love you so much, Natalie."

Nat let herself be held for a second before pulling away. "Mom, no. You can't give up. Tell her, Kit."

I opened my mouth, but no sound came out. My hands and feet were numb. My brain had been shredded in a blender. Mom's gaze settled on me. It pleaded for understanding, for me to take her side.

When I didn't respond, Nat whipped her head toward me. "I've had to be the bad guy our entire lives, while you got to be the favorite. But you're not going to have a mother soon if you don't give her a little tough love for once."

Something cracked inside me. "Mom, please. If you won't do it for yourself, do it for us."

"That's enough, girls." Mom pulled us both close.

In the boiling trailer I blinked, feeling that familiar wave of nausea. No part of me wanted to do this exercise. I could come up with a make-believe story, an easier one to swallow and share—about a mother who was overly critical of grades or wouldn't let boys come to the house. Before I could stop myself, I plucked a couple of strands of hair from my head. The relief was instantaneous. I was righted again, like when water at the car wash streamed down the windows, clearing away the dirty soap.

Ruth broke the silence. "Talk to your parent about this memory. You can start out by retelling the story or you can launch straight into your feelings. But I want you to have an honest conversation, say whatever you've been holding back all these years. Imagine you were to write Mom or Dad a letter, but then never mail it. How free you would be to tell the truth, no matter how poorly that truth might reflect on you. Today is not about judgment. It is about clearing space for ourselves to heal. Don't worry about taking turns with your partner. You should talk over each other. You can scream. But I want you to stay grounded. No violence." She paused. "You may begin."

Jeremiah and I hesitated, listening to the voices around us for cues. Most of our classmates spoke in hushed, hissed tones.

But Sofia wailed right from the start. "How could you? Your grand-daughter died, and instead of comforting me, you said she brought it on herself."

My eyes popped open, widening at the accusation. The voices rose in anger.

"How many times did you use me as your punching bag?" Raeanne spat.

"I shouldn't have stolen your money," Sanderson said.

"How could you let her drown?" April said. "You were supposed to keep us safe."

Ruth's voice was featherlight in my ear. "Please keep your eyes closed, dear. Focus on your own memory."

My eyes snapped shut. Jeremiah's voice wavered when he spoke. "If you'd had one ounce of compassion, none of this would have happened." His voice was so cold that goose bumps pimpled my arms.

He hesitated when he noticed I wasn't speaking. "Anything you want to say, Kit?"

I took a long inhale. "You left us. We needed you."

"Atta girl," Jeremiah said.

"We would have been okay if you'd lived." I felt guilty for blaming my poor dead mother, who, on top of battling lifelong depression and terminal cancer, now had to carry the weight of my failures too. I wished my sister was sitting across from me instead of Jeremiah. She understood loneliness better than anyone, how it became a barnacle.

By now the room was soggy with misery. Sofia and Raeanne were yelling. Sanderson rocked, apologizing over and over to his parents, slowing only when Ruth murmured something in his ear. I snuck a peek at Gordon. Straight-backed and unmoving, he sat in the corner. I couldn't tell whether his eyes were open or closed.

"His death is on you too," Jeremiah said.

I trembled, overwhelmed. I didn't have time to think about whether I wanted to participate—I just did, so my voice wouldn't be notably absent from the crowd's, like when they did the group "om" at the end of a yoga class. If I didn't keep talking, Jeremiah might get self-conscious again that I was eavesdropping on his conversation.

"You should have fought, Mom," I said a little louder to match the volume of the rest of the mob. My mind whirled. "Why weren't we worth sticking around for?"

"You're doing so well," Ruth said. I wasn't sure whether she was talking to me or Jeremiah. "Keep going."

"I should have been there for you. I'm sorry," I said, then voiced the thought I'd had thousands of times: "This is all my fault." I'd been easy on her when I should have been tough and tough when I should have shown compassion. I was vomiting on my own feet in Vegas while she took her last breaths. She mattered more to me than everyone else combined, yet I had totally and utterly failed her. I hung my head, desperately fanning myself.

Ruth moved away, then shouted to be heard over the cacophony. "Good, everyone, very good. Now be still."

The room quieted, reeking of sweat and body odor. I needed air.

"Take a photo of your memory and put it in the middle of a crisp white bedsheet."

I pictured my mother slumped at the kitchen table, upset that we were ganging up on her. I put the image in the bedsheet.

"Bring the four corners of the sheet together, and close it with a bungee cord. You can't see the photo anymore. The memory is trying to tug free, so it may jump around inside the sheet. Do you see it?"

I did as I was told, wrapping the bungee cord around my mother's betrayed expression.

"Now hurl that wrapped-up memory as hard as you can against the wall. Let me hear the sounds of your efforts."

People began to grunt, as if they were trying to push a building off its foundation. Someone howled. Jeremiah's hand sliced the air, and I imagined he was actually trying to whip away his memory. I hesitated, not wanting to throw my mother against the wall. Could we not open a single window in this sweltering trailer? I longed for a breeze, for escape.

"Come on, Kit. You can do it," Ruth said.

I imagined spinning the bedsheet over my head faster and faster, until finally I let it go. My butt rose off the ground. I stopped myself from wincing when my mother crashed against the wall. Instead of panicking over how crazed I felt, I tried to focus on the marvels of the brain, to reflect on the power of imagination.

"Begin to come down, class," Ruth said. "Start to let those intense emotions drain from you. Let the rage go. Let the grief go. Let the confusion go. Let the fear go." People started to calm. "Are you a little lighter after ridding yourself of the weight of that memory? A lot lighter for some of you?"

Even with my eyes closed, I could tell the room was brightening. Ruth was slowly raising the blinds. My classmates breathed deeply, no longer panting. Only Sofia was still whimpering—"my poor baby," she said over and over.

The insanity began to feel like a dream. A roomful of adults had gone mad—now we were supposed to pretend like everything was okay?

"Thank your partner for accompanying you on this journey," Ruth said. "Then focus on your breath."

Jeremiah mumbled his thanks. What had his mother or father done? Had he been referring to his brother's death?

"Now lie on your backs and get comfortable," Ruth went on. "You may want to stretch your arms overhead or curl up in a ball on your side. Let the position you need choose you. It's time to indulge in twenty minutes of self-care."

I spent the entire time rationalizing what I had done. Why had I gone along with them? Why had I shared something so deeply painful and personal? Did I feel any better for having done it? I was mortified that these nine people had possibly put together the morbid pieces of my family story. I was unnerved I had so easily been swept into the exercise.

But I felt a little lighter, having shared a piece of my guilt and anger and fear aloud. To hear how many other people were furious with their parents or bore a backbreaking load of shame. To discover I wasn't the only terrible daughter or son in the room. I was a little lighter.

When the twenty minutes had passed, Ruth guided us into seated positions. She turned the lights all the way up. We moved our pillows into a circle. Ruth asked us to close our eyes again and breathe to her counts for a few minutes.

I studied each face. They were all so sincere—they believed in these exercises. Jeremiah was concentrating so hard his brow had furrowed.

"One final exhale," Ruth said. "Everyone open your eyes, please."

Ten pairs of eyes opened.

"There." She beamed. "Don't you feel better?"

18

TO BOISTEROUS CHEERS I bowed at center stage. For some the nightly ritual comprised a warm bath, a sheet mask, a good book. Mine was a standing ovation.

"Thank you, Dayton." I grinned at my audience. I never felt higher than when a crowd was chanting my name. As I lay in bed at night, their cries looped in my head.

I am goddamn invincible.

I scanned the theater once more, searching for a familiar face. My sister, Jack, was meant to attend tonight's performance. After all that fuss about moving as far away as possible in college, she had ended up back where she started, a fifteen-minute drive from our childhood home. I couldn't locate her in the crowd. Perhaps she had changed her mind.

When the curtain descended, I sauntered offstage, closing my dressing room door behind me. I paced the room and waited for the adrenaline rush to recede. My tour had begun three months ago, during which I'd performed in a different city every day, and my shows were gaining traction. A local radio station had invited me for an interview. A fan had recognized and approached me while I was out to dinner the previous evening. Soon I would hardly be able to keep up with all my correspondence. Beneath me, at the mere age of twenty-four, a wave was building, swelling. A good night's rest had become an impossibility.

There was a knock at my door. I opened it, and the oxygen fled my body.

"What are you doing here?"

Sir pushed past me to enter the dressing room. "Free country, ain't it?"

I hadn't seen my father since he'd dropped me off at college six years ago and I was shocked by how rapidly he'd aged since then. What was once blond had silvered. Jowls were firmly settled, beer gut complete. The lines across my father's face ran deep as a bulldog's, unhappiness embedded within each one. He watched me grumpily.

"I didn't expect you to come tonight." I swallowed. "You never got back to me."

"Your sister made me."

"Where is she?"

He shrugged. "Ran into an old friend from high school."

"Where's Mother?"

"Sicker than ever. Hardly leaves the house."

I cast my eyes to the floor. "I'm sorry to hear that." This felt like an out-of-body experience, talking to my father as formally as if he were a stranger.

He sniffed. "You'd know if you ever came home."

I vowed to keep things civil. I would not take his bait, wouldn't let him ruin the afterglow of a virtuoso performance. "It's hard with the tour schedule."

He scanned the room, mouth puckered. "Never had your priorities straight, did you?"

"You told me to go out and be somebody. My whole life you said it. That's what I've been doing."

"You think tricking people into eating spiders makes you hot shit?"

"It's not the act itself. It's what it represents."

He crossed his arms. "Were there not enough respectable careers for you to choose from? You had to go and pick this one?"

My insides were wilting, but on the outside I bristled. "I'm a headliner, Sir. I have my own tour."

He stabbed a finger at the door. "You were tramping around that stage like a common street whore."

I stopped my mouth from falling open. *He's right. He's absolutely right. I'm worthless, a talentless hack.*

"W- . . . w-with all due respect, sir," a voice said outside the doorway, "you're talking to one of the preeminent mentalists of our time."

In walked a brawny teenage boy, seventeen or eighteen, with honey eyes and a crooked nose. Sir and I both stared at him.

Sir turned to me, gesturing at the boy with his thumb. "Who's this little snot rag?"

I shrugged. I had never seen him.

"I couldn't help b- . . . b-but overhear," the teen said, "because I was eavesdropping. Did you know her show tonight sold out? And, by the way, Madame Fearless is the first female mentalist to get a national tour?"

My father inspected the boy like he was from another planet. "Big whoop."

"It *is* a big whoop," the boy said. "You may not like magic, although frankly I can't see w- . . . w-why you came tonight if you don't, but how many stages have you ever stood on? How many people have paid their hard-earned money to hear you talk?"

Sir was at a loss for words, something I'd witnessed only once or twice in my life.

"Not many, I'm guessing. If this is how you treat people."

Sir's teeth clenched. "I'll talk to my daughter however I damn well please."

Surprise wrinkled the boy's otherwise flawless skin. "Oh, you're her father, then?" He considered me. "Guess you drew the short straw on that front. Sorry to hear it. My dad's a b- . . . b-bastard too." He shrugged.

The corners of my lips twitched.

Sir's face was beginning to purple. "I oughta smack you into next Tuesday."

The teen grinned. "I w- . . . w-wouldn't, sir. I played football for Aldsville, so I'm pretty good at taking hits. Used to making them too." He continued smiling, delivering the threat as merrily as if he were wishing Sir a happy birthday.

"How dare you talk to me that way?" Sir said.

"How dare you talk to her that w- . . . w-way?"

"W-w-w-way," Sir mocked him. I cringed.

"Well done, sir." The boy nodded toward my father. "Punch me right in the stutter. It's a low blow, and not an entirely original one, but a blow nonetheless. I have to warn you, it'll take much w- . . . w-worse than that to send me running." He rocked onto his heels and put his hands behind his back like he was happy to stand there all night.

Sir glared at me. "You gonna do something about this punk?"

My father was wrong about me: I *did* have something to offer; I *was* talented. Someday I would change the world. "I think you should go," I said.

"I knew it was a mistake coming here. I told your sister as much."

No one said anything. I stared at Sir, willing him to leave.

Finally he did. "Don't bother showing your face around these parts again."

"Gladly," I said loudly enough for him to hear.

He stormed out of the room, shoulder checking the boy on his way. The teen barely moved, rock solid. Once Sir was gone, the air returned to my lungs.

"Thank you."

The boy smiled sympathetically. "As I said, I've got a model like him at home."

I remembered myself then, that I was to be the nonpareil of fearlessness. I squared my shoulders, forced my chin to higher ground. "I don't need other people fighting my battles for me."

"Of course you don't. You're Madame Fearless. But sometimes it's nice to know someone has your back."

Something loosened inside of me. "Call me Rebecca." He nodded but made no move to state his intentions. "How can I help you?"

"You don't remember me?"

I squinted.

"From your magic show. W- . . . w-when you were in high school."

"I performed that show three times a week for four years." I put a hand on my hip. "Might you narrow it down for me a touch?"

"I was your assistant in the handcuff routine," he said at the same time I recognized him. He was the boy in the second row at the show Sir and

Mother had attended, the one I'd bungled due to the provocations of the drama club. A lifetime had passed between then and now.

I shook his hand. "Remind me of your name?"

"Gabe." He grinned. "I've b- . . . b-been excited for this show for months. It was fantastic."

"You flatter me, Gabe."

"You deserve it. You were a master up there."

"Generous of you to say." I paused. "Do you want me to sign something? Take a photo?"

"Actually, I was hoping I could offer *you* something. I w- . . . w-wondered if you might need an apprentice."

I considered the quickest way to turn him down while he prattled. True, I desperately needed an assistant, but the plan was to find my hire through a temp agency. This jaunty boy was emphatically not part of the plan. "I'm studying public relations, so I could help you get the w- . . . w-word out about your shows."

He was in college, then, older than I'd thought.

"I'll take care of whatever you need, like a p- . . . like a p-personal assistant."

"What's in it for you?" I asked suspiciously.

"I've always w- . . . w-wanted to be a magician."

"Then why don't you put your own show together?"

Gabe shifted his weight. "My dad w- . . . w-wants me to go into a steadier line of w- . . . w-work. Find something more lucrative."

I stared down my nose. "What is it your father does?"

"He owns a p- . . . p-pizza chain." Gabe's face turned crimson. He stared at his tattered sneakers. "He says I'll never make it as a magician anyway if I can't even spit out a line."

Silence inched its way into the room and hovered uncomfortably. *How many fathers had trampled the dreams of their children? Would it never stop?* I gritted my teeth.

"What about your mother?"

He shrugged.

"As I recall, you had a younger brother," I tried again. "Is he supportive?"

"W- . . . w-when it's me and him, sure. Otherwise he goes along with w- . . . w-whatever Dad says."

"Siblings are unreliable that way, aren't they?" I said darkly.

He nodded at his shoes, chewing his lip.

"Well, in my experience parents rarely know what they're talking about."

Gabe peeked up, so unguardedly full of hope that it made my chest twinge. His face clouded. "I'm not the type of guy they p- . . . p- . . . let onstage."

"Not so long ago women weren't allowed onstage either," I said evenly. "The only person who has the power to stop you from being what you want is you." He broke out in a grin, and I had the rather merciless impulse to add, "You're going to need a much thicker skin if you want to make it in show business."

He nodded. "I want to learn the ropes as best I can."

What was the responsible action here: give him a leg up or dissuade him from a life of rejection and setbacks? I recognized the fire in Gabe. Had Evie ever once tried to extinguish mine?

When he sensed my vacillation, he said, "B- . . . b-but I'm not asking for charity."

I wrinkled my nose. "I'm not the philanthropic sort."

One "yes." That was all he wanted. How long had I been saying I wanted to help others, to pass on all I had learned about the art of fearlessness? I had ambitions of effecting change on a grander scale, but perhaps I was putting the proverbial cart before the horse. I could practice with Gabe, loosen fear's grip on him. I was far too intelligent to believe in chimerical concepts such as destiny, but I allowed for the occasional stroke of serendipity. What more fitting first pupil could I ask for than a boy under the thumb of his father?

"I'd work you to the bone. Your university classes would look like child's play."

He bobbed his head again. I watched him for a time, searching for a sign this was a mistake. I found him slightly annoying, a bootlicker, too cheerful and fawning. He was ignorant of social decorum. Possibly he would expect us to be friends or to share our feelings occasionally.

I strode to my purse on the makeup counter and pulled a business card from it anyway. When I turned around, standing in the doorway behind Gabe was my sister.

I started. She was wearing too much makeup in all the wrong places, leaving the resultant impression that she had recently returned from a hard day's work in a coal mine. A grin stretched sloppily across her face.

"Sir left," I said. Gabe turned to see whom I was addressing.

"I know," Jack said. "I'm here to see you."

I collected myself and handed Gabe my card. "Call me first thing Monday."

He pumped my hand with the exuberance of a first-term politician. "You w- . . . w-won't regret this. I promise."

Oh, but I would. In my entire life I would never regret anything more.

19

Kit

I SCANNED THE cafeteria. I had thirty minutes before my second one-on-one with Rebecca, but April and Georgina were both on cleaning duty.

At the farthest table I spotted Jeremiah. He was hunched over a booklet with a pencil in hand, whistling to himself. I approached tentatively, not wanting to be a bother. He was working on a crossword.

"Is it okay if I sit here?" I asked.

He glanced up. "Only if you help me with this puzzle."

I grimaced, taking a seat across from him. "I'm hopeless at crosswords. Not smart enough."

"I bet you're smarter than you think." He stuck the pencil behind his ear.

"Yeah? Would a genius almost burn down the cafeteria while using the microwave?" I reddened at the memory.

Jeremiah winced. "Good point. Maybe you're not that bright."

I laughed.

He twisted his crossword book so we could both see. Half the puzzle was filled in. "Seventeen down: Chicago-style prohibited condiment."

I thought for a second. "Ketchup."

He counted the squares, then grabbed his pencil. "Bingo. Twenty-three across: popular nineties shopping board game."

"Mall Madness. You're giving me the easy ones."

He raised an eyebrow, gestured at his thick beard and bear-shaped physique. "Do I look like the target consumer for Mall Madness?" I laughed again. "I've never even heard of it. Like I said, you might be smarter than you give yourself credit for."

I shrugged.

He consulted his puzzle. "Forty-two down: surname of Dwight Schrute's nemesis."

"Oh, come on. You're telling me you've never watched *The Office*? H-a-l-p-e-r-t."

"I was spelling it wrong." He filled in the letters. "And of course I did. Don't tell me Jim is your favorite or I'll have to ask you to sit elsewhere." He put a hand to his chest. "Or Pam, heaven forbid."

I made a face. "Obviously it's Michael. But can we talk about how seriously underrated seasons three through five Andy Bernard is?"

"Only if we first discuss that Creed is the actual hero of the show. Minute for minute he adds more humor than any other player."

We smiled at each other.

Jeremiah twirled the pencil between his fingers and stared at the puzzle. "My brother used to help me with these when we were younger. I took care of history and politics. He knew all the art and Hollywood ones. He loved old movies." A far-off gaze crossed his face. "One summer he made me watch all of the Oscar winners. I whined through every single black-and-white film—*Why couldn't we watch* Superman *for the fiftieth time like the other kids?* He ignored me, naturally."

He leaned back in his chair, stroking his throat. "Now every year on his birthday I rent the latest Best Picture winner. I get popcorn for me, Junior Mints for him—which I always end up throwing out. What kind of ghoul likes Junior Mints?"

I held up my hands to say *Not me.*

"Only my dumb brother." Jeremiah drew stars in the margins of the crossword page. "We were a good team."

"You miss him."

"Yup."

"I'm so tired of people telling me it's going to get better." I kept my eyes on the stars. "It doesn't get better, does it?"

He made a noncommittal noise. "I'm not fighting for every breath anymore. The pain's less sharp, but it's still there. I wake up some mornings and don't see his face first thing. That hurts in its own way."

"I don't want to stop seeing her face. Ever."

"I know."

I checked my watch. "Shit, my one-on-one's in a couple minutes." I lingered at the table, not wanting the conversation to end.

"You'd better not be late. Take the shortcut through the back door."

"That's what she said," I called as I ran.

MINUTES LATER I sat across from Rebecca on the couch in her office. She wore a formfitting black tee and trousers, her feet bare, toenails painted the color of dried blood. She studied me warmly. I forced myself to maintain eye contact. I wanted to be a tidal wave.

After half a minute of silence, she pursed her plum-shaded lips. "Have you come up with your mantra yet?"

I nodded uncertainly. Night after night I had obsessed in bed over what it should be. The task felt like a test I needed to pass. I had even tried coming up with something about a tidal wave but decided that was too kiss-assy, even if it was true.

Rebecca waited, watching me. She had too much self-control to repeat the question or drum her fingernails on the chair's arm. For as long as it took, she would sit there patiently.

I toyed with the rubber band on my wrist. "Die with memories, not dreams."

Her eyes gleamed. "One more time, with confidence."

I puffed up my chest, summoned false bravery. "Die with memories, not dreams."

Her face split open into a grin. "It's perfect." I let out a sigh. "How clever you are."

"You think so?" I asked doubtfully, hopefully.

"We must work on your self-confidence. We don't *think*—we know. How will this mantra guide you?"

"It'll remind me not to be afraid. To take risks. To live the life I actually want instead of the one I think I should have." I'd gotten the idea from April's preaching.

Rebecca nodded once. "Already you're taking more control. Only two weeks in and see how you've grown. Tell me your impressions of Wisewood."

"It's been wonderful. Everyone is so kind and open here." I tucked my hands under my legs. "The guests are different than I expected."

She waited for me to elaborate.

"They're so sure about leaving their old lives." I turned to the window—another sunny day. "Most of them don't feel guilty for leaving their friends and family."

She put up a hand. "Why should they? Your fellow guests are the ones who have been deserted. Sanderson is here because his parents kicked him out when he needed them most. Ruth left because her entire community ostracized her instead of practicing forgiveness. Debbie came to Wisewood to flee an abusive partner. Neutralizing a threat doesn't always mean staying to fight. Sometimes it means running for your life."

I nibbled my lip, considering this.

"Your peers have been rejected by their neighbors, siblings, and parents. Just like you have."

I whipped back to face her. "How did—"

"I know all about you, Kit." She leaned toward me. I swallowed. "Everyone in your family has treated you poorly," she said tenderly.

"That's not true."

"Really?" She sat back, eyes full of sympathy. "How about your father?"

I jiggled my leg. "I'd hardly call him family. He started an affair with his coworker when my mom's depression got bad. He left for good when I was three." I picked at a scab on the back of my hand—I'd burned myself last week helping Debbie remove a few trays of chicken from the oven. "He calls us on our birthdays and Christmas. My sister talks to him, but I don't pick up."

Rebecca played with a silver pendant dangling near her cleavage. She had a small birthmark in the middle of her chest. "And your mother?"

I stiffened. Mom was never the first to let go of a hug. She had taught us how to build a fire and roast marshmallows. She told ghost stories that made us squeal but wouldn't cause nightmares. She took us camping in the back-yard, sleeping with us in the tent. We used to fight over who got the last kiss from her before bed—she'd move back and forth between our little cheeks until we were both asleep, so we never knew who did.

"She was amazing," was all I could manage.

Rebecca tilted her head, considering me. "I know she was, but she missed out on a lot too, didn't she? Dance recitals, school plays, and the like?"

My mouth fell open. How did she know?

"She did the best she could." I clutched Mom's scarf.

"Was the best she could good enough?" She gazed at the silk around my neck.

"I can't bad-mouth my mom."

Rebecca's violet-gray eyes glittered. "I know this is difficult. The goal of these meetings is to help you achieve fearlessness. As you work the path, you'll find that the more honest you are with others and especially yourself, the faster you'll progress. Your mother had weaknesses."

"We all do."

"She chose victimhood. She turned away from you when you needed her most."

"You don't choose depression. Just like you don't choose cancer or ALS. She fought hard her entire life."

"Kit, who got you ready for school in the morning?" Rebecca smiled sadly. "Who put your outfits together and made sure you were fed?"

I bowed my head. "Mom and Nat both did."

"From what I understand," she said kindly, "your sister took on the bulk of the responsibility."

"How do you know all of this about me?" The only people I'd confided in here were April and Georgina. I didn't think either of them would divulge my secrets, but now I was doubting myself. I hadn't explicitly asked them not to share my stories about Mom—but come on, that was common sense. This stuff was personal.

"Does it matter?"

"I told my friends those stories in confidence."

She leaned in again. The pendant swung across her breasts. "You should be careful who you call a friend. And even more careful about who you trust. How well do you know any of these people?"

I flinched. April hadn't said a word about her loved one's drowning since the transference exercise, and I didn't feel right pushing for more details. That class had taken on a sacramental quality—what was shared in the trailer stayed in the trailer. Still, though we hadn't discussed April's accusation, the three of us had discovered a lot of common ground in two weeks. April's parents had also divorced when she was young. Georgina had been caught shoplifting as a teenager, same as me. They both wished their first times had been with someone different. I did too. I stared at my feet. I thought we were friends.

"Listen to me: this conversation is not an indictment of your mother. She clearly had many strengths if she raised a daughter as strong and bright as you." Rebecca ducked her head, trying to get me to look at her. "Resist the urge to defend her in here. We're all conditioned to accept bad behavior in order to maintain peace within the family unit. To present that unit as happy and functional to the rest of society."

"Is that conditioning or loyalty?"

"Conditioning. Sugarcoating our memories only impedes us on the path to our Maximized Selves. I don't want you to condemn your mother—only to admit that, at critical times in your life, she failed you."

I blew out a long, reluctant breath. "I guess you're right." If what I'd admitted was true, why did it feel like a betrayal?

Rebecca closed her eyes. "You're tougher than you know, Kit. I have no doubt you'll work the path quickly."

I brightened. Some of the uneasiness subsided.

"Now about your sister. Natalie, isn't it?"

I glanced at her warily.

"She's always been available if you need her, but doesn't she admonish you every time you try to explain your unhappiness, your desire for more from the world?"

That had definitely come from April or Georgina or both. I'd said as

much about Nat when we were talking in my room the other night. The
duplicity stung.

I gnawed my bottom lip. "She wants to make sure I'm healthy and
happy."

"Are you?"

I stared.

"Happy?" she prodded.

I gazed at the bookshelves behind her. Random titles jumped out at me:
Into Thin Air by Jon Krakauer, *Can't Hurt Me* by David Goggins.

"For the most part," I said too late.

She leaned forward to finger the rubber band around my wrist. "What
about this?"

My stomach turned. "What about it?"

"You snap it to stop yourself from pulling out your hair, do you not?"

My face flooded with red-hot shame. I'd tried to be careful, to keep it
private. The urge to pull coursed through my fingers. I sat on my hands
again.

"When did you start?"

Talking about it deepened the urge, like thinking about an itch you
weren't supposed to scratch. "After she died."

"Do you feel guilty about her death?"

"I feel guilty about a lot of things."

"Then you're not happy, Kit, are you?" She sat next to me on the couch.
"Not if you have to punish yourself like this."

I willed the heat to leave my cheeks.

"Don't be embarrassed." Rebecca pulled my hand from under my leg and
held it. "We'll work this out together. By the end of your time here you won't
need that anymore." She gestured to the rubber band. "You'll see."

The mix of mortification and hope and mortification at my hope—the
way I glommed onto any glimmer of it so desperately—brought tears to my
eyes. I blinked them away before she could see. I would never be as strong as
Rebecca.

"Let's bring the conversation back to your sister." She patted my hand.
"She wants you to be her version of happy, not yours. How many times have
you tried explaining as much to her?"

This process wouldn't work unless I made myself vulnerable. If I couldn't be as strong as she was, I could at least be as honest. "Many."

"How many times have you gotten through?"

I pressed my lips together, sending a silent apology to Nat. "None."

"What does Natalie think about you being here?"

"She thinks it's a waste of my time and money." I bit the inside of my cheek. "She doesn't believe in this stuff."

My sister had been like that since we were kids. I'd wanted to pretend our neighborhood playground was an amusement park, and she would list all the reasons that was impossible. I'd wanted to make the LEGO building a few inches taller, and she'd launch into a lecture about architectural stability. We'd be lying in the park on summer break and I'd say I heard the music of the ice-cream truck, and she'd say no, I didn't, that the ice-cream man didn't come on Mondays.

Why can't you believe? I wanted to ask her.

Rebecca nodded knowingly. "So Natalie has also turned her back on you by minimizing your needs. Notice I did not call them wants, but needs. Because I believe you are in critical danger. Even as you sit here composed in front of me, you are crying out for something more."

I trained my eyes on hers. So far all I had accomplished was feeling awful about my family and realizing my new "friends" were gossips. I badly wanted Rebecca to be wrong about the people in my life. She wasn't.

She tucked a strand of pearly hair behind her ear. Tattooed on the inside of her wrist in white ink was a single word: ENDURE.

She folded her legs into a pretzel. "Rest your head on my lap."

I did a double take.

"Your body is tense. We need to relax you in order to continue making progress during this session. A brief temple massage usually does the trick."

I let her guide my head onto her crossed legs. She ran her fingers through my hair, gently tugging it away from my face. I closed my eyes, felt pressure on both temples. Soft finger pads massaged in small circles. I lay there, anxious at the strangeness of letting a woman I barely knew hold me this way. But after a couple of minutes, my breathing slowed. My shoulders relaxed. My head felt jiggly.

"There we go," she cooed. "That's it."

I listened to both of us breathe. She matched her breath to mine. The world outside the office doors was quiet. I pushed aside thoughts of Mom, Nat, April, Georgina.

"Describe the moment you decided to join Wisewood."

I kept my eyes closed. "The application form had been sitting in my in-box for a week. I was at work on a Thursday afternoon, eating leftover pasta for lunch, when I had this strange déjà vu. I tried to remember if I'd had ziti the day before or the one before that, but I couldn't. I couldn't remember when I'd made it or what I'd eaten for lunch any day that week." The pitch of my voice rose. "For a minute I couldn't remember what day of the week it even was—they all blended together; they were all the same—and I panicked."

My shoulders had tensed again. Rebecca grasped and massaged them. "Relax," she sang. "Relax."

I lowered my tone, tried again. "I'd been going through the motions, sleepwalking through each day. I'd shower, go to work, eat, work some more, go home, watch TV, go out for drinks, go to bed, get up, do the same thing all over again. Every single weekday. For a year. I got scared that the next time I snapped out of it, I'd be forty or eighty or somewhere in between and diagnosed with something terminal. When I couldn't sleep that night, I filled out the application."

I'd tried to find meaning in my life. After Mom died, I moved to New York, thinking a new city might do the trick. When it didn't I took that Thailand trip, staying in hostels to keep costs down. I considered going back to school but already had thirty-three grand in student loan debt—the thought of adding to it sickened me. Instead I found the receptionist job. I'd describe the ennui from time to time to coworkers and then Nat, but no one understood. They suggested I find a new career or get out of New York. I tried to explain it wasn't the job or the city—I'd felt as trapped in Tempe and San Diego—but they still didn't get it. Another month went by.

I opened my eyes. Rebecca was watching me from above. I sat up, pushed myself to the other side of the couch, and wrapped my arms around my knees. "I kept thinking, what if this is the rest of my life? What if I look back and I've done nothing but eat leftover ziti for four decades?"

"Which is why you came here."

"Right. I like that every day is different. I can hear myself think again."

She studied me through long eyelashes. "I'm sensing a 'but.'"

I let go of my legs and put my feet on the floor. "I miss my sister." I tugged the edges of the scab again. I knew I shouldn't pull it off. Nat would have told me to leave it. More likely, she would've rummaged through her purse for Neosporin and a Band-Aid. I never had Band-Aids on me.

"Yes, she can be unsupportive," I said, still working at the scab, "but she'd also do anything for me. We haven't talked much since Mom . . . you know. I've been acting like her passing was Nat's fault, but it's not."

"Are you ever going to rip that thing off? Or are you going to torture yourself forever?" Rebecca stared at my hands.

I winced and stopped picking. "It's starting to heal. You're supposed to leave them alone."

"Where's the fun in that?" She winked.

Rebecca smoothed her platinum hair, dark fingernails like spiders scuttling down her scalp. "It's common for students to get lonely or homesick during their first month here. But I promise if you throw yourself into the program, you'll find your tribe.

"Best of all, your fellow students aren't content to walk through life like sheep in a herd. They want to make a difference like you do. They're not interested in clocking in and out, in binge drinking and watching. They'll be more supportive in helping you find your way than your sister ever was."

I chewed my lip. To not be ridiculed constantly, to spend my days with others who understood what I was searching for. I thought back to the parental transference exercise, to being surrounded by people willing to do whatever it took to create a more meaningful life for themselves.

"You also have me." She moved her legs so our knees grazed. "We can help each other, you know."

My eyes flitted to her face.

"I think you're exactly the person Wisewood needs."

20

GABE EXCUSED HIMSELF from my dressing room, grinning and stuttering his thanks. He hurried down the hall, leaving me alone with Jack.

She swept into the room and wrapped me in a hug, like she hadn't spent most of her adult life avoiding me. I kept my arms by my sides.

She pulled away. "I'm so proud of you. The crowd loved you up there, *Madame Fearless.*"

I nodded. "Thank you, Jack." I hadn't seen my sister in forever. The clumsy makeup application aged her well beyond twenty-seven. Somewhere along the way she had also acquired a nose ring, which struck me as desperately jejune.

She hesitated. "I go by my real name now."

I raised my eyebrows, surprised my sister had finally grown some cojones. "I see. And what is Sir calling you these days, Abigail?"

Her face darkened as I knew it would. Standing up to the entire world was one thing. Standing up to your father was another.

"Want to get dinner?" she asked, eager to change the subject. "My treat. Let me run Sir home first."

At least she had the common sense not to invite him.

Thirty minutes later she joined me at a family-run trattoria. The first glass of red disappeared quickly for both of us, but Jack guzzled hers like there was a drought in Tuscany. She stared at her glass afterward; she was waiting for me to say something, though I could not fathom what.

By the time our meals arrived—a spaghetti Bolognese for her, chicken cacciatore for me—I had been updated on every last detail of Jack's life. Based on what she had told me, I had even less in common with my sister now than I had as a child. She would soon marry her college boyfriend, produce a few offspring, and continue to run her small marketing firm that serviced clients in western Ohio. Her life was positively midwestern. I couldn't believe someone with such a checkered childhood could evolve into something so uninteresting.

"Too bad Mom couldn't come tonight," Jack said, halfway through her third glass. "She would have loved the show."

"Would she?" I sat back against the viscid red leather booth. "She's too busy kowtowing to our father to form an opinion of her own. And based on the verbal review he gave me, he'd rather be burned at the stake than forced to watch another of my performances."

Jack's eyebrows jumped. "Geesh. What did he say?"

"The usual. I'm an abject failure; my career is disreputable. This time he compared me to a common street whore, which was a new touch."

She winced. "I thought he'd behave himself."

I gazed at my sister. "When on earth has he ever done that?"

She squirmed under my glare.

"Why did you even bring him?"

"I thought it'd be good to get the family together. You invited him, didn't you?"

I wished I never had.

"I was trying to be nice," she said.

I crumpled my paper napkin and placed it atop my half-eaten meal. What meager appetite I'd had to begin with had vanished. "Now's a fine time to start."

My sister watched me, her lips pressed together. I'd meant for my words to cut her, but saying them felt like shoving a knife into my own gut.

"Is this the point where you tell me it was my fault?" I pushed the napkin harder into the sauce, watching the white paper turn tomato red. "That if I'd only been more like you when we were young, he wouldn't have been so awful?"

"Not at all." Jack swallowed. "I didn't know the stuff from our childhood still bothered you."

I scowled at the other patrons slurping their noodles, wiping orange sauce off their chapped lips and mottled chins. "It bothers me that you'd come to my show and act like we were the best of friends when you've spent most of our lives pretending I don't exist."

She flushed. "I was trying to break free. Start fresh."

"Some of us were still locked up. I needed you."

"I shouldn't have lumped you in with him. I get that now. I'm sorry for shutting you out."

Some apologies, even when heartfelt, were laughably inadequate.

"I stuck my neck out for you all the time." I struggled to steady my voice. "I got into the boat at Lake Minnich so you wouldn't get in trouble. You knew how scared of the water I was, yet you all but let me drown."

"I dove in after you. I saved you."

Saved me? Anger and sorrow were both symptoms of weakness, fear manifesting in different forms. Anger was unquestionably easier.

"There would have been no need for saving if you'd stood up to him in the first place," I said. I wanted to hurt my sister and protect her from me all at once. Why couldn't I let this go? What right did I have to impart wisdom to others when I was stabbing my finger in the same tired old wounds?

"Where would that have gotten us? Tossed in the water side by side? Him deserting me on some random beach and leaving me to find my own way home? Mom frantically searching for me in the dark with a flashlight?"

"He never laid a hand on any of us."

"I was afraid that one day he would. Listen, I'm sorry I didn't protect you back then. And for ignoring you in college. I'm trying to make up for it now." She gestured at the meals on the table between us. "I'd like for us to be closer."

I thought about taking her in my arms. Instead I crossed them. "Why now? Why'd you wait until my star was rising to reach out?"

She rolled her eyes. "I admire the success you've had, but let's not get ahead of ourselves. You're a long cry from people using you for your 'fame.'"

I fought the urge to claw at her face. What had she said when I called to tell her I was dropping out of school to go on tour? *Can't you choose a career that isn't so . . . embarrassing?* She had always doubted me. She still didn't believe in my mission.

"I've spent the last year trying to reconnect with you," she said. "You're the one who keeps blowing me off."

How does it feel, dear sister? I'd come to this dinner with two options: I could restart our relationship, or I could make her feel as unwanted as she had me. I didn't relish my choice, but I would stand by it. I wanted her pain more than my happiness.

When I studied my sister, I no longer saw the girl with whom I'd built forts and chased lightning bugs. I saw the hundred times she'd dodged my calls or glanced the other way. At eighteen Jack had moved across the country to begin anew, but ever since, she had been sliding into the quicksand of fear. The return to Ohio, the number of dinners, card games, and movies she surely now shared with Sir. How could she invite him into her life after all he had done? She was weaker than I could have imagined.

I pinched the crook of my arm under the table until the skin broke.

"I don't think you deserve to be in my life," I said. Not all of them could be saved. Not all of them were worthy.

Jack's mouth fell open. She sat there, blinking and speechless. "That is so harsh."

I put my purse over my shoulder and slid out of the booth.

"Runs in the family."

21

Kit

J U L Y   2 0 1 9

I WANDERED OUT of Rebecca's office and down the spiral staircase in a daze. My feet carried me toward the cafeteria. Outside in the blinding sun I was vaguely aware of guests tending the vegetable garden, carrots and kale on the left, zucchini and peas to my right. Contradictory thoughts battled for headspace.

No one gets to criticize my family but me.

She's right: they have failed me. They've loved and protected and saved me— but they have also failed me in hundreds of tiny and not-so-tiny ways.

Isn't that normal? Don't all parents and siblings fall short at one time or another?

But do all parents fall as short as mine have?

What's so wrong with wanting to take six months off to improve my life? What right does Nat have to make me feel bad?

I stood in the cafeteria doorway, trying to clear my head. Across the room Georgina waved. I frowned and made my way to the table where she and April were sitting.

"Bologna sandwiches again," Georgina said by way of greeting. She wore a turquoise maxi-dress that made her eyes appear even greener than usual.

She scrunched her nose. "What's a girl gotta do to get some mayonnaise around here?"

"Mustard would be even better," April said.

They began to debate the merits of Dijon versus honey mustard. Once I'd picked up my own sandwich, I sat across from Georgina and next to April.

April was gushing about a lecture she'd attended that explained how to separate one's self-worth from career achievements and failures. "This is what's been holding me back." She jabbed a finger at the notes in her journal. "This is why I haven't quit my job."

Georgina listened, nodding when she connected with something April said. Which of them had blabbed to Rebecca? Georgina was more of a gossip, but April was more devoted to the program. I took a bite of the dry sandwich.

Georgina nudged me with a bony arm. "You're quiet today."

April's eyes darted around, searching for Raeanne—she was worried we were going to get in trouble for breaking the no-touching rule again—but Raeanne was busy scolding a couple of teenagers nearby.

I shrugged and kept eating. Should I bring it up? I didn't want to rock the boat. After a few weeks of our spending nearly every waking hour together, I'd become closer with these two than with the high school and college friends I'd lost touch with.

"How'd your session go?" April asked.

"She's intense." They both nodded. "She knows a lot about me and my family." I hesitated, then decided I had to know. "Stuff I hadn't told her."

"She's so intuitive," April said. "She guessed right about my family dynamics too."

"She wasn't guessing." I shoved the last bite of sandwich into my mouth. They both stared at me, waiting for an explanation.

"Did either of you tell her anything?" I kept my voice steady, wiped my palms on my jeans.

Georgina tried to catch April's eye, but April was peering at me.

"The stuff I told you about my mom and sister?" I said.

Their eyes widened. The seconds of silence between my question and their answers were excruciating. My heart pounded in my throat.

"Of course not," Georgina said.

"Those aren't our stories to share," April said.

I nodded and set my plate aside, considered letting it go—but couldn't. "I can't figure out how else she would know. You're the only two people I've told at Wisewood."

April's and Georgina's eyes met for a second before they turned back to me.

"She's counseled so many guests," April said. "She must know the clues to watch for. You can tell she has excellent intuition."

"She knew Nat got me ready for school in the mornings. That my mom missed my dance recitals." I flushed.

No one said anything for a minute. My face got hotter and hotter.

"That is strange." Georgina spun the chunky rings around her fingers. "But like I said, I didn't say anything. April says she didn't either." When I didn't respond, she added, "It sounds like you're accusing us." When I still didn't say anything, she stretched her swan neck. "Which I don't appreciate."

"I'm not accusing anyone of anything. I'm just confused."

"Did you ask her how she knew?" April said.

I nodded. "She said it didn't matter."

The silence that followed implied they agreed with her. Maybe they were right and I was making something out of nothing.

"We would never do that to you," April said, heart-shaped face brimming with sincerity. "You can trust us."

"This could be a good thing," Georgina said. "Now you have everything out in the open."

"You're right." I bobbed my head, unconvinced. "I'm sorry, you guys. I don't know what I was thinking. This place is messing with my brain." I cleared my throat. "As for the condiment debate, I'd kill for some Cholula. Drown out the taste of bologna."

Both women chuckled. The tension at the table lifted.

I stayed a few more minutes to make sure they weren't upset with me, then begged off before the lunch hour was over, claiming I was behind on chores. I cleared their trays in addition to my own as a gesture of goodwill. I waved as I left them, hoping I hadn't stirred up bad blood. April and Georgina were sharp, funny women, and I liked hanging out with them.

But as insightful as Rebecca might have been, she wasn't omniscient. I didn't buy that she had intuited all those details about me after one hour-long meeting.

One of them had to be lying.

I just didn't know who.

I left the cafeteria. The sun scorched my shoulders. I fanned my face, twisting my hair into a ponytail before letting it drop down my back. I wished a storm would break this heat, that fall—or an air-conditioning unit—would arrive. When the weather became stubborn like this, there was nowhere to go to escape it.

I opened the back door to Rebecca's house and took a right. In the laundry room twelve baskets of clothes and towels waited on the floor to be washed, dried, and folded. I opened the doors to the four industrial washers and loaded the tubs. I measured the detergent, trying to distract my thoughts.

I would've shared the stories in class or during a one-on-one anyway. So what if someone had gossiped and gotten carried away? I told myself it didn't matter, vowed to forget the whole ordeal. The unease in my stomach lingered.

It wouldn't hurt to branch out, to make some new friends. I'd been so preoccupied with April and Georgina that I had paid little attention to the other guests. It was time to stop worrying about everyone else—what Nat would think of Wisewood, what Rebecca thought of me. I needed to focus on what I thought.

I closed the four washer doors. The drums spun. I sat on the tiled floor and leaned against a dryer. I glanced at the ceiling—all that separated Rebecca from me. I wondered how she spent her lunch hour. I'd never seen her in the cafeteria. What was she doing at this moment? What had she meant when she said I was exactly what Wisewood needed?

Absentmindedly, I touched my hair. I'd wrapped my fingers around the first strands when I realized what I was doing and reached for the rubber band. I studied my hands, the small patch of angry brown skin with pink edges.

I ripped off the scab.

22

GABE STRAIGHTENED THE coffin's black silk lining for the third time. I smacked his hand.

"Enough fussing," I said. "The room is sublime."

We inspected the gallery that had become our second home. The roof, twenty feet above us, was made of skylights and exposed wooden beams. Columns the size of ancient tree trunks supported the ceiling. Single light-bulbs, hanging from long wires, were scattered about the space. The night sky with stars for eyes peeked in through the roof, twinkling with curiosity about the impossibilities rumored to take place here.

Per usual, the immaculate white walls had been cleared of all sketches, paintings, and photographs. For this performance we had created six-foot-tall letters from black masking tape, sticking a single word to each gallery wall.

FEAR
WILL
KILL
YOU

He clapped, beaming. "This is all because of your genius."

I took his face between my hands and rested my forehead against his. "Where would I be without you?"

It was no longer enough to swallow glass or spiders as I had throughout the *Fearless* tour. Such feats had become humdrum by the mid-eighties. There wasn't enough risk involved; I wanted to push further. I wanted my life on the line. That was how *Madame Fearless Presents . . . Suffocated* was born. What better way to demonstrate fearlessness than by holding a plastic bag over my head until consciousness deserted me?

Gabe helped me plan that first show in '85. He found this Brooklyn gallery, which would go on to serve as our locale for nearly every performance. The monstrous movie screens on two of the walls had been Gabe's idea, a way to cram my brand of uncomfortable intimacy down our spectators' throats. It was also his idea to turn my work into onetime events instead of something I replicated in theaters across the country. I tried to put on a new show annually but sometimes two or three years slipped by before I could perfect a feat.

After that first performance, I fretted that only a dozen spectators had attended. How was I going to transform the lives of the masses if the masses didn't show up?

Then I met The Five.

Gabe's smile disappeared when his focus returned to the center of the room. "Are you sure about this?"

I clucked my tongue and let go of his face. Gabe did this before every show: agonized about my safety, brooded that perhaps this was the piece where we had pushed too far. The wrinkle between his eyebrows warmed my insides, though I'd never admit as much. Encouraging worry was the antithesis of what I stood for.

"Dearest, I love you, but we don't have time for this." The audience would file in ten minutes from now. The cameraman had set up his equipment.

"But—"

"Gabriel, how can we preach the importance of fearlessness if we don't exemplify it ourselves?" It was best to cut him off before he gained momentum. If he sensed his argument had legs, he would run it into the ground.

For eight years Gabe and I had spent night after night in my dreary studio, brainstorming ways to push my mind and body while subsisting on little more than noodles. Spaghetti, macaroni, ramen; whatever was cheapest that week was what we ate out of plastic bowls, my feet in his lap as we covered the laminate floor with ideas, sketches, fantasies. When he stressed about the bills, I held him until his shoulders drooped; when I was creatively stymied, he massaged my temples. Many of these nights Gabe did not return to his own apartment but slept like the dead in my bed. When the sun began its uphill climb, we too resumed our efforts.

I rubbed my tongue along the backs of my teeth, pausing at the small grooves where the two halves had fused back together. If I could bisect my tongue with garden shears, if I could wrap a plastic bag around my head, if I could go a year sans speaking to another human being, how was this endeavor any different? These performances were the primary reason I lumbered out of bed at daybreak. Nothing else made my blood fizz the same way.

Gabe sighed. "Aren't you afraid of anything?"

I sometimes questioned why he had stuck around for so long, could not comprehend why a man who rollerbladed for fun would elect to spend his time in the underbelly that was my world. As soon as he'd moved to New York to work for me, I'd found him the best speech therapist in Manhattan and used nearly all of my savings from the *Fearless* tour to fund the sessions instead of reinvesting the money in my work. I waited in the lobby during every meeting, held my ear to the door to make sure the therapist wasn't too tough on him. Gabe's confidence skyrocketed, and I went to bed beaming.

After a few years in Brooklyn, he ceased the palaver about becoming a performer in his own right. We were stronger as a team, he said. He'd rather operate behind the scenes. I supported this decision because I knew he, not his speech impediment, was the one making it. He was a support team of one, the only person who had never questioned my need to maim my body over and over. In exchange for his loyalty, I withstood his worries.

I turned my back to Gabe, gesturing for him to zip the last inch of my black bodysuit. The ensemble was custom-made and hugged every curve. I felt more alive, more awake, than I had in years. I was primed.

"Confirm with the doorman we don't have any surprise visitors, won't you?" I asked.

Gabe made for the door and disappeared into the night.

The week prior I had run into my old college roommate, Lisa, whom I had talked to sparingly in the last decade, in part because I was still miffed that she'd assumed I would fail in this career, but mostly because these things happen. People fall apart as life takes them down divergent paths. She begged me to lunch right then and there. By the time we had Niçoise salads in front of us, she had laid the ruins of her life in my lap. Three years earlier she had married a sturdy, jovial man who began cheating on her six months into their union. I thought surely the only dilemma would be whether she had the funds to buy her own home, and I was worried she might ask for a loan I was in no position to give. Instead she wanted to know how she could move forward with this man who had deceived her for three-quarters of their wedded life. *You're always giving advice on fearlessness,* she said. *How do I stop being afraid he'll cheat again?* Once I managed to scrape my chin off the floor, I told her she had misunderstood my teachings. The fear she must now battle was a fear of loneliness. I pointed out that her husband had stopped cheating only because Lisa caught him; more specifically, Lisa's octogenarian dry cleaner found a pair of crotchless underthings stuck in her husband's suit sleeve. She needed to leave yesterday. Lisa staunchly refused, insisting she could save her marriage. I tried appeals to both the head and the heart, but neither worked. She sat there, clinging to a thread that had already snapped. How weak this woman was whom I had once called my closest friend. How beyond saving too. I ended the lunch by telling her she was much too tall to be a doormat. I suspected I would never hear from Lisa again, but some small part of me thought she might sneak in tonight, sabotage my performance because I had everything I wanted and she had nothing, not even the art gallery she had once dreamt of opening. Lisa worked at a bank.

I couldn't help them all.

The door to the gallery opened. We were getting close now. The pre-performance jitters would soon begin in earnest; they were the only way I kept myself honest, the lone indicator of whether what I was trying was risky enough. The queasy stomach, the sodden palms, the rattletrap legs: I used to view all of them as weaknesses. Now I understood they were the body's way of telling us we were alive. Or perhaps that was merely the story I told myself when I couldn't control my fear. I watched Gabe make his way across the space. I was more at ease the closer he came.

"She's not here," he said when he reached me.

I struggled to keep the relief off my face. "How long is the line?"

"It's a good-sized crowd." He grinned.

"Oh, I could kiss you."

Gabe flushed, one of those unlucky fools who wore his emotions on his face. He was perhaps a little in love with me, though I had made clear years ago that nothing amorous would transpire between us. I never would have gambled our partnership on something as fleeting as love.

"And The Five?" I asked.

"Waiting outside with the rest." He riffled through his backpack. "Have you had your granola bar yet?"

I sighed. "Gabriel, how am I supposed to get in the proper frame of mind when you're droning on about snack bars?"

"You definitely skipped it." He dug until he pulled said bar from the depths of the bag, examined the label, then glanced up, confused. "I thought the blueberry ones were your favorite."

I cleared my throat and clenched my gluteus, which always made me feel powerful. "Your job is not to feed me. It's to extract every drop of endurance from my body so I can apply it toward the work. Everything—"

"Is in service to the work," Gabe finished. Under his breath he said, "Can't endure on an empty stomach."

I gazed at the dark rings under my assistant's eyes. The sweat on his face had dried, and now his skin lacked luster. He went on and on about nutrition and exercise and sleep but took none of his own advice. He had been over-exerting again. I fought the urge to run my fingers through his sandy hair, to rest the back of my hand against his forehead.

"Perhaps you'll take a few days off after tonight."

He checked his watch. "Thirty seconds until doors open. Take your mark."

I nodded, standing in front of the pedestal and stepladder. On top of the pedestal rested the coffin, black with ornate finishes. The coffin maker had put his best foot forward, knowing a photo of his product might make it into tomorrow's papers.

Spectators began to trickle in, whispering their exhilaration. Goose bumps pricked my skin. My heart pounded. This was it, my next opportunity to secure my footing in the annals of history.

How long would I be able to withstand the pain this time?

I spotted The Five the moment they walked through the door. The two boys had long scruffy hair; the three girls had sheared theirs close to the skull. They all dressed in baggy silhouettes and chunky boots.

At my first show I had barely registered the five young people dressed in black, eyes wide as believers'. I would later learn they'd been only seventeen at the time. Some of them had broken curfew to attend.

After the second show, a year later, they introduced themselves nervously, said they attended a school near my gallery. They'd seen the flyers Gabe had put up around their campus, found themselves intrigued. One of them blurted that they loved what I had to say about fear. The others bobbed their heads.

Before my third show they shyly revealed they wore all black as an homage to me. They said they had no interest in following in their parents' footsteps, questioned whether college was the right path even as they sat through lectures and exams. They were bored with drinking every night but had nowhere else to funnel their almost manic eagerness; they buzzed with passion but were unsure what to be passionate about. I was only eight years older than them but they treated me like an oracle. They had watched and re-watched old *Fearless* footage, they explained. I saw the potential immediately.

After my fourth performance I began to see them weekly, spending hours talking through their questions and concerns. They were afraid of everything but badly wanted not to be. I helped them summon the courage to live fearlessly. When one of the girls came out to her parents, they shunned her. I let her move in with me until I found her a place of her own. When one of the boys dropped out of college like I had, I offered him a job so he wouldn't feel like a failure. When a third member of their circle broke up with her high school sweetheart, I smoothed her hair while she sobbed. One by one we celebrated each of their twenty-first birthdays with a trip to the local watering hole. They couldn't believe their first legal drinks had been paid for by *the* Madame Fearless.

Now, at this fifth show, they stood before me, dutifully dressed in black, as they had the past seven years. They knew better than to approach me before a performance but snuck in subtle waves hello. I winked.

By now they all worked for me. Their mission was to spread news of *my* mission as far and wide as they could. Even if I'd had the wherewithal to pay them, they wouldn't have heard of it.

Thus far The Five's outreach had only doubled the attendance numbers, an underwhelming improvement. But as I took in their awestruck faces and the concentration with which they watched me, I reminded myself it was the depth, not the breadth, of my reach that mattered. If I could transform even five lives, wasn't that worth more than stuffed-to-the-gills galleries or raving press accolades?

The door at the far end of the room clattered closed. Once the space had quieted, I turned to face the ladder, clearing my mind of any thoughts but of the task before me. The ladder's three rungs had been replaced with butcher's knives, which I admit added little to the challenge other than a bit of showmanship.

Never waste the spotlight's beam.

I climbed the ladder's first rung with my breath held, distributing my weight evenly the way I had practiced thousands of times. The audience gasped. On the second knife I met a similar success, but on the final I moved too quickly, too eager to enter the coffin. The arch of my right foot dug into the knife's blade, but I would not allow myself so much as a wince or whimper, not when the camera was projecting my face on the ceiling, not when my believers were counting on me.

I forced myself to take my time settling in, to fan out my hair on the black silk pillow like a Disney princess, if any of them had been enterprising instead of utterly useless. In minutes the lid would close. The crowd would swarm, snapping photo after photo. At that point, a smirk would dance on my lips. I would show them all how unafraid I was of the dissipating supply of oxygen. Let them one day show their grandchildren the face of the most fearless person who had ever lived.

I am goddamn invincible.

I stopped fiddling, barely noticed the warm blood trickling down my foot. I folded my hands across my belly as though I were already dead and took one final, effortless breath. To Gabe, I said, "I'm ready."

Fear was etched into every crevice of his face, but he obeyed. Inch by inch, he lowered the thick Perspex lid until it latched closed. Immediately I felt the smallness of the space but reminded myself I was sheltered, not trapped. The difference between a cocoon and a straitjacket was perspective.

Under no circumstance was Gabe to release me; he would leave me to my fate until the agreed-upon time. I watched him poised above me, his arms extended, a boy playing ringmaster. He held a stopwatch in the air for the spectators to see. The cameraman focused on the timer's face, displaying 0:00 on the ceiling.

"Welcome to *Madame Fearless Presents . . . Entombed*," Gabe said. He clicked a button. The numbers began careening upward.

I could scarcely breathe.

23

Kit

WHY I STAYED

During a class on grief management, I told the story. I said I was by my mother's side every hour I wasn't working while she slowly died of cancer. I had planned to skip my friend's bachelorette party, but Mom insisted she'd be fine for the weekend. She had the in-home nurse, plus Nat had driven in to watch over her. So I went to Vegas. I let loose. When I got a call from my sister twelve hours in, I threw up. She didn't want to tell me over the phone but I made her because I couldn't move off that square of concrete until she'd said the word. When she did I crumpled, skinning my knees. I told my classmates I'd regretted taking the trip every single day since the phone call. I wanted my goodbye.

Ruth had Sofia retell my story as if it were her own. Afterward she asked if I thought Sofia was a bad person based on her actions. Absolutely not, I said. How could she have known? Sanderson suggested I write Mom a letter. Debbie said it was okay to talk to her like she was still here. Rebecca said the best way to honor Mom was to live a life brimming with possibility, glossy with fearlessness. She said I had to shine as brightly as Mom's scarf.

I began attending the five a.m. yoga class. I hid in the back row, rusty after months without practice. I focused on my breaths, let sweat pour down my face, didn't wipe it away. Pose after pose, my muscles burned up the guilt, gobbled the fear. After a week I moved to the middle row. Another week and I was in front. The new guests viewed me as their example.

Ruth encouraged me to put my own class together. I demurred but she kept pushing, secured special approval from Rebecca. *Non-staff never get to lead classes,* Ruth said. *We all see so much potential in you.* I took a whole day to plan it—I wanted to get the sequences perfect for my students. My favorite part was the end of class, when I got to tell the others how strong they were, how worthy of love.

Because of the exercise, I had more energy. I took on more chores. I tended the garden every afternoon, plucking garlic and arugula, unearthing potatoes. Once in a while I'd rest, squeeze soft dirt between my fingers, let the sun kiss my face. I mowed the lawn and skimmed debris from the pool. My skin tanned from the time outside. My arms grew toned with the physical labor. My face remained round and full—for the first time I didn't care. I stopped criticizing my body, quit assigning it shapes of fruit.

In the evenings, after I'd finished all my chores, I roamed the island. I memorized the cabin numbers and which guest lived in each one. I spent hours walking the inner perimeter of the hedge wall, running my fingers along the leaves while deep in thought. I discovered a second door, also half-covered by bushes, built into a different part of the hedge. I wondered what the staff did beyond these walls.

To help me overcome my fear of public speaking, Ruth put me in charge of a beginners' class. Although Jeremiah had plenty on his plate with his new job as Wisewood's accountant, he offered to help me prepare. Like Nat he was organized, a planner, but unlike her he wasn't intense about it, kept things fun—literally whistled while he worked. With his help the course quickly came together. On my first day he sat in the back row. When I posed a question that was met with a shy but awkward silence, Jeremiah raised his hand and filled the void before panic could paralyze me. After class he said he'd enjoyed himself so much he was going to take my entire course.

Every day I stood in front of ten people and asked what they were afraid of. I told them we weren't ashamed of our bruises here. I watched as my students took baby steps toward their own fears. Somewhere along the way

I forgot to dread public speaking. I no longer trembled in front of a crowd. I came to like the sound of my voice.

During one class, Jeremiah described his crushing guilt for not being there when his brother died. He'd been in a freak accident, so Jeremiah couldn't have predicted or prevented it. Still, he was stricken, believing he somehow should have saved his brother. I told him I talked to Mom every morning. I'd asked for her forgiveness over and over until I didn't need it anymore—I knew I had it. He began to try some of my recommendations, took me aside a few weeks later and thanked me, said they were working. I'd done that. I had eased another human being's pain.

Every morning I watched the sun rise, every evening it descend. I marveled at how little I had noticed before, how rarely I'd paid attention. One night in particular will stick with me always—the moon was the smallest of slivers, clouds empty of birds. The sun had just disappeared, striping the sky burnt red and cool blue, the hue in between them amber and untouchable. *Like a painting,* I thought. How had I been lucky enough to wind up here?

Fall arrived. The temperature dipped. I pushed my shorts to the back of my closet. I drained the pool and stored the outdoor furniture in the shed, breathing cold air deep into my lungs. My meals with April and Georgina whittled from five days a week to three to one. I'd forgiven them for gossiping about me to Rebecca—though I still didn't know which of them had—but couldn't ignore how often their conversations turned to life beyond the island. They wondered what political news they were missing, debated which app they'd use first when they got their phones back, described the family member they were most excited to hug. They didn't want to talk about Wisewood, at least not all the time.

Instead I began eating with Jeremiah, who always had a pencil behind his ear and that book of crosswords in his back pocket. In between asking me for the answer to five down and whistling Lady Gaga's "Poker Face," he opened up about his divorce, his strained relationship with his deceased father, the weight he'd been struggling to lose since college. As I became closer with him, I got to know the rest of the staff too, members who had been here for years, for whom there was no such thing as life post-Wisewood. While tackling lawn care with me, Raeanne told me the horrors she'd experienced as a child and later as a long-haul trucker, and I began to understand her steely exterior. I watched Ruth fuss over Sanderson, saw how tightly she held him when she thought no one was paying attention, the way his shoulders relaxed into her embrace. As a group we scanned the list of advanced courses, considering what we should take next. I realized with a start that Nat wasn't chiming in. I hadn't heard her voice in some time. Mom's either. It was only me in my head.

Here I woke to the chirps of sparrows instead of sirens. No guns, no viruses, no planes falling from the sky. There was no longer a need for pepper spray or a key between my fingers. I was safe.

My hands were always busy now but my mind was newly quiet. The urge to pull my hair weakened. I tossed my rubber band in the trash. At first my wrist felt off-balance, too free. After a week I stopped noticing its bareness. I remembered Rebecca's promise during our second session—that soon I wouldn't need the rubber band anymore. She had been right. The pink scars healed; the skin blended. My hair grew back.

Three months in, she offered to let me use her computer. I could check my e-mail, the news, social media, whatever I wanted. The laptop sat at her desk, beckoning, but I had no urge to answer. What was waiting on the other side? Lapsed insurance notifications, wedding announcements, sleek travel photos posted by strangers I used to admire. You couldn't swipe left or right on me anymore. What difference did it make that Congress was still gridlocked and Rachel was pregnant with her second? The machinery of the world had kept churning without me, I without it. I told her thanks but no, thanks. Her eyes shone. She pulled a cell phone from a desk drawer, dangled it in front of me, and asked if I'd like to call anyone. A former coworker, perhaps? A neighbor? Natalie?

For the first time in my life, I was content. I had finally stopped reaching for my phone. What could I hope to gain from one call anyway? I had Jeremiah and Raeanne and Ruth and my students, I told her.

I have you, Teacher.

24

Kit

I STRODE INTO Teacher's office, a clipboard tucked under my arm, at four o'clock sharp.

"The gutter on the west side of the house has been repaired." I checked my notes. "Same with dryer number four. Sanderson left to make the grocery run. I reminded him to double up on nonperishables in case the storm is worse than we expect."

Teacher peered up from the legal pad on her desk. "What would I do without you?"

I warmed at her praise like a lizard on a desert rock.

"As for my students, I think nine of them are ready to move on to intermediate courses." I turned the page on my clipboard. "Jocelyn is doing particularly well. Yesterday she set a new guest record in the pool—sixty-five laps without stopping."

"You hypnotize me, you know that?"

After three months here, I had gotten used to the intensity of Teacher's attention, though it still made my stomach flip.

"What about the tenth student?"

I frowned. "Should we re-enroll him in the beginners' course with a different instructor? He's still showing up late to class, not making much of an effort." I tugged Mom's scarf tighter. "Jeremiah searched the student's room like you said. He found a cell phone in the desk drawer."

"Send him home."

My eyes widened. "But—"

She slapped her own face, hard. I gawked. "That's what sneaking a phone here feels like to me. The program has to come first. We don't do three strikes." She calmed. "You know that, Kitten."

I swooned. She had never used a nickname for me before. She rose from her desk chair and gestured for me to join her on the velvet couch. We sat close together. The right side of her face had a red handprint where she'd struck herself. She rested her hand on my knee, danced a finger in little circles around the bone. My spine tingled.

"I have to be able to count on your judgment if I'm going to bring you on as an employee."

I gasped. She bit back a smile.

"Seriously?" I had hoped this would happen but knew Teacher preferred to keep her staff small. According to Jeremiah, the only reason he'd been brought on was to organize Wisewood's finances. He claimed Teacher didn't even like him that much—the disarray of her bookkeeping was that bad.

She pointed at my clipboard. "You practically are one already. I think it's time to make it official."

My head spun. "So I would live here . . ."

"Indefinitely. You won't have to leave when your six months are up. You won't have an income but you'll get a free room, free meals, free course work. No more worrying about taxes and the rest of the government's headaches. We'll help with the student loan. We're here for you." She squeezed my knee.

I considered what I'd be leaving behind: happy hours with my coworkers, walks through Central Park, mirrors, the internet, Domino's at two a.m. When I came here, I never intended to stay.

I had spent the past weeks reimagining my career. Maybe the key was avoiding office gigs. I thought I'd like working outside or with animals. I'd toyed with moving to Colorado or Wyoming. I could become a nature guide, host white-water rafting trips. When I'd mentioned my ideas to Teacher, she'd told me the world beyond Wisewood wouldn't care about my Maximized Self. No matter where I moved or what job I took, they would try to change me. At the time, I was deflated. But she could've been grooming me for this job all along.

Teacher's face had turned stony. "If you're not interested, I'll find someone else." She gripped my knee. When I squeaked in pain, she released me and shifted away.

I had finally found peace. I'd met people who understood me. But I still hadn't apologized to Nat for treating her like the bad guy after Mom's death—before it too, if I was being honest. At the very least, I'd have to let her know I wouldn't be returning to New York in January. Could I live here for years to come? For the rest of my life?

"Don't make me ask again."

I would make amends with Nat. I could always leave Wisewood if I changed my mind. I didn't have to stay forever.

My eyes welled. "I'm shocked is all."

She softened. "What's the matter?" She leaned in to rub my back the way Mom used to. I could think about Mom now without feeling a gaping loss in my chest. Wisewood had done that for me.

"You're the first person to tell me I'm special. My entire adult life, the question has been how much I have to conform. I never considered I don't have to change at all."

"That's the power of our program." Teacher clasped my hands in hers, ran her thumbs over my knuckles. "Is that a yes?" Hope crept into her voice.

"I'm in." I beamed. "A hundred percent."

"Excellent." She dropped my hands and rose from the couch. "I'll have Gordon bring you a contract." She went back to her desk and resumed writing in her notepad.

I stood on trembling legs. "Thank you for the opportunity, Teacher. I won't let you down." She waved in acknowledgment but didn't glance up. The work was so important to her.

As I turned to leave she said, "I doubt those friends of yours will approve."

I stopped in my tracks. "April and Georgina?"

"They don't have your best interest at heart." She was still scribbling away. "Trust me."

Had they been talking about me again? "I hardly see them anymore."

I waited but Teacher didn't say anything else, so I left the office and hurried down the staircase. I ignored the heaviness in my chest, focused on my happy news instead. I couldn't wait to tell the others.

I rushed outside into a gloomy October evening. The temperature had dropped to the fifties. The sky was dim by five these days. A bitter draft zipped past me, hinting at harsher weather to come. The motion-sensor lights along the walkway clicked on as I loped through the garden. We had harvested most of the fruits and vegetables in the past couple of weeks. Without the bounty the tracts resembled cemetery plots. I thought of Mom back in California, waiting for me to put flowers on her grave. When was the last time Nat had visited her?

I shook my head. Today was a day to celebrate. This was what it was like to be good at something, to be valued. I let out a small whoop and reached for the cafeteria door. I was starving.

Most of the staff sat at their regular table, all wearing party hats. Was it someone's birthday? I made a beeline for them. "I have news!"

A grin broke out on every face, though Jeremiah's was slow to form. I'd have to check in with him later, make sure he was okay.

"Is this what I think it is?" Sofia bounced in her chair.

I nodded and did a silly victory dance. Everyone began to clap.

"We're so proud of you, dear." Ruth leaned toward me and winked. "I'm the one who suggested you for the job."

I'd begun to thank her when Debbie emerged from the kitchen. Her apron was stained with egg yolk, and flour was smeared across both cheeks, but she was glowing as she carried a messy round cake toward us. She held it in front of me. "It's three layers," she announced. "Your favorites: chocolate, peanut butter, and cheesecake. Took me a few tries but I think I got it right." The cake was covered with lumpy yellow frosting—my favorite color. She'd written *Congradulations, Kit* and drawn a smiley face in purple icing. A lump formed in my throat.

Raeanne peered at the cake. "You spelled 'congratulations' wrong."

Debbie's face fell.

"I love it, Debbie," I said. "Thank you so much."

They had known my job offer was coming, had never doubted that I'd accept. How had they been so sure?

She brightened. "Should I cut us all pieces?"

"Where's Gordon?" Jeremiah asked. "Shouldn't he be here?"

Raeanne rolled her eyes. "Probably on another one of his secret missions."

"Let's give him a few," Ruth said. "It's the nice thing to do."

"How come he gets to come and go as he pleases," Raeanne asked, "while the rest of us have to follow the rules?"

"We have to celebrate somehow," Sofia said. Her eyes sparkled as she shot out of her seat. "Group skinny-dip!"

Sanderson and Jeremiah laughed, but the women didn't.

"Group balcony jump," Sofia tried again, prancing on the tips of her toes. I assumed she was joking, but no one was laughing anymore.

"Calm down, dear," Ruth said. "We'll have the cake soon enough."

Sofia shook her head for a beat too long. "We're supposed to be more alive than everyone else, aren't we? What happened to leading by example?" When no one answered, she threw up her hands. "Fine, I'll celebrate Kit alone." She took off for the door with surprising speed.

Ruth sighed, slumping in her chair. "Every day I break my back for you kids, and this is the thanks I get?"

"I'll go," Jeremiah said. Raeanne raised an eyebrow, but he ignored her. "I'm proud of you, kiddo," he said to me as he jogged after Sofia.

An urge to hug him washed over me—but of course I wouldn't.

I gestured to the kitchen. "I'm going to grab some food while we wait for Gordon. Thank you guys again." I grinned at my new quirky family and left to grab a plastic tray. Pot roast again. I filled my plate and was about to head back to the staff's table when a voice nearby called my name. I swiveled. April.

She was sitting with Georgina, waving me over. I paused by their table. "Maximized day," I said, trying the phrase on for size. It sat awkwardly in my mouth but I was sure I'd get used to it.

"Eat with us." Georgina patted the seat next to her. "We haven't talked in forever."

I gazed longingly at the staff table. They were deep in conversation, likely discussing plans for the newest course that Teacher wanted to create for advanced students—Increasing Your Pain Tolerance. Resigned, I sat next to Georgina and began to eat.

"What's with the party hats?" she said. We'd been sitting in silence for at least a minute.

"I actually have some exciting news." I grinned. "Tea— . . . Rebecca offered me a staff position." Something told me the two of them would find it weird that I called her Teacher now. I shouldn't have cared what they thought— fear of rejection was getting the best of me.

"Here?" Georgina said.

"Permanently?" April asked.

I nodded, my smile fading at the doubt on their faces.

"Congratulations," April said.

"Yeah, congrats," Georgina echoed without enthusiasm.

We ate in silence for another minute. I could hear April chewing the tough meat.

"So you're just going to live here forever?" Georgina finally asked.

I shrugged. "As long as it's working for me, why not?"

April nodded quickly. "I've learned a lot here too." She hesitated. "What about patching things up with Nat?"

"I've been trying to get a handle on my own improvement before I rope her in."

"What about your career?" Georgina said.

I snickered. "What career?"

"Getting married, then? Having kids? Sex?" The joke fell flat when I didn't laugh.

I shrugged again. "I'm making a difference in people's lives." I pierced a chunk of potato with my fork, said to the spud, "I thought you'd understand."

"If you're happy, I'm happy," April said. She reached for my hand. I jerked it away. These two were always forgetting the no-touching rule.

"We're watching out for you. That's all," Georgina said.

No, they were trying to hold me back. This was a six-month lark for them, a story for the grandkids. They would forget everything they'd learned as soon as the ferry returned them to Rockland. Teacher had been right about these two.

"Some of us take this program seriously."

"I never would have signed up," Georgina said, "had I known taking the program seriously required lifelong confinement."

April shot her a glare. I blinked rapidly, trying not to cry.

"Why can't you be happy for me?" I stood and picked up my tray.

April startled. Georgina's mouth fell open. For once she had nothing to say.

I headed for the staff table. "Enjoy the rest of your stay."

25

GABE STUDIED ME, clutching a fire extinguisher to his breast. "You're a specter." His eyes shone. "Floating in midair. I've never seen anyone so breathtaking."

Ordinarily the gallery's concrete floors stole the warmth from my feet, but tonight my feet were not on the floor. Tonight I stood atop a three-foot-tall barstool made of metal. On my body was a long-sleeved, floor-length gown with a six-foot skirt that hid the stool. The pattern of the dress was nothing spectacular, a simple white sheath one might mistake for a bedsheet. The material of the dress, however, was as critical as that of the barstool. It was a common cotton, not unlike the bed linens, draperies, and clothing found in households the world over. Highly flammable.

"But what if something goes wrong?" he said, handsome despite the thin sheen of sweat covering his face.

I gestured at the extinguisher.

"I don't like it." He tucked his chin. In the rare moments when Gabe felt the need to stand his ground, he avoided eye contact. I had warned him that this automatically put his opponent in a dominant position, but he couldn't help himself. Gabe was the lamb, not the lion.

The soft fabric of the dress billowed off me. "How fortuitous then that you're not the one setting yourself alight." I winked.

He sighed; when up against me, his was always a losing battle. He rummaged through his bag and held up two tubes of lipstick. "Instigator or Caviar?"

I motioned to the black shade, daubed some across my lips, and handed it back to him. "Shall we?" I arched an eyebrow.

Gabe nodded but wouldn't meet my eye. He set down the extinguisher and pulled a lighter from his pocket. Earlier The Five had placed tea lights around the edges of the room, all that would separate the spectators from me. Gabe walked from candle to candle, holding his lighter to each wick.

When he'd finished, Gabe strode to the circuit box. A few seconds later, the lightbulbs switched off. Darkness consumed the gallery but for the glimmering tea lights. One could be forgiven for finding the space romantic, at least until the action began. I stood stock-still on my stool, a nine-foot-tall grim reaper dressed as a cherub with black lips.

"Break a leg." Gabe's whisper rippled across the room. I blew him a kiss. He headed for the door.

A few minutes later the audience entered, invading the space like ants on a picnic blanket. Most of the faces were new; The Five had been hard at work these past months. I had worried that as they reached their thirties, they would tire of our mission and politely cut ties with me. On the contrary, their resolve never wavered, though one of them had married and two more were dating each other. They had all acquired day jobs, but *this* was their true calling. I was their vocation.

Two figures strode toward me. One of The Five held a camera with a glowing red light on her shoulder. The other was Gabe. He picked up the fire extinguisher, had insisted he be the one to hold the salve. "I'm right here." He pulled the lighter from his pocket once more. "You sure?"

I ran my fingers down the bodice of the dress. A shame to waste it. I fluffed the skirt a final time, then settled my arms at my sides, letting them dangle, feigning nonchalance. I was ready and willing to do whatever it took to enlighten my followers.

"Now," I said.

Gabe stepped toward me. The lighter clicked when he flicked it open. A tiny blaze illuminated the fright on his face. He, the antipode of fearlessness, crouched and held the lighter to the back of the skirt until the white cotton caught. The spectators gasped. All they had known coming in was the show's title: *Madame Fearless Presents . . . Aflame.* Perhaps they had seen the intentionally vague marketing posters. Perhaps they had their suspicions. Perhaps they now regretted buying their tickets. It was too late to turn back, for all of us.

As the flames inched closer to my untouched skin, I did not scream.

When at last they took me, I wanted to.

MY EYES FLUTTERED open. One of The Five stood in the corner of the room, aiming her camera at me. An oxygen mask covered my nose and mouth.

"She's awake," the camerawoman said.

I moved my gaze in the direction from which she was speaking. Sleeping in the fetal position across two chairs, next to my bed, was Gabe.

The air around me reeked of failure. We were in a hospital.

The camerawoman nudged Gabe awake. He leapt to his feet and leaned over me. "If you need anything at all . . ."

I closed my eyes.

SOMETIME LATER I opened them again, struck by the monotony of the act. Open and close, open and close, over and over until they failed to open one final time.

I noted that the oxygen mask had been removed, but something else was restricting my facial muscles. I reached up to touch my cheeks and saw my hands were bandaged. I waggled my chin. My face was swathed as well, with holes for my eyes, nostrils, and mouth. I waited for a searing pain to consume me, for the flames to rise anew. Instead I felt nothing. Perhaps I was on a heavy dose of morphine. I glanced down at my body. Every visible part was covered in clean white dressing.

Still pain did not besiege me.

Have I done it? I thought wildly. *Have I become immune to pain?*

Already I was cooking up seminars, weeklong conferences, research studies that would methodologize what I had accomplished. I needed to package the process so my achievement could be realized by others. I was a sorceress; I had created actual magic.

I rotated my head to peer out the window. The Five stood by my side, horror-struck by whatever they saw lying in my hospital bed but trying not to show it. A couple of them held bouquets and "get well" balloons.

"We've already started an online fundraiser to take care of your medical bills," said one.

"Six hundred dollars so far."

"Plus our own thousand bucks."

"What would I do without you, my angels?" I winced, throat on fire.

"Okay, that's enough. Give her some space," Gabe said from the other side of the bed. With great effort I turned to him. He gestured to the food on the tray table, careful not to touch me. "I put extra honey in the yogurt, the way you like."

"How long did I last?"

"Let's get some food in you." He scooped a spoonful of yogurt, held it to my mouth. When I scowled at him, he let the spoon fall back into the plastic cup. "You have third-degree burns on seventy percent of your body."

"Did the entire dress ignite?"

He wiped away a fat tear. "You went into cardiac arrest in the ambulance. The EMTs had to use a defibrillator to bring you back. You're going to need skin grafts. That could mean a blood transfusion."

We had anticipated burns, possibly a few bad ones. We had not expected defibrillators or that the fire would raze me quite this thoroughly. Still, I had, once again, proven myself fearless. I would forever have the scars to substantiate my claim.

Always, always, was I aware of the unblinking red glow of a recording device. Something Gabe never understood: the show demanded to go on. I cleared my throat. "If the next word out of your mouth is not 'yes' or 'no,' you're fired."

He staggered backward. "Yes. The dress burned all the way to your neck, like we planned."

DAYS LATER I told Gabe to summon The Five to my hospital room.

"You've already done so much for me," I said once they were assembled, "so I'm loath to ask you to do more."

"Anything," they chirped.

I stared gravely at each of them.

"Who here has O blood?"

One of the girls nervously raised her hand.

I studied her. "I want you to make a donation. In case I need a transfusion during surgery."

The girl paled. "I'm terrified of needles."

"I know it's a big ask," I said softly. "I wouldn't make it if I didn't need it."

"The hospital must already have plenty of blood," she stammered.

"That's hardly the point, is it?" I cocked my head. "You all said you would do anything for me."

"*I* would," one boy said.

"I'd love to donate," said a second girl. She turned to her friend, whose face had greened. "Think of the honor of having *your* blood flowing through the veins of Madame Fearless."

They all glowered at the green girl.

"It's an honor, for sure." Her hands shook. "But I've been deathly afraid of needles my whole life."

"Oh, come on," one of the boys said.

I held up a hand. "All of you, leave us." They shuffled out of the room. "You too, Gabe," I said when he hung back.

He hesitated. "This doesn't feel right."

"Get out," I said through gritted teeth. I didn't bother to turn and catch the wounded expression I knew I would find as he marched out the door.

A woman can tolerate only so much weakness.

Once it was just the green girl and me, I patted my bed. She sat but wouldn't meet my eye. I held her hand.

"I'm sorry," she said. "I don't want to disappoint you."

"You could never." I tucked a strand of auburn hair behind her ear. Over the years, all the girls had grown out their locks. "But what am I going to remind you?"

She sniffed. "That the fear of pain is worse than the pain itself."

"Such a bright girl." I tipped her chin toward me. "Do you remember how scared you were to tell your parents you were gay all those years ago? You couldn't sleep. You were vomiting between classes. Your grades suffered.

And then Mom and Dad kicked you out, which was horribly painful. But what happened eventually?"

"They reached out," she said in a small voice. "They apologized, said the way they'd reacted was their single biggest failure as parents. They told me they loved me unconditionally." The tiniest of smiles. "They asked for my forgiveness."

Warmth spread across my chest. "Do you know why they reached out?"

"I assume guilt was eating away at them for those couple months."

"Probably so. And perhaps a little bird had been calling them weekly, reminding them how lovely their daughter was, how much they'd regret not being a part of her life."

She froze. "You were the one who changed their minds?"

I nudged her. "We can't let fear stop us from doing what's right."

Silence settled between us, save for the various beeps of hospital machinery. The green girl was less green now. Her gaze swept up and down my body cast. She leaned forward.

"I'll do it," she said, resolute. "I'll give you blood."

I patted her hand. "Good girl."

I ENDED UP not needing a transfusion, but she didn't need to know that.

LATER, WHEN WE were alone, Gabe clenched his jaw. "Why the hell didn't you stop the show when you knew you were about to pass out?"

I gripped my half-finished Jell-O cup. He had the nerve to challenge me while I was caught in the throes of a bacterial infection? "Not 'stop.' 'Quit.'"

He squinted one honey eye, tilted an ear toward me as if he'd misheard. "Excuse me?"

"I don't quit. My name, my entire body of work, is built on not giving up. I endure; that's what I do. I cannot conclude these performances a loser." I threw down the Jell-O.

He guffawed. "You're telling me you'd rather be a dead winner?"

"I'm not even hurting. I think I've finally done it, Gabe." I tried to assuage the hysteria in my voice. "I've rid my body of pain."

"Will you listen to yourself?" He frowned. "You're not in agony right now because you've burned all of the pain-sensing cells in your skin. Are you delusional enough to believe you're immortal?"

"Watch your tone."

"Don't talk to me that way." He narrowed his eyes. "You're my partner, not my mother."

Partners? How many times had he put his life at risk? Thank God our livelihood depended on my bravery and not his. Apparently he was under the mistaken impression that because we had paid our bills with his inheritance once or twice, we were on equal footing.

It turned out that a pizza franchise could be quite lucrative. When Gabe's father expired last year, he had left his son millions. Gabe invested wisely, and we had dipped into the funds only the couple of months we struggled to eke out an existence. But it took considerably more than capital to manifest a career like mine. Without my coattails to ride, Gabe would be nothing, a nobody.

I slammed a hand on the hospital tray, sending it clattering. "I didn't hear you vociferating about your independence when I paid for your speech therapy. Where was your indignation then?"

He blinked a few times. "I've offered to repay you for those sessions. Several times."

Ungrateful—that was what he was. "You'd still be choking on your *w*'s if it weren't for me."

I regretted the sentence as soon as it flew out of my mouth. Some part of me yearned to squeeze his hand and apologize, but the bigger part was furious that after all this time, after the countless hours I'd spent coaching and leading by example, Gabe was still this fearful. He was supposed to be stronger by now, to support me unconditionally. If I wanted an overbearing man in my life, I would have remained in touch with my father.

"Take that back." Now he stuttered only when he was especially grieved.

"I don't see our wrists handcuffed together. The door is right there."

"Fine." He stomped toward it. "I quit."

"Good riddance." The door slammed.

I lay my head against the starchy pillow. The longer I proclaimed the gospel of fearlessness, the more I knew the world needed my teachings. Rather than uproot their fears, the masses let them grow and grow until their paths were choked, dreams forgotten.

Take Evelyn Luminescence. This woman had been my mentor. The boldness of her art had transformed my own. In her prime she said and did what few others dared, put her art before love, before everything. Where was she now? Teaching finger painting to toddlers at a patrician nursery on the Upper East Side. She told me that at her age she needed steadiness, both in income and in emotional state. Less turbulence, more predictability. I knew what was behind the about-face: a fear of failure. She was afraid of the slow fade into artistic oblivion. Rather than wait for defeat, she had removed herself from the arena. The world was poorer for it.

I sat in the hospital bed alone, aware of a slowly encroaching pain that wanted to eat me alive. Mind over matter, though; I would create my own reality. So long as I believed I was immune to this pain, it would be true. Gabe was the delusional one.

I turned on the television for a distraction. A black-and-white Western was playing, which made me think of my father, which made me wonder whether he had heard about any of my performances. If he had, Sir would find my stunts, complete with stopwatch and recitations on endurance, gussied up but familiar. A sadist he unequivocally was, but at forty I was willing to concede he'd taught me most of what I knew about fearlessness. Because of him I'd become invulnerable to fear. I knew how to swallow pain, to repurpose it as a source of power. Admitting as much was out of the question. We hadn't spoken in sixteen years.

As I waited for the nurse to check on me, my thoughts kept drifting guiltily back to Gabe. He had always been good to me. He didn't deserve to be mistreated. Still, he perennially forgot one simple fact: there was no shortage of Gabes, Lisas, and Evelyns on the planet, people who clutched their fears like dead loved ones without a clue how to let them go. He had to learn he was the replaceable one between us.

Nobody cared about the pawns. They were too busy watching the queen.

26

Kit

OCTOBER 2019

TEACHER AND I sat on the velvet couch in her office on a Monday in late October, door closed, discussing the progress I'd made on the Mom front.

"It's not my fault she died." I fingered the cool silk around my neck. "You made me understand that."

"I'm so proud of you. You've begun to let go of the emotional attachments to which you once clung so tightly."

I bent my head. "Thank you, Teacher."

I had been an official Wisewood staff member for almost a month. In that time I'd worked fourteen-hour days, sweeping out the shed, mulching the vegetable plots, and reorganizing Teacher's kitchen and pantry. I learned that she ate different foods than the rest of us—brie and prosciutto and an organic fig jam from a farm stand twenty minutes outside Rockland. Gordon had to take a bus to get there; no wonder he was gone all the time.

As a team, the staff had created a syllabus for the new Increasing Your Pain Tolerance class. Everyone's eyes lit up when I suggested incorporating superglue into the curriculum. They called me brilliant, our secret weapon. I floated through the rest of that day.

At night I still wandered the campus. I found myself returning to the

Staff Only doors, putting an ear to the wood but hearing nothing more than the sounds of the forest. Every time I reached for the brushed-steel handles, I held my breath. Every time they were locked, and I didn't know whether to be relieved or disappointed. I was one of them now—when would I be allowed beyond these walls?

Teacher leaned toward me. I caught a whiff of her crisp perfume. "The next step is ridding yourself of material attachments."

I peered at her. "I already did. It's all in storage. I left everything behind when I came here."

"Not everything." She peered at my neck.

I gaped. "My scarf?"

"It'll be good for you." She watched my grip tighten on the fabric. "That scarf is a noose."

"It's not." I let go of it. "I'm keeping her memory alive."

She tapped the star tattoo on my temple. "You can store memories of Peggy right here. You're holding on to the past."

She might've been right, but I still didn't want to give it up. "What if I keep it in my dresser? So it's not with me all day."

She shook her head. "Your reluctance proves my point." Her tone hardened. "Do not allow fear to control you."

I stroked the silk and peered out the window. A dense fog slunk closer and closer to the house, threatening to overwhelm us.

"Do you trust me?"

"You know I do."

"Then get rid of it. You'll never be free so long as you wear it."

We sat in agonizing silence. I studied her features for a flash of ambivalence— maybe I could change her mind. It was a foolish thought; she appeared more steadfast with every second.

"It only took Debbie a month to hand over her old engagement ring," Teacher said. "Twelve years she was engaged to that abuser, yet she found the strength almost immediately to shed any reminders of him. You, on the other hand, have been here almost four months."

I couldn't think of a single thing to say, so I knotted my hands in my lap and stared at them. Her eyes bored into me.

She sighed and looked away. "The rest of the staff knew you wouldn't."

I glanced up in surprise. They had all been so warm and encouraging. I remembered Debbie's lumpy cake, how we'd all eventually come together, huddled and laughing, to eat it.

"I defended you, told them to give you a chance. Won't I be the fool with egg on my face?"

When I found my voice, it was shaky. "What would you do with it?"

"Not to worry—I'll keep it safe." She extended a hand, waiting for me to acquiesce. She wouldn't take no for an answer.

Maybe she was right—she had been about everything else so far. How could I be truly fearless if I had Mom wrapped around my neck every day? I'd be distracted from our mission until I apologized to Nat, set things straight, and put the mistakes I'd made around Mom's death behind me. It was time to close that chapter.

I undid the scarf, and hesitated before dropping it in Teacher's outstretched hand. She closed her fingers around it. I pushed down a spike of regret—more weakness I had to overcome.

"Good, Kitten," she said, happy again. I let out a small sigh of relief. "How brave you are. You can share this progress with your class."

I thought of one student in particular, a man who had lost custody of his daughter. Everything here reminded him of her: the way Sanderson ate his sandwich crust first, the shape of Orion in the night sky, a classmate's flamingo-patterned socks. He'd flown six hundred miles for a reprieve but couldn't outrun his memories. I tried to be an example for him, a light at the end of his tunnel of grief.

I nodded, staring at Mom's scarf clenched in Teacher's hand. I'd barely taken it off in two years. My neck felt exposed.

Teacher walked the scarf to her desk and tossed it in a drawer—I couldn't see which one. She rested both palms on the desk, leaning over it, waiting for me to focus on her. When I did, she slid open the utensil drawer. "I have a reward for you."

She pulled out a navy envelope, glided back toward me on the couch, and placed it in my hands. Written on the envelope in spidery handwriting was a single word: *Kit*. She gestured for me to open it.

Inside was a thick card filled with the same looping cursive.

Dear Kit, the letter began, *you have come so far during your time here. Four months ago you never would have relinquished your mother's scarf.* I scanned the rest, picking up phrases like *cordially invite you* and *exclusive opportunity* and <u>*total*</u> *secrecy.* I felt Teacher's laser beam glare on me. I read through it a second time, more slowly.

When I'd finished reading, I looked up. "What's the Inner Circle?"

III

I must eliminate any obstacles
that impede my path to freedom.

27

Natalie

KIT IS HERE, in my cabin, sitting on the bed. I freeze on the thresh-old. For most of our lives my sister has had chest-length, straight blond hair.

Now it's buzzed close to her scalp.

Like everyone else on Wisewood's staff.

The rest of her looks the same: round cheeks, bright eyes, a small star tattoo on her left temple. She wears jeans and a yellowing T-shirt, her coat slung over my desk chair. She appears healthy, content, not a scratch or bruise on her. No sleepy expression suggesting a drugged state. No tears to imply harm. Actually, she's beaming.

She's okay.

She's okay, she's okay, she's okay.

My shoulders drop. The weight lifts off my chest. An ache builds in the back of my throat. Part of me thought I'd never see my little sister again.

I run toward her with my arms extended. She shrinks back on the bed, stopping me short.

"We have this no-touching rule," she says.

That's why Gordon jerked away when I tapped his arm.

I step back, surprised. Kit has always been the touchy-feely one, climbing into laps, linking arms, playing with hair.

Most people don't hug like they mean it. Our hugs are too quick, a chore to be hurried through, a formality. Not Kit's. She grips you like a life raft and doesn't let go, leaving no doubt how much she loves you. No one gives hugs like Kit.

She got that from Mom.

I long to wrap my arms around Kit and Mom—more accurately, for them to wrap theirs around me. I want to shove my nose into the hair Kit has left to make sure it still smells like apples. I know I broke the rules by coming here, but I was expecting a warmer welcome than this. *She's not even happy to see you.* The ache in my throat deepens. I keep it together.

Kit raises an eyebrow. "So? Did you happen to be in the neighborhood?"

As I survey every inch of her, my gaze keeps drifting back to her fuzzy head, the bare neck and ears, the features that are too big for her face now. There's no getting around it: the haircut is horrible.

"What happened to your hair?" I blurt.

Self-consciously she runs a hand over her head, then bristles. Her voice has an unfamiliar edge to it. "What are you doing here, Nat?"

My stomach drops when I remember the accusatory e-mail. I swallow the truth, find a different one. "I'm worried about you." She stares, waiting. "I haven't heard from you in six months. I tried e-mails, texts, calling, but you haven't responded to any of it."

"I don't have my phone or computer. I told you I wouldn't." She brightens. "Anyway, you have nothing to worry about. This experience has been incredible. For the first time since she died, I've moved past the Mom stuff."

I'm nauseated with regret but can't go down that path yet. It's too soon. I'm not ready. I tell myself not to be critical right off the bat. I decide to gather information, assess, and make a plan, nothing more.

"What have you been doing all these months?"

"Oh God, I'm so busy. I teach classes and yoga; I keep Teacher's calendar organized; I get to serve her breakfast every morning. I plan special Wisewood functions. Last month I put together a party for Teacher's sixtieth. It was magical, all of us dancing on the beach in the moonlight. She's also invited me to sit in on some of her sessions, to offer my input after the guest has left. There aren't enough hours in the day."

"Are you a therapist in training, then?" I've never seen her so driven, so invested.

Kit shrugs. "I help out where I'm needed. This is not me heading down the path to becoming a licensed psychologist, if that's what you're asking."

"What path *are* you heading down?" I try to phrase the question with curiosity.

"The path to my Maximized Self. It's not a career ladder, Nat. Here I don't need to worry about what I want to be. I don't have to pick one thing. Your sister is a real renaissance woman." For the first time she smiles at me.

My sister is a real idiot, I think.

"Are they paying you?"

"They pay me in free classes and housing and food," Kit says as if she's won the lottery.

My sister sees no issue with working a full-time job without payment. She doesn't have reservations about cutting herself off from the real world. She has no intention of leaving Wisewood, possibly ever.

I'm losing her.

Kit pulls herself to standing. "I still have a few things to do for Teacher."

I glance at the wall clock. "She works you hard."

"She doesn't make me do anything. Only I can work the path."

I quell a violent urge to tear her away from this place, remind myself to keep the peace.

She peers at me. "If there's nothing else, I better get going."

I consider telling her right here and now, letting the secret pour out of me. But now that I'm actually staring her in the face, my resolve slips. I can't turn our first conversation in half a year into one that will destroy her. I'll tell her in the morning instead, then head back to Rockland.

"I'm so glad you're okay. Look, I'll be out of your hair tomorrow. I've gotta go back to work."

"Actually, you'll have to stay a few days."

I watch her, questioning.

"A bad storm is coming through, so we're grounding the *Hourglass*. It'd be unsafe for you to make the crossing."

"Oh," I say, uneasy at the prospect of staying here more than one night. This reunion has been formal and awkward, not at all what I pictured.

"Once the storm passes, Gordon can take you home." She heads for the door, then turns back. "Why'd you tell him I e-mailed you?"

My mouth dries. "He said he couldn't put family members in touch with guests. I figured if I said you reached out first, he might help me."

"So there was no e-mail?"

I hesitate, loath to lie to my sister again, then shake my head anyway.

Kit nods, thinking. "You know, he's more compassionate than you'd guess, Gordon." She opens the door. "You should've told him the truth."

28

Kit

I WOKE TO pounding at my door. Groggy, I opened my eyes and flipped the alarm clock toward me. The neon numbers announced it was 3:15 a.m. The person at the door knocked again.

"Kit. Open up."

I pulled myself out of bed and shuffled to the door, swinging it open. On the other side stood Raeanne, dressed in baggy jeans and a flannel shirt. Her expression was urgent, life-or-death. Anxiety overpowered my drowsiness.

"What's wrong?"

"You're going to be initiated," she said, barely able to contain her excitement. When I looked confused, she added, "Into the IC—the Inner Circle."

"Right now?" My heart pounded. *In the middle of the night?*

"Everyone's waiting for you." She rushed into my room. "Hurry and get dressed."

"Who's everyone?" I rubbed my eyes. "What do you mean, initiated?"

She sighed. "Will you get dressed already?"

I went to the bathroom to change into jeans and a sweater. When I came back out, Raeanne was riffling through my desk drawer. She slammed it closed.

"Sorry," she said guiltily, moving toward the door. "Teacher asked me to search for something."

"What is it?"

She waved me off. "Never mind. We'll be late." She handed me my key card and yanked open the door to a brisk autumn night.

"Have I done something wrong?" I pulled my sweater sleeves so they covered my hands.

"*Shhh.* You'll wake gen pop." Since joining Wisewood's staff, I had learned that Teacher and my coworkers referred to the guests as "gen pop" behind their backs, short for "general population." The phrase sounded harmless enough but there was a certain superiority behind it—gen pop were the less committed among us.

Raeanne turned on her heel and took off in a jog. I dashed after her. Wisewood was bathed in midnight blue, peopleless. I glanced at the sky, millions of stars cold and distant.

"Raeanne, what were you looking for?"

She wove among the guesthouses, not slowing. "Teacher has us do routine checks on each other to make sure we're all following the rules. I'm sure you'll be searching my stuff in no time."

Was that supposed to make me feel better? Did it?

I trailed her past the vegetable garden to the hedge on the west side of the island. We stopped at one of the STAFF ONLY doors, and my breath hitched. This was it—I was finally going beyond the wall.

Raeanne peeked over both shoulders, scanning the campus, then pulled a ring of keys from her pocket. She slid one of them into the lock and pushed the door open, signaling for me to go through.

I had roamed every inch of the island but never here, never through these doors. All those times I'd jiggled the handles, curiosity had overpowered fear, but now fear sliced through me. What was waiting for me out there? I shook off the weakness. My fellow staff members would never lead me into harm's way.

"Where are we going?" I asked.

"It's a surprise."

Raeanne locked the door and pulled a flashlight from her pocket, illuminating our path. Pine and rich earth perfumed the air around us. Nearby an owl hooted. We rushed through the forest, sticking to the narrow trail strewn with tree needles and moss. I was walking so fast that I barely registered my surroundings, other than clusters of spruce so tall and dense that I could no longer see the starry sky. I pictured the trees as a gang of Slender Men—spider-limbed and faceless, waiting, watching, following—and stuck as close to Raeanne's six as I could. Insects gossiped; twigs snapped underfoot. I tugged the cuffs of my sweater tighter, swatting branches from my face.

After a while the forest gave way to enormous blocks of granite. In the dark I couldn't see the ocean, but I heard waves slapping at the shore. We had reached the edge of the island.

On the granite stood a handful of people. They turned when they heard us approach. My pulse quickened.

I recognized Ruth first and let out a huge sigh—she wouldn't be involved in anything untoward. I stepped onto a boulder beside her as she winked. Next to Ruth was Sanderson, hood pulled up, hands crammed into his sweatshirt pocket. I was surprised to see the cook Debbie here, beaming at me, but not at all surprised to find Sofia bouncing in place. Raeanne strutted to her own spot on the rocks, pulling a toothpick from a coat pocket. Rounding out the group was Gordon, standing at a distance with his arms crossed. None of them looked like they'd been roused from sleep.

Ruth checked her watch. "We'll have to start without Jeremiah." I perked up at my friend's name, glad he also belonged. "Gather round."

The group formed a tight circle. I felt a spike of disappointment—I'd been hoping Teacher was part of the IC too.

Ruth gazed at me. "Welcome, Kit, to Wisewood's Inner Circle. Sometimes it's hard to remember how fortunate we are when we're all so busy. Lord knows I can barely keep up with the workload, what with the daily chores and classes, plus the planning of these things falling to me every time." She glanced around the circle accusingly, then perked up. "Then again, no one else has my experience, which is why Teacher only trusts the job to me." A few bodies tensed. Ruth frowned at Raeanne as soon as she opened her mouth, prompting her to close it again. "Tonight should serve as a reminder to each of us how wonderful this place is."

"So wonderful," Sofia said, already starting to tear up. Debbie took a subtle step away from her.

Behind Ruth the tide was low. The moon bounced like a spotlight off the sea life scattered across the boulders: rockweed, whelks, and periwinkles.

"We're so thrilled you're—"

The trees rustled, stopping Ruth mid-sentence. We all froze. There was someone or something in the forest. A bulky figure rushed onto the rocks.

"Sorry I'm late," Jeremiah said, hands on his knees.

"Can you not fit a watch around that tree stump of an arm?" Raeanne grumbled as everyone relaxed again.

"Sorry," Jeremiah repeated, still panting. "I got caught up."

"Doing . . . ?" Gordon asked.

Jeremiah straightened, ignoring him.

"What were you caught up doing?" Gordon said again.

A hush fell over the group. Jeremiah stroked his beard, which he had let grow bushy. He hesitated a second too long. "Helping Teacher with tax stuff."

At three in the morning? Even I, the newcomer, could tell he was lying.

"At this hour?" Gordon said.

Another uncomfortable silence. I was sure whatever reason Jeremiah had for being late was a legitimate one. He could've had a breakthrough he wasn't ready to share. Or Teacher might have asked for his help, told him to keep things confidential. I wanted to defend my friend but now was not the time to cause trouble. I tried to catch Jeremiah's eye. He was busy returning Gordon's glare.

"Why don't you mind your own fucking business for once?" Jeremiah finally said, tired.

Ruth gasped. Raeanne smirked. Everyone shifted nervously except Gordon, whose face and statuesque stillness gave away nothing as he stared at Jeremiah.

Sofia bounced harder on her toes, goggling at the horizon. "Can we jump in now?"

That broke the spell. Jeremiah turned away from Gordon and stood next to me, mouthing, *Sorry.* I smiled and his shoulders slackened.

Ruth stepped up. "Unless one of you wants to lead this ceremony, no more outbursts." She fixed each of us with a scowl. No one said a word. "Let's get in the water."

My fellow students slipped out of their shoes and hitched up their pant legs.

"Cannonball," hollered Sofia, running toward the sea.

"Sofia, don't," Ruth called. "The water's not that—"

Sofia jumped in. We all peered over the boulders, waiting. A couple of seconds later she resurfaced, shrieking about how cold it was. Ruth sighed.

Everyone else eased off the rocks. I gasped when the water bit my toes, then ankles, then knees—it couldn't have been over fifty degrees. Ruth and Sanderson were last to get in. She squeezed his hand when she thought no one was looking, and he smiled back. The group waded deeper, forming a circle around me like a shiver of sharks. I waited, trying to stop shaking. I didn't want them to think I was scared.

Once Sofia had quieted down, Ruth said, "The Inner Circle is a group of students that are more committed than the average guest to pursuing their Maximized Selves. The six months of classes are a good start, but we need the opportunity to put what we've learned into action. Think, for example, of becoming a lawyer." She paused. "After completing years of course work, you don't simply begin arguing in a courtroom. First you have to pass the bar exam. Do you understand?"

I nodded, mind racing.

"The way we test ourselves is through Quests of Fearlessness. Some members call them q's for short. In each quest we attempt to master a universal fear."

She stopped again. I felt like I should say something. "How many quests are there?" My legs were numb.

"No one knows," Debbie said with wonder.

"Teacher does," Raeanne said.

"With every completed quest, you move one step closer to your Maximized Self," Ruth said. "None of us knows what a quest entails until the first of us tries to complete it."

Sofia spoke up, water dripping from her head. "They're the most life-altering experiences you'll ever have."

The others nodded.

"Teacher will never ask you to complete a quest until she knows you're ready," Ruth said. "In order to be initiated you have to pass your q1. The Quest of Judgment."

Butterflies swarmed my stomach. "Tonight?"

She tipped her head forward.

The people here didn't judge the failures of my past—they wanted to better the Kit standing in front of them right now. When I'd joined Wisewood back in July, I had hoped I might return home with a few strategies to break harmful thought patterns. I wanted to loosen the noose of guilt around my neck. Never in my wildest dreams did I think I'd come this far, find the philosophy I had been searching for my whole life.

"I'll do it." My teeth chattered.

Ruth beamed. "First we have to get you clean." She joined me in the center of the circle, told me to lie on my back in the water. I did as instructed, sopping sweater and jeans pinned to my freezing limbs.

"From water you were born, and in water you shall be reborn," Ruth said.

Without warning she yanked my head under with both hands. I screamed at the icy shock, swallowing salt water in the process. I coughed and swallowed more. Ruth's grip on my head tightened. She was stronger than she appeared.

What if she didn't let me back up in time?

My arms and legs began to thrash, and liquid coursed down my throat. My lungs heaved in protest. Above me Ruth was indistinct, soft-edged but monstrous in the dark. I clawed at her hands with my fingernails.

She lifted me out.

Ruth let go of my head and patted my shoulder. In the moonlight I could make out her glistening eyes.

"You're ready for q1," she said.

Sanderson finger whistled. Raeanne hooted. Jeremiah bit his lip. My adrenaline receded as I took in all their eager faces. After a couple of minutes I quit trembling. Between coughs I grinned. My throat and nostrils burned but I didn't care.

The fear was the point—this was what I'd signed up for.

"Now," Ruth said, "let's go find Teacher."

29

I POKED MY head out of the khaki tent that had been erected on the lip of the ice. Dawn had turned the yawning sky the hue of cotton candy. On the frozen lake ahead, a man in a snowsuit bored a perfectly symmetrical hole in the ice with a power auger. Beneath the ice rushed bitterly cold water. Nearby The Five watched him work. He had almost finished the job.

Behind the tent, an unending expanse was carpeted in snow. The snow was blue, almost lavender, the sky reflecting in the flakes. Bald trees dotted the rolling prairie. Wooden fence posts separated the large swathes of land, though for whom or from what one couldn't tell. The fences were handmade, the posts uneven in width and height. A handful of them staggered at forty-five-degree angles, as if they could not bear the weight of one more barbaric New York winter. On a low-hanging branch a red-bellied woodpecker cheerfully went to work, the only one not grousing about the breath-stealing cold.

I pulled my head back inside the tent and zipped it closed. The space was cramped, barely big enough for two, plus the rack of dry suits, booties, and masks. The space heater blasted, pooling sweat inside my suit. I turned to Gabe, who handed me my boots. "I hope you're right about this," he said.

With forced patience I set down the boots. "We've been over this."

"Would it have killed you to choose a different stunt?"

"I should change *my* performance because *you're* afraid?"

He struggled to keep his composure. "Can you blame me after what happened with *Aflame?*"

I scrutinized my hands. From knuckles to wrists puckered angry red
scars, the only parts of my body with permanent disfigurement from that
performance. The rest of the scars, corporeal and otherwise, had faded with
skin grafts and physical therapy. I still stood by the show. The photos were
glorious, worth every second of pain and the months of recovery. One of
them even made a local newspaper.

Ten months after deserting me in the hospital, Gabe had returned to my
side, as I knew he would. Our work was finally beginning to take off, but with
each new exploit being more dangerous than the last, I fretted over my fans. I
couldn't bear to endanger them; for the first time I had forbidden an audience
from attending my performance. The masses would have to settle for a taped
viewing. While I worried about my fans, Gabe worried about me. We quar-
reled incessantly over my safety. What had once been endearing now stifled.

"We should've hired a safety crew," Gabe said.

"That's what The Five are here for."

He rolled his eyes. "They're not qualified."

"You brood too much." I wrenched on the dry hood, signaling the end of
the parley. Gabe pulled the boots onto my feet, then extended the neoprene
gloves. I slid them over my sullied hands, marveled at my body made flawless
again. The mask came last. Together we slipped it over my face. Gabe tightened the strap on the back of my head.

"You didn't watch your best friend go up in flames."

"Oh, Gabriel, it was five years ago. Enough sniveling."

He crossed shaking arms. After all this time, he was still afraid.

I had failed him.

"Join me," I said suddenly.

"Where?"

"In the water. You've only ever endured my lectures. You're overdue to put
the lessons into practice."

Gabe blinked. "You must be joking. I haven't done any training."

I knew in my gut this was the solution he needed. It was the right thing
to do. "You don't have to stay in as long as I do. Just experience the sensation

of true fearlessness running through your veins. Perhaps then you'll understand why I do what I do."

He shook his head. "I'll take your word for it."

"Oh, come on. Any of The Five would die for this opportunity."

"I'm not them. I have a job to do here, in case you've forgotten. Your safety is my top priority."

I waved him off. "The Five will serve as my safety crew. They don't need a sixth running the show."

"I don't—"

"You can come up with as many cockamamie excuses as you want. We both know the real reason you don't want to." I paused. "You're afraid."

He glanced away.

"Gabriel." I took his hands in mine. "Do you believe in my—*our*—mission?"

"Would I be here if I didn't?"

"Then when are you going to stop letting fear run your life? What happened to the Gabe who knocked on my dressing room door so many years ago, demanding an apprenticeship? The one who called my father a bastard? Who moved to New York despite his own father's warnings?"

"Don't go there." He thrust out his chin. "I've got nothing to prove to a dead man."

"But you have something to prove to someone else. Someone much more important." I clasped his shoulders. "I see the way you gaze at me before I start a show. Jealously, longingly. Some part of you wants the chance to shine as I do. I'm giving you that chance right now. Prove to yourself you're every bit as brave as Madame Fearless. I'll be by your side the entire time."

Gabe sighed, but there was a glimmer of something in his eyes. "You won't take no for an answer, will you?"

I laughed. "I can promise you this much. You're going to feel goddamn invincible."

OVER THE YEARS, the question I had been asked most frequently: how do you quit being afraid?

You didn't, not entirely. You learned to ignore your body's warnings to stop, turn around, go back before it's too late.

I squinted up through the murky green water at the round hole in the ice, head pounding. Brain freeze was not uncommon in ice dives; cold water did not mix well with the soft tissues of the head. ThermoKline, the company from whom we purchased the dive gear, had guaranteed any head pain would attenuate quickly, thanks to the innovative features in their new line.

My crew tugged on the yellow safety rope to which I was harnessed. I tugged back, our signal to let them know I was well. Calmly I breathed through the regulator, bubbles dancing away from my body. I turned to Gabe and flashed him a thumbs-up. He returned the gesture. His woe was for naught. We would host no slips or stumbles here. We had spent hundreds of hours training for this performance. Headache or not, I was ready.

The Five had strenuously objected when I announced Gabe would join me in the water, citing the same safety concerns he had. How many more years would it take me to eradicate the beliefs that society had drilled into them? How long until they understood they were all as capable of fearlessness as I was? In that regard, my mission had fizzled. The point of these performances was to inspire others, to make them believe they too could live a life sans fear. Perhaps I needed to rethink my approach.

A camera appeared above the hole. I lifted a hand but did not wave. I wanted to acknowledge my fans with a solemnity appropriate for the occasion. Our intention was to make a feature-length documentary this time, to expand my reach to as many souls as possible. The Five had suggested I record voice-overs for the film in which I would share my knowledge with the rabble. We would call it *Madame Fearless Presents . . . Frozen.* Hundreds of thousands, even millions, could absorb my teachings. I would revolutionize the psychological lives of the masses like Freud and Jung before me. I'd show my domineering old man once and for all how wrong he was.

I moved away from the hole and imagined The Five starting the stopwatch. I considered the inky water around me, could not quite grasp how dark it was down here, not when I knew the sky to be bursting blue overhead. Gabe aside, another living soul did not stir in these parts, although how could I be certain about that? At this moment some primordial creature might be rising from its slumber on the lake floor. Fangs and claws—remember those old bogeymen? I was a silly girl then, one who had no idea that the monster in the boat was much worse than anything that dwelled underneath it.

How many points would this challenge be worth, Sir?

Depends if you get it right.

This was nothing like Lake Minnich. This time I had a choice.

I HAD NOT expected invincibility to be quite so laborious. For the past hour I'd sensed I was breathing through an increasingly pinched straw, as though something were obstructing my hose. The regulator I'd chosen was a model not yet on the market but rigorously tested, I had been assured.

I felt a tug on my rope. I pulled back. I would continue to do so no matter how shallow my breathing became, no matter how tightly the chill wrapped itself around my bones. I would not return to land until the record had been beaten.

Did the achievement even count if it didn't hurt to get there?

Time slowed to the drip of a leaky faucet. Over and over I recited my mantra. Through the hourglass more sand passed. I closed my eyes and breathed in for four seconds, ignoring the obstruction of my airflow, out for four seconds. In, two, three, four. Out, two, three, four.

When I felt a pat on the arm, my eyes flew open. Gabe pointed toward the ice, signaling he was going to get out. I gave him a thumbs-up. I was surprised and more than a little proud that he had lasted this long. I began another four-second breath: in, two—

I sputtered as water leaked into my mouthpiece. I blew the liquid out before it darted down my trachea and into my lungs.

The rope strained.

I tried to breathe deeply again. This time I inhaled a dull chunk of ice, sending me into a coughing fit. Gabe turned to check on me, stopping his ascent. I pressed the purge button. Still I had trouble breathing. My regulator must have frozen. Those pricks at ThermoKline had sworn their equipment would hold up in water colder than this. In hundreds of practice dives, not once had this malfunction occurred.

The Five heaved the rope a second time.

I resolved to move on to the backup regulator, as we had prepared for worst-case scenarios. I peered down but couldn't find the neon yellow hose. Gabe slowly made his way back toward me.

The Five jerked a third time. I cursed their neediness. Clearly I was occupied with the task of saving my own life. Could they not be brave for five minutes of their sorry existence?

Finally, with Gabe's help, I located the backup mouthpiece, which had curled itself around my neck. I tried to untwist it, but my fingers were clumsy in the thick gloves. I panicked at the thought that I might drown down here blundering like an imbecile. It has been well documented that when humans are cold, they become less sensible, which is the only way I can explain my next action.

Since the gloves were impeding my efforts, I removed the right one and grabbed the alternate regulator with my bare hand. Success! Gabe shook his head wildly. Abruptly I was towed through the water. I gaped at the lake's surface. The Five had disappeared from view, evidently having decided to pull me out.

I glanced at my watch, distressed, and reached my naked hand toward the underside of the ice. *More time,* I wanted to yell. A hulking form leaned over me; I hoped it was the camera. I envisioned the photo: my five fingers spread wide, palm shoved against the ice like glass, burn scars visible, a million tiny bubbles of breath surrounding the hand, proof of life, of something trapped beneath the surface.

Perhaps we could put the image on T-shirts, I thought dizzily as my hand wilted.

The safety rope yanked me toward the hole in the ice. I had trained far too hard and long to surrender this easily. I could correct the issue if they'd give me the chance.

What's the only way you're going to succeed?

Through my willingness to endure.

I let go of the backup regulator and fumbled with the harness instead. I was breaking every rule in the scuba handbook, but I also wasn't an average diver. No matter how Gabe scoffed, I was absolutely certain that I had become immune to pain. As long as I remained levelheaded, danger would not find me. I unhooked from the safety rope and thrust my body downward. Gabe made a noise and reached for me, but I kicked my arms and legs to escape him. Once I was firmly out of reach, I relocated the backup mouthpiece, movements labored and awkward.

Gabe floated above me for a few seconds, then unclipped his own harness.

I frowned. This was not part of the plan. Gabe hadn't spent hundreds of hours acclimating for cold-water dives; he couldn't hold his breath underwater for six minutes in case of an emergency; he didn't have gear tailor-made for his body. He was supposed to return to the surface and leave me to my performance. He would pay for this. I'd send an army of seahorses after him. I giggled at the thought, bubbles erupting from my mouth as I swam farther down.

Above Gabe a few arms stretched through the hole into the lake. What were they thinking, sticking sockless arms into freezing water? Gabe swatted at them. I propelled myself a few feet lower so no one could reach me. After every gasp for breath, every invasion of water and ice, I cleared my regulator. I glanced at my watch again. What time did I want it to be? Why was my throat frosty?

The creatures above blurred, flailed, descended farther into the water. Head, shoulders, limbs, trunk. I thought fish demons resided at the bottom of the sea.

Perhaps this *was* the bottom, I mused. Perhaps I was topsy-turvy. I peered down, then up, then down, then up. Conclusion inconclusive, I ruled.

The brute, pale and bloated, lurched toward me in the murky depths or tops. I tried to swim away—I did—but my limbs were made of broken china. My eyes went black, black as a silk sleeping mask, black as a father's promise.

No sleep for you tonight, sweets.

Final snapshot: another fiend reaching through the hole, eerily reminiscent of an auger, the fiend not the hole, thin on bottom, broad up top. What was the drill's name? How long ago that seemed, another dimension altogether. Had I ever been dry?

I came to, choking, colder than I had dreamt possible. Serious-looking people scuttled and strapped and poked and prodded. In and out I went. Au revoir! Sirens, sirens, sirens, the soundtrack to my journey. How many times had Gabe raced behind them, chasing me to the emergency room like we were two children playing tag?

This time we shared the hospital wagon. That's what they told me later; I don't remember any of it. Not the blue face or the hot saline drip or the hearse that pulled around back.

One week later I was discharged and sent home. Meanwhile, my best friend in the world, the one who froze to death, was burned to ash.

30

Natalie

JANUARY 9, 2020

THE NEXT MORNING I step outside to a sheet of gray hovering low in the sky. The wind whoops, threatening to steal my hat. But there is no downpour, no strike of lightning or boom of thunder. The clouds look like they might open any minute into the storm Kit prophesied last night. For now, the island holds steady.

I get to the cafeteria right as it opens. After grabbing bland cereal and a tub of yogurt, I choose a seat with views of both doors to watch for Kit. Today's the day. I'm going to take her aside first chance I get.

I feel like I might be sick.

I force myself to eat anyway, itching to take out my phone (nestled safely in my sports bra) while I do. It's been almost twenty-four hours since I checked in with my team, and I'm dying to know how yesterday afternoon's briefing went. When was the last time I went this long without opening my inbox? College? My breath hitches at the thought of triple-digit notifications, a screen chicken-poxed with red circles. *What if someone needs me?* I squeeze the bridge of my nose.

The door squeaks open, and Gordon walks through. He heads up the aisle, stopping at my table. I fake-smile a greeting.

He cocks his head. "You've parted your hair on the other side today."

I nod, vaguely creeped out, still unsure whether he's the one who's been following me.

"I hear you found your sister?"

"I did."

"And?"

"She's in good spirits," I admit.

His gaze flicks to my barely touched cereal. "Once you finish eating, we'll make the return trip."

"Kit said something about a bad storm."

"Not for another day or two. We'll leave today."

Why is he in such a hurry to get rid of me? "Kit said—"

"Ms. Collins is hardly a meteorologist," Gordon interrupts. "Nor is she a sailor. We'll leave this morning."

I'm tempted to take him up on it, to ditch this island of misfit toys and forget about confessing altogether. So many times I've wondered whether Kit would actually want to know. She's happy here, doesn't want me interfering. I have plenty of work back home.

But something about the island is off. Someone e-mailed me for a reason. I assume the e-mailer is also the one following me around and messing with my clothes, but where do I go from there? There's no shortage of cagey weirdos here: Gordon and the big guy who yelled at him, the bald woman babbling about new blood, our boat guide Sanderson. Any of them could be the e-mailer.

The more I think about it, the more I think it probably wasn't Sanderson. I'm pretty sure he was trying to escape this place; if all he wanted yesterday was a daylong bar crawl, why pack such a huge bag?

A few more days at Wisewood won't kill me. The extra time will give me a chance to convince Kit to come home. And as much as I'd like to fantasize otherwise, I can't leave without telling her about Mom. I nod to myself, resolved. I'll e-mail my boss to let him know I'll be out of touch for the rest of the week. I could message Jamie too, although she probably hasn't even noticed I'm gone, what with the baby and all. I think of who else I need to notify and am mortified when I can't come up with anyone.

"Nah," I say, "I'm not going anywhere until the storm blows over."

Gordon's nostrils flare.

I pick up my spoon, take a bite of cereal. "Do I need to tell Rebecca?"

He stands there for so long that I assume he's dreaming up creative ways to murder me in my sleep.

"I'll tell her." He turns on his heel.

My whole body relaxes once he leaves the building. I dawdle over the cereal, waiting for my sister. After forty-five minutes she still hasn't shown, so I clear my spot and head out.

I weave around the cabins. Guests chat in groups of twos and threes. They all wave to me before turning back to their conversations. No Kit. I'm about to give up and return to my room when I spot her outside the trailer, holding an open cardboard box. "Kit," I call as I race over, heart throbbing. "Can we talk?"

"I only have a minute." She gestures with her head at the trailer. "I'm free after my class, though." Maybe I'm hearing only what I want to, but I swear I detect a trace of hope in her voice. "What's up?"

The timing's not right. I'll have to wait until the class lets out. Instead I ask, "Does Wisewood have housekeeping?"

"Just a laundry crew on Sundays."

I suck in a breath. "Then someone broke into my room while I was searching for you yesterday. They moved my sweater from a shelf to a hanger."

Kit stares. "So? The laundry group was probably trying to be nice, cleaning up after you."

"I thought you said they only work Sundays."

She shrugs. "Someone might've been doing a last-minute check that the room was cleaned and ready. Your arrival wasn't exactly planned."

"It's not only that." I lower my voice. "Someone is following me around the island. Peeking in my cabin windows."

"Nat, come on. You can't be serious." She shifts the cardboard box to her other hip, shuffling the contents.

I peer into the box. Inside are thousands of thumbtacks. I glare at her. "What are these for?"

"If you want to find out, you'll have to sit in. I've got to go."

I glance at one of the trailer windows. A familiar-looking man with a beard is watching us, rubbernecking to hear better. When my eyes meet his, he jolts out of the frame.

"Next time. Let's talk after, though."

She shrugs and disappears inside the trailer. A few stragglers hurry in behind her. After that I'm alone again. I step off the walkway and head toward the hedge wall, looking over my shoulder, formulating a plan. Where are the most likely places for cell service? Rebecca's office, if she has one? Her bedroom? The staff must use computers or phones for guest reservations; maybe they confine their technology use to designated areas.

A lightbulb flickers. I pick up my pace, walking along the hedge until I reach the door with the STAFF ONLY sign. I try the handle again. This time it turns.

I push open the door and step through.

HUNDREDS OF SPRUCE trees surround me. Between the trees is a narrow, soft path, carpeted with pine needles and slush. I follow it. The forest is quiet. A few birds chirp in the distance, but I don't hear any signs of human life. No rustling or breathing or footsteps. I'm alone. After a minute of winding around lanky evergreens, the path forks. I take the path on the right.

Once I'm thirty feet from the hedge, I unzip my jacket, reach down my T-shirt, and pull my phone out of my bra, then hold down the button to turn it on. I tap my foot, glancing between my phone and the woods around me. They keep still. The silence begins to feel unnatural. I want someone by my side. No, I want to get out of here.

Finally the home screen loads: "No Service."

I swear under my breath. If I walk deeper into the forest, surely I'll find a building out here for the staff. They aren't taking breaks in the middle of the woods. I put my phone in my pocket and keep walking, lungs aching from the cold.

A minute later the path tapers off. I could squeeze between a few clusters of trees, but none of the ground appears more well-trodden than the rest. I choose a cluster and walk for a while until the forest becomes too dense for me to continue. I retrace my steps, worried I'll lose my sense of direction and forget where I started. I choose a new cluster to squirm through. I spot something white ahead, a stark contrast to all the greens and browns. I approach the thing cautiously, choke back a gasp when I see what it is.

A skull.

It's a bird's, or was once. The beak is long like a pelican's, eye sockets empty. I wonder how the bird ended up here, where the rest of its body is. All color and life rotted away a long time ago, but I can't make myself step around it.

I turn back, picking up the pace, checking my watch. I've been gone for only twenty minutes, but it feels like hours. I begin to jog.

What if the path doesn't lead anywhere? What if it's a bunch of dead ends? This could be part of some weird trust exercise that classes go through. I picture Gordon bringing a bunch of blindfolded students out here, leaving them to find their way back. I would have screamed.

Nearby something snaps.

I freeze. My chest thrashes. Slowly I turn around.

Gordon isn't there. No one is. I glance down. A broken twig lies under my right foot. I'm not being followed. I rub my forehead, considering whether to return to the hedge door. I don't know my way around Wisewood. What kinds of animals live on islands in Maine? What if I get lost and no one can find me? The island seemed pretty big when we were ferrying in.

I walk for another minute, then stop short. Ahead is an old building covered with wooden shingles. It looks like it hasn't been used in decades. In the movies there would be a grizzly man waiting inside with a hatchet across his lap, his entire family bleeding out on the floor at his feet. Every cell in my body tells me not to go any closer.

I creep down the path, stop in front of the building, and put my hand on the doorknob.

It's locked.

I exhale, flooded with relief, and begin to circle the building, searching for a window. On the left side I find one. I cup my hands around my eyes. No one's inside.

It's an old schoolhouse. Along one wall are short bookshelves filled with dusty tomes. In the center of the room I count three rows of four wooden desks. On some of them lie open textbooks. At the head of the classroom is the teacher's desk, a blue globe atop it. The chalkboard is filled with frenzied scribblings I can't read. Above the board is a sepia-toned map of the United

States. A broom leans in the corner. The room has a *Little House on the Prairie* vibe, a feeling that the teacher and pupils will be back any minute.

My insides curdle, pushing me to get away from this place, out of the forest. I pull my phone from my pocket and watch the signal status change from "No Service" to "Searching." I tap my foot. Back to "No Service." I check the Wi-Fi options. Nothing. The battery is down to thirteen percent.

I'm so concentrated on my phone that I don't register the approaching footsteps until they're right behind me.

A voice growls, deep and pissed.

"Who the hell are you?"

31

MY LIFE CLEAVED in two: before Gabe died and after. *After,* I chronicled to the police every blunder at the lake: the faulty regulator, the bumbling hands, the inexperienced rescue team. I explained that I had somehow come unclipped from the safety rope, that Gabe had attempted to extricate me. A tragic accident, they determined. Case closed, sympathetic stares.

The Five were not so kind. The day after I was discharged from the hospital, they showed up at my small apartment, not to help me grieve and heal, but to quit. They didn't know the specifics of what had happened beneath the ice but said a man's life had been needlessly wasted. They no longer wanted to be part of my mission. They weren't even sure what the mission was anymore, but they'd dedicated—nay, wasted—more than enough time on a cause that was going nowhere. They said I had used them, manipulated them, made them unwilling accessories to a crime. It was time they moved on. As I lay on my sofa, heartbroken and heaving, they tearfully wished me a good life. I begged them to reconsider but the disgust on their tongues was palpable. Their callousness filled my lungs with cement.

After, I could not bear the simultaneous loss of my five greatest believers plus my only friend. Who but they had ever understood what I was trying to achieve, the revolution around the corner? With Gabe and The Five the dream had been within reach. Without them the load was too heavy.

After, I escaped. With no confidants left in New York, there was little point in my staying. I longed to flee to the most remote place possible, a haven sans memories. For the last decade of her life, my aunt Carol had spent her summers on an island in mid-coast Maine. To my mother's chagrin and father's joy, we didn't hear from Aunt Carol for months at a time; she had strayed as far off the grid as she could. I rented a one-room cabin from the same woman Aunt Carol had.

After, I didn't leave my new refuge. Why bother when everything reminded me of Gabe? I began keeping score again: –10 for not eating, –20 for not sleeping, –30 whenever it stung to breathe. I passed the days in a half-conscious state, nodding off only to wake to the sound of a man choking on water, gasping for air.

Serves you right.

There weren't enough points to count all my weaknesses.

MONTHS AFTER GABE died, his lawyer located me. Gabe had left me everything. I knew his father had bequeathed him a sizable inheritance but was unclear exactly how much. When the lawyer handed me a check for fourteen million dollars, I laughed until I sobbed (–2) and sobbed until I retched (–3). I put the check in the top drawer of the cabin's rickety dresser.

I waited for the fog to subside, wondering whether it ever would. What if The Five had been right? What if the principles I believed in were all wrong? If I had no wisdom to impart, then what was my reason for being? Why bother sticking around at all? Weeks, then months, then years both flew by and dragged, as though some higher power couldn't decide how best to punish me. I didn't believe in such a thing, but in those days I wanted to.

My mother had never forgiven my lack of faith, which even now made me want to throttle her. Didn't she understand how much easier life would be if I could swallow that a benevolent dictator had everything under control? Did she not appreciate how much less I would suffer if I believed in a magical place called heaven instead of Gabe's bones withering to dust? Religion was a comfort. To believe was a privilege. Mother could go on insisting that *everything happened for a reason* until she was blue in the face; that was what believers told themselves, so they wouldn't have to admit that life was unthinkably cruel in its randomness. I could force myself to trust in a higher power no more than the believers could accept that no one was watching out for them, that there was no grand plan tailor-made for their souls.

One day I walked the island out of sheer ennui and found an old canoe at the far end of the property. With my landlord's permission, I took it out on the water. The next day I felt aches in muscles I hadn't exerted in years. It was a good ache, a much more manageable pain than the variety I'd been suffering.

I began to row every morning for three, four hours. Initially I remained in the boat, watching the sun light the sky on fire and paint the water blood orange. Later I pushed off for unexplored shorelines, finding corpses in every quarter: empty shells, frozen starfish, bird skulls. I collected them all, laid the bouquets of cold meat on the floor of my canoe. I picked beach peas and sea celery. Straight from the rockweed I plucked and ate soft-shell crabs. Over time I grew bolder still, pulling my canoe from the sea so I could wander the islands, through untamed meadows and mossy thickets, deserted quarries and crumbling cemeteries. I discovered meadows of Queen Anne's lace, hedgerows of rugosa. I spotted goldfinches, puffins, black guillemots. All around me life persisted, apathetic to my pain and plight. The indifference was somehow soothing. I was awake as I hadn't been in decades. I itched with a desire to start anew.

On the fifth anniversary of Gabe's death I realized where I'd gone wrong.

It wasn't that my principles were unsound. The Five had hung on my every word in the early days. I could still hear hundreds of theater seats bouncing closed as my fans leapt to their feet at the end of *Fearless*, could smell their sweaty exhilaration when they were freed from pain and fear. I remembered rushing back to my dressing room mirror after each show for a glimpse of that orgasmic flush, understanding I, too, had been transformed.

No, the issue was not my teachings. The issue was the venue.

How could I get through to the public when a much louder and more powerful force was breathing down their necks? What hope did I have of changing hearts and minds so long as every poor lost patsy was caught up in society's expectations? If I could get them out of their environments, away from their cities and jobs and families, perhaps then I could effect lasting change.

Had Lisa not feared loneliness, she would be happy. Had Evelyn not feared failure, she would still be an artist. Had Jack not feared parental estrangement, she would be free.

Had Gabriel not feared danger, he would be alive.

I could bear to surrender not one more soul to fear. My inheritance from Gabe could give me my second act, an opportunity to shift the spotlight. I studied the violent waters around me and thought, *Why not here?* Where better than the middle of the sea to prove I wasn't afraid of my own death or anyone else's? What better daily reminder that control over fear required constant vigilance? Five years could fall like sand through one's fingers. With an entire ocean between us and the mainland, my acolytes could leave behind their unhealthy habits and relationships. They could start anew.

I hurried back to my cabin and told the proprietress of my plan. She tipped me off to a newly available island, listed by a family who had fallen into financial duress. The grounds had been in their name for generations, but no one had lived there for half a century. I paid a hefty price for it, considering the state of disrepair. A construction crew knocked down the ramshackle main house and built my own glass palace in its place. They cleared the land for fifty guest rooms and two class trailers. The pier, gate, and hedge wall came later. I left only the old schoolhouse to remind us of the importance of self-education.

In the summer of 2012 I opened our doors. Here my new flock could forget past calamities. We would be safe from naysayers, thanks to heightened security. This was our chance to escape the viciousness of the real world. Madame Fearless was dead, but from her ashes rose a phoenix named Rebecca.

I am goddamn invincible.

I could help the common man if he gave me one more chance. The masses made the world go round but couldn't stop their own lives from spinning out of control. If the people learned how to challenge their fears, they might evolve into the idealized version of themselves of which they had always dreamt, the one I spoke about in *Fearless*, the person I'd spent all my life trying to become. A *maximized self*, if you will.

I knew the way. They only had to follow.

32

Natalie

I JUMP ABOUT twelve feet in the air, shoving my phone in my pocket before whirling around. A fifty-something woman, dressed top to toe in Carhartt, stands on the path. The sight of her shaved head enrages me. She drops her wheelbarrow full of tree branches and puts her hands on her hips. Has she seen my phone?

"I was trying to find the bathroom and got lost," I say. "I'm new here."

The woman scowls, a definite Southern twang to her speech. "You were looking for the bathroom past a 'Staff Only' sign? I was born at night, honey, but it wasn't last night."

"It was an honest mistake."

She marches over to me, stopping nose to nose. "I think what happened is I caught you snooping." She pulls the toothpick from her mouth, teeth yellow and uneven. "Come with me."

The woman takes giant strides, dragging me by the coat sleeve without touching my arm. I try to pull away but her grip is firm.

"Is this necessary?"

She grunts. "We get people like you all the time. Entitled, think the rules don't apply to them."

I yank free, stop walking. "You don't know anything about me."

"Yeah, you stay here, princess. See how long it takes you to find your way back."

She has a point. I hurry after her.

"You come here with your demands and designer clothes and shiny hair, subtle as a heart attack. Meanwhile, no one sees me even though I'm a full head taller than you. Ever think about why that is?" She doesn't give me time to answer. "'Cause I don't stomp around the dang woods breaking twigs and cussing my head off, whining that the whole world is out to get me. Quiet sinners get a lot further than loud ones."

She taps her temple, never slowing or hesitating as we march through the forest. A few minutes later, I spot the door I came through and let out a breath, barely hearing her now that I'm safe again.

The woman opens the door and shoves me through. "You gotta be more fox, less hound, if you want to give 'em the slip." She closes the door behind us and jabs at the large black letters: STAFF ONLY. "Next time, listen to the signs."

She trudges toward Rebecca's house. I think the ordeal is over until she turns around, waving her arms. "I don't got all day, princess. Let's go."

The 'princess' insult has worn thin, but I think better of crossing this woman. As we speed-walk across the now-busy grounds, people watch us curiously.

"I'm Kit's sister," I say, hoping that holds sway.

"I know exactly who you are."

My heart throbs. Is she the one who e-mailed me?

By now we've reached the garden behind Rebecca's house. The clouds loom, thick and ready to burst. I have never seen so much gray in one place.

The woman pulls a walkie-talkie from her back pocket and lifts it to her mouth. "Kit, you there?"

A few seconds later, my sister responds, "Kit here. Go ahead."

"It's Raeanne. I've got your sister with me in the garden. Caught her nosing around the forest." She flashes daggers at me. "Where do you want me to bring her?"

"I'll be there in five." Kit sounds annoyed.

"Roger that." Raeanne puts the walkie-talkie back in her pocket, crosses her arms, and glowers at me. The wind punches us over and over.

We wait in tense silence, me glancing everywhere but Raeanne's face while her volcanic glare bores into me. My sister appears a few minutes later.

"Thanks, Rae. I'll take it from here."

Raeanne shakes her head and lopes away.

My sister frowns at me. "What were you doing in the forest?"

I finger the phone in my pocket. "I got lost trying to find my way around."

She stares at me, suspicious.

"What's that schoolhouse in the woods?"

"Keep your voice down," she says, making sure no one overheard. We walk toward the cabins. I expect the heavens to open any second, but still no rain. Gordon was right about the storm. We stop at number four. Kit lets us inside, watching me. My stomach buzzes at the thought of being alone with my sister. This is the chance I've been waiting for.

Her room looks the same as it did when I was snooping yesterday. "When did you become a neat freak?"

"That's all you have to say to me?" She bows her head, collects herself. "You can't wander around, trespassing wherever you like. Some of the staff are already pissed you're here."

I sit on her bed. "Gordon?"

She nods, tucking her feet under her on the chair.

"He told me this morning that the storm won't hit until tomorrow or the day after. Insisted the water was perfectly safe to travel today. When I told him what you told me, he said, and I quote, 'Kit is not a sailor.'"

"He doesn't know what he's talking about. I've driven the boat plenty of times."

"I sense some animosity between you two."

"He was Teacher's right hand for years. And then I got here." The corners of her lips twitch.

"Kit, weird shit is happening on this island. These people are either crazy or dangerous or both. How can you work alongside them?"

She crosses her arms with a stony expression.

I gesticulate at the window. "There are no blinds in any of the cabins."

"We don't keep secrets here." She gazes outside. "Removing the blinds was my idea."

My eyes bug out. I'd thought my sister was a foot soldier blindly obeying orders. Now, as I consider the walkie-talkie she's been given, the classes she leads, her access to Rebecca, I recognize with horror how quickly she's moved up the ladder, how high her perch actually is.

"What's your plan, Kit? To live here indefinitely?"

"I don't know." She tenses. "It's freeing not to have every day planned within an inch of its life."

"Plenty of careers allow for spontaneity in the day-to-day." She opens her mouth to protest, so I speed up. "I know it's not only about the work. You love not being tethered to technology. So set limits on your phone use, leave your laptop off all weekend, spend Saturdays hiking or hanging out at the beach instead of watching TV. You want fewer responsibilities? Come live with me. Did you know I moved to Boston?" Her eyes widen. "No, you didn't, even though I texted you about it a bunch of times, begging you to visit."

She peers at me. "Why Boston?"

I pick at my thumbnail. "Same reason you went to New York. I wanted to get away from all the memories of Mom. Boston was the only branch that had an opening for a strategist, so that's where I transferred."

"Do you like it there?"

No, I think. "Yeah," I say, and take a breath before rattling off the pitch I've prepared. "We can rent a two-bedroom apartment. I'll pay the bills until you find work that makes you happy." To have a friend, let alone my sister, in my adopted city is almost more than I can hope for. I lean over to grab Kit's hand, but she twists away from my touch. "Your friends miss you. I miss you."

Kit shakes her head. "You don't get it. I *am* happy. Wisewood is what makes me happy."

"You're seriously going to stay here long-term?" Visions of Friday night *Parks and Rec* binges fade. "What about dating or starting a family of your own? That stuff used to matter to you. Does it not anymore?"

She clears her throat. "Not really."

My heart bangs in my chest. She doesn't care about anything more than Wisewood. I don't know where to go from here, have no idea how to change her mind.

"You're not going to change my mind, Nat. This is not an indictment of you. You don't know how glad I am to see you, even though you've gotten me in trouble."

"Then why haven't you called or texted a single time in the past six months? Gordon told me the guests are allowed to reach out to family members."

"I wasn't trying to hurt you, but I knew we'd end up having this conversation. I wasn't ready to have it then. Teacher thought you might try to change my mind, and then I'd head back to the outside world with you and be totally miserable. I know you think I'm a selfish brat for choosing to be here, but this is the most content I've been in my entire life. I don't know how to make you understand."

"What's so great about this woman, anyway? I have yet to see her."

"That's because she's tied up with a new project." Kit's eyes shine. "She'll change your outlook on life, Nat."

"She has all of you jumping through hoops. Some of the people here seem brainwashed." *Like you*, I don't add.

Kit grimaces. "Scientists have proven it's not possible to empty a person's head against their will. You can't take over someone's mind. Brainwashing is a concept popularized by Hollywood. The idea gives family members permission to blame an outside authority instead of their loved ones."

Exactly what someone who has been brainwashed would say.

"Everyone at Wisewood has made this commitment of their own free will. No one's being coerced into anything."

"Just because she's not holding a gun to your head doesn't mean she's not planting ideas in your mind."

"We *want* new ideas to be planted in our minds! That's the whole point of a self-improvement program."

"I've gotta be honest, Kit." I pause. "Wisewood sounds like a cult."

She works her jaw for a minute. "'Cult' is a derogatory label that society puts on a group of people whose beliefs they either don't understand or don't agree with."

"This place isn't normal. No internet, no phones, no connection to the rest of the world."

"What's so great about normal? People are terrified of everything now. They climb corporate ladders, scared their stuff isn't good enough because it's not the *newest* or *biggest* or *best*. They do juice cleanses, afraid their waistlines are too big, then binge drink, afraid their nights are too boring. Climb, buy, eat. Climb, buy, eat. Like hamsters on a wheel. Overdrugged, overstimulated, over the life they're killing themselves to keep up with. Why do you have to bash a different way of life? Let me be happy."

Neither of us speaks for a while. I listen to my sister take deep breaths in and out. I don't want to leave her here. I don't want to resume life without her. How can she be okay with never talking to me? Does she value our relationship so little? We're the only family each of us has left.

"I don't know how to protect you." My voice wobbles. "This place is awful, and you can't see it."

Kit sniffs. "Do you remember the Christmas I was nine and you were twelve?"

I shake my head. All our childhood Christmases blend: me wrapping Kit's presents, baking cookies for her to leave Santa, tiptoeing downstairs to eat them once I was sure she was asleep, writing her thank-you notes in big block letters, carefully smudging them with charcoal so she would be convinced he'd come down the chimney. After being up all night, I usually passed Christmas Day in a tired haze.

"I'd wanted this one Barbie for months. She wore a yellow jumpsuit and heels and had her hair in a ponytail like I did. When I ripped off the wrapping paper Christmas morning and saw what was inside, I'd danced around the room, shrieking with excitement. Mom sipped coffee in that bathrobe with the cats on it. You had just opened the Girl Talk game." She chews her lip. "I shoved my Barbie toward you, begged you to look. Do you remember what you did?"

A knot forms in the pit of my stomach. "No."

"You rolled your eyes." I cringe. "So I tried a second time. This was *the* Barbie. I just wanted you to see how cool she was. The second time you told me to get it out of your face."

I rip a hangnail. My cuticle begins to bleed.

"The third time you turned to me and said"—here Kit adopts a psychopathically cold tone—"'Aren't you a little old for Barbies?'"

I swallow.

"All of a sudden that nightgown I was wearing, the one with Ariel and the purple ruffles, seemed babyish. I took the Barbie out of the packaging to show Mom how much I loved it, but I felt like a two-year-old whenever I brushed Barbie's hair or slipped the plastic heels on her feet. I looked stupid making her walk and talk. A month later I stopped playing with dolls. For good."

The worst part is not the act itself (though that was mean enough) but the fact that I have no recollection of it, whereas my sister has carried it with her for decades. So much for us remembering only the wrongs we've committed, not the ones committed against us. I open my mouth but can't think of a single redeeming thing to say.

Kit watches me with red eyes. "You're not going to take Wisewood's sparkle from me."

"I'm sorry." It's not enough; I know it's not.

"I'm not denying the rules here are strange. Every system has flaws. Wisewood is no different. But we focus on the positives of the program."

I've lost the will to fight my sister. She's fallen under the spell of a group and an ideology I can't understand. If she insists this place makes her happy, then fine.

"Understood." I raise my hands in surrender. "I'm on your side, okay?"

A knock at the door makes us both jump.

"Ms. Collins, are you in there?" Gordon calls.

"I'm busy," Kit says.

"Please open the door."

She closes her eyes. This time her tone is icy. "I said I'm busy."

A pause. "Very well. I'm taking the boat out, so you'll have to—"

Kit leaps from the bed and opens the door. "We're not supposed to leave."

Gordon draws himself to full height. Even so, he's shorter than she is.

"It's snowing," she says.

Still he doesn't speak.

"Where are you going?" she asks.

His gaze swings toward me. "Are you sure you want that answer right here, right now?"

My sister glances at me.

"Kit, I have to tell you something," I say, remembering my reason for being here. "We're not done."

"Yeah, we are." She follows Gordon outside and closes the door.

33

Kit

OCTOBER 2019

WE WADED OUT of the water and put our shoes back on in silence. Debbie offered a towel she'd brought especially for me. Even after I dried off, my teeth still rattled so hard my jaw hurt. When he saw my knees knocking, Jeremiah handed over his jacket.

I shook my head, pointing to my soaked sweater and jeans. "It'll get wet."

He shrugged. "It'll dry."

I flashed him a tired smile and zipped the coat to the top. I was instantly warmer, though the ends of my hair had hardened to icicles. The members of the IC began heading single file into the forest. As I followed Sanderson, Jeremiah close behind me, I tried to work out what the Quest of Judgment might encompass. Were they going to list my sins and dole out punishments that fit the crimes? I imagined standing in front of a panel of my peers. *For stealing candy from that convenience store when you were thirteen: ten blows against the knuckles with a ruler. For getting your high school best friend arrested: three days without a single meal. For being a negligent daughter: kneel on broken glass until your skin is speckled with blood.*

I might have to pass judgment on someone else.

"It's not as bad as you're imagining," Jeremiah said from behind. I nodded, stomach roiling.

A drizzle began to fall, forcing us to pick up our pace. Like a cabin-fevered child, Sofia rushed up the pine cone–strewn path, ducking and dodging wayward branches, shouting the entire way. The rest of the group was solemn, which did nothing to calm me.

Soon the woods smelled of wet bark. Our shoes squeaked in the mud. My lungs ached with every intake of cold air. I prayed whatever came next would be inside, ideally somewhere with a fireplace. Jeremiah whistled "Party in the USA," maybe trying to ease my nerves, break the heavy silence.

He'd gotten through the first chorus when Raeanne said from the front of the line, "I swear to Christ, you musta swallowed the most tone-deaf canary that ever lived."

He stopped whistling, and the group fell silent again. I didn't like how edgy everyone was tonight, the way most of them were trying to mask it with false cheerfulness. I wanted to know what they knew.

After a while we came upon a small building. In the dark I couldn't see much other than walls of weathered shingles. I strained for the roar of the sea, but it was gone. My cheeks were raw, windburned.

Sofia was waiting for us at the wooden door, hands on her knees. Ruth nudged me to the front of the pack.

"To think I once qualified for Boston," Sofia wheezed.

I startled. Outside of class, the staff rarely brought up their lives before Wisewood. "The marathon?"

She nodded, composing herself.

After one more deep breath, she grabbed the door handle and pushed me into the pitch-black void of the building. I squeaked in protest at the same time the cold room flooded with light. I squinted, trying to adjust to the change.

We were inside what resembled an old schoolhouse. Teacher sat at the head desk at the front of the classroom, hair coiffed, clothes dry. Next to her desk was a tripod with an empty phone mount fixed to the top.

She rose, gesturing to a desk in the middle of the front row. "Please take your seat."

I glanced over my shoulder. The rest of the IC had filed in behind me.

"Don't worry about what the others are doing," Teacher said.

I nodded and walked toward the front of the room, holding her gaze the entire way. I sat in the student's chair, wooden and hard, and heard my peers slip into their own desks. I didn't dare look away from those violet eyes until they'd released mine. My muscles twitched, heart palpitated.

Teacher walked up and down the rows, greeting each student with a squeeze of the hand. Some members bowed their heads; others grinned. Gordon approached the tripod, pulled an iPhone from his pocket, and settled it sideways into the mount so the back of the phone was facing us. He tapped the screen a few times, then stepped away, back against the chalkboard, watching the phone.

Fear slithered down my spine. He was recording us.

For the millionth time I wondered what, exactly, Gordon's job was at Wisewood. Ruth and I taught, Debbie cooked, Sofia healed. Raeanne managed the garden, mowed the lawn, shoveled snow, cared for the land. Sanderson drove the boat, made grocery runs, had a head for plumbing and electric. Jeremiah balanced Wisewood's books. None of us knew what Gordon did other than hang around Teacher's office and occasionally disappear on top secret missions.

Teacher returned to the front of the room and waited for the group to settle. I wiggled my toes, still couldn't feel them.

"Kit, I'm thrilled to welcome you to your q1, the Quest of Judgment." Teacher sat gracefully atop her desk. She steepled her fingers, brow furrowed. "Why have you been chosen for the IC?" My mouth fell open as I scrambled for an answer. "Why have all of you been chosen?" She peered at the others. "The people in this room have been through the worst of life's tribulations. You have suffered unimaginable grief, losing the people who mattered most to you via death or rejection, sometimes both. You have been beaten bloody, had your spirits broken. You have lost your battles with addiction."

I snuck a peek over my shoulder. Most of the students had their heads down, tracing the wood grains of the desks with their fingers, but Raeanne and Sofia were staring at Teacher, unblinking, breath held.

"When I look at your faces, I don't see victims," Teacher said. "I see survivors. I see fighters."

Sanderson beamed at his desk. Ruth nodded. Raeanne whooped.

Teacher began to pace the front of the room, speaking more loudly.

"Each of you has the chance to exemplify fearlessness, to assist greatness in others." She stopped and wrung her hands. "I hope the veterans among you will provide that assistance tonight. I cannot do the work alone. I need every single one of you right now." She examined us. "We must push forward as one."

"Hear! Hear!" Sofia said. The others bobbed their heads. I leaned my ears into my shoulders, trying to warm them on Jeremiah's coat.

Teacher turned to me. "During your time here, Kit, you've addressed specific fears with me. But the Quests of Fearlessness are about mastering universal fears, fears that almost every human being struggles with at one point or another. The first of those fears is of judgment." She smoothed and resmoothed invisible creases in her black wool trousers, put her hands in her pockets. "We waste so much time during our brief lives worrying what others think of us. We fear their reactions to our outfits, our weight gain, our hair loss. We fear what they'll think if we dance at a wedding or down the sidewalk."

I nodded, rubbing my upper lip against my nose to warm it, chiding myself to quit fidgeting and pay attention.

Teacher sighed deeply. "But we also fear judgment of our bigger decisions. We worry others won't approve of our jobs or our homes or our partners. At Wisewood, we believe it's impossible to reach our Maximized Selves so long as we're worried about other people's judgments. Q1 is a way to move past that judgment."

Though I wouldn't have worded it that way at the time, fear of other people's judgments was one of the reasons I'd signed up for Wisewood. I would do whatever it took to be rid of the fear. I vowed to exemplify fearlessness, to make Teacher proud.

She winked at me. "You don't have to look so anxious. You'll be fine."

I realized I was gripping the desk. I let go and forced myself to breathe.

"Better," Teacher said. "We host q1 in this former schoolroom to remind ourselves that we are all students—yes, even me—constantly learning and evolving." She paused. "Close your eyes."

I fought the urge to bolt from my seat and out the door. The rain started coming down harder, bouncing off the shingles. I did as she'd said.

"Imagine the worst thing you've ever done. You might have to dig for it, but most likely, it surfaced right away. It's something you've never forgotten, probably a guilt you carry. Nothing to do with your mother—that's ground well covered by now. Are you thinking of something?"

I hesitated, then nodded.

"That guilt is heavy, isn't it?"

"Yes," I said, eyes shut.

Save for the driving rain, the room was sarcophagus quiet.

"Now," Teacher said, making me jump, "imagine removing that guilt from your shoulders. Would you like that?"

I nodded again.

"I'd like it too." Teacher's voice was getting closer to me. My eyelids fluttered. "What you're going to do is share that misdeed with everyone here, so that you may be free of it. Once you release the burning secret, you'll begin to recover. And with recovery, you inch closer to your Maximized Self. You may open your eyes."

When I did, her face was up close to mine, her irises glowing. She took both of my hands in her own papery palms. "I know you can do this."

I opened my mouth, but she cut me off before I could say a word. "Begin by stating your full name, Kitten."

"Katharine Frances Collins." My face burned. "One time I got behind the wheel after a night out and drove home. It wasn't a long trip, but still, I could've gotten a DUI. Or worse."

Teacher's face fell. She dropped my hands, her ankles cracking as she pulled herself to standing. She glared down her nose at me. "I hope I haven't misjudged inviting you here. We expect a serious infraction, an admission of true vulnerability. You're not telling us the whole truth."

I unzipped Jeremiah's coat, sweating. How did she know?

She ogled the others, walking the rows again. "Why don't the rest of you share your own q1 admissions? Reassure Kit she's not the only imperfect being in the room?"

I struggled to erase the fear from my face. This was my one chance, and already I'd screwed it up. A familiar urge began to build in my fingertips.

Debbie spoke first. "I stole from the diner cash register when I was short on rent."

Teacher laid a soft hand on Debbie's back.

"I planted my stash in another employee's locker so my dad would fire him instead of me," Sanderson said. Teacher winked at him.

Ruth flushed. "I wrote bad checks to get enough money together to move to Maine." Teacher nodded her approval. It took all of my self-control to keep my face blank. Ruth, of all people, had committed fraud?

Sofia began to speak, but Teacher held up her hand, shifted her focus to me. The urge to pull, to yank, zipped through my forearms toward my shoulders. *Not now.* One of the desks creaked as someone moved in their seat.

I ducked my chin. "You're right—I was holding back. The thing I didn't say before is that while driving drunk"—I sucked in a breath—"I had a crash."

Teacher's expression darkened. "You mock the principles we stand for." She leaned in, lowered her voice so only I could hear. "These early quests are about building camaraderie too. If you act like you're a saint, better than the rest of them, that's hardly going to bring you closer, is it?" The urge rushed up my neck, wrapped itself like a vise around my throat. Teacher backed away again, gestured to Sofia to continue.

The doctor jiggled her leg so hard her entire body wobbled. "Each time my daughter went missing, I was desperate." When her voice wavered, Teacher was at her side in an instant. She pulled a pack of tissues from her pocket and handed one to Sofia, then nuzzled her lips to the distraught woman's ear. Sofia listened, squared her shoulders. "I wrote Oxycontin prescriptions for Rosa's junkie friends so they'd tell me which drug den she was hiding out in."

I nibbled at the inside of my lip until I drew blood, the tang of iron a relief. Rain battered the roof. Teacher pulled Sofia in for a hug, then turned her scrutiny to Jeremiah.

His voice shook when he spoke. "I cooked the books at work."

I gaped at my friend as his face drained of color. He wouldn't meet my eye, was busy watching Teacher's pained expression. She made a fist of strength, patted him on the shoulder. He nodded and sat up taller.

"Boohoo, you buncha small potatoes," Raeanne said, folding her hands behind her head and leaning back in her seat. "I killed two men."

I did a double take. This was the wildest transgression of all, yet I had little trouble imagining it. Was it true? Had she? Teacher stopped in front of

Raeanne's desk. She rested her palm on her own chest for a moment before moving it to Raeanne's. I couldn't see Teacher's face but knew by the shine in Raeanne's eyes that Teacher must've been beaming at her. I longed for that wholehearted approval.

Still gazing at Raeanne, Teacher said, "I'll give you one more chance, Katharine. If you want to join this group, you need to give us an admission worthy of entry. No more wasting our time."

My heart pounded. Sweat trickled down my hairline. My chest felt like it was breaking out in hives. What was this supposed to resolve, again? I had lost the thread. Maybe what we were doing was wrong.

But we had an accomplished doctor and a CPA among our numbers, and they saw nothing wrong with the process. Fraud aside, Ruth was one of the kindest, most decent people I'd ever met, and she wasn't alarmed. If Wisewood was off, the rest of them wouldn't have stuck around, dedicating five or six years of their lives to this place. I shook my head, trying to focus. Teacher had warned me about thoughts like these.

I scooted forward on my chair, palms leaving sweat prints on the desk. Rain poured down the windows.

"I crashed because I hit something." I put my head in my hands, dizzy. "Someone."

The bodies in the desks leaned forward hungrily.

"I didn't go back to check . . ." I trailed off. A deer had run out of the woods across a poorly lit road. I hadn't seen it until it was too late. The ordeal had lasted seconds, the animal limping back into the woods before I'd stopped my car from spinning. I'd clipped a deer, not a person.

Hadn't I?

A grin spread slowly across Teacher's face as she made her way toward me. Guilt gave way to relief. "Kit," Teacher said, tousling my hair, "you are now one step closer to your Maximized Self."

The room erupted in applause. I felt nauseous.

"What about you, Gordon?" Raeanne said when the cheers had died down. "Always behind the camera, never in front." She stole a nervous glance at Teacher.

Gordon, who hadn't moved an inch since he'd leaned against the chalkboard, now cleared his throat. "This is Kit's q1, not mine."

"Everyone else shared," Raeanne said.

"I answer to Teacher, not you."

Teacher tilted her head. "Do you think you're better than the rest of them?"

For the first time since I'd arrived at Wisewood, surprise—and pain—crossed Gordon's face. He stepped in front of the phone, speaking directly to the camera. "The worst thing I've ever done is provoke an enemy at work who later murdered my wife and son while they were asleep in their beds."

A few people gasped, everyone but Teacher shocked. With complete control, Gordon removed the phone from the mount, collapsed the tripod, tucked it under his arm, and walked out of the schoolhouse, letting the door bang closed.

"Should we go after him?" Ruth asked Teacher, worried.

Teacher patted Ruth's arm. "Leave him be." She returned to the front of the room, began pacing again. "More so than before, you understand the dangers of the outside world. Make our guests—your students—see how stunted their lives were before they came. Remind them they're much safer here than they ever were out there. When guests leave Wisewood, they do so at their own peril. They return to abuse, abandonment, even death. But when they stay, we can watch over them, bring those with the most promise into the fold. Like we've done with Kit." She softened. "Congratulations on passing your q1, Kitten."

The applause this time turned into a standing ovation. I blushed, trying to shake off my apprehension. It wasn't like the recording would ever see the light of day. So what if I'd exaggerated the details—I had completed my q1!

Yet even as I delivered a short thank-you speech, even as the rest of the IC cheered my name, a vague disquiet coursed through me. For the first time in a long time I yearned for my sister.

"One more thing before you join IC ranks," Teacher said with a wink.

Raeanne grinned and stepped forward with a pair of electric clippers.

34

Natalie

JANUARY 9, 2020

FOR HOURS I wait in Kit's cabin, dreading her return. By dinnertime she and Gordon still haven't turned up, but the promised storm has. Slushy snow pelts the island, then changes its mind and turns to hail. I stop in my room before heading to the cafeteria to eat with Chloe, who sits with a few guests her age. After dinner the kids invite me to a "feelings circle" in one of their rooms. I tell them thanks but I'd rather have rattlesnake venom injected into my gums.

Instead I decide to find Kit.

I've been waiting for the right moment to come clean with her when the reality is there won't be one. There is no perfect setting or situation to deliver news that will shatter your sister, not to mention that in the twenty-four hours I've been here, I've spent the entire time distracted and looking over my shoulder. The sense of being watched, of eyes unseen, is omnipresent. As soon as I get this off my chest, I can go home. Before something worse happens.

I pull the hood of my parka over my head and brace myself as I leave the cafeteria. When I see how hard the hail is coming down, I pick up my pace. I've almost reached the cabins when a pellet shoots me in the back. I yelp.

I hurry around the innermost ring to room number four and pound on the door so Kit will hear me over the storm. I take shelter under the skimpy overhang while I wait. Kit doesn't answer. I knock again. Still she doesn't come to the door. I run around the other side of the building and peek inside.

She isn't here.

A tremble that starts in my shoulders spreads to my arms and legs.

Where is she? Where is my sister weathering this storm? What if she's stuck at sea with Gordon? Maybe she couldn't stop him from leaving. What if their boat capsized? I picture her being tossed around in the water like a piece of driftwood, shredded to unrecognizable pieces.

I bow my head, negotiate with a presence I badly want to be listening.

Take whatever you want. My job, my apartment, my health. Just don't touch a hair on her head.

Thirty seconds later, I'm back in my cabin. Hail bounces off the roof. I walk to the window and peer out. No one there.

I kneel next to the bed and reach my hand between the mattress and frame, keeping an eye on the window. I scoot over an inch or two, grasping at nothing. I glance from the window to the bed, lifting the entire right side of the mattress off the frame.

My phone isn't there.

I drop my forehead to the floor. It isn't under the bed. I shake out the sheets, comforter, and pillowcases. It isn't in the bed. I check the nightstand and desk drawers, though I know I didn't hide it there.

The crystal clear memory of a couple of hours ago plays as I ransack the room. I came straight from Kit's cabin to mine and deposited my phone in between the mattress and frame, practically in the middle of the bed. The phone couldn't have been spotted unless someone was searching for it. Or watching from the window when I stashed it. I whip my head toward the panes, but they're all empty. I swallow.

I try to recall whether the contract had any clauses about confiscating belongings, but I skimmed it too quickly. I might've agreed to being robbed. I turn over my purse and duffel bag, letting the contents of each spill onto the floor. I search every pocket, every inch of the room.

My phone is nowhere to be found.

A familiar wave of panic rises.

Nearly a decade ago I had just started my first job post-college. After-work drinks turned into closing down the bar. I didn't check my phone for hours. When I finally fished it out of my purse, I had forty-two missed calls from my mom. All the breath left my body. I called her immediately, not bothering with the voice mails. She didn't answer, so I listened to the first message. In it she cried that she couldn't cope anymore and pleaded for forgiveness. She said she'd had enough, went on this way for three minutes until the carrier cut her off.

I stumbled into a taxi, trying her number again and again, squeezing my phone against my ear until my hand was white. It turned out she'd had too much chardonnay and passed out on the couch with her own device in hand. I put her to bed and vowed never to ignore my phone again.

Even now that Mom's dead, even though I have no service on the island, I can't stop the tightness spreading across my chest. I tell myself Kit will understand. I'll have to admit I lied about not bringing my phone here, but she knows the history. Her new outlook on life doesn't matter. She's still my sister. She will help me.

I'll never lie to her again. Let her be okay.

I dash back to her room, dodging hail the size of golf balls along the way. This time I don't bother with the door, but go straight to the cabin window and gaze inside. The room is still dark. It's eight p.m.

I trudge back to my room, resigned to the fact that most of the clothing I've brought to Wisewood is damp. I slump on the desk chair, wet clothes and all. The cafeteria will be closed by now. Who would be the most likely to help? Whose cabin number do I know besides Kit's? I kick the desk and swear.

At nine I try Kit's room again. No answer then or at ten or eleven. At midnight I give up, trying not to freak out. *Where is she?* I don't know how, but I'm sure Rebecca is behind this.

After pacing the room for an hour, I give up. At this time and in this weather, I can't do anything to get my phone back or find my sister. I'll go to the cafeteria right when it opens tomorrow and demand to have my property returned. I will confide in Kit as soon as I figure out where she is. I lie in bed, vacillating between fear and anger. Sometime around two thirty, I lose steam. My eyelids grow heavy.

I WAKE TO a repeated tap on my forehead. *A leak in the roof?* I think groggily.

I open my eyes. The moon illuminates the room. Someone is standing over me. I scream and recoil from the intruder. The person is tall and thin and wears a bank robber's mask.

"Who are you?" I pull the comforter up to my chin. Hail beats the cabin walls.

In a low tone the woman says, "Let's go." She's dressed in all black.

"How did you get in my room?"

"Do you want your phone back?"

I start but there's no sense in lying. Someone must have seen me trying to use it in the forest. Probably Raeanne. I curse myself for being so stupid, then nod.

Trying to blink the sleep from my eyes, I shrug on my parka and boots. The woman doesn't give me time to get my scarf and hat before nudging me toward the door.

"I don't have my key," I protest.

She ignores this and heads off. I glance at Kit's cabin when we pass, but it's too far away to see inside. Snow pummels us as we pick our way through the circles. The cold is brutal, bone-chilling. A gale shrieks past us. None of it bothers the masked woman.

"Who are you?" I ask again.

She doesn't respond. The obvious answer is Raeanne, but it could be any staff member; I've met only a few of them. What if it's a guest gone crazy? I brush away the fear. How would a guest know about my phone?

We walk in the opposite direction of the big house. Maybe we're going to this woman's room. Soon after, we clear the cabins. Okay, my phone could be in the class trailer. When we pass the trailer without stopping, I lick my lips. There are no more buildings ahead, only the hedge.

The masked woman stops at the same Staff Only door that Raeanne yanked me through earlier in the day. Yesterday, technically. She unlocks it and motions for me to go through. Could they be keeping my phone in that schoolhouse? I freeze, rooted to the spot.

"Tell me where we're going."

She steps toward me. "Keep moving."

"Not until you tell me what's going on."

She pulls something from her pocket, twirls it once between her fingers. A button clicks, and a blade ejects: a box cutter.

My legs feel weak. I back through the doorway, keeping my eyes on the knife. The masked woman drifts behind me through the forest, commanding the occasional "right" and "left." Even in the frigid storm, I can feel the steam of her body heat at my back. I picture what would happen if she tripped and stumbled forward, if the blade was still out. I walk faster.

After what seems like forever, she tells me to stop. I look around but don't see any buildings, only tree branches heavy with snow. They offer some shelter from the weather, but I'm already covered in powder.

"Where is it?"

She stays silent.

"You had no right to steal my shit."

Still she says nothing. Who is this woman, so cold and controlled?

"I want my phone back."

Motionless in spite of the storm, she stares through me. "You should've read your contract."

"Listen, I'm sorry for breaking your rules." I hate my pleading tone.

The masked woman watches me for a while. I force myself to wait her out.

"Stay here 'til someone comes for you," she finally says.

Every hair on my body stands on end. The arteries in my neck pulse. "You can't be serious. It's freezing outside. We're in the middle of a snow-storm."

She leans over me. "What Teacher says goes."

I remember the bloodcurdling scream when I first arrived at Wisewood. How many people has she punished this way? "I want to see my sister."

She plays with the box cutter, expelling and retracting the blade.

"What about my phone?"

She shakes her head.

"There has to be another way. Please."

The woman brandishes the cutter in my face. I shrink from her. We stare at each other, breathing heavily in the snow.

"Don't follow me." She steps backward, still holding out the knife. "No one's a tough guy when they're bleeding out."

Her feral eyes never leave mine. One gingerly step at a time, she moves away from me, blade at the ready. I want to cry out. Instead I watch her go until I can no longer see her shadow, until she disappears into the darkness.

35

THE GIRL STEPPED into my office and froze.

"Something the matter?" I asked from my desk, closing the notebook in which I'd been scribbling.

She stared at my neck, eyes protuberant.

I fingered the scarf. "I thought it was time to test your fear of grief again. Not to mention it gets chilly this time of year." I rose from the desk, carried my mug of green tea to the sofa, and gestured for her to join me. "How does it make you feel to see me wearing it?"

She opened and closed her mouth like a fish out of water. Finally she shrugged. "It doesn't make me feel anything."

If she forced that nonchalance any harder, she'd choke on it.

She cleared her throat. "I'm thinking about calling my sister."

I frowned. "Why?"

"In the same way that scarf has been holding me back," she said, squirming, "so is the lack of closure with Nat. I feel guilty about the way I treated her after Mom died. Well, before she died too."

I had heard from my own sister recently via e-mail. Apparently Sir had had a stroke while doing laps in Lake Minnich, nearly drowning. Beer gut aside, he'd always been a healthy man, but now, at eighty-two, the left side of his body was paralyzed and he was battling a blood clot in one of his lungs.

He may not pull through, Jack had warned. *You need to come home as soon as possible.*

As if she'd known our father's imminent death wasn't enough to move me, considering the way he'd treated me throughout his life, she had added, *He calls me Abigail these days. He's been asking to see you, even before the stroke. He is a softer man than the one you knew, a better father.*

I admit the idea of him beckoning to me, needing me, gave me pause. But how could I lecture my flock if I myself succumbed to a fear of loss? Besides, my father didn't deserve a final absolution. When I was a child, he'd demanded strength. Now, as an adult, I would show it to him. I wanted his dying thought to be one of regret for the way he had treated me.

I ground my teeth, waiting for my pulse to slow. (–1)

"Might this be the fear of disapproval having its way with you? You can't stand to know your sister is out there, judging the decisions you've made."

The girl considered the question. "I don't think so. Once I clear the air, she and I can go our separate ways."

One had to tread carefully. "I hardly think *you're* the one who owes *her* an apology."

"I know you're worried she'll try to convince me to leave Wisewood, but I'm strong enough to ignore her opinion. I don't care about her disapproval anymore."

"If you knew what I know about her, I doubt you'd be so eager for a reunion."

She tilted her head. "What do you mean?"

I let the silence hang between us.

She scooted forward on the couch, hands clutched. "What do you know?"

"From everything you've told me about your sister, she's a classic skeptic. There's nothing wrong with that—I have more than a healthy dose of skepticism myself—but it risks annihilating every shred of optimism. People like Natalie and I are resilient. We are doers; we take care of the weak among us. But we also have a tendency to behave like bulls in china shops. In our eagerness to defend, we steamroll. We have a hard time letting others resolve their own dilemmas."

The girl deflated, leaning back against the sofa.

"You will not get the closure you want," I said softly. "You think she'll accept and protect you, but ultimately she'll watch out for herself. Sisters are fallible that way."

"You're right. It was a stupid idea."

I patted her knee, the epitome of magnanimity. "Ideas are only stupid if you make hasty actions of them. I'm glad you brought this one to my attention. Now, what updates do you have for me as regard your peers?"

She shifted uneasily. Since her q1, I had tasked the girl with reporting any gossip or disobedience among her fellow IC members.

"Sanderson is less engaged than usual. But then, we're all working so hard that it's tough to say. He might've taken on too much."

I sipped my tea. "I didn't realize there was such a thing as taking on too much when you're working on a mission as important as ours." I sniffed. "Do you no longer find what we do compelling?"

"Me? You know how much I believe in the work. I'm down to four hours of sleep a night. But maybe Sanderson isn't up to the—"

I raised a hand. "That's enough. Let's not unnecessarily bad-mouth our colleagues. What else?"

"Gordon is pretty interested in Jeremiah's whereabouts ever since my initiation. He gives him the third degree if he's so much as a minute late to something."

I smirked at my mug. "Gordon can be a bloodhound, sniffing out anyone uncommitted to our cause. He is fiercely loyal to me." My jaw clenched. "Jeremiah, on the other hand, I have my doubts about."

"What'd he do?" she asked, failing to keep her voice steady.

"It's not so much what he's done as a feeling I have." I forced myself to blink. "I don't like the way he smiles at me."

She wrinkled her nose. "He admires you. He's so dedicated to the cause."

Perhaps this one was not to be trusted either. My foot jiggled, though I loathed fidgeting. "I understand he's become something of an avuncular figure to you." I could stay seated not one minute more. I stood and paced. "I want you to stop spending your free time with him."

A flush crept from her cheeks to her neck. "Teacher, I'm sorry but . . . I think you have this all wrong."

"Ruth too." I wrung my hands. "They might be working together."

The girl rubbed a hand over her head. Downy hair had begun to sprout from her scalp. She bit her lip. "Jeremiah and Ruth both work tirelessly to improve Wisewood."

How naïve she was, even after all of my tutelage.

"Mark my words, someone will slip up at some point. When they do, the cameras will catch them."

She blinked. "Cameras?"

"The monitoring system."

"What monitoring system?"

"Did Gordon not tell you? Everyone in the IC knows."

She stared stupidly.

"We have cameras in the rooms." I waved a hand around my head. "They're all over campus."

The girl struggled to keep her face neutral.

"It only takes one bad actor to bring down the entire ecosystem." A crackle of energy ran all the way to my fingertips, a great swelling of power (+2). At times like this I was a conduit. I knew not from where the message came, only that I'd been called to deliver it.

I am goddamn invincible.

"That's why you have to keep an eye on your fellow students, to pick up whatever the cameras miss. I don't relish having to ask for reports behind their backs, but mainland ideas are so deeply ingrained in us that they're difficult to let go of. Gen pop has a hard time acclimating to this lifestyle for a few measly months, so imagine how difficult the transition is for the staff. Anyone who comes from that mainland brings with them treacherous ideas. Every time the *Hourglass* drops off a new group of guests, we risk subterfuge. This is why I pontificate about loyalty. Do you understand?"

She nodded slowly.

"Good. Now, do as I say, and avoid who I tell you to. Unless you want your own allegiance called into question more than it already has been."

Her mouth fell open. "Who . . . ?"

"Who hasn't?" I raised an eyebrow. "They all worry they can't trust you."

"They can," she sputtered.

"Normally I consider my judgment sound, but I must say I'm having second thoughts about bringing you into the IC. You're more loyal to these side friendships than to me."

"That's not true."

I toyed with the scarf. "If you want to take Gordon's place at my side, I must be confident of your devotion."

She jerked her head, undoubtedly surprised to hear me speak so baldly of the staff hierarchy. She shouldn't have been. Honesty at all costs was my policy.

"What can I do?" she asked mousily. Was there anything worse in a woman than meekness? "To prove my devotion?"

I considered the question for an inordinate amount of time, debating whether she was up for the challenge. Perhaps it was too soon.

She rubbed her hands on her jeans, waiting.

"I think it's time you took your q2."

She went completely still. "It's only been a month or so since my q1."

"Are you saying you're not ready? Would you prefer I give this opportunity to one of your peers?"

"No. I'm ready. I'll do whatever you think."

I sank next to her on the couch and laced my fingers through hers.

"That's my girl."

36

Kit

ALL THIS TIME I'd been trying to figure out whether it was April or Georgina who betrayed me.

Neither had.

Since Teacher had told me about the cameras, I'd begun searching the island for them. They were everywhere. In our guesthouses they resembled smoke detectors. In the classrooms and cafeteria they were disguised within photo frames. They were even nestled in the hedge foliage. Wherever we went we were watched: around the pool, inside the shed, by the staff doors. I was sure all of it had been Gordon's doing. I'd figured out his role here: head of security. His handiwork was how she knew everything. She wasn't reading our minds.

She was watching us.

The abandoned inside jokes, the lost laughs, the late-night discussions— I'd thrown away my friendships with April and Georgina over nothing.

Anger stirred my gut as I paced the second-floor corridor of Teacher's house a few minutes before midnight. Just because I didn't see any cameras didn't mean they weren't there. On the wall was an oil painting inspired by Munch—a bald woman clutched the sides of her head, face melting, mouth frozen in a shriek. The painting was disturbing enough on its own, made worse by the fact there were six copies of it, three on each side of the hallway.

Every time you had a one-on-one with Teacher, you had to walk past the sextuplets with their haunting eyes. Maybe they were a reminder to face our fears—or what would happen if we didn't.

I REACHED FOR my own bald head, still not used to it. Teacher had said this was one more way to sever our connections to the past. If I had no hair I couldn't pull it out. Sometimes I missed the warmth on my neck or the messy bun piled atop my head. I missed matching my hair to my mood. I missed feeling pretty. Plenty of women with buzzed hair were gorgeous, but I was no Natalie Portman. I didn't need a mirror to confirm the cut was bad for me. I just knew.

Pretty is frivolous, I chided myself. *A fear of rejection.*

I was waiting to be summoned into a spare bedroom that Sofia used to treat ailing guests. An exam table with leg stirrups stood in the center, surrounded by three rolling cabinets packed with medical supplies. In the corner were crutches that had never been used. Teacher kept the medicines in a locked cabinet in her office. No one could say Wisewood was unprepared in case of an emergency.

I pressed my ear to the door, heard shuffling and hushed tones, but nothing that would give me any clues. I wished Teacher would tell us ahead of time what our quests were; not knowing bred anxiety. Probably this was a pre-quest test. We had to be unafraid before the q's and during them.

A quiet knock at the door made me jump.

"Kit," a voice said. "Knock back when you're ready."

I stood tall and thumped. On the other side was Sofia, buzzing with excitement. Behind her the room was dim, lit by a handful of candles. I stepped inside.

They had moved the exam table to the front of the room. Pillows covered the rest of the floor: two neat rows of three. On each pillow kneeled an IC member: Gordon, Ruth, and Debbie in the first row; Sanderson, Raeanne, and Jeremiah in the second.

"Kit, welcome to your q2. You will now begin"—Sofia paused dramatically—"the Quest of Pain."

My insides heaved.

"Throughout life we all suffer emotional pain, but there is physical pain as well. Pain is a fact, an inevitability." Sofia cocked her head. "Or is it?"

She leaned uncomfortably close. "Want me to go first? I'd die to take mine again."

All I could manage was a terse shake of the head.

Sofia shrugged and handed me a kernel of plastic. "You're supposed to put this in your ear."

"For what?" I examined the earbud before sticking it in my right ear.

"Just in case. I need you to get on my table now."

My entire body trembled. I climbed onto the exam table and lay on my back.

"Pain is a choice," Sofia said to the rest of the group. "Research has shown that pain is exaggerated by fear. If you're relaxed and believe whatever you're about to go through won't be painful, then you'll feel none or only a tiny fraction of the pain you'd experience if you were afraid. Therefore, the key to ridding ourselves of pain is to first face our fears."

Sofia lowered her voice. "Roll onto your stomach."

I flipped over and rested my forehead on the backs of my hands. Sofia washed up at the sink in the corner, then pulled on latex gloves.

Have you lost your mind? Nat popped into my head. *Get the fuck out of there.*

A different voice filled my right ear. "What on Earth is Jeremiah doing?"

Teacher.

I lifted my head and glanced at my peers on their knees. In the second row Jeremiah wobbled. I couldn't answer Teacher even if I'd known what to say—I only had a receiver, no microphone. I pictured her sitting in her office, Mom's scarf wrapped around her neck. She'd started to wear it daily.

Raeanne flashed Jeremiah a dirty look, leaning out of his path as he swayed toward her. "For Pete's sake."

"Dude, are you okay?" Sanderson said, brow wrinkled.

Jeremiah tipped forward onto his hands and knees. "Sorry. I need a minute."

"Do you have low blood sugar?" Sofia rushed to his side.

He waved her off. "I get squeamish easily. Don't worry about me."

Sofia lit up. "A quick dive in the ocean would revive all our spirits." She peered around for any takers, found none.

"We need to stick to the plan," Gordon said.

"How we gonna do that if this lily liver passes out?" Raeanne grumbled.

"Leave him alone," Ruth warned as she squeezed Debbie's shoulder—the cook was watching Jeremiah with tears in her eyes.

No-touching rule, I thought involuntarily.

"Ignore me and keep going, guys," Jeremiah said.

I might have found such a dramatic reaction panic inducing, but he didn't know what was coming either. He'd never been to a q2.

"Ask him why he hasn't attempted his own Quest of Pain yet," Teacher said. I bit my lip. The last thing I wanted to do was kick my friend while he was down. "Don't you want to help Jeremiah on his journey toward fearlessness?"

"Why haven't you done your q2 yet, Jeremiah?" I asked.

He glanced up, surprised, face ashen.

"Point out he's been in the IC longer than you have," Teacher said.

Why was she making my q2 about Jeremiah? This was supposed to be an opportunity for me to take another step closer to my Maximized Self. Couldn't she and Jeremiah have this conversation during a one-on-one? What was the point in shaming him?

"Do you want to hinder his work on the path? Can you live with yourself if all that hard-won progress is lost?"

"You've been in the IC longer than I have," I said just loudly enough for everyone to hear. I prayed they all knew this was coming from Teacher. Surely Jeremiah understood I wanted to get this over with as much as he did.

"Don't speak until he answers," Teacher said.

The silence that ensued had to be more painful than whatever Sofia was planning. No one stirred. Jeremiah stared at me. In a thin voice he said, "Because I'm . . . scared."

"Perhaps he doesn't belong in the IC after all."

I laid my forehead back down, praying Teacher would let this go.

"Say it."

I mumbled the words. "Maybe he doesn't belong in the IC after all."

"Don't get smart with me. You may be my favorite today, but that doesn't mean I won't punish you tomorrow."

Heat spread across my cheeks and neck. I wanted to get back to the quest.

"I warned you about him," Teacher said after what seemed like a lifetime. "Tomorrow you tell Jeremiah that if he's thinking of abandoning this community, I have no problem sending the video of his q1 to his former employer."

I stifled a gasp. The day after my initiation, I had confronted Jeremiah about his admission. How long had he been cooking the books? Did anyone at his company know?

He'd gazed at me sadly. "I thought you knew me better than that by now. I made it up, Kit. I bet at least half of those confessions were exaggerations— . or straight-up lies—to outdo each other. To win points with Teacher."

Half of me was relieved I wasn't the only one who had embellished their secret. The other half was disappointed—were we freeing ourselves from judgment if our transgressions were invented? What was the point?

"Carry on," Teacher said in my ear.

Color had returned to Jeremiah's face, so Sofia left his side and smoothly resumed preparations. She picked up an alcohol swab from her metal tray and tore it open. She patted my right leg until I relaxed, lying like a cadaver on her table. She wiped the swab across the pad of my right big toe. My breath hitched.

"The mark we wear on our toes is an homage to all that we've learned," she said. "The three points of the triangle represent Wisewood's three principles. The triangle plus trunk form an evergreen tree to remind us where our rebirth originated. And the triangular *Q* plus the *F* beneath it stands for 'Quests of Fearlessness,' the reason we're all here tonight."

It's just a tattoo. I exhaled, thinking of the star on my temple—I'd gotten it the week after Mom died. Nat thought I was crazy then, and she would think this was crazy now. But how was q2 any different from a man branding his girlfriend's name across his chest? A family commemorating the death of a loved one with matching angel wings? We wanted a way to express our commitment, a daily reminder of what we were working toward. All of this was pain with a purpose. Teacher often reminded us that pain was fear leaving the body. In our case, it was especially true. With every quest, we were one step closer to fearlessness. I didn't know how to make Nat understand.

She's not here, I reminded myself. *Don't let fear of judgment get the best of you.*

If my sister *were* here, she'd say that I followed Teacher around like a puppy, with a head empty of opinions or reason, but she would be wrong. I knew Teacher manipulated me. I knew she played all of us against one another, keeping us closer to her than to each other. I knew she told me what I wanted to hear to strengthen her hold over me.

But I cared less about the *reasons* behind her actions and more about the actions themselves. Every wink, every compliment, every hug—they made me feel needed. Most of the time, it didn't matter if she was telling the other students the same things. I craved her approval. Teacher telling me I was special was more important than whether it was actually true. I was willing to overlook serious flaws if it meant being loved. Who among us wasn't?

I tolerated these manipulations because they pointed me in a direction I already wanted to go. Teacher wasn't trying to force me to wear a skin that didn't fit, to push for a life I didn't want. She could be harsh but she was also right—fear was a monster of our own making. Fear held power over us only if we let it.

You're a tidal wave, Kitten. You're exactly what Wisewood needs.

"Sanderson? Raeanne?" Sofia said. The two of them rose.

Sanderson cleared his throat. "I'm not totally down with . . ." Raeanne grimaced at him. He swallowed and approached the table.

"You take her legs. You get her arms," Sofia said.

Clammy hands clamped my ankles; a dry pair grabbed my wrists. I reminded myself Teacher had said touching was allowed for quests as long as we didn't enjoy it. I willed myself not to think about how much time had passed since I'd touched another human being—besides her—in a non-classroom setting, but a number materialized anyway: six and a half months. I refused to think about my mother's hugs or my last boyfriend's kisses. I ignored the blasphemous thought that touching was a form of socializing, and socializing was what made us human.

I focused on lying still on the table, wondering if Raeanne could feel my pulse jumping out of my wrists. Sofia laid a comforting hand on my back as she talked about the importance of pain, how it made us stronger.

"Showtime," she finally said. Her knees popped as she lowered her head even with mine. She dug her nails into my arms. "I want to thank you for doing this. For bringing her back."

I peeked at the doctor. "Who?"

She pointed to a stool in the corner of the room. "Rosa. Whenever I feel most alive, like right now, when I can feel the blood zinging through my veins, my daughter visits me. You brought her here tonight."

She was speaking figuratively, right?

Raeanne nudged Sofia out of the way. "Let's get moving, Doc." She took

Sofia's spot by my head, pulled the toothpick from her mouth. "Time to be brave."

I rested my chin on the table and held Raeanne's gaze. I would not think about the potentially hallucinating doctor about to put a needle to my foot.

"It's gonna hurt a lot," Raeanne said, breath rancid, "but only for ten minutes. Only for a hundred breaths in and out, and we'll do them together. You ready? You'll breathe with me?"

I nodded, unable to stop quivering. I had a frantic thought that I needed to know what was coming and glanced over my shoulder.

In Sofia's hand was a cautery pen. The tip glowed red.

Raeanne brought my head back to face her. "Soon you won't be afraid of pain anymore, I promise."

I had been expecting a bunch of tiny bee stings, like with my star tattoo, but when the tip of the pen touched my toe, a white-hot pain sliced through me. I jerked and screamed.

"Hold her still," Sofia said.

The pressure on my arms and ankles intensified. The pen kept moving. When the smell of burned flesh hit my nostrils, I stopped moaning. I could barely feel my foot anymore.

At last fear was leaving my body.

37

Natalie

JANUARY 9–10, 2020

I WAIT, CROUCHED under a spruce. Hail ricochets off the trees. When I've convinced myself the masked woman is gone, I dart down the same path she took, trying to retrace our footsteps. But she must have brought me out here on a roundabout route; none of my surroundings are familiar. Actually, all of it's too familiar, one grove of trees identical to the next. I feel like I'm in a maze. The same eerie sensation I've had since first setting foot on this island settles over me: I'm being watched.

I scope the forest, chest thumping, afraid to yell for help.

"Hello?" I call.

No one answers.

What kind of guru leaves someone to freeze to death?

The weather's not letting up. Snow falls thick as fog. My parka is warm enough for arctic conditions (thank baby Jesus), but my hair is wet, ears frozen. I pull up my jacket's hood, cutting off my peripheral vision. I push it back down, scared of what I can't see.

Why did I follow her out here? How could I be so stupid?

I'm about to call out again when I hear a cracking sound. I whip around but don't catch anyone behind me. For a minute, maybe more, I stand there.

Nothing but the endless deluge of hail. I hear the sound again, and this time I'm sure it's the sound of knuckles cracking.

Is she fucking with me?

I turn a slow circle, the trees closing in on me. I listen for more cracking, but all I hear is the wind. I probably imagined the noise. I decide not to wait to find out.

I run, sure I'm fleeing something but no idea what. Blindly I push my way through clumps of branches. The branches claw at me; needles cling to my jacket. I need to be more methodical if I'm going to find this door but I can't think over the wailing of my lizard brain: faster, faster. I don't see the tree root on the path until it's too late.

My boot catches on the root. I grunt as I fly through the air, and bite my lip hard when I come down. The heels of my hands catch the brunt of my weight. I lie for a second, facedown, and imagine Wisewood's troops closing in on me. I see them turning me over, blood weeping from my eyes and ears and nose. I picture them tossing my waxen corpse into a hastily dug plot, my hair filled with writhing worms. My mouth is frozen in a silent scream.

Nothing happens. No one comes. I sit up and assess the damage. My palms are scraped; my mouth aches. I lick my lower lip. It's bleeding and beginning to swell. I wiggle my ankles. Nothing is twisted or sprained. I'm okay.

I bring my knees to my chest. The masked woman warned me that *what Teacher says goes.* Could she have been Rebecca? Would she stoop to such dirty work?

No way is this a run-of-the-mill self-improvement program. Either a staff member has gone rogue or Rebecca has institutionalized psychological warfare. Is this how they keep guests and staff in line, by terrifying them into submission? Kit has been rushing around, doing Rebecca's bidding, since the moment I got here. She has them all trained like dogs. When I get off this godforsaken island, I'm going to drag that woman through the mud until she's buried.

I take a deep breath. I have to keep moving. I haul myself to my feet.

I don't know how long I walk for. At some point my hands and feet go numb. After a while I stop noticing my runny nose, my throbbing bottom lip. When, at last, a dark wall looms ahead, I nearly sob with relief. I inch between the wall and trees, fingering the fake leaves as I walk along the hedge. Finally I reach a door, feel twin spikes of pride and fear. Who's waiting on the other side? I reach for the handle, overwhelmed by déjà vu.

The door is locked.

Irate, I pound on it, no longer caring what awaits me. I keep hammering long after I've bruised the side of my hand. I call for help until my throat is hoarse. I'm met with total silence. I don't hear a single creature stirring in the woods at my back. I have no way of getting through or over this wall.

No one is coming to get me.

I find the biggest tree nearby and nestle myself underneath it, out of the snow and waning hail. I set my watch alarm to go off every twenty minutes so I can do jumping jacks and butt kicks to warm my core. I recall the year I resolved to meditate more: ten minutes every day. I summon those lessons now, try to find some inner Zen, tamp down the voice screaming that I'm going to die out here.

Then I wait.

MANY HOURS LATER the sun rises. The sky looks like a bruised cheek, smoky purple against blotchy peach. The effect is ghastly, casting a jaundiced glow over the island. Still the snow tumbles; still the wind howls. Something caws overhead, but I can't see it from my spot under the tree. By now the adrenaline coursing through my body has faded, but I haven't slept at all. I've been staring at the door, willing it to open, hour after hour after hour, until I'm sure my pulse is a clock external to my body, something everyone else can hear but is ignoring.

A key turns in the lock. I scramble out of my hiding place, brush the tree needles off of my coat. The door swings open. I brace myself.

Kit pokes her head inside. "Nat?"

I squeak something unintelligible, never more relieved to see my stupid fucking sister. Kit peeks over her shoulder, steps into the forest, and closes the door behind her. In her arms are my hat and scarf.

She thrusts them toward me, then recoils. "Your lip."

I jam on the hat, teeth chattering. "Get me out of here."

She nods, eyes wide. "I came as soon as I found out."

I wind the scarf around my neck. "Let's go."

She opens the door, and I sprint out of the forest. I take off for my cabin. Kit plods along behind me, panting hard. When I reach the front door, I double over, hands on my knees. "Tell me you have the key."

She pulls a key card from her pocket and unlocks the door. I shove her inside. She lurches away from my hands.

When we're both safely in the room, I slam the door behind us. I wrench off my coat, grab the comforter from the bed, and wrap it around my body, teeth still clacking. My lower lip feels like it's grown another lip on top of it. Kit quietly takes a seat in the desk chair. I pace the room, a new rush of adrenaline zipping through me.

I glare at my sister. "What is this place?"

She glances at the smoke detector on the ceiling. "I know the methodology can be extreme but—"

"Kit, I was left alone in the woods in January for"—I check my watch—"five hours."

She nods as if this has been a regrettable turn of events. "I don't always like the treatments either."

"I didn't sign up for any treatments," I yell.

"It's sometimes hard to see during a learning experience what the takeaway is supposed to be, but there's always a method to Teacher's madness."

I wheel around on her, dropping the comforter. "So the woman who left me for dead was Rebecca?"

She screws up her face. "Of course not. She's way too important to administer treatments."

"Who was it, then?"

She shrugs. "Someone on staff."

"Raeanne?"

Her eyes flit away from mine, which means yes.

Between gritted teeth I ask, "Who told you where I was?"

Kit presses her lips together, refusing to speak. She doesn't have to.

"I want to talk to Rebecca. Now." The mystery of the anonymous e-mailer is no longer so mysterious. If Rebecca didn't send it herself, she certainly had something to do with it. No one and nothing in this place is untethered from her puppeteer's strings.

"Impossible."

"And then I want to get off this island. As soon as humanly possible."

I follow her gaze to the snow beating the window.

"You can't go out in this weather. It's unsafe."

"More unsafe than being left outside in twenty-degree temperatures? I could have gotten hypothermia out there, Kit. I could've died."

"Your fear of pain is taking over."

To stop myself from throttling her, I stomp into the bathroom. Twelve hours ago, I vowed to some fairy in the sky that I would die for Kit. Now I want to kill her instead.

I go to look in the mirror, then remember—oh, wait—there are none in this hellhole. I wrap a starchy bath towel around my hair and wet some toilet paper, wincing as I blot the cut on my lip. Even without a mirror, I can see how puffy it is. When I come back out, Kit is staring at the ceiling again. I stand in front of my sister, get in her face. "Raeanne threatened to stab me with a box cutter."

Kit's face clouds over. "She shouldn't have done that."

"You think?"

"We try to avoid violence here."

I snort, then lower my voice. "When the water is safe to pass, I'm getting out of here. And you're coming with me."

"Oh." She blinks a few times. "No, Nat, I'm not. I'm not going anywhere. This is my home now."

"You know what I think? I think this is a cry for help. You want to get away from here but can't because Rebecca has brainwashed you into thinking that leaving would be the end of the world."

"I already told you brainwashing isn't a valid scientific concept."

"Let me talk to Rebecca."

"Not a chance." Kit's entire body tenses. "You're going to insult her and humiliate me. I didn't need your meddling before Wisewood, and I sure as hell don't need it now. I came and got you from the forest because I wanted to help you, nothing more."

My sister's newfound assertiveness surprises me. I point to my swollen lip. "Do I look helped?"

"You're the one who brought your phone here."

"*That's* the big violation?"

"You lied to us."

"You know why I don't like to be without my phone, Kit."

"This was an opportunity for you to get over that."

I glare. "Where were you all night, anyway? I went to your room half a dozen times. I was worried sick."

"I was trying to stop Gordon from doing something stupid."

"What's that guy's deal?"

My sister scowls at the smoke detector. "He's Teacher's pet."

And you aren't? I think, raising an eyebrow.

She turns her head sharply toward me, and I worry I've voiced the thought aloud. "You don't know a thing about me anymore, Natalie."

I study her sheared scalp and dull skin. Her dimples have vanished; the lightness has gone out of her eyes. I try to find traces of my sister, but she's a shadow of the whirlwind she once was. She's harder, tougher.

I realize she's right.

She tilts her head. "Earlier you said we needed to talk."

"Now's not the time."

She squeezes her left hand into a fist, then relaxes it. "Now is a perfect time."

"Let it go, Kit. I'm not in the mood."

"I've grown a backbone since we were kids. You're not in charge anymore. You can tell me now or not at all."

"Fine," I say, eager to spit the words out, excited for the pain they'll cause, scared by my own depravity.

"Mom planned her death. And I helped her."

38

Kit

I HAD NO reason to limp. Now that I'd passed my q2, I was free of pain.

Still, I stepped gingerly as I tidied the trailer after class, emptying the wastebasket and straightening chairs. To distract myself from my throbbing foot, I jotted down some quick notes—which students were stagnating, how I could help. A burning pain shot up my leg from my toe, making me wince. I hoped it wouldn't take long for the tattoo to scab over.

Tattoo? Nat sniped. *Why don't we call a spade a spade? You've been branded. Like fucking livestock.*

It's a symbol. I'm not scared of pain anymore.

How can you believe in this shit? she screeched.

I gritted my teeth. My sister had been telling me how and what to think our entire lives. She thought she was smart because she didn't believe in anything. When I was in third grade, she haughtily informed me Santa wasn't real. Mom would've been happy to keep playing him—smudging thank-you letters with chimney soot, eating all the cookies—until we left for college, had Nat not ruined the illusion.

When we were teenagers my sister decided she no longer believed in God. She pointed out the logic flaws, the inconsistencies in the stories we'd grown up learning at CCD. But it wasn't enough for her to stop believing; she also had to spurn anyone who still had faith. She didn't see belief the way I did: as a comfort, a reassurance that someone or something was out there, keeping the scales between good and evil tipped toward good—or at least balanced. So what if I wanted to believe life wasn't random and pointless? So what if I needed my existence to mean something? In the end, what did it matter whether the believers or nonbelievers were right? Our beliefs affected the here and now.

Nat prided herself on sniffing out what she perceived to be bullshit. She thought her doubts made her better. I thought they made her miserable. If I kept letting her butt in, she would ruin Wisewood for me the same way she'd ruined God.

I opened the trailer door. A burst of freezing air slammed into me. I tucked my chin into the warm fabric of my coat, dreading that glued-together-nose-hairs sensation this weather brought. The sun struggled to peek through clouds the color of dirty mop water.

I could see why we had so few guests during this time of year.

On days like this I missed the Sonoran Desert of my childhood—the unrelenting dry heat, the cowboy-shaped saguaros, the shocks of fuchsia and strawberry bougainvillea. Back then I had wondered why anyone would subject themselves to the miseries of winter year after year. I had become one of them, muttering for months straight about dark days and biting cold.

No sooner had I locked the trailer door than I saw Jeremiah standing a few feet away, whistling an attempt at nonchalance. I automatically reached for my hair, found only scalp.

I hadn't called on him in class that morning or even made eye contact—partly because Teacher had told me to cut ties with him, partly because I was avoiding passing along her threat.

"How's the foot?"

I glanced around. No one from gen pop was nearby. "All good, thanks." I headed for the cafeteria, signaling an end to the conversation.

Jeremiah walked alongside me, matching my pace. "It looks like you're limping." I didn't respond. "You should get a gel or lotion or something from Sofia. Help it heal faster."

"I already have."

He went to tap my arm but I twisted out of reach. "You sure you're okay?"

"I told you I am. Why do you keep asking?" In the back of my mind, I noted faint sobbing coming from one of the guesthouses.

"Because you were *branded* last night."

"Keep your voice down." I stopped short and peered around. We were still alone. "Are you questioning the q's?"

"Are you not? You've scarred your body for life."

Jeremiah had never spoken so brazenly—he must have been terrified about his own q2.

"I see it as a badge, not a scar. And you'd better join me soon."

"Or what?"

"Or Teacher said she'll send your q1 to your old boss."

Jeremiah glared. "I never should've . . ." He trailed off.

The nape of my neck tingled. "You're not having second thoughts about the IC?"

He studied me. "What are you going to do if I say yes?"

I hesitated. My q2 had rattled him more than I'd thought. "I have to do what's best for Wisewood. We all do. So why don't you think long and hard before you say something you'll regret. I can't have my loyalty called into question." *Again,* I didn't say.

His face turned red. "Don't you care about anything more than her?"

Where was this animosity coming from? "I thought you admired her too."

"Pretty hard to admire a liar."

My mouth fell open. "What are you talking about?"

He shuffled his feet, regret plain on his face.

"Tell me."

"Forget it."

"Tell me," I said more forcefully.

His gaze shifted to the tiny camera affixed to the roof of a nearby guesthouse. You wouldn't have noticed it unless you were searching for it—but it was pointed straight at us. He glanced back at me, then tipped his chin a fraction of an inch toward the hedge. I blinked twice and left him standing there. Mind racing, I walked an indirect route to the outskirts of campus, chose a spot away from any doors or cameras. A minute later, Jeremiah joined me. The trees beyond the wall swished, eavesdropping and whispering, passing secrets along like a game of telephone.

When he was sure we were alone, Jeremiah stepped toward me, his eyes wild, fists shaking. A growl escaped his throat.

"Rebecca killed my brother."

39

Kit

I STARED OPENMOUTHED at Jeremiah, too shocked to speak.

"When we were kids," he said, "my parents took us to see a magician at the high school two towns over, this girl wonder named Rebecca. She chose my brother as her assistant for a handcuff trick. Gabe was transfixed. He'd always been interested in magic, but from that moment on he was obsessed."

He told me about Teacher's life before Wisewood—her Madame Fearless persona, the death-defying stunts, Gabe's role as her business partner of twenty years, how she'd mistreated him yet ended up with his inheritance.

"It's her fault Gabe's gone."

"I thought your brother died in a freak accident."

"He drowned in a half-frozen lake. During one of her shows."

I choked on a gasp.

"Even if the whole thing was an accident, she's still responsible for his death."

I rubbed my hands together to warm them, trembling in the cold. "Jeremiah, that's ridiculous."

He barked a laugh. "You don't know her like I do. I've spent years researching her, this place."

A new fear sprouted in my ribs: Teacher's safety. How had I so misjudged this man? All his devotion and swooning had been a lie.

"You're hoping to do what, exactly?"

He gestured at the island around us. "She took my brother from my family long before he died. Now she's doing the same damn thing to the people who live here. I can't let her keep endangering people, ripping them away from their loved ones. This is bigger than Gabe."

"What are you going to do?" I asked.

Sweat glistened at his temples. "Make her take responsibility. That woman has been manipulating and abusing her followers for years. Somewhere along the way she must have screwed up. If I find proof of that screwup, I'm handing it over to the police. If I can't . . ." His expression clouded. "I'll get justice my own way."

The cold had snaked down my collar, up my sleeves. I itched to inch closer to the house—I had to warn Teacher as soon as possible. "Have you found anything so far?"

Jeremiah tugged at tufts of his beard. "A lot of crazy shit has gone down here, but no one besides me is willing to talk about it, either because of the NDA or they honestly believe this crap is for their own good." He wrinkled his nose. "I don't know where Gordon hides that phone with the blackmail videos from q1, but I sure as hell haven't been able to find it. I've been through Rebecca's files, her journal. Not a single goddamn reference to Gabe in there—can you believe that?"

I shook my head, debating whether he was beyond saving. "I don't think you've thought this through."

"I've thought about nothing *but* this for years."

Teacher had been right about him all along.

He gripped my wrist, breathing hard. "My sabbatical is almost over." He wouldn't let me shimmy free. "I only have a few weeks left before I go home. She has to pay for what she's done."

Suffering from burnout, quitting his job, never wanting to leave Wisewood—everything Jeremiah had told me was a lie. Desperation radiated from him in waves so thick it scared me. I thought we'd made progress in class but knew from experience that grief manifested in unpredictable ways. His brother had died nearly fifteen years earlier, yet Jeremiah was still hung up on the accident. Maybe I could put a stop to this harebrained scheme before he got hurt.

"You need to take a step back and rethink this 'plan.' Do you know how many lives you could ruin? I'm sorry about Gabe; his death was tragic, to be sure. Teacher probably could've been kinder to him. I'm sure she's made mistakes in the past—we all have." My heart thumped in my chest. "Even visionaries mess up from time to time."

Jeremiah glared at me. "You know what I found in the desk of your *visionary*? Files with each of our names on them. That's right—there's one that says 'KIT' in big black letters." My stomach turned. "I only had time to flip through my own, but it was filled with background on me."

I thought it at the same time he said it: "That's why Gordon is gone all the time.

"Teacher has him digging into our lives," he added.

"How do you know it's Gordon?"

He gave me an "Oh, come on" roll of the eyes. "I checked his file—"

"I thought you only had time to look through your own."

"I had to see what I'm up against. You have to be a loon to dish the dirt on yourself as well as everyone else."

Or loyal, I thought.

"You know what he used to do before Wisewood?"

I wanted to cut him off, to tell him I didn't care, but was too curious to walk away.

"He was a private investigator. That story he told about his family during your q1? It was actually true. Some socialite hired him to figure out whether her husband was cheating. She got everything in the divorce, including full custody of the kids. The guy was so pissed he hired two hit men to take Gordon out. Some wires got crossed, and they shot his wife and kid instead. Both of them died a few days later in the hospital." Jeremiah shook his head. "It's like a bad Liam Neeson movie."

"If Gordon snoops on people for a living, how have you not been caught? How has he not made the connection?"

"I'm not sure Rebecca's told him about her past. He probably doesn't even know who Gabe was." Jeremiah watched me, wary. "To be safe, I signed up for Wisewood under a friend's name. Guy I went to college with. We have the same build, used to get mistaken as brothers all the time. He works in accounting too. Keeps a low profile online."

My head spun. "Your name isn't even Jeremiah?" He raised an eyebrow. "What is it, then?"

He pressed his lips together and shook his head. He no longer trusted that I would choose him over Teacher.

I gawked at him. "Does your friend know you've stolen his identity?"

His jaw hardened. "As if losing my only sibling wasn't bad enough, Rebecca ended up with fourteen million dollars of my family's money. I wouldn't be surprised if she kept Gabe close all those years to get the cash."

It's not true, I told myself. Teacher couldn't be blamed for inspiring such fervor in the people around her. If they wanted to give their money to her—to Wisewood—that was their choice.

"My family's success built Wisewood. I feel accountable to the guests here. People are being fooled and robbed. I have to put a stop to it."

Fooled and robbed—he didn't believe any of our principles. I had admired this man. He'd helped me plan my classes, let me talk about Mom long after everyone else had grown bored with my grief. I didn't know a single thing about him, not even his name.

He lowered his voice. "I've kept my head down the entire time I've been here. I've trusted no one, avoided getting close to people. I couldn't risk getting caught." He softened. "Then you came along. Despite my better judgment, I let the wall down. You're a good kid, anyone can see that, so I prayed you wouldn't be invited to the IC. When you were, I told myself I could watch over you, keep you safe. I was delusional." He rubbed his face. "Blackmail is one thing—I sat idly by for that—but I can't watch these monsters mutilate your body. I'm telling you all of this because I care about you, Kit. I won't let Rebecca hurt you the way she's hurt my family."

I stuck out my chin. "She would never."

"She already has. She's got you under her spell."

I was sick and tired of everyone telling me they knew better than I did what was best for me. All Jeremiah cared about was his own preposterous story—he didn't care whom he hurt to prove it. I thought of Teacher's demise, Wisewood's collapse, and felt light-headed.

I checked my watch. "I'm supposed to have lunch with Ruth. We're going over lesson plans."

"Please, please don't out me. I don't know what she'll do."

I chewed the inside of my cheek, then slogged toward the cafeteria, leaving my former friend alone in the cold.

"They're in alphabetical order," he called. "Top left drawer of her desk."

40

Natalie

I REGRET THE words as soon as they've left my mouth. How could I be so spiteful? I reach for my sister's hand, but she pulls away.

"What are you talking about?" Her voice shakes.

"Mom didn't die unexpectedly," I say as gently as I can. "She had me set her up with an assisted-dying physician so she could go on her own terms."

The blood drains from Kit's face. Guilt-stricken, I gaze out the window. The snow has slowed. I watch the lazy descent of each flake as it swirls toward its final resting place. I think of tongues and eyelashes and the open palm of a tiny mitten, all the homes the flurries claim as their own. I remember Kit and me standing on a sidewalk in snowsuits during a trip to visit our uncle, two kids with our heads tipped back, like we'd seen on TV, like those women leaving the cafeteria.

I make myself continue. "She begged me, Kit. She told me she asked you first, but you said no. She wanted to do it while you were gone. She was trying to spare you the pain."

Her lips are turning as white as the rest of her face. "I told her no because you and I agreed we wanted her to fight. I never said goodbye."

I sit on the bed and stare at my feet. "She told me she said her goodbye.

Before you left for the bachelorette party, she told you how much she loved you, how proud she was."

Kit's eyes harden. "*I* didn't get to say goodbye to *her*."

Neither of us says anything.

"You took that from me." A single tear spills down her cheek. "You got to hold her hand and tell her you loved her. Comfort her while she took her last breaths."

I don't deny it. My head begins to throb in tempo with my lip.

Kit wrings her hands. "Did you both think so little of me that you thought I couldn't cope? That I would rather miss out on saying goodbye to my own mother than face the pain?"

I soften my tone further. "I was carrying out her wishes, Kit." How many times have I cursed Mom for putting me in this position, cursed myself for agreeing to it? Surely Mom knew I couldn't lie to my sister forever. She couldn't have expected I'd take her secret to my grave.

"Bullshit," Kit spits. "This was your last chance to be her favorite. To be the one she chose for once."

I flinch at the truth of it. For years I've spent night after sleepless night lying in bed, interrogating my motivations. Did I truly act out of selflessness, a desire to help our mother, shoulder the emotional burden, and bring a horrible wish to fruition? Or did I, the lifelong third wheel, want to be the only daughter at her side while she lay dying? I go cotton-mouthed every time I debate it.

Kit clutches her chest like her heart is giving out. "I can't believe my own sister would do this to me." I hang my head. "You've kept it from me all this time. For two years I wanted to crawl out of my skin with guilt for not being there. You were never going to let me be there." She leans over, hugging her chest to her thighs. "This is the worst thing you've ever done."

"I'm sorry," I say almost inaudibly, wishing I could take her in my arms but knowing she'd only push me away because that's who Kit is now. My bear-hugging, hair-braiding, piggybacking sister has become untouchable.

"I'm sorry," I say again.

We sit for a long time, me with my head bowed on the bed, her folded in half on the desk chair. The sun finishes rising. The snow stops. Still we sit there, not speaking. Sobs, a tantrum, a lecture—anything would be better than this gulf of silence.

"Say something. What are you thinking?"

She lifts her face off her knees, eyes tired in a way I haven't seen since Mom's funeral. She opens her mouth to speak.

I hold my breath.

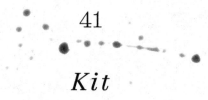

41

Kit

DECEMBER 28, 2019

I PULLED THE laptop out of the bottom desk drawer and turned it on, drumming my fingers on the keyboard while keeping an eye on the closed door. Teacher's bedroom and office were the only rooms on the island without any cameras. I had thirty minutes until she was showered and out of the bathroom.

A splash of color in the drawer caught my eye. The laptop had been sitting on top of a painting. I picked up the canvas, then saw there were two more underneath. I laid them all on the desk—eight-by-ten-inch paintings of a woman from behind. Teacher was the subject. In one a plastic bag was tied over her head. In another her body was on fire. In the third her head was turned to the side, blood gushing from her tongue. In the background of every painting was an audience, wide-eyed and dazzled.

In the bottom left corner of each canvas was an identical set of illegible initials. I flipped the paintings over. Scrawled on the back was a message: *Yours in fearlessness, The Five.*

I had no idea who The Five was, but Jeremiah had been right about this much: Teacher had once been a performer.

The computer's home screen loaded and requested a password. Panicked, I opened the top left drawer of the desk. It was full of hanging file folders.

Halfway back was a tab for each IC member, filed alphabetically like Jeremiah had promised. The one with my name on it called to me. I ignored it—I wasn't here to pore over my file. I only wanted to see if Jeremiah's story was true.

For two weeks I had agonized over what to do. I'd stopped talking to Jeremiah, knew I should report him to Teacher—the confession sat on the tip of my tongue—yet something stopped me. I didn't know what she or Gordon would do if they found out who Jeremiah was. Their punishments tipped toward drastic more often than not.

Every day I kept this from them, I was putting Teacher's well-being at risk, but as I watched Jeremiah go about his routine, I couldn't picture him hurting her. The reality was he'd gotten nowhere with his zany theories. Maybe I could let him ride out this last week and return home without anyone getting hurt. I found myself eating less and less at mealtimes, unable to stomach my own duplicity. I was weak for wanting the easy solution, a traitor for betraying Teacher.

I brought my attention to the front of the drawer. The first folder was labeled "Passwords." I reached in and scanned the tidy spreadsheet. Teacher must have made this—no way would Gordon have okayed a printout containing all of Wisewood's security information. I found the random password he had assigned the laptop and entered it with my breath held. For half a year my face had not been bathed in the glow of LED light. I hated myself for breaking my fast.

The desktop loaded.

I clicked on the Chrome app and typed *Gabriel Cooper*. More than eighty million results popped up. I tried *Madame Fearless* instead. The first entry was a Wikipedia page. I clicked the link and scrolled to the career section.

Fearless. Suffocated. Dark. Split. Alone. Entombed. Awake. Upright. Aflame. Frozen (canceled).

Some of the performances included photos. Under *Aflame* was an image of a younger Teacher and a sturdy man, his arm slung over her shoulders. He had the same crooked nose as Jeremiah. I glanced at the caption: *Madame Fearless and assistant Gabriel Cooper before Aflame, 2000.*

I swallowed. I wanted this ill-fated man with floppy hair and golden eyes to have nothing to do with Jeremiah. Yet I couldn't ignore their similar smiles, the dimpled chins.

The *Frozen* section was shorter than the others, with no accompanying photos:

> On January 3, 2005, Madame Fearless attempted to break the record for time spent submerged in thirty-five-degree water. A tragic accident and lack of safety crew led to the drowning of her assistant and the cancellation of the performance. She has not performed since. Her current whereabouts are unknown.

I scanned the page again, but there were no other mentions of Gabe, nothing to confirm Jeremiah's wild ideas. I didn't doubt he believed his hunch with all his heart—he wouldn't throw his life into disarray otherwise—but his certainty didn't make it true. Then again, had he ever given me a reason to think he was unhinged? Recent confession aside, I'd known Jeremiah to be a rational guy—smart, thoughtful, and composed. Even now he didn't strike me as the conspiracy theorist type.

The question I'd firmly shoved to the depths of my subconscious wriggled its way to the surface: was it so hard to believe Teacher would manipulate someone to extremes?

I sat for a minute with my hands on my knees. Slowly I reopened the top drawer, then found the file with my name on it. My hands shook as I flipped through the pages. First were copies of official documents: my birth certificate, college transcripts, the three speeding tickets I'd gotten as a teenager. Next came the lists: distant relatives, former employers, and old addresses— my childhood home in Tempe, the San Diego condo Mom and I moved into after her diagnosis, the Brooklyn studio I fled to once she'd passed. There was also a Boston residence. That must have been a mistake. I'd never even been to Boston.

The last was a copy of a death certificate. I squinted at the tiny print. Name of decedent: Margaret. Ann. Collins. I felt pinpricks at the backs of my eyes. I had never seen this.

I was examining the second row—date of birth, age, sex—when a bold headline halfway down the page caught my eye.

CAUSE OF DEATH
Immediate Cause: CEREBRAL METASTASES
Underlying Cause: SQUAMOUS CELL CARCINOMA
   OF LEFT MAIN BRONCHUS

Inside the Cause of Death box, someone had used a blue pen to add a note in small, neat letters. I recognized the handwriting from the to-do lists Teacher dictated to him: Gordon.

DDMP2.

He had vehemently circled the characters. I stared at it, trying to crack the code. When I couldn't, I turned back to the laptop.

The first search result for DDMP2 was a pdf entitled "Preparations for the Last Day" from the End of Life Washington website. The second was an *Atlantic* article: "How Aid-in-Dying Doctors Decide Which Drugs Actually Work." The third was titled "The Complicated Science of a Medically Assisted Death."

I stopped breathing.

I clicked the first link and read as fast as I could. I flew past words like "diazepam," "digoxin," "morphine," and "propranolol" until I understood— DDMP2 was a drug, a mixture of four medicines that made terminally ill patients fall asleep, slip into a coma, and die.

I slammed the laptop shut and clutched my chest. If Gordon was right, Mom hadn't died because it was her time. She'd died because a doctor had given her some pills. I squeezed my eyes shut, picturing her gaunt in bed, staring down eternity alone.

I reopened the computer, head spinning. After clearing the browser history and cookies, I powered down the laptop and shoved it back into the drawer.

But she hadn't been alone, had she?

I traveled back to that patch of concrete on the Vegas strip. The aftertaste of Bacardi coated my tongue—I hadn't been able to stomach rum since. I was vaguely aware that my knees were skinned and bleeding as I clutched my phone. What had Nat said? How had she reassured me?

I've been by her side the whole time. She didn't go alone.

She knew, then. They both did. Mom knew. Natalie knew. They had made a pact, a plan to get rid of me, and then they jumped, hands held, leaving me behind.

Everyone I trusted had lied to me.

"Sick" wasn't a strong enough word. I pushed the chair back from the desk and jammed the heels of my hands into my eye sockets. I choked back a howl, but a whimper escaped.

I didn't know how long I'd been sitting there when the room chilled. I sensed her presence before she said a word.

"What do you think you're doing?" Teacher asked from the doorway. Every time I'd opened that door, every single time over the past six months, it had creaked like it was going to fall off its hinges, sending echoes throughout the entire house. Yet the one time I saw Teacher enter the room, the door was silent. How could you explain something like that? How could you spend any amount of time around her and remain unconvinced she was extraordinary?

I pulled my hands from my face and met her eye. "I have to tell you something."

42

Natalie

KIT GLARES AT me. "I know, Nat."

I frown. "Know what?"

"How Mom died. I've known for weeks."

I freeze, mouth open. The e-mailer had told her, then.

My sister's voice cracks. "I didn't want to believe it. I told myself, no way you two were capable of such deceit. I've never wanted so badly to be wrong about something." She works her jaw. "That's why I wanted you to come here, so you could explain that I had it backward."

"Wait, *you* sent the e-mail?" I say, dizzy.

"Figures this is the one time I'm right."

"How did you find out?" She scowls as my brain struggles to compute the facts. Then I remember.

The second attachment.

Mom's death certificate with *DDMP2* written neatly in blue ink. Someone must have shown Kit the document.

My tongue feels fuzzy. "Why didn't you pick up the phone? You could've asked me to come out."

"What, and give you the chance to prepare some sob story? You hadn't even thought about telling me the truth until I threatened it out of you."

"You're wrong." I take a rickety breath. "I thought about it every day. I couldn't figure out how to do it in a way that wouldn't devastate you."

"How about not lying to me in the first place?"

My chest tightens. "If you had just signed the e-mail . . ."

"Gordon monitors the account, so I couldn't. He would've known I was having a setback and reported it."

A pounding builds in my ears. My pulse jabs at my throat. "Is that what this is about? Impressing Rebecca? She matters more to you than getting closure on Mom?"

Kit narrows her eyes until her pupils are barely visible. "Are you fucking serious? Don't put this on me. You were scared for a few days, and suddenly *I'm* the sociopath?" She jumps to her feet. "You let me panic for two years. How many times did I cry to you about how guilty I felt? Every single time you kept it going. *You* could've given me that closure."

"I know." I drop my head in my hands. "I know, I know, I know. I have no excuse other than it's what Mom wanted. For once I actually listened to her."

"What a time to grow a conscience."

"I deserve every insult you've got." I scoot forward on the bed. "I even deserved being left in that forest. Not because of the phone, but for what I did to you. I've been a shitty sister." My chin quivers. "I'll spend the rest of my life making it up to you, I swear."

She shakes her head. "It's always too little, too late with you."

"Kit, I'm the only family you have. We need to stick together."

She turns on her heel and heads for the door. "The people here are better family than you ever were."

"You don't mean that." I suppress a mortifying urge to cry.

She sniffs and glances out the window. "Skies are clearing up. It's time for you to go."

43

Natalie

JANUARY 10, 2020

KIT SLAMS THE door behind her. I stand in the middle of the room with my arms wrapped around my waist, struggling to formulate a plan on no sleep. The big sister in me wants to run after her and patch things up, but my sense of self-preservation is screaming to take Kit at her word and leave now. I feel a little better knowing some anonymous e-mailer isn't out to get me; still, the staff here has messed with my stuff (twice), stolen my property, and threatened me at knifepoint. I don't want to stay any longer than I have to.

One step at a time. First, I'll pack. Then I'll get my phone back. I'll demand a meeting with Rebecca. I chew on my knuckle.

Then I'll make one last pitch to get Kit to leave with me.

Either way, Gordon's driving me back to Rockland within the hour.

A few minutes later, I've thrown all my clothes and toiletries in the duffel. I lift the bag to my shoulder and check the cabin. I linger in the doorway, afraid to leave the room. I don't want to go back out there, where Rebecca's goons are waiting.

Tugging on my wool hat, I force myself over the threshold and hike through the powder toward Rebecca's house, keeping an eye out for someone official-looking. I'm halfway there when I spot a stocky older man marching across the grass. He wears a thick raincoat and galoshes.

Gordon.

He's animated in a way I haven't seen before. An excited flush has replaced his staid expression.

I block his path. His glasses are rain-spattered, strange since it's not snowing anymore. He wipes the glasses clean and frowns when he sees who's standing in his way.

"I'm ready to leave," I say. "How do I get my phone back?"

"I don't have time right now, Ms. Collins," he says, hand clenched.

When I see what he's gripping, I stop breathing.

44

Kit

CALMLY I CLOSED my file and put it back in the desk drawer, my gaze never leaving Teacher's.

"You were right about Jeremiah." I sat back in her chair. "He's not who he says he is."

The fury in her eyes changed to fear. She closed the office door. I rose from her desk, motioned for her to join me on the sofa. We each took a cushion, knees grazing. I squeezed one of her hands.

"I'm sorry for snooping. I was scanning his file to see what you already knew." Out of habit I reached for Mom's scarf, but it was wound around Teacher's neck, not mine. "Gordon's been keeping tabs on the wrong guy."

Teacher smoothed her hair behind her ears, then folded her hands in her lap. With forced restraint she asked, "Whom should he have been examining?"

"The guy you know as Jeremiah? That's not his real name."

Spots of color bloomed across Teacher's pale face. Her hands were clasped so tightly her knuckles had turned white. "Shall we sit here all day or are you going to disclose his identity?"

"Your old manager, Gabe Cooper? Jeremiah—whatever his name is—is his younger brother."

Her jaw fell open.

"He's here for revenge. He wants to topple Wisewood. And take you down with it."

I had never seen her speechless. I counted backward from five—still she didn't speak. Her neck muscles strained, nostrils flared.

She looked like she wanted to kill me.

"I told him the suggestion was absurd," I hurried to add. "That he was being ridiculous."

"Ridiculous?" she repeated softly, violently. She lifted the glass bowl of china shards off the coffee table. "Balancing a platter on your head for an hour is ridiculous."

She whipped the bowl at the wall. I gasped as it shattered. "'Treasonous' is the word you're looking for," she roared.

"This man is deranged. I think you might be in real danger. We have to get you off of Wisewood."

Teacher paced the room, crunching in leather boots over glass and porcelain. "No, we must fight back."

I shook my head. "Neutralizing a threat doesn't always mean staying to fight. Sometimes it means running for your life."

Our eyes met across the room.

She stopped pacing, face pallid. "Then take me away from here. We'll depart as soon as I pack my bag."

"There's no time. We'll leave out the side door. Grab your parka on the way." I paused. "Do you trust me?"

Teacher nodded, wide-eyed. After all these months, she finally believed in my devotion.

I made sure the coast was clear in the hallway, then moved carefully down the spiral staircase. The house was a tomb. We snuck outside, directly across from the same Staff Only door I'd entered for initiation. That night in the water—my rebirth—was a million years ago. I hurried Teacher through the hedge entryway. We stuck close to the wall as we made our way around the island to the front gate.

The sky was a patchwork of moldy clouds. I hurried to move faster than nightfall—I had only an hour of sunlight left. When the iron pickets of the gate came into sight, I craned my neck for a view of the water. The *Hourglass* bobbed dutifully at the pier. A shaky laugh escaped my lips. I nodded once to Teacher. We made a run for it.

"Go ahead and get in," I said, panting, when we reached the boat. Fingers frozen, I unwound the ropes from the cleats, jumped in behind her, and pushed the *Hourglass* back from the pier.

We'd made it. No one could stop us now.

I paused for a moment to watch Teacher, huddled there on the L-shaped seat. She pulled Mom's scarf tighter around her neck, more exhausted senior than revolutionary. This was a big day for her.

"Thank you, Kitten. I knew I could count on you."

I tipped my chin. "Let's go for a ride."

I turned back to the task at hand: getting us far away from Wisewood as quickly as possible. I started the engine and grabbed the steering wheel. We'd been driving for only a minute or so when Teacher cried out.

I whirled around, half expecting to find her sprawled on the floor or gone altogether, having leaned too far over the side of the *Hourglass*. Instead she was transfixed, her mouth forming a perfect O. I followed her horrified stare back to the pier.

Silently watching us with his hands in his pockets was Jeremiah.

45

Natalie

JANUARY 10, 2020

I POINT TO the dripping scarf in Gordon's hand. A lump fills my throat.

I dig a thumbnail into my palm, leaving a crevice in my skin. The pain focuses me. "Where'd you get that?"

He pulls the scarf to his chest. "It's Teacher's."

"It was my mother's." One of Mom's regulars at the bar had it custom-made for her. There are no others like it.

Gordon glowers. "Ms. Collins gave it to Teacher a few months ago. She's been wearing it ever since."

My temples pulse. How dare she give away one of the few remnants of our mother? "How did you get hold of it?"

"I need to talk to Ms. Collins."

"Why is it wet?"

"I found it."

"Where?"

We both peer at the scarf. Gordon's hands are shaking. I glance up at his face. His eyebrows are knitted together.

"Gordon, where is Rebecca?"

"Gone." He presses a fist to his mouth.

I gape at him. "What do you mean, *gone*?"

"I haven't seen her in weeks." His voice trembles. "She was convinced that some of the staff had turned on her. She'd summon me in the night, positive that intruders were lurking outside her bedroom door." His words come faster. "I followed up on every suspicion, every supposed lead, but couldn't find any evidence to substantiate her claims. It's healthy to be cautious, but . . . I think she'd slipped into paranoia." He shakes his head, puts his nose to the wet scarf. "This reeks of seaweed and salt water. Her scent is gone."

He chucks the scarf at me. The wind howls around us, shoving me off-balance.

"Then what?"

He drags his fingers down his cheeks. "Ms. Collins said Teacher demanded to be driven to the mainland, that she wouldn't be safe here until we'd 'neutralized the threat.' I'd been stuck in a half-day workshop, didn't know she was gone until Ms. Collins had returned with the *Hourglass*. She told me Teacher wanted us to operate the business as usual in her absence." He cracks his knuckles. "Supposedly Teacher put Ms. Collins in charge. No one was to know she wasn't at Wisewood, not even the other staff members." Gordon wrings his hands. "I haven't heard from Teacher since."

My stomach turns. "Rebecca left Wisewood before I ever got here?"

He nods.

Then the order to steal my phone, to torment me in the forest, hadn't been Rebecca's idea.

It was my sister's.

46

Kit

I GRIPPED THE wheel of the *Hourglass* as she bounced on the water.

"The sea is irascible today," Teacher said from her perch.

I calmed my breathing. "We'll be okay." I waited a few seconds. "Should I head to Rockland?"

She quit jiggling her leg. Her eyes had plum-hued rings beneath them. "You know I'll never set foot on the mainland again. That wretched society has cost me everyone and everything I held dear."

"Where should I take you, then?"

"This was your plan. Figure it out." She mumbled something about Jeremiah, how she'd always known there was something wrong with him.

After that we drove in silence. With each wave the *Hourglass* rode, an old stopwatch slid back and forth across the dashboard. When I couldn't take another second of the rattling, I flung the watch into the bucket of my seat. Then there was nothing but the pounding of the current. I slowed the boat.

Every bone in my body warned me not to, but I steeled myself and turned around anyway. With control I asked the question that had been pounding in my head since I'd seen the death certificate: "Why didn't you tell me how my mom died?"

Teacher stiffened. Her eyes widened a touch.

I felt everything tightening—my jaw, my shoulders, my hands—and forced them to slacken. "You knew she signed up for assisted death. Why'd you keep it from me?"

Traitor! my brain shrieked.

Teacher made a noise in the back of her throat but said nothing. A seagull squawked overhead.

"You preach that even white lies are poison," I said.

This woman gave you a new life.

"What happened to honesty at all costs?"

This is how you repay her?

Teacher had tamped down the surprise, recovered her haughtiness by now. "Are you calling me a liar?"

"I'm asking you to explain yourself."

"Let's talk about this some other time." Teacher waved away my words like mosquitoes, as if to say, *We can hardly worry about you when my life is on the line.*

A ball of fury had been building deep in my chest since I'd realized Jeremiah's story was true, since I'd held my mother's annotated death certificate in shaking hands. For hours I'd swallowed my anger, kept it simmering beneath the surface so I could do what needed to be done. Now that rage cracked, spilled out, broke free. My tongue itched to lash.

"How come your moments of need are always more urgent than ours?"

Teacher gave me a scathing look. "Have we not discussed your pitiful mother enough in my office? This sounds like a path regression."

People had always underestimated me. Easygoing, amiable Kit—*She'll go along with whatever we say; nothing but empty blue sky in that head.* Teacher still didn't understand what this was.

A final chance.

"I can't have my favorite student backsliding, can I?" she cooed.

Yesterday that comment would have been enough to appease, to nourish, to silence. It had taken me far too long to recognize that she saw me—saw all of us—as a tool, not a person. Mom's death certificate was something to hold over me, to control me with if I ever stepped out of line. In an instant Teacher could have released me of my guilt and suffering; instead she'd let me writhe in it for half a year.

She patted the seat next to her, but I stayed put. "Do you know how special you are to be this close to me? To be the one to save me?"

She loves you, a voice whispered.

I used to agree that Teacher was irreplaceable. Everyone on the island believed *she* was what made Wisewood special. Only recently had I come to understand it was the principles, the workshops, the community. Together we had all turned Wisewood into magic. If I was a cog, then so was she.

"Is this a game to you?" I said. "A social experiment to see how far you can push people? Do you even believe in your own program?"

"Don't you dare insult me."

"Wisewood's principles mean something to me. To all of us. I value being in the IC. I take the quests seriously. You've built something more vital than power games."

She glared at me. "I was merely trying to protect you. I knew you would suffer setbacks if you discovered your mother and sister had been colluding against you."

She wants to keep you safe.

No, she was an egomaniac with big dreams who had manipulated me into becoming her lackey. Why had I ignored the signs? How had I been so completely taken in? I was as furious with myself as I was with her.

"Since when has our pain mattered to you? The more the better—isn't that right? You love nothing more than to jam your finger in our open wounds and twist."

"Keep this up, and I'll send you home."

For six months she had been the sun—my entire world revolved around her. Just when I'd rid my body of grief, that impossible heaviness was coming back. "You can't do that."

"Wisewood is my island." She jabbed the cushion. "I'll do as I please."

My heart pounded. I could not bear to leave this place—not when I'd made so much progress, found my people, improved the lives of other students.

If the cleric abused his power, you abandoned him, not the faith.

"Yes, Teacher." I bowed my head. "I'm sorry. I was out of line." A not-small part of me meant it. She sat back in her seat, satisfied.

The thing about friendly people was that if you pushed them hard enough, they snapped like anyone else.

I drove and drove, waiting for my gut to tell me we had reached the spot. After forty-five minutes I found a tiny island miles from its neighbors. I circled it to ensure there was no sign of life within the small thicket at its center. Teacher didn't notice. She scoped the fog-riddled horizon behind us, as if expecting Jeremiah to come skulking out of the mist any minute. I stopped the boat near the island's shore.

"How about here? Not exactly the Ritz-Carlton, but you'll be safe. It's only for a few hours."

She nodded but didn't move. I wanted to turn the *Hourglass* around.

As soon as I returned to Wisewood, I would tell Gordon, teary-eyed, that Teacher had demanded I take her back to Rockland. I'd say she was convinced that someone on the island was out to hurt her, though she wouldn't say who. She'd given me no contact information but mentioned she might go back to Ohio—she had some unfinished family business there. In the meantime we were to keep Wisewood going, no matter how arduous the task became. "Arduous" was a good word, a Teacher word. He would believe the command had come from her mouth.

I could already hear him lecturing me for giving in to her erraticism. He would lay the blame in my lap, never in hers. I would suffer his reprimands. Eventually he'd become suspicious, search high and low for his beloved teacher. By then it'd be too late.

I know for a fact you're braver than you think.

I cut the engine and picked up the small silver ladder. She recoiled when I walked past her with it. I set the ladder off the back of the boat. She eyed it, unmoving.

"Here." I leaned over her feet. "I'll help you with these."

"I'm capable of taking off my own shoes."

It took her what felt like hours to remove her boots and socks. Once she had, she carried them, ghostlike, to the ladder. She clung to the top rung, eyes squeezed shut. What a curious woman; I never understood the things she feared, considering all those she didn't. She stepped from the rung onto a boulder.

"We'll take care of everything back home. I'll come for you as soon as I can."

Like a deer in headlights she stared, oblivious that she was transitioning from one reality to the next. For a moment I wondered if she knew. Was she onto me?

Then she straightened her back, claiming every inch of space that all six feet of her took up. "Thank you, Kit. For all of it." She turned away.

You're exactly the person Wisewood needs.

"It's been an honor," I said with a knot in my stomach. If she heard me, she didn't acknowledge that she had. She moved slowly over the boulders, never turning back.

It took everything in my power not to call out to her. *For Wisewood,* I thought as I returned the ladder to the boat's floor. *For Wisewood,* I chanted silently as I used an oar to push the boat from the boulders. *For Wisewood,* I reminded myself as I restarted the *Hourglass*'s engine.

Bile rising, I watched Teacher's streaks of lustrous white hair disappear in the arms of the birch. The forest devoured her whole.

I drove away.

As I sped through crest after crest, tears freezing my eyes, the sense that I had forgotten something nagged at me. Halfway back to Wisewood I realized what it was.

My mother's scarf.

47

Natalie

IT WAS YOU.

I want to believe Rebecca was the one who messed with my sweater, stole my phone, concocted my punishment in the forest. It has to have been her or Gordon or Raeanne.

Anyone but Kit.

I can tell by the way that Gordon meets my eye, unblinking and indignant, that he doesn't know what happened to me last night. Raeanne isn't smart enough to be the brains behind any operation. She's a private, not a general. I want to sink to the thawing snow.

"Teacher was right, per usual," Gordon says. "I would have protested an extended absence, but had I known she felt that unsafe, I'd have helped her plan a short-term getaway. She must have known that."

How could you? I think. *You left me in the woods to freeze to death.*

"In seven years, I've never gone this long without speaking to her. The first week we made do here. By the second, I sensed something was off, though Kit had warned me Teacher could be gone for months. I made a couple calls and began taking the boat out. I visited other islands and the mainland, asking around. No one has seen her."

You knew taking my phone would make me sick, the memory it would dredge up.

Gordon removes his glasses and rubs his eyes. "This morning I was patrolling and found this." He pulls the scarf from my shock-frozen hands. "On a buoy."

I clear my throat, find my voice. "She could've lost it in a gust of wind. While Kit was driving her."

A pained expression crosses Gordon's face. "The buoy was six miles in the opposite direction of Rockland."

My mouth falls open. He pinches the skin at his throat, then pushes past me. "I have to find Ms. Collins."

I follow him, unable to make the facts compute. It's possible Rebecca's with her family, and they're shielding her from Gordon so she doesn't get pulled back in. (I would do the same given the chance.) Or Rebecca could have grown tired of Wisewood and had Kit cover for her. Or maybe there's been an accident, one that Kit is scared of getting caught and punished for. Could my sister have come up with this convoluted cover story, fooling everyone for weeks?

Gordon lifts a fist to Kit's door. I stand close behind him. "No touching." I back away a few inches.

We both still when we hear raised voices coming from inside.

"You need to get out of here today," Kit says.

"I would've gladly left weeks ago," a man says. "But I'm not leaving without you."

"I've told you a hundred times—I'm not going anywhere. I swear to God, if you don't go now, I'll tell Gordon who you are."

Gordon pounds on the door. The argument ceases immediately. Seconds later the door swings open.

"Who exactly would that be, Jeremiah?" Gordon says.

Kit's eyes blaze like a cornered animal's. Beneath the fear I see exhaustion, sorrow, a need for a hug. My sister couldn't have ordered Raeanne to leave me in the woods; she must have had something less severe in mind, and Raeanne got carried away. The Kit I know wouldn't be able to stare at my bloodied, swollen lip, knowing she's responsible for it. The Kit I know would've drowned me in apologies by now.

The man she's arguing with is the burly one who confronted Gordon when I first got to Wisewood. Both he and Kit assume stony expressions, refuse to say a word.

Gordon shoves the scarf toward Kit. "I found this on a buoy east of Wisewood." She gawks at the fabric. When she doesn't say anything, he adds, "Ohio is *west* of here, in case you've forgotten."

"This was Mom's," she says to me as if I wouldn't remember, as if we're alone in the cabin. My chest tightens. She tries to take the scarf from Gordon.

He yanks it back. "How do you explain this turning up so far from Rockland?"

Kit peers at him. "What are you suggesting?"

Gordon's face turns aneurysm scarlet. "I called Teacher's sister in Ohio. They haven't heard from her in years."

Kit studies the old man. "I dropped her off at the harbor. She told me she was going to Ohio, but maybe she didn't." She bites her lip. "Why would she lie?"

What have you done?

"Was she sick of Wisewood?" she muses.

"This place was Teacher's home," Gordon says. "We meant everything to her. She wouldn't desert us, especially not for the mainland. She said she would never go back there, not so long as there was breath in her lungs."

"Yet that's exactly what happened." Kit jabs a finger at Gordon's chest without actually touching him. "You're letting a fear of abandonment control you. I told you she wants us to keep Wisewood going. We have to do that whether or not she comes back."

"Wisewood is nothing without Teacher," Gordon rails.

"What do you suggest we do? Send everyone home? Wait around and cross our fingers that she turns up?"

"I say we redirect our manpower toward finding her. And don't stop until we do." He glares at Kit. "You're awfully composed for having lost your mentor."

"One of us has to be. Seven years pursuing fearlessness, yet you're sniveling over the first setback."

"Sounds just like her," Jeremiah says under his breath.

Gordon wheels around and puffs out his chest. "And you. I know all about you."

Jeremiah raises his eyebrows, unimpressed.

"Teacher knew something was off. You were always asking about her past, dodging quests, nosing around the office. She insisted I dig into you. I should've done a more thorough job before she disappeared, but once she'd fled, that got my attention. Do you know what I discovered, Jeremiah?" He emphasizes the name.

No one speaks.

"That you enrolled here under a stolen identity." I blink, but the others don't appear surprised. "Your name is David Cooper." Gordon pauses. "And Cooper happens to be the last name of Teacher's former assistant."

"I don't know what you're talking about," Jeremiah says.

"Gabriel was your older brother. He had an accident while working for Teacher. Fourteen years later you show up on her doorstep, and now she's gone." Gordon takes a threatening step toward Jeremiah. My head spins, trying to keep up. "What did you do to her? Where is she?"

"I have no clue," Jeremiah says, "but I'd like to kill her myself when I find out."

Gordon glances back and forth between Jeremiah and Kit. "Have you been working together all along? Plotting her demise from day one?"

Jeremiah snorts. "You're off your rocker," he grumbles at the same time Kit says, "Don't be ridiculous."

Gordon takes another step forward, and is now nose to chest with Jeremiah. In spite of their height difference, I fear for Jeremiah more than for Gordon. "You will leave this island immediately," Gordon says, "but know that for the rest of your days, I'll be watching. If you switch jobs, if you remarry, if you have children, I will know. You won't be able to buy a coffee or push your kids on the swings without feeling my eyes on the back of your head. I will follow every single move you make, and when I find out what you did, you will pay."

Jeremiah crosses his shaking arms. "Unless Kit comes with me, I'm not going anywhere."

"Yes, you are," Kit says. "You're leaving now. If you won't go willingly, we'll find another way to get rid of you."

She glares at Jeremiah, her lips a flat line. After a minute he sighs, opens the cabin door, and bangs it closed behind him. The door rattles on its hinges.

Gordon turns to Kit. "Don't think for a second that you're scot-free in all of this. I don't know what you've done, Ms. Collins, but you can bet I'll be back once I figure it out."

Kit puts her hands on her hips. "So that's it? You're going to ditch Wisewood?"

He gazes out the window. "I'll return when I have Teacher with me."

The corners of Kit's lips turn up. Gordon doesn't catch it, but I do.

"Then take my sister with you," she says. "She's been dying to leave Wisewood since the minute she arrived."

Finally I speak up. "I want to talk to you first, Kit. Alone."

"I have nothing left to say."

I grind my teeth. "Then you can listen."

"I need to pack a bag," Gordon says. "I'll meet you at the pier in forty minutes."

Kit puts her hand out. "I'll take back that scarf."

"Not a chance. It belongs to Teacher." He heads for the door.

I block his exit. "You said it doesn't smell like her anymore."

"I'll keep it safe," Kit says.

Reluctantly Gordon gives it to her. "You Collins girls are nothing but trouble."

"So you've mentioned." I move aside to let him pass. He storms through the doorway. "Don't forget my phone."

We watch him go.

"Walk me to the pier?"

Kit shrugs, then pulls on her boots and coat. We walk side by side down the path as the sun slinks free from the clouds.

"What did you do?" I say.

"Carried out Teacher's orders."

"It doesn't add up. This woman who craved control, who worshipped the spotlight, left without giving her devotees a chance to prostrate themselves?"

"She feared for her life." Kit shoots me daggers. "You know nothing about Teacher."

"I'm trying to learn."

"No, you're not. It was a mistake to ever bring you here. I don't know what I was thinking."

"Can you look me in the eye and honestly tell me you dropped Rebecca off at the harbor in one piece? And haven't seen her since?"

She stares straight through me. "Yes."

I click my tongue. She weaves through the rings, leading us toward Rebecca's house. Along the way a few guests wave. She wiggles her fingers back like she doesn't have a care in the world.

"Kit, listen to me carefully. I don't know what you and Jeremiah, or whatever his name is, have done. When Gordon figures it out, he'll go to the authorities. Come home with me now, before it's too late."

"How do you still not get it? I'm not leaving."

"Is this because you're pissed about Mom?"

"Nat, come on. I have more important things to worry about."

I shake my head. "I hate what this place is doing to you."

"This place has made me strong. And you can't stand it. You have no identity if you're not my savior."

Stung, I search for traces of the little sister I raised and protected. She's gone. I send up an apology to my mother. I've failed her too.

We pass the pole with the cream-colored arrows and make our way around the side of Rebecca's house. I'm running out of time. At what point does societal obligation upend the familial one? If Kit and the others are hurting people, don't I bear some responsibility to stop them? How many future guests might be left in the cold or threatened at knifepoint because of an insignificant misstep? How many families have lost their loved ones forever to this impenetrable world?

Mom's dying wish was that I keep Kit safe. Could my sister go to prison for whatever she's done? Would she be safer locked up than left here? Kit would say it isn't my job to answer these questions. She's her own lifeguard now; she's made that much clear. I make one more stab at saving her.

"Either you get on that boat with me now," I say, "or I'm going to the cops when I get back."

She stops dead in her tracks. Her eyes narrow. She purses her lips, trying to tell whether I'm bluffing.

Even I'm not sure if I am.

48

THE BOAT PULLS away from the shore. I survey my temporary abode: a wild island the length of an Olympic swimming pool, the width of three lanes, possibly four. The nearest patch of land is a light-year away. The longest swim of my life, I suppose.

I return my socks and shoes to my feet. I have not slept well these past weeks, what with the constant threats to my welfare. My eyes ache from the wind. I long to lie down somewhere soft and warm, unwatched.

I wander for a while. A forest in shambles—that's all there is to it. A parking lot for seaweed. No berries or critters. Not that I'm hungry anyway.

My eyelids are heavier than my boot-clad feet. I sit on a bed of moss. The girl said it would be a few hours until she returned. What could be the harm in a midday nap?

Decades ago, I read a story in the newspaper about a close-knit community that used to lower traitors upside down into a well by their ankles or lock them in a six-by-four-foot box. They beat them with hoses, wrapped snakes around their necks. Imagine the efficiency of fighting fear and crushing dissent in one fell swoop. I nod off to the image of that dreadful brawny man in handcuffs, features drenched with remorse.

I smile as I succumb to the land of dreams.

———

WHEN I WAKE, night has fallen. The girl and my rescue party have not yet come. It must be taking longer than she had expected to vanquish our foe. I try not to worry, tell myself to be patient. Much easier to sleep through the chaos. I pull my parka tighter around me, return my head to the earth, and fall back into a fitful sleep.

ON DAY TWO, I spend groggy hours at the shore. No matter how long I sleep, I cannot shake this exhaustion. I am dizzy, light-headed, full of dry. Well over twenty-four hours have passed since I took in sustenance. This knowledge causes a stirring within. I try to catch a fish with my raisin hands. When the water takes my hands from me, I give up on flounder. I think grass and twigs might not taste so bad. I am correct.

ON DAY THREE, I discover pine cones are edible (+2).

ON DAY FOUR I can't be sure it actually is day four, but I believe it to be so. I think I've been watching my watch, or is my watch watching me? It's the one called a watch, after all. Should it perhaps be called a wrist clock instead?

No one has come for me. In fact, I've not seen so much as a ship, any sign of human life, so I may be forced to swim. It is unlikely I could make it from here to Rockland, even with my powerful stroke and superior technique, so I will settle for the place from which I came.

I scan north, south, east, west. I don't know which is which, but I know I inspect all of those directions because I turn a complete circle. None reminds me of my kingdom more than the others. Was I blindfolded coming out here? That can't be right.

Am I blindfolded now?

———

O N D A Y F I V E I crow like a wild thing, head flung back, arms raised, a marathon photo finish. I glance around, waiting for my accolades, then remember I am stranded, alone, not at the end of a performance. I'm not doing anything that warrants applause.

That's not true. I'm surviving.

I march straight into the water, not bothering with bearings. I will swim in some direction until I hit land, and then someone will take me to my people.

I get no deeper than my ankles before the chill stings me through my boots.

Now my boots are soaked.

Drat.

What if my people are on their way to liberate me right this instant? Best to stay put.

I S L E E P O R don't. I know not how long but not too long because my feet are too cold to let me. Strangely, even after the rest, I don't feel clearer. I seem to have been abandoned, but that cannot be accurate. I am beloved.

I have a horrifying thought that takes hours to form but eventually barrels over me: what if I continue waiting here in vain until it's too late for my feet, that they've reached a state of numbness that will no longer allow me to use them as propellant devices? Will I swim in this bulky coat or remove it? Shall I wade stage left or right?

There are rather too many decisions required of one in adulthood.

T H E T I M E I S nigh. The rescue party is lost or nonexistent. Others may fear the sea, but not an enlightened one like Madame Fearless.

I have been training for this challenge all my life. I will think of it as a second attempt at *Frozen*, my chance to redeem a prior failure.

Idly I wonder what the record is for a long-distance swim in the Atlantic. *I am goddamn invincible.*

AT FIRST I enjoy the bracing slap against my face. Water wakes in a way that alarms and name-calling cannot.

Soon, though, I find it hard to breathe. I do not panic. I keep paddling and kicking, remind myself this is merely a large Lake Minnich.

What's the only way you're going to succeed? he grunts.

Through my willingness to endure!

Did you prove your father wrong if no one saw you do it?

My arms tire, for I am a mere mortal, not impervious to the deleterious effects of hypothermia, as proven in nineteen-ninety . . . eighty . . . the aughts. I think about turning back, but when I do the parking lot appears miles away.

Just-in-case thinking is for losers, he growls.

He is awfully loud for being so far away.

I swim until I can't feel my limbs. I imagine my trunk as a china platter, a landing strip for seagulls to rest their weary wings. I spot a sea green buoy with a number one spray-painted on it, and I grab onto it, pulling myself up and out of the water. I am filthy hot; I am burning up. I tell myself I'm not, this is one of the symptoms, I have trained for this, I know what to do, but still my brain cannot convince my body. It is my body that convinces my brain that this is a rare case in which I truly am burning up, so I give in, so I free my neck, so I remove the scarf. I can't recall how it came to be in my possession in the first place. I leave it behind and return to the water.

CAN ONE SWIM and sleep simultaneously? I cannot remember a time I was not swimming, and now I long to stop. I care not if that makes me a loser.

My legs are below instead of behind me. I don't recall granting them permission to run amok, but I'm too tired to castigate. Too cold to regret.

Like a carousel, their faces whirl past me: Sir, Mother, Jack, Lisa, Evelyn Luminescence, Gabe, my staff. All those miserable human beings have failed me. Who have I ever been able to rely on but myself? Who but me has been dependable one hundred percent of the time?

I suffocated. I split. I bled. I burned. I froze. I freeze.

I let go.

I have endured enough.

49

Kit

I EXAMINE NAT as though seeing her for the first time.

What did I tell you during our second session? Natalie has never had your best interest at heart.

I flex my neck, then continue walking. We pass the front of the house, stopping at the wrought iron gate. I punch a code into the panel. The door swings open.

"I wish you wouldn't," I say, "but I can only control my actions, not yours."

Police interference has always been a possibility at Wisewood, though Teacher said the NDA was enough to silence the rare unhappy guest. If not, Gordon has employed a few scare tactics once or twice to ensure our secrets stay secret.

If Nat goes to the cops, if they locate Teacher, they'll find no evidence of a struggle. No signs of foul play. She was the one who refused to return to the mainland. What had I done besides carry out her wishes?

You destroyed the one woman who accepted you as you were.

The gate closes behind us. We clomp down the path toward the pier.

"I don't understand you," Nat says, trying to slow me down.

I speed up. "You probably never will."

Teacher's absence is best for Wisewood. She distracted us during our q's, ate up our time with never-ending tests of loyalty, pitted us against one another. She put us all at risk—Jeremiah was determined to take her down and would've gladly crushed Wisewood to do so. Now that I've eliminated the threat of her, he has the justice he wanted. If he ever speaks to the press, then I will too. I'll explain that Rebecca Stamp is no longer affiliated with Wisewood, that we didn't know how Madame Fearless treated her employees in the past, though perhaps we should have guessed. Teacher will never again hurt my peers or students the way she hurt Jeremiah's brother, the way she hurt me.

My sister watches me expectantly.

"Someone has to uphold this institution," I tell her.

Teacher was Wisewood, but Wisewood is not her. The staff designs the courses, teaches the classes, conducts the quests. We bring students to the island and lead them through orientation, guide them every step of the way. Ruth and I can lead one-on-ones. We can do this without Teacher.

Don't flatter yourself. Without me, Wisewood is a washed-up commune.

Teacher gave birth to a movement that has outgrown her. This is the natural order of things: mothers age, languish, die, while their offspring move on without them. Teacher's principles were right, but her means of implementing them were wrong.

If the mother makes the baby sick, you remove the baby from its mother.

"God knows Gordon isn't capable of protecting Wisewood's values," I add.

Unlike Jeremiah, Gordon will never let this go. He won't return to Wisewood without Teacher by his side—he has no attachment to this place, only to her. Just as well. We don't need Gordon to keep Wisewood going. The community doesn't depend on any single person. It's bigger than that. It's about to get much better.

Naturally I'm concerned about releasing him back into the world, but he's an old man. Without Teacher to serve, he'll become rudderless. Time will do what time does. I hope before then he finds peace, a way to pursue his Maximized Self in the outside world. Though I don't like him, he has as much of a right to work the path as I do. Jesus didn't get to kill the disciples he found grating.

The *Hourglass* is in sight, floating at the end of the pier. The sun warms my face. Only a couple of months until spring.

"I can't believe you're willing to do literally anything to keep Wisewood going." Nat says this like it's a bad thing.

You're a tidal wave, Kitten.

I imagine my sister marching into the police station, demanding they dismantle everything we've worked so hard to build. I see Debbie returning to Carl, collecting bruises like baseball cards. Raeanne is forced into the back of her truck, four hands holding her down. Ruth is alone in Utah. Sofia weeps nightly at her daughter's grave site. Sanderson is back on the streets, begging for booze. We've already had one close call with him.

A few days ago he confided to Ruth that he was leaving for good. He claimed it had nothing to do with drinking—he felt stronger than ever but had changed his mind about Wisewood and wanted to return to his family. But we all knew better than that. Luckily Ruth reported the plan to Gordon, who jumped on the *Hourglass* to save Sanderson right before he snuck away. I shudder to think what might've happened if we'd lost him.

Principle I: I want to live a life in which I am free.

I replace the ghastly images with a memory. All of us stand around a bonfire, swaying with the trees and singing "Hallelujah." We've constructed our own family here, one without lies or judgment. None of us is better than another. No one wins or loses. No one is overweight or underpaid. No one is doing life wrong. We love one another as we are.

I can better this place. In some ways I already have. Take the blinds, for instance. Putting cameras in the guest rooms was too much; we don't need to monitor our students every minute of the day. It's enough to remove the blinds from the windows, to prove to one another we have nothing to hide. The cameras will soon come down—the one in my cabin already has.

The only person with the potential to cause real trouble for Wisewood is my sister. She is lonely and determined and has all the energy in the world. She could upend our fragile ecosystem. She could take my family from me. What wouldn't she do to get me back under her thumb? Teacher warned me.

Principle II: As long as I fear, I cannot be free.

We reach the end of the pier, stare out at the sparkling water. How gentle, how inviting, it appears now, no longer a thrashing and crashing monster.

My sister and I stand shoulder to shoulder. For a second I forget the weight of the responsibilities that have landed in my lap. I gaze at her.

I'm seven; she's ten. I ask Mom if we can go to a baseball game. We don't have the money, but instead of telling us that, Mom hands out glittery tickets the next afternoon. Numbers have been tacked to folding chairs in the living room. She makes a big show of ushering us to our assigned seats. She turns the kitchen into a concession stand, giving out Monopoly money to pay for tubs of popcorn and paper cups of soda. During the seventh-inning stretch, she makes us stand and belt "Take Me Out to the Ballgame" along with the crowd on TV. It's one of the best days of my life.

The tickets were written in Natalie's handwriting. So were the seat numbers. So were the prices at the concession stand. All of it was my sister's doing. She let Mom take the credit.

Principle III: I must eliminate any obstacles that impede my path to freedom.

I check my watch. Gordon and Jeremiah will be here in a few minutes.

I glance at my sister. She's gripping her duffel bag, watching me with a face full of fear. I wonder what she's so scared of: Gordon? This place?

Me?

"Forget them." I wipe away a tear and point to the *Hourglass*.

"Let's go for a ride."

Acknowledgments

When I started working on this book, I had no idea how much more difficult it would be to write than my first novel. Over the course of two years and seven drafts, I wrestled this story into its final shape. My work was made easier by, and I am indebted to, the following people—

My readers! You have countless ways to spend your free time, and I'm honored you've chosen to spend some of it with my books. Your insights, comments, and questions have been sources of both joy and reflection. Thank you for giving me the boosts I need to keep writing.

My tireless agent, Maddy Milburn, plus the rest of the team at MMLA, especially: Emma Dawson, Liv Maidment, Giles Milburn, Valentina Paulmichl, Georgina Simmonds, Liane-Louise Smith, and Rachel Yeoh.

My editors, Amanda Bergeron in the US and Max Hitchcock in the UK. I told you at least once that I'd bitten off more than I could chew with this story. You guided me with patience and brilliance through draft after draft . . . after draft. . . . You get the picture. Without you, there would be no book—or not one anyone would want to read, anyway. Three years in, I still can't believe how lucky I am to work not only with the two of you, but with the geniuses that are Sareer Khader and Emma Plater as well. Thank you to Eileen Chetti and Emma Henderson for such thorough copyediting.

My publishing teams, who continue to amaze me. To the Berkley team: Loren Jaggers, Danielle Keir, Bridget O'Toole, Jin Yu, Emily Osborne, Dan Walsh, Claire Zion, Craig Burke, Jeanne-Marie Hudson, Christine Ball, and Ivan Held. To the Michael Joseph team: Jen Breslin, Gaby Young, Christina Ellicott, Lauren Wakefield, Vicky Photiou, Elizabeth Smith, Hannah Padgman, Sarah Davison Aitkins, James Keyte, and Catherine Le Lievre. And to the Simon & Schuster Canada team: Nita Pronovost, Shara Alexa, Felicia Quon, Rita Silva, Jasmine Elliott, Greg Tilney, and Kevin Hanson. You all work so hard to get my stories into the hands of readers, and I will never stop thanking you for it.

The doctors, nurses, and other medical professionals who generously offered their knowledge when Google wasn't cutting it: Kimmery Martin, Duncan Alston, Laura E. Hudson, Arnaldo Vera-Arroyo, and my cousin Shannon Soukup. Thanks as well to Savitri Tan and Jeanne Marie-Hudson for connecting me with these individuals. Any errors are my own.

John Drury for taking me on a tour of mid-coast Maine in his boat, which was the single most helpful day of research throughout the entire writing process. Thanks too to photographer Peter Ralston, whose stunning pictures brought the region to life for me once I was back in the UK. I hope my descriptions are half as good as his photos.

Dave Pfeiffer for help with engineering quandaries, Scott Demar for answering my accounting questions, and my uncle Mike Soukup for guidance on all things competitive swimming.

All the librarians and booksellers who have been unbelievably supportive of my fledgling career, especially Mary O'Malley, Pamela Klinger-Horn, and Maxwell Gregory. My heartfelt thanks as well to the Bookstagram community, particularly Abby of @crimebythebook.

My fellow authors. You've been so gracious with your time, and I'm beyond grateful to be a part of this community. A special thank-you to those who were kind enough to write blurbs for my books: Ashley Audrain, Diane Les Becquets, Kirstin Chen, Lee Child, JP Delaney, Samantha Downing, Teresa Driscoll, Tarryn Fisher, Melanie Golding, Laura Hankin, Lisa Jewell, Sandie Jones, Gilly Macmillan, Margarita Montimore, Liz Nugent, Amy Stuart, C. J. Tudor, and Wendy Walker. I know you receive loads of ARCs. I'm so appreciative you took the time to read one of mine.

Taylor Wichrowski for imagining Rebecca's pre-Wisewood career visually with your show posters. To Sheila Wichrowski for reading an early draft. To Ali O'Hara and Allison Jasinski for providing feedback on jacket copy, as well as decades of moral support and free therapy.

My parents, Ron and Kathy Wrobel, for accompanying me on my research trip to Maine. I promised you three days of adventure—I think it's safe to say I kept my word!

My sisters, Jackie Malich and Vicki Wrobel, to whom this book is dedicated. Everything I know about being a sister I learned from the two of you. I hope I've been good more often than bad, and that I didn't abuse my power as the eldest too often. Special thanks to Vicki for designing Wisewood's logo and to Jackie for always letting me sing the girl parts of Disney songs (not that I gave you much choice). I love you both to the moon and back.

Finally, to Matt, who has requested the title of Alpha Reader so many times I'm finally breaking down and giving it to him. For reading all of the drafts, for problem solving in and outside the book, for keeping faith in this story every time I lost it. What a ride the past decade has been. Here's to the next one.